Help us Rate this book...
Put your initials on the
Left side and your rating
on the right side.
 1 = Didn't care for
 2 = It was O.K.
 3 = It was great

	1 2 3
	1 2 3
	1 2 3
	1 2 3
	1 2 3
	1 2 3
	1 2 3
	1 2 3
	1 2 3
	1 2 3
	1 2 3
	1 2 3
	1 2 3
	1 2 3

DATE DUE 7/20

CHASING THE WHITE LION

Center Point
Large Print

Also by James R. Hannibal and available from Center Point Large Print:

The Gryphon Heist

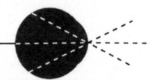

This Large Print Book carries the Seal of Approval of N.A.V.H.

CHASING THE WHITE LION

JAMES R. HANNIBAL

Center Point Large Print
Thorndike, Maine

This Center Point Large Print edition
is published in the year 2020 by arrangement with
Revell, a division of Baker Publishing Group

Scripture used in this book, whether quoted or
paraphrased by the characters, is taken from the
King James Version of the Bible.

This book is a work of fiction. Names, characters, places,
and incidents are the product of the author's imagination
or are used fictitiously. Any resemblance to actual events,
locales, or persons, living or dead, is coincidental.

The text of this Large Print edition is unabridged.
In other aspects, this book may vary
from the original edition.
Printed in the United States of America
on permanent paper.
Set in 16-point Times New Roman type.

ISBN: 978-1-64358-565-9

The Library of Congress has cataloged this record
under Library of Congress Control Number: 2019956942

CHAPTER ONE

Volgograd,
Russia Wharf District
Present Day

The cabdriver cast a nervous glance at the alley's unlit streetlamps and blacked-out windows. An old man in a mud-stained coat stumbled out of the darkness and passed through his headlights, muttering in the singsong voice of the permanently delirious. The cabbie honked his horn and shouted at the bum, then turned in his seat with a wrinkled brow. "*Vot? Ty unveren?*"

Here? Are you sure?

Talia Inger smiled, answering him in flawless Russian, refined at the Central Intelligence Agency by America's top accent coaches. "Oh yes, my friend. This is exactly where I want to be."

She climbed out and paid him, slipping in an extra five thousand rubles because he hadn't wanted to drive to that side of town in the first place.

The driver thumbed through the money and gave her a soft, worried smile, as if his next words might be the last she'd ever hear. "You are a nice lady," he said in his native tongue. "I will stop at St. Peter's and light a candle for you."

Talia reached through the open window and squeezed his forearm. "*Spasibo*." She took in a deep breath as he drove away. The night air stank of drizzle and old fish.

Glorious.

The entrance to the *Som*—the Catfish—lay at the base of a stairwell halfway down the alley. Like many of the most interesting places in the world, the Catfish could be found only by those who already knew where it was. The bar had no webpage, no neon sign, just three Cyrillic letters scratched into a black-painted iron door. Talia pulled it open and absorbed the blast of heat, noise, and cigarette smoke that greeted her, then waltzed past the bouncer like she owned the place.

Several sets of eyes turned her way. Most of the men seated at the bar or tucked into the dark booths were murderers and thieves. Talia didn't fit the profile, but she didn't care. She could handle them. She picked the beefiest patron looking her way and met his eyes with a disgusted glare. "*Na chto ty smotrish', izvrashchenets?*" *What are you staring at, pervert?*

He growled and went back to his drink.

The others laughed.

A wooden table near the back sat empty, lit by the faint red glow of the liquor shelves. Talia pulled out a three-legged chair and checked the clock on her phone. Three minutes until her target arrived. In the meantime, she was content to sit and wait—to soak it all in. Volgograd, still known to most Americans as Stalingrad, was Cold War Russia trapped in time. For Talia, this place embodied all her preconceived images of intelligence work.

A seedy bar filled with the refuse of Siberia's prisons.

A rendezvous with a greedy criminal ripe for the turning.

A shot at several years' worth of vital counter-terrorism intelligence.

Like she'd told the cabbie. This place—this dank, smoky, dangerous place—was exactly where she wanted to be.

Her fish entered the bar a few minutes later. Oleg Zverev remained true to his file photo, down to the blue leather motorcycle jacket. Talia guessed he thought the padding in the shoulders made him look bigger. He thought wrong. Compared to the big gorillas and lithe jaguars at the bar, Oleg looked like a rat wrapped in a blue leather blanket.

The bouncer stepped in front of him, folding his arms, and for a moment, Talia worried she might have a problem. The rat answered with a sour look. The gorilla chuckled and stepped aside.

"Vera Novak." Oleg spotted Talia at the table and greeted her with the cover name she'd given him. She stood to take his hand, and he held her fingers far too long while his eyes passed up and down her form. "What a *pleasure* to finally meet you in person."

What mass delusion made men from every culture think women enjoyed leers and innuendo? Talia slipped her fingers from his grasp. A little sweat. A little hair product. Gross. She sat again and wiped her hand on her jeans under the table. "You can speak Russian, Oleg. I'm fluent."

"I want to practice my English. Besides, it is safer. The overgrown morons around us can barely speak their own language, let alone another."

The music blaring from behind the bar—some Russian knock-off of nineties American metal—would cover their conversation, but Talia didn't argue. "Suit yourself."

"I will. First round is on me. What do you want?"

"I'm here for business. Not a date."

The corners of his mouth turned up as he walked away. "Why can it not be both, eh?"

Moments later, he returned from the bar with a bottle of vodka and two tumblers, which he filled well past the customary level. "*Zdoróvye.*" He tossed his drink back in one gulp.

Talia slid hers aside with the back of her hand. "Nice place you picked. A lot of . . . atmosphere. What kind of name is Catfish for a bar?"

"It is good name. In Volga River, catfish is king.

He is top of food chain, up to five meters long and three hundred fifty kilograms." The rat took her tumbler, swallowed its contents, and poured two more. When Talia's flat expression didn't change, he spread his hands. "*Three hundred fifty kilograms,* Vera. The *Som*, Volga catfish, is bigger than mako shark."

"The Mako. Now *that* is a good name for a bar."

"You Americans. No imagination." Oleg slid the tumbler in front of her.

Talia pushed it aside again.

He frowned. "Fine. Business. What can best forger in Russia do for Vera?"

"The question you should ask is, What can Vera do for you?"

"Okay. I bite. What can Vera do for me?"

"Make your bank account grow." Talia produced an envelope, fat with cash.

The flaring of Oleg's nostrils told her she had his full attention. "I am listening." He leaned across the pocked tabletop, bringing with him the stench of cigarette breath and perfumed hair, and reached for the cash.

Talia snatched the envelope away. "Not so fast. This is one hundred thousand US, a good-faith payment to show that my employer is serious. First I want to know you're serious as well."

"What kind of relationship?"

"The profitable kind."

Oleg let his eyes drift around the bar in

poorly feigned disinterest. "I have many such relationships. My identities are best in Russia." He pressed his thumb and forefinger together and kissed them with a loud *smack*. "*Best* in Russia. I am not copy-shop hack making fake passports. I build complete identities. Documents. Digital histories. Life stories. A hundred thousand will buy your boss five identities." He raised his chin. "In fact, make it ten. I give him new customer discount."

"*Her*. My boss is a woman."

The rat raised an eyebrow. "How modern. I cannot wait to meet her."

"You never will. And she doesn't want new identities. She wants copies of the identities you create for others."

The leer dropped from Oleg's face. "Perhaps my English fails me. It sound like you want me to betray my clients."

"Don't think of it as betrayal." Talia lifted her hand, revealing the full thickness of the envelope—the weight of all that money—and watched Oleg lick his lips. "Think of it as a bonus. You'll get paid twice for every identity you create."

The rat's Adam's apple dipped. "A bonus. Yes. I like that." His fingers crept across the table, seeking her permission.

"Go ahead, Oleg. The money's yours." She owned him.

Oleg drew back the lapel of his blue leather jacket and tucked the envelope away. "It is very good deal. But tell your boss *I pass*."

As if the statement were a command, all the rough patrons at the bar swiveled their stools to glare at Talia. Others emerged from the booths.

Oleg laughed, zipped up the jacket, and patted the envelope inside. "Did you think I would not find out who you were, Miss *C-I-A?* Identities are my business." He slapped both hands down on the table. "Like I said. You Americans. *No imagination*."

CHAPTER TWO

Volgograd,
Russia Wharf District

Talia leaped up from her chair, leveling her Glock.

In the same instant, a meaty hand wrapped the barrel and tore it from her fingers. One of the Russian gorillas stepped out from behind her and handed the weapon to Oleg.

The rat laughed, holding Talia's Glock in one hand and the vodka bottle in the other. "Nice try. But you cannot save yourself. This was your last mission, Miss CIA Agent."

"You mean, 'CIA officer.'" The correction came from the bar—from the only patron who hadn't turned at Oleg's signal.

The rat lowered the bottle. "What did you say?"

"My friend, here, is a CIA case officer." The man kept his back to them, face buried in an untouched drink. "She was trying to turn *you* into an agent. Get it right."

Talia knew the voice, despite the fake Russian accent. Adam Tyler. "What are you doing here?"

He swiveled the stool, bringing his face into view. The accent vanished. "Looking after you."

"I don't need looking after."

"Hey!" Oleg waved the bottle and gun in the air. "Who is this guy?"

Tyler ignored him, keeping his focus on Talia. "Are you sure? I count fourteen hostiles. One of them already has your weapon."

"Fifteen. You're slipping. And I can handle them."

Tyler glanced at Oleg. The two shared an incredulous look and asked the same question in unison. "Oh really?"

"Yes. Really."

With a grunt, Talia lifted the little table and launched the two vodka tumblers. She swatted one with an open hand, sending it flying at Oleg to shatter on the bridge of his rat nose.

At the same time, Tyler left the stool to bring a closed fist down on Oleg's forearm.

The Glock fell. The rat clutched his bleeding face and ran for the door. "Kill them, you idiots! Kill them both!"

The Russians converged. Talia's world descended into hairy, nicotine-scented mayhem.

Her first target, the gorilla who'd torn the Glock from her hand, caught a knee in the groin, followed by an uppercut that met his face as he doubled over.

Another Russian dived for the Glock, but Tyler soccer-kicked him in the temple, and the weapon slid into the dark space under a booth. Talia had no chance to go after it. A thick arm caught her in a choke hold. She clawed at it, fingernails slipping on hair and sweat.

As she fought for breath, a figure swept in from her left, swinging a bottle. Talia cringed, but the bottle connected with her attacker's head, not hers. The sweaty arm went limp.

She grabbed the bottle-swinger by his lapels, jerking his face into the light. "Finn?"

Michael Finn—Tyler's forever-shadow and daredevil cat burglar—pumped his dirty blond eyebrows.

Talia pushed him away. "I should have known."

Finn gave her a self-assured smolder, the one she never knew whether to love or despise. "The count was fourteen," he said in his Melbourne accent. "Not fifteen. You included me. So—" He paused to level an oncoming attacker with his elbow.

"So, Tyler was right, and I was wrong. Yeah, I get it. Do you really have to be here?"

"Someone's gotta look out for Tyler while he's looking out for you."

One of the Russians pinned Talia's arms with a bear hug. She drove her heel repeatedly into the man's instep, shouting with each stomp. *"I don't . . . need . . . looking . . . after!"* The hold loosened. She ducked out and shoved the Russian back over an empty chair. He fell at Tyler's feet and got a face-full of boot.

The three fought their way through the bar with

chair legs and liquor bottles, until Talia reached the bouncer—the biggest gorilla of them all.

He crossed his arms and growled, "Where you going . . . *little girl?*"

Behind her, Tyler knocked out his last opponent, raised a gun, and fired three rounds into the ceiling.

The gorilla stepped out of their way.

Tyler walked past, slapping the weapon into Talia's hand as he started up the steps to the alley. Her Glock. He must have dug it out from under the booth while she was talking to Finn.

As she followed, she checked the mag. Plenty of rounds. "You couldn't have used this earlier?"

"What? And skip all the fun of a full-on bar brawl?"

A third member of Tyler's team waited beside a Toyota HiLux pickup. The big Scottish pilot, Mac Plucket, stood by the cab, holding Oleg by the collar of his jacket. Oleg's kicking feet were a good six inches off the pavement. "Evenin', lass. Your wee friend here offered me a hundred thousand dollars ta let him go."

Talia and the other two climbed into the back of the truck. "And what did you say?"

Mac produced the envelope. "I accept."

"You forgot *let me go* part." Oleg swung his fists at Mac, never connecting.

"Good point, lad. My mistake."

"That's our Mac." Talia held Oleg in the

Glock's sights as Mac heaved him into the truck bed. "Talk." She kneeled beside him and shoved the gun closer. "There's no way a little rat like you pierced my cover. Who tipped you off?"

In place of an answer, blood spurted from the rat's lips. Bullets riddled his body. More rounds plinked off the HiLux. A black sedan raced up the street with a shooter hanging out the passenger window. Someone in the bar must have made a call—likely someone who didn't want Oleg giving any false identities.

Finn lifted the Russian's body as a shield.

Tyler pulled Talia down and pounded on the bed. "Mac, get us out of here!"

The trees of Volgograd weren't large, but they were everywhere, lining even the busiest streets. They grew in the empty lots and the train yards, gradually turning a gray former Soviet city into Sherwood Forest. Now the forest whipped past while gunfire splintered every trunk.

Talia rolled over to yell at Tyler. "A pickup truck? This is what you chose for an urban rescue?" They both lay on the bed, keeping their heads below the cover of the tailgate and the dead forger. She raised herself on an elbow, emptied the Glock, and dropped down again to change magazines. "Poor turning radius. Limited cover. Limited speed." She slammed her spare mag home and chambered a round, passing the weapon to Tyler. "Why bring a 4x4 when a lighter, faster vehicle will do?"

The next volley hit the trees to their right. Tyler raised the Glock with one arm and fired blind. Glass shattered. Tires squealed. Talia stole a glance over the tailgate and saw the sedan back off four car lengths, one headlight shot out.

How did he do that?

Using the Glock, he gestured at the road ahead. "*That's* why we needed a 4x4."

She looked forward through the cab. The end of the street was coming on fast, and beyond it, nothing but a mile-wide stretch of the Volga river, guarded by a dirt berm. Mac hit the curb at full speed, bouncing Oleg up into the air. The body landed next to Talia with an ugly *thud*.

She gave Finn a look.

He shrugged. "Sorry, princess. I didn't have as good a grip as I thought."

The truck barreled over rough ground, and it took all Talia's strength and coordination to avoid smacking her head repeatedly into the bed. She could barely speak. "This will slow them . . . down . . . but they'll still . . . be coming. Your plan . . . won't work."

"Oh, it'll work," Finn said. "Trust us."

What were they up to? The engine surged. By now, the river had to be close. "Mac?"

"Hang on!" Finn shouted.

The HiLux roared up the berm and sailed out over the river. Talia went weightless, floating in space with the dead Oleg.

The truck splashed down with water flying high on all sides. Talia groaned and pressed up to her knees and saw Mac climb out through the driver's window just as the river began pouring in.

He cast a sour look at Tyler. "Ya said I'd get to fly on this partic'lar job. Ya didn't say I'd be flyin' a truck."

A motorboat pulled alongside them, piloted by a young black woman, Darcy Emile, Tyler's chemist and demolitions expert. She helped Mac into the boat first and gave him the wheel before helping the others into the back. "Nice of you all to *drop in,* yes?" she said to Talia in a singsong French accent, handing her a towel.

"Hilarious." Wiping the river from her eyes, Talia looked warily back at the berm. Where Darcy went, explosives were sure to follow. Something was about to go boom.

She hoped.

Before following the rest of the team, Tyler took the time to strap Oleg into the sinking truck with a set of tie-downs.

"What are you doing?" Talia asked.

"Keeping options open."

The Russians had carried enough momentum to drive the sedan to the top but not over. Five men piled out, all armed with submachine guns.

Talia pulled Tyler into the boat. "You've given them the high ground. If you've got another trick up your sleeve, now's the time."

"Oh, ye of little faith." He pulled a wet handkerchief from his rear pocket and scrubbed at a spot of Oleg's blood staining his jacket. "Darcy, you're on."

"Wait." The French woman watched the pack of thugs with interest, as if watching lemurs at the zoo. "I want to see their smiling faces, yes?"

A fusillade of bullets peppered the water, and more than a few poked holes in the fiberglass at the back. Mac revved the engines. Everyone but Tyler shouted at the chemist.

"Darcy!"

"Yes, okay. Here goes."

With a tremendous *foomp,* an entire section of the berm rose skyward. Five thugs and one car went flying on a cushion of dirt.

Finn poked Talia on the shoulder and laughed. "I told you it would work."

CHAPTER THREE

Ban Doi Henga Refugee Camp
Thai/Burma Border
Mae Hong Son Province, Thailand

Nine-year-old Thet Ye jogged barefoot down the steps of the wooden church, squinting in the early light as he scanned the main road of the refugee camp. "Hla Meh?" He didn't see her.

A few girls sat in the dirt and played *e-keb*, tossing a stone in the air and sweeping up pebbles with their hands. Hla Meh was not among them. Other children raced, rolling woven bamboo hoops past a line of wobbly houses, also bamboo. Hla Meh was not among those either.

What had become of his best friend?

She could not have gone far. Hla Meh had better *not* have gone far. Only a few minutes remained before the school day started. Attending classes beneath the thatch shelters beside the church was a privilege. He didn't want Hla Meh to lose hers.

At the bottom of the steps, Thet Ye caught the shoulder of another boy, Aung Thu. "Where is Hla Meh?"

"Who knows? Your best friend is a girl. You never know *what's* going through their brains."

The other boys often picked on Thet Ye for

choosing a girl as a best friend. He gave Aung Thu his usual answer. "When you best her in a foot race or take the ball away from her in a soccer match, maybe I'll pick you."

"*Psh*." Aung Thu flopped his hands in the air and walked up the steps.

The church steps. The butterfly. "Hla Meh!" Thet Ye ran around the church to the thin patch of wild grass separating the building and the jungle. Hla Meh had chased a butterfly in that direction before Thet Ye had run inside to get a drink of water.

"Where do you think she lives?" Hla Meh had asked him.

"Wherever the other butterflies live, of course."

"And where is that? We should find out." Hla Meh followed the creature from the rail of the church steps, to the shoulder of a girl playing e-keb, to a stalk of grass at the rear corner of the church. And Thet Ye followed Hla Meh, until he became thirsty.

Fresh water was not so easy to come by in the mountain refugee camp. Thet Ye knew that well. His mother had given him the daily job of walking down to the river with empty jugs and trudging back with full ones. Lately she boiled the water. The teacher at the school had taught her how. But the church had fresh, cool water, brought in each week by the American group that helped the pastor open a school. Thet Ye could drink as much as he liked. And he had, leaving

Hla Meh to follow her butterfly to its home.

"Hla Meh?" Thet Ye jogged to a stop in the middle of the grass patch. She wasn't there.

Something rustled in the trees. "Hla Meh?" They weren't supposed to go into the jungle, but Hla Meh was not always good at following the rules. He ran toward the sound.

The morning sun faded quickly to dim green shadows. Thet Ye pushed a tangle of vines aside, stumbled over a dead branch, and then paused to listen. The rustling continued, ahead and to his left. "Hla Meh?" At a small clearing, near the base of a big *yang na* tree, he found her. Thet Ye let out a huge breath. "Hla Meh."

"I lost the butterfly." Hla Meh picked at the underbrush with a stick. "She was right here, but then I lost her."

Girls. Aung Thu had been right about one thing. You never knew what was going through their brains. "We have to get back. School is starting."

"One more minute. I know she's here. Look at that tree. It *must* be her home."

"Her what?" Thet Ye struggled to understand Hla Meh's words sometimes. When distracted, she often reverted to *Kayah*, her native tongue. Most of the children in the school had grown up in the camps and learned Thai from an early age. But Hla Meh had crossed the border from Burma with her mother, fleeing the most recent purge of Christians. Thai came harder for her.

Nearly everything came harder for her. It was the main reason Thet Ye had taken her on as a best friend.

"There she is!" Before Thet Ye could stop her, Hla Meh pushed apart a pair of saplings and disappeared again.

He chased after her, but a few steps in, he caught his toe on a low vine. He crashed into Hla Meh, and the two tumbled down a hill into a larger clearing.

Thet Ye groaned, sitting up. "Now look what you've—" He stopped. Hla Meh's eyes had grown wide with fear, staring at something behind him. He turned.

Three men wearing the camouflage uniforms of soldiers glared back at the children—two a little younger than Thet Ye's father and one teenager. The teenager had been digging. The shorter of the two older men took a menacing step toward Thet Ye and his friend. He reached for them with a grubby, burn-scarred hand.

CHAPTER FOUR

Ban Doi Henga Refugee Camp
Thai/Burma Border
Mae Hong Son Province, Thailand

The soldier lifted Thet Ye to his feet and dusted him off. "That was quite a tumble." The instant he spoke, his uniform and the burn scars on his hands became less frightening. Many grown-ups and teens at Ban Doi Henga had similar marks. A great fire had burned the camp on the night Thet Ye was born. It was the reason for his name— Brave Life. His mother always said he'd come out to brave the fire instead of hiding.

But these soldiers were not from the camp.

When the short soldier tried to help Hla Meh to her feet, she scrambled back. He looked at her hard, then the hardness evaporated, and he smiled. "Where are your teachers, little ones?"

Behind him, the other soldier barked an order at the teen, and the boy continued his work. This sparked Thet Ye's interest. "What are you digging for? Are you looking for treasure?"

The soldier's face turned serious. "Landmines. And that is why this area is off-limits. This jungle is a war zone."

Thet Ye knew that well. His parents had been

driven into Thailand because of that war, the same as Hla Meh and her mother.

"Do your teachers know you are here?"

Thet Ye shook his head.

"I see. Well, that is a big problem."

"It is?"

The man looked past them through the trees. "You attend the new school in the camp, yes?"

Thet Ye nodded.

"Your teachers are responsible for your safety, even before the school day begins. If the government finds out they let you wander into a mine-filled jungle, the school will be shut down."

"But we love our school. Isn't that right, Hla Meh?" Thet Ye looked back at his friend, but she only continued to stare at the soldier. Her eyes remained as wide as Thet Ye had ever seen them.

The man paced back and forth for a few moments, then crouched down to the children's level. "How about this? I will not tell anyone you were here as long as you do not tell anyone. That way, your teachers will not get into trouble. Do we have a deal?" He offered his hand.

Thet Ye shook it, feeling the strange smoothness of the burn scars. "Deal."

With a helpful point from the soldier, Thet Ye and Hla Meh made their way back to the church. She held his hand the whole way, so tight it hurt. Thet Ye did not want to offend his friend, but he could not allow the other boys to see them holding hands. He wrenched his hand free before they pushed out from the last of the vines. Even then, Hla Meh said nothing. She ran off to the school shelters where the day's session was starting.

Thet Ye did not tell the teachers about the soldiers. Hla Meh remained silent the whole day as well, though she had never agreed to keep the secret. After school, Thet Ye caught up to her in a muddy track between bamboo houses, a shortcut to the newer section of the camp. The narrow gap between thatched roofs left them both in shadow.

"You're going to stick to the deal, right?" He took her hand from behind.

She jerked it away.

One minute she wanted to hold his hand, the next she did not. Aung Thu seemed wiser by the second. "What's wrong?"

"There is no deal—not with those men."

"But what about our teachers? Those men could tell the government. They are soldiers."

"They are *liars*. They are Burmese militiamen who hate us."

Now Thet Ye understood. He'd heard stories of the war, but Hla Meh had lived it. She had seen the militias destroy her village. He tried reassuring her. "No, silly. The soldiers were nice to us, and they spoke Thai."

"*You* speak Thai. But you are not from Thailand."

Thet Ye could not argue. None of the children

in the camp belonged in Thailand, even those born there. Refugees did not belong anywhere. He shook his head. "Yes, but the uniforms."

"Militias wear uniforms too." Hla Meh sat down and cried.

Oh, how he should have listened to Aung Thu the Wise. At a loss, Thet Ye kneeled in the mud and held her shoulders.

Hla Meh leaned into him. "Do you know what happened to Peh?" she said between sobs.

Thet Ye knew enough Karenni children and grown-ups to understand that by *Peh*, she meant her father. He swallowed. "No." He'd asked about her father not long after they'd met, on the day the school opened, but she had turned sullen, so he had never asked again.

"Peh stood up to them, men wearing uniforms *just like those*. They came to purge the village of Christians. He said someone had to stop them."

Her sobs grew stronger. Thet Ye held her shoulders. If a grown-up saw, they wouldn't understand, and he would be in trouble. But what else could he do?

"*Mua* tried to hide my eyes. She tried to pull me into the trees, but I saw Peh. I saw him fall. They shot him, and then they burned our church to the ground." She looked into Thet Ye's eyes. "If they could do that in our village, they can do it here too."

27

CHAPTER FIVE

Gagarin Airfield
Saratov, Russia

Talia listened to the gear of Tyler's Gulfstream 650 swing up into the well.

Tyler's gear. Tyler's Gulfstream. Tyler's rescue. She was grateful, sure, but did he have to hover around her like a helicopter mom? She sank her aching body into soft white leather and frowned across a walnut table at Finn. "Where's Val?"

The Aussie opened his mouth to answer, but Darcy cut him off, squeezing between his knees and the table to take the window seat. "Russian hotels do not meet Valkyrie's standards." She sat down and breathed on the window, drawing shapes in the fog.

"What she means is, Val had a previous engagement."

Darcy joined a pair of circles to a triangle. "But our Val has a lot of these *previous engagements,* yes?"

Valkyrie, the team's grifter, had missed several of Tyler's outings, and the darkness in Darcy's tone told Talia it had become a sticking point. To be fair, Talia had missed a lot as well. Her promotion to the Russian Operations desk in the Directorate's Russian Eastern European Division—REED for short—had come with a mountain of new work and plenty of travel.

In Talia's first six months, Mary Jordan had sent her out on no less than eight high-visibility assignments—Estonia, Siberia, Rostov, Kirov. Tyler's little off-the-books charity projects, like undercutting a corrupt banker in Zambia or removing a drug lord from the Chilean parliament, had taken a back seat to Talia's day job.

"So," Finn said. "Oleg got the drop on you. Do all CIA officers take such a slapdash and devil-may-care approach to the job?"

"I didn't need rescuing." Talia felt a snide remark brimming on Tyler's lips and shifted her glare his way, cutting him off with a preemptive denial. "I didn't."

"Of course you didn't."

"And I don't need babysitting."

"Of course you don't. I never thought you did. Volgograd was an anomaly, an intersection of operations. It was a onetime thing."

"Except for Moscow," Finn said. "Don't forget Moscow."

"And what about Minsk?" Darcy had fogged up the window again and was drawing what Talia took to be a dollhouse blowing apart. "Talia was in the embassy across from our hotel, yes?"

Tyler pulled a finger across his throat in the

international *Please shut up* sign. "Thank you, Darcy. Thank you very much." He tilted his head, motioning for Talia to join him in the next set of seats.

As Talia followed, Darcy raised her drawing finger. "And Vladivostok. Was not Talia the woman you were watching at the port authority building in Vladivostok?"

"Yes," Tyler said without looking back. "Yes she was. Again, thank you. So helpful."

When they came to the rear table, he stepped aside and offered Talia the forward-facing chair, a thoughtful gesture implying he knew she always preferred to face forward while flying. Yet somehow it irked her. Tyler knew so much about her. Too much.

Before they'd met on Talia's first mission for the CIA, Tyler had spent fifteen years watching her from the shadows. A guardian angel. Except this guardian angel had assassinated her father. She'd forgiven him, and with his help, she had returned to the God her father loved. But those fifteen years of watching made her uneasy. Now it seemed he hadn't given up the habit.

Talia crossed her arms. "Shouldn't you be flying the plane?"

"Over Mac's dead body. I'm a hobbyist. He's a professional. I know when to step back."

"Do you?"

A spark in his green eyes acknowledged he had

walked right into that one. "Okay, so I picked a few jobs with locations near your assignments. Let's call it operational overlap. Can you blame me?"

She let her hard stare do the talking.

"I get it. You're trying to leave the past behind, and that's good. But the fact is, your past is still a big part of your present."

The two had covered the same ground time and again. Tyler and Frank Brennan, Talia's first section chief at the Agency, believed a spy known as Archangel had ordered her father's death nearly sixteen years earlier. And they believed this spy was still haunting the CIA. But Tyler had no more proof than a cryptic name on a fifteen-year-old slip of paper.

Talia wanted—needed—Archangel to be a figment of the past so she could put her father's death and Tyler's part in it behind her. She tried pushing the conversation in a different direction. "Let's talk about how you lied to me a moment ago. You said Volgograd was an intersection of operations when you know full well you were just shadowing me."

"You're wrong. I didn't lie."

Up to that point, the exchange had been something of a tennis match. Despite Talia's attempts at gravity, Tyler had been playing a game. The quiet *court jester who could kill you but probably won't* thing was part of his DNA.

Talia had gotten used to it. But in that instant, the commander inside him took full control, like someone had flipped a switch.

Tyler laid his hands on the table. "We knew Oleg was on to you, Talia. That's why I brought the team to Volgograd. That's why Finn and I were in the bar." He lowered his chin, keeping those green eyes locked on hers. "Someone at the Agency sold you out."

CHAPTER SIX

Talia knew her attempt to turn Oleg had gone horribly wrong, but Tyler had jumped to an extreme conclusion. "You're overreacting. Oleg was vermin, but he was connected. Maybe one of those connections broke through the curtain."

"You're not listening. We *knew* Oleg broke through the curtain."

He let the statement hang. Talia had learned the same technique at the Farm. Create unacceptable silence. Force the target to engage. Was Tyler aware he was working her like a mark? "Okay. I'll bite. How did you know?"

"Livingston Boyd."

"The young investment mogul whose penthouse we broke into before the Gryphon heist?"

"Correct."

Dozens of constellations sparkled in the panoramic window beside the table, so high above the Russian cloud deck. A million lights, all fixed in place no matter how fast the Gulfstream flew—as inescapable as her past.

Tyler pressed on with his explanation. "We

33

broke into Boyd's London penthouse to catch up with Finn on the Fabergé carriage job, but I had an ulterior purpose. I had Finn steal a thumb drive from Boyd's desk."

"The thumb drive I found in your laptop," she said, turning her gaze to the panoramic view, "with the list of buyers for Ivanov's hypersonic missiles."

"Correct. Boyd isn't the energy stock and real estate wunderkind he pretends to be. His wealth comes from other sources."

The lists of buyers on Tyler's laptop appeared in Talia's eidetic memory. She couldn't have blocked out the image if she tried. "So Boyd was the Englishman mentioned in our Dark Web intercepts—Ivanov's arms broker."

Full circle. Talia had taken the conversation in a new direction, and Tyler had led her right back around. During the operation to stop Ivanov from selling hypersonic tech and launching a missile against Washington, DC, Talia had unmasked Tyler as the assassin who killed her father. Archangel had given the order.

She took her eyes from the unmoving stars. "You think Boyd is linked to Archangel."

"Ivanov practically told us so." Tyler eased himself up from the table and crossed the aisle to the rear galley. "Murderer or not, he had no reason to lie at the time. He told us his contact at the Agency gave him the idea for the attack and the arms sale and brought him the broker—Boyd. If Boyd was Ivanov's link to Archangel, then he can be our link to Archangel as well."

She read his expression. Confidence. "This isn't pure speculation. You've done some homework."

"Not me. Eddie."

"Eddie?"

"Who else would I go to for high-level hacker work?"

Unbelievable. "You're using my best friend behind my back?"

Talia had met Eddie Gupta at Georgetown and found an instant connection. Together, they were a foster care kid and a child of foreign diplomats, out of place among their Ivy League peers. The Farm had followed. Same class. Afterward, they'd been assigned as a pair to Frank Brennan's Other branch within the Clandestine Service, then promoted to REED. "Eddie is supposed to be working with me now, at the Russian Ops desk."

"He is. But let the kid have a hobby."

"Eddie is a geek. By definition, he has a hundred hobbies."

A spark in the eyes. The court jester again. "And working for me is one of them."

"Tyler . . ."

"The encryption on the thumb drive had a digital fingerprint—subtle, but definitely there. Eddie cross-referenced this fingerprint with data from the Gryphon heist and intercepts on the Dark Web. We were looking for connections to our CIA traitor, and—"

"*Alleged* CIA traitor."

"Sure. If it makes you feel better." Tyler opened the galley's mini-fridge. "Ginger ale? I stocked up before we left." He offered her a bottle.

Talia accepted. "So you were looking for connections, and . . ."

"And the markers kept taking us to remote servers." He fiddled with the other drinks in the fridge, pausing too long for her comfort.

"What servers, Tyler? Where?"

Again, he prolonged the silence, pouring himself a glass of Perrier. He returned to the table just as Talia took a swig from her ginger ale. "You're drinking straight from the bottle these days? What would Conrad say?"

She lowered it quickly, nearly choked on the fizz. He had set her up for the wisecrack by not handing her a glass in the first place. The tennis match was in full swing. She didn't want to play. "Tyler. The servers."

"They were everywhere. All across the globe. No discernible pattern. But fragments of Boyd's digital fingerprint kept popping up. We've been following them for months."

Talia's eyes widened. The team's little excursions. "Zambia?"

"And Chile. You were with us for those. But

Moscow, Minsk, and Vladivostok were about Boyd as well. I never had to work at keeping our efforts close to your operations. There were too many options, too many rabbit trails to chase." He finished the water in his glass and filled it halfway with the remainder from the bottle. "Eddie hasn't nailed down the architecture yet, but it's clear Boyd has his fingers in criminal operations in every major city, from London pickpockets to human traffickers in Rangoon to forgers in Volgograd."

Talia dropped her half-empty ginger ale into a cupholder. "And that brings us to Oleg."

"One of his Dark Web posts had a digital marker matching Boyd's network, so when you were assigned to his case, Eddie placed a RAT on Oleg's home computer—a remote access tool that gives us screen and keylogging access, among other things."

"I know what a RAT is."

"Sure you do. Sorry." Tyler grew deadly serious. "A data packet came in unsolicited from the network. When Oleg opened it up, there were three simple words. 'Vera Novak. CIA.' "

"You think the tip-off came from your mystery spy, routed through Boyd's network?"

He touched his nose.

The story had merit. Talia had learned to trust Tyler, but she had been placing her trust in Eddie far longer. Not even Mary Jordan, chief of

REED, fully appreciated the hacker asset the CIA had gained when Eddie signed up. She looked down at her hands, searching for a handle on the implications.

"The data packet came from Boyd's network," Tyler said. "But the information *had* to come from the Agency."

She shook her head. "You're making a leap. Most covers are throwaways. They're only the first curtain."

"Throwaway covers leave a black hole. They don't point the mark to the CIA."

"Yes, but—" Motion in the panoramic window caught Talia's eye. The stars remained still, but the cloud layer was rising. Or rather, the Gulfstream was descending. "Is Mac landing the jet?"

"Nothing gets past you. Sorry, Talia. A quick ride home might tip off our traitor to my involvement. We got you out of Volgograd, but you'll have to find your own way out of Russia."

They left her standing in a dark hangar on the outskirts of Kursk. No passport. No luggage. Just her Glock and a wad of rubles. Darcy offered a finger-wiggling wave from the lighted cabin. Talia didn't wave back. She watched the Gulfstream take the runway, then trudged off across an empty field toward the highway.

"Thieves."

CHAPTER SEVEN

Washington, DC
Potomac River

Talia and her foster sister, Jenni Lewis, walked a racing shell out to the Georgetown dock on the Potomac. They worked by the orange glow from the boathouse and the small lights clipped to their caps. The sun had not yet risen.

"Way enough," Talia said in an even voice—the *halt* call. In the US rowing dialect, it sounded like *wane-off.* "Roll to the waist."

The girls rolled the boat from their shoulders to their hips, and Talia winced against the soreness from her Volgograd bruises. A long-sleeve shirt and windbreaker hid the marks. She didn't need any uncomfortable questions from her sister.

Talia gritted her teeth, trying not to let the pain show. "And . . . down." They bent at the knees and set the shell in the water.

Without a word, Jenni threaded the first of her two oars through an oarlock. Talia did the same. They had chosen a *double* for the morning, a two-person sculling shell requiring two oars for each rower. For months, even as the weather grew colder, the sisters had rowed together on Tuesday and Thursday mornings before sunup.

To make up for lost time, they also rowed the day after either of them returned from a trip, like that morning—a Friday.

They settled into their rolling seats with their backs to the bow and locked their feet into the shoes fixed to the push-boards, known as *stretchers*.

Talia laid a hand on the dock's edge. "Ready?"

"Ready."

"Push away."

Jenni had taken the stern seat, leaving the bow seat—and all the steering—to Talia. "How about a balance exercise?"

"I'm game if you are. In three, two, one, go."

Both girls raised their oars from the water and used their cores to keep the boat upright. No easy task. They held it steady for a few seconds, aided by the river's momentum, until the shell wobbled and dipped.

"Hold steady," Talia said.

Jenni let out a laughing yelp. Her left oar slammed into the water.

Talia got a face full of ice-cold Potomac. "Thanks," she said, sputtering.

"Sorry. But you know you'll be getting a lot wetter on Sunday. You're going through with it, aren't you?"

Talia had made a profession of faith a few weeks after the incident with Ivanov, when Tyler had helped her let go of a lifetime of anger. She was ready to tell the world through baptism, but Jordan's constant assignments and Tyler's side jobs had forced her to reschedule on three occasions—a strange conflict between the yearning of her spirit and the world's practicality. "Nothing will stop me this time. I promise."

"Good. Let's get moving upstream."

Jenni went silent until Talia got the boat turned against the current. A false move would dump them both into the freezing drink. Talia worked the bow straight upriver and made the starting call.

"At the catch." She compressed her body against her knees, ready for the first drive. "Row!"

Together, Talia and Jenni pushed with their legs, drawing the oar handles back and the paddles forward, willing the shell into motion. "One . . .Two . . . Three . . . Four . . ." Talia set a sharp pace in the hope of keeping Jenni's lungs well-occupied. But in the quiet of her mind, she was thinking, *Here it comes*. Silence had never been Jenni's strong suit.

"So? How was your trip? Did you see anything interesting? Meet anyone new?"

Annnd . . . there it goes.

"Yes . . . I did." Talia let her answers out with the strained exhalation of each drive. The bruising on her ribs screamed.

"And?"

"Turns out . . . he wasn't . . . my favorite person." She never lied to Jenni. Would she offer vague and evasive answers? Yes. Lie? No.

Neither the recovery phase nor the drive phase of each stroke—the breathing in and the breathing out—affected Jenni's ability to converse. "Sorry to hear it. But, you know, that happens to you a lot."

"People are people . . . What can you do?"

It had become a common problem following every trip. Jenni's genuine concern and inquisitiveness made her an asset to the State Department's public relations branch and a good foster sister. It also made Talia's life challenging. She tried to get her talking about her own life. "What . . . about you? Anything come up . . . while I was gone?"

"Actually yes, and it's weighing me down. Can we talk about it?"

"Yes." Talia tried not to sound too relieved. "Yes we can."

Jenni let up on the pace, forcing Talia to compensate to keep from rocking the boat. That was new. Jenni rarely slacked off during a workout. "It's not fair, Talia."

"What's not fair?"

"Life. Everything. I mean, I know God has a plan, but . . ." She lifted her oars out of the water and rested them on the surface to hold the balance of the boat.

"But what?"

"It's the refugee crisis."

"Oh." Talia wanted to be sympathetic, but sometimes Jenni needed a push toward reality. There were millions of refugees. Precious few ever made it to the US. Two weeks earlier, Talia had interviewed a married couple arriving from Ukraine, ferreting out intelligence on Russian border incursions. The couple had waited five years for resettlement after separatists drove them from their home. "Jenni, I know it's sad, but there's always a refugee crisis."

"I know. I know. But it's all over the news right now. Especially Myanmar. Tens of thousands displaced in religious purges. State PR is getting hundreds of calls a day."

"And you're fielding a lot of those calls." Only a year and a half out of college, Jenni was at the bottom of the State Department food chain. That meant answering phones.

"So many. People want us to do something. I have to regurgitate the same old lines. 'We're doing all we can. We're working through the proper channels. It's a delicate situation.'" She spoke each phrase as if it were poison. "And then there are the children."

"The children?" Talia's own strokes stopped. Her oars skimmed the water's surface. "What children?"

"Children in the camps are going missing.

Myanmar won't acknowledge they were ever born. The host countries, Bangladesh and Thailand, won't register them. There's no paper trail." She glanced back at Talia, wobbling the boat. "How do you find a child that doesn't officially exist?"

"That must be hard to deal with."

"Day in and day out, Talia. The calls never stop. Don't they know I want to fly a jumbo jet over there and grab as many as I can?"

Talia balanced her oars with one hand and looked back. "I know it's hard to see, but you said it yourself. God has a plan." She set her oars in the water again. "Come on. One more mile."

CHAPTER EIGHT

Lobéké National Park
Southern Cameroon

Anton Gorev scanned the forest preserve through the scope of his Fabrique Nationale Ballista rifle. He'd broken visual contact and advanced ahead of his targets to take up a position on a rocky perch.

He'd lost sight of them for an hour, but it mattered little. In another life, a Spetsnaz drillmaster had taught him that the hunter who understands his quarry's mind is never far off the trail. Gorev had taken on a new name since then, and a new face, but the old lessons still applied.

A gap in the trees revealed a family of elephants—a bull, two females, and three calves. The bull's tusks were clean and white from a recent dip in the river. They stood out well against the deep green of the foliage, making him tempting prey for Kweku Okoro and his men. The poachers would come. Gorev would wait.

He traced his scope along three potential avenues of approach before he acquired his targets, crouching in high grass five hundred meters from the elephants. Okoro and his men would take their time, avoid spooking their prize.

They had no concerns about interruptions from the preserve's rangers, because Okoro kept the local commander in his pocket with bribes. That sin also granted Gorev the freedom to stalk him.

With a gloved hand, the Russian brushed gravel and grit away from a broad stone and stretched his body out flat. He settled the Ballista on its forward bipod, pressed his shoulder to the stock, and put his eye to the scope. A minor adjustment brought Okoro under the crosshairs. But Gorev didn't pull the trigger.

He watched.

Two of the poachers carried Chinese AK-47 knockoffs. Okoro, however, carried a bolt-action Holland & Holland Nitro Express elephant gun. A traditionalist. Gorev respected that.

The old English big-game hunters had walked this same African forest with the same weapon, but they'd trekked with local carriers who bore the weight of the gun until the hunters were ready to shoot. Not Okoro. In nearly forty-eight hours, Gorev had seen him set the weapon down only to eat and sleep. He carried it like a scepter. Gorev respected that too.

The Russian brought his eye back from the scope and frowned. Boyd was making a mistake. He dialed his smartphone using his trigger hand, with the tip of the thumb and forefinger cut away from the glove. A live video feed opened on the screen.

Livingston Boyd scowled at the camera from a white shag rug in the great room of his London penthouse. "Anton. You're calling sooner than expected. Is the job done?"

Is the job done? Another Englishman too high and mighty to carry his own gun. Gorev took a moment to consider his answer. His own bearish visage would look enormous on the eighty-five-inch LCD monitor above Boyd's fireplace. That always annoyed his young boss. Did Gorev dare annoy him further? "Eh . . . Not yet, boss. I have . . . question."

"You have . . . *k-vestion?*" Boyd mimicked Gorev's accent. Before the Russian could respond, Boyd's eyes shifted to the lower portion of the monitor. "Wait. You're bouncing this call off the satellite? You know this line comes with risks."

"It is important."

"I'm sure you *think* it is."

Gorev checked his targets. Now that he knew their location, he could watch them without the scope. They had advanced, but not far. "I have concern about our plan for Hawk Three One Four. He is strong. An asset."

Boyd lowered his chin and raised his eyebrows. "Our plan?"

"Your plan. Forgive my English, please."

"I will not." The Englishman paced in an oval on his rug. "Hawk Three One Four . . ." He scratched his temple, as if killing a poacher in

Cameroon was an easily forgotten piece of his Friday. "Remind me. Which field mouse did this guy eat to earn his wings?"

"Field Mouse Eight Zero Zero Seven Five. Another poacher, across border in Nigeria. A wise move. For consolidation."

Boyd snorted. "A lazy move. For convenience. Hawk Three One Four is old, Gorev. You know how I don't like the old ones."

Gorev bristled at the comment. In Boyd's eyes, anyone over thirty-five belonged in a home. Or better still, a grave. Gorev was over thirty-five. "I think his experience is asset."

"Do I pay you to think?"

The correct answer to that question depended on the day. "*Nyet.*"

"*Nyet.*" Boyd spat out the word. "Look. I brought you in after the fiasco in the Black Sea because you had one extremely valuable contact and one true talent. The contact was a bonus. Your *talent* is what led me to give you a job, a new identity, and generally save your former-Soviet bacon. Use that talent now." He stepped closer to the monitor. "Or should I send an anonymous tip to Interpol, alerting them to your presence in Cameroon?"

Gorev tensed his jaw. "*Nyet.* I do as you ask."

"Good. Here's what you don't see. I've got Jackrabbit Four Eight Two Five on the hook in Yaoundé. He's younger and hungrier, building a top-notch ivory distribution network. If I hand him your hawk's supply chain, costs go down and profits go up. What makes me happy, Anton?"

"Costs down and profits up."

"*Da*. The old makes way for the new. Circle of life. Law of the jungle." He picked up a remote from his coffee table. "Now go do your job. And make it quick."

"Why quick?" Boyd had never cared how the job was done before. "For mercy?"

"No, you Neanderthal. I need you at the new towers in Bangkok . . . like yesterday. The contractors are botching up my game floors. You know how I feel about my games. Get down there and scare them straight." He pointed the remote at the camera. "Boyd out."

The screen went blank. Gorev stared at it for a long time, then returned his attention to the valley below. His targets had closed on the elephant, putting Okoro within a comfortable range for the big Nitro Express. It wouldn't be long now.

Gorev's rifle needed only a minor shift on its bipod to adjust for the new angle. After checking the chamber, he inched forward and pressed his shoulder against the stock. He moved his eye to the scope and waited until Okoro rose to a knee and lifted the elephant gun.

A shot rang out across the valley.

The family of elephants lumbered off into the trees.

Okoro teetered to one side and dropped.

Gorev had fired first.

He kept the Ballista trained on Okoro. One of the poacher's men rushed into the scope's view and picked up the Nitro Express—the ruler's scepter. Gorev fired again.

The next man, the last of the poachers, understood. He left the scepter where it lay and tore off through the scrub, surely to tell others what he'd witnessed. The new blood, Boyd's handpicked replacement for Okoro, would encounter no resistance when he moved in to take over the operation. For all Boyd's entrepreneurial brilliance, Gorev doubted whether he knew how to send such a message.

CHAPTER NINE

CIA Headquarters
Langley, Virginia

"Good mornin', Skinny." Luanne, the full-figured barista of the CIA's very own internal Starbucks, rested a hip against her counter. "What's new?"

Talia gave her a thin smile. "No skinny for me, today. I need the good stuff."

"I don' know if I can allow that."

"It's just one drink."

"Mmm-hmm. Like I ain't heard *that* before." Luanne twisted the steel cup in her hands, wiping it out with a dishrag. "Look, honey. I give you one with the good stuff today, one tomorrow"— she raised her eyes to Talia's—"and the next thing you know, my little Skinny looks like Frank Brennan."

"I'll never let it go that far. I don't have the cheek structure for the mustache."

"Funny, but you know what I mean. You're on the edge of a sugary, slippery slope."

"Look, I don't pay you to talk." Talia tapped a finger on the counter and gave her a wink. "I pay you to pour."

"You hardly pay me at all." Luanne shot a glance at her tip jar, then threw the rag over her shoulder and went to work on Talia's leaded white chocolate mocha. "So what in the world's got you turnin' to the caffeinated dark side?"

"Something happened in the field." Talia slipped a dollar bill into the jar. The conversation had reached a gray area. Luanne worked inside the CIA. She'd been vetted, but Talia could only say so much. "Someone may or may not have tried to have me killed."

Luanne didn't miss a beat. "Oh, is that all?"

She shoved the steamer down into Talia's full-fat milk and raised her voice above the hiss. "You know where you work, right? This ain't the Department of Agriculture, although I hear it's pretty cutthroat over there." Luanne poured the milk. "This is the C-I-A. Just 'cause someone tries to kill you ain't no reason to go mopin' around, drinking high-calorie death coffee." She worked the syrup bottle, pumping squirt after squirt of flavored sugar into the cup. "In this business, when someone tries to kill you, you track 'em down and kill 'em right back . . . or at least lock 'em up."

"This is different."

"No it ain't. You only think it's different." She sprayed a small mountain of whipped cream into the cup and pushed the finished product across the counter.

Talia said nothing. She stared down into the softness of the cream.

"Listen, Skinny. You know you're gonna take my advice before it's all said and done. Why not save us both the time and get started now?"

The coffee would go on Talia's running tab. She picked up the cup, feeling its warmth, and turned to go. "I wish I could."

"Mmm-hmm." Luanne turned as well—hips first, head second. "Go on then, girl. Wander off mumblin' and grumblin' into your big ol' dessert. But when you've settled things, I expect you to come back so I can have my 'Told you so.' "

Talia and her *big ol' dessert* took an elevator six floors down to the black marble halls and clear cubicles of REED. But before heading to Russian Ops at the heart of it all, she turned down a nondescript hallway. At the end was a door, marked by a brass plate.

OTHER.

One corner hung a nanometer south of level.

Inside, Frank Brennan lounged behind his desk with a fragment of donut in his hand and a large napkin tucked into his collar. The napkin had failed to catch all the powder, leaving his plaid shirt dusted white.

"You've got a little something . . . ," Talia said, circling a finger around her entire blouse. "And also . . ." She moved the finger to her upper lip, indicating his bushy mustache.

Brennan shoved the last of the donut home.

"Thanks." He whipped the napkin from his collar and made a failed attempt to clean up. The smears of white made a nice abstract pattern, shifting the focus away from the pit stains. "Welcome back. I'm glad you're not dead."

Had the broom-closet office shrunk even more in the two weeks Talia had been away? She glanced at an empty workstation in the corner. "I see they haven't replaced me."

"No one can replace you."

"You're sweet."

"As sweet as the creepy uncle you only see at Thanksgiving." Brennan rubbed the remaining powder out of his mustache. "I assume you and Tyler had a chat. How much did he tell you?"

"The whole story."

"He never tells the whole story."

"Okay." Talia lifted the box of donuts from the corner of Brennan's desk. The day was just getting started and only two remained. "He told me enough. And before you start, I haven't bought into the whole *Oleg's tip came from the Agency* thing."

"That's fair." He took the box away from her. "Hands off. You don't work here anymore."

"I was going to throw them away."

"Over my dead body."

"Exactly what I'm trying to prevent." Talia glanced over her shoulder, checking the door. "To be clear, you and Tyler think Jordan is Archangel."

A hard stare was all the confirmation Brennan would offer.

"Look. Jordan's harsh. But an abrasive boss isn't necessarily a traitor. I learned that lesson with you six months ago. I'd hate to make the same mistake twice."

Brennan sighed and steepled his fingers over his spare tire. "So, what's your play?"

"Business as usual. Keep my eyes open."

"And if she sends you out again?"

Talia shrugged. "I go out."

"Risky."

"Comes with the job. Ask Luanne. She'll tell you."

"And what about Tyler?"

Talia scrunched up her nose. "What about him?"

"If Jordan sends you out again, you'll keep Tyler in the loop. Right?"

Talia flicked his donut box with a finger and laughed. "As if you won't. I know where he gets his intel." She started for the door.

"By the way, young one," he called after her. "I picked up on the thinly veiled insult earlier. For your information, I was never an abrasive boss."

"See you, Frank." She let the door to OTHER fall closed behind her.

CHAPTER TEN

CIA Headquarters
Langley, Virginia

Eddie Gupta saw Talia coming. She watched him duck behind his bank of monitors when she entered the gleaming intelligence palace known as Russian Ops, still called *The Russian Ops Desk* by all who knew of its existence.

The central branch of the Directorate's Russian Eastern European Division had shrunk to just that—a desk—after the dubious end of the Cold War. The Agency's operational focus shifted to counterterrorism, and funding for old-school espionage against America's favorite foe had diminished. But in recent years, thanks to the almost mystic talent of its chief, Mary Jordan, to put officers in the right places at the right times, the desk had once again bloomed to a full branch. And Talia was its rising star.

This hadn't earned her a great many friends.

"Terrance." She gave a *'sup* chin lift to a passing case officer, a veteran of the branch. Terrance had scored a seat at Russian Ops four years earlier and had dug in like a tick. He favored bow ties, although he refused to see any correlation between his fashion choices and his glaring lack of field assignments.

He answered with a curt smile. "Welcome back. I hear you got your asset killed. Nicely done."

"He wasn't an asset. Not yet."

"Oh, that's right. You never landed him in the first place."

She glowered at his back as he marched up steel-grate steps to his cubicle. Russian Ops had reached its lateral limits, and Jordan had added staircases and a few upper-level cubicles— sought-after real estate, like the top bunks at summer camp. Terrance had already declared to Talia she'd never get his.

"Eddie . . ." Talia approached the geek's desk. He didn't answer from behind the monitors, but she heard a sneeze and a juicy sniffle. "I know you're there."

He rose like a prairie dog peeking out of its hole, assuming a prairie dog could hold a handkerchief to its nose and wear wire-rimmed glasses that were perpetually sliding out of place. A second hand appeared, palm up, holding a little box of chocolates.

Gifts were not really a thing between them. Talia set her coffee on the edge of her desk and folded her arms. "What's this?"

Eddie traded the handkerchief for his phone, showing her a text message on the screen.

She knows.
Arriving today.
Run, hide, or bring gifts.
Maybe all three.

The sender was listed as UNKNOWN. "Tyler?"

"Finn, I think." Eddie looked at the screen as if trying to decide. "You can almost hear the Melbourne accent." He brought the chocolates to her and offered them, lowering his head. "Look. I'm sorry. I should have told you I was working on Tyler's project."

"I get it. And you're forgiven. Sending him to Volgograd saved my life." She accepted the gift. "But don't tell him that."

The designation NC-1701-D was stamped in gold print on the clear plastic top of the chocolate box. She turned it over. "Hey. This says 'Free with your purchase of *Star Trek: The Next Generation* commemorative Christmas socks.'" She lowered the box. "And it's dated two years ago."

Eddie scrunched his shoulders. "I was pressed for time."

The chocolates went straight to the trash bin under Talia's desk, and she followed Eddie back to his monitors. Hundreds of lines of alphanumeric code rolled up his left screen in a continuous stream. Corresponding graphs and tables flashed up and down on the center and right screens. "Wow. What are you working on?"

"Oh this? This is my screensaver. Makes it look like I'm doing Jordan's bidding when she walks by." Eddie clicked his keyboard. The code and graphics dissolved, revealing a flat global map that took up all three monitors. Arcing red and yellow lines joined cities all over the world. "*This* is what I'm really wor . . . wor—" He sneezed. Hard. His glasses clacked down on the keyboard.

"Are you sick?"

"It's nothing. Probably spring fever."

"It's the fourth of December."

"Whatever." Eddie wiped his nose, put the glasses back on, and went to work again.

The map coalesced into a globe on the center screen. Some of the yellow lines ran to satellites, hopping from one to the next before returning to Earth.

"The Volgograd save came from a breakthrough I had in Tyler's project." Eddie zoomed in on a bird in geostationary orbit over the South Atlantic. "But this morning I had another one. Big—like someone handing me a cheat code for *Legend of Zelda*. Suddenly hidden rooms and side quests were popping up everywhere."

A diminutive woman of Korean descent walked by, hair pulled back into a tight ponytail— another Specialized Skills Officer like Eddie. She glanced at the screen with interest.

Eddie hit a key to bring up his screensaver.

He swiveled his chair and motioned with his handkerchief for the woman to keep moving. "Eyes to yourself, Sue Lin. These are my screens, not yours. You're not cleared for this."

Sue Lin let out a huff, hugged a stack of files to her chest, and walked on.

Talia looked down her nose at her friend. "Can a guy with your social skills afford to alienate a girl like Sue Lin? You two have a lot in common."

"I don't need her." Eddie swiveled his chair back to his screens. "I have Darcy."

"Meh . . ." Talia made a face. " 'Have' is a strong word when you're dealing with the French female Unabomber." She hit his keyboard to unlock the screens. "Okay. I heard *cheat code* and *Zelda*. Give me the Geek-to-Normal translation please."

"I got an alert at four a.m., another hit from the digital marker Tyler and I traced to Boyd."

"Like the one that told you Oleg's tip-off about Vera Novak came from Boyd's network."

"Right. And since I knew you were safe, I rolled over and tried to go back to sleep. But the image of the marker called to me. I saw it every time I closed my eyes, like when Rey kept seeing visions of Kylo Ren, and she—"

"We both promised never to speak of that movie again."

"Yeah. Sorry." Eddie clicked on the satellite, opening a window of constantly shifting data.

"Anyway, the encryption fragment from the alert kept poking at my brain, especially the six-digit preamble."

"Again, Geek-to-Normal, please."

He captured a screenshot of the shifting data and blew it up to fill the center screen, showing her several columns of code. "Here. Look at these. Each one is a data packet passing through this satellite on its way to somewhere else. Keep in mind, lots of networks use this same satellite."

"Okay . . ."

"Okay. Data packets entering a satellite acquire little riders, tour guides that help the packets navigate an internal maze. And it's a moving maze—walls shifting, doors opening and closing—all designed to make a finite digital space as efficient as possible."

Eddie was still talking above her geek level. Talia flipped back through images of his words to make sense of them. "The six-digit codes are *tour guides* that help the data find its way."

"Exactly. Picture an army of tour guides who all speak different languages. When the satellite encounters a new encryption language, it builds a new tour guide with a new code." Eddie sniffled, circling one of the columns with his cursor. "Look at this."

She stared at the column, blinked, and shook her head.

He rolled his eyes. "You're looking at a new

six-digit tour guide, unique to Boyd's encryption. In short, the marker led us to the satellite and its tour guide, and the tour guide led us to Boyd's unique encryption pattern. Now we have a treasure chest *filled* with trackable data fragments."

She retrieved the coffee from her desk. She felt like she would need it. "You know, you could have led with 'treasure chest of trackable data' and skipped the rest."

"But then you wouldn't fully appreciate my genius. Anyway, pieces of the puzzle are falling into place every hour now. It's incredible, unlike anything we've ever seen."

He was too excited, skipping key parts of the story. Talia took a swig and cringed at the level of sugar. Luanne had been right. She'd gone a step too far. "Be specific, Eddie. *What* is unlike anything we've ever seen?"

"Boyd's criminal network. Our British wunderkind has put together a global crime syndicate on a scale as yet unheard of."

Eddie paused to blow his nose, leaving her hanging—and a little disgusted—for several seconds. He clicked his mouse, and the digital camera flew from city to city. Blue glowing labels popped up everywhere next to warehouses, coffee shops, and skyscrapers. Each was a code with two letters and a string of numbers—FM60915, JR2937, CO852.

"Those labels. What do they mean?"

"Members? Users? I've broken out portions of a few messages so far. Think of it like playing *Wheel of Fortune*. I think F-M is field mouse. C-O is cobra."

Talia wrinkled her nose. "Why is Boyd using animal—" Talia stopped mid-sentence. What was she doing? She flipped Eddie's monitors back to the screensaver. "I don't care." She said it to herself as much as to the geek. "And I don't want to care. This is Tyler's crusade, not mine."

Eddie swiveled around to look up at her. "You have to care. We're trying to find a traitor." He dropped his voice to a whisper. "We're trying to find the person who ordered the hit on your father."

"And I wish you the best. But don't you get it?" Talia pulled the rolling chair over from her desk and sat beside her friend. "Holding on to my anger over Dad's death crippled me— physically and spiritually. I can't run back into that darkness."

"So you're just . . . moving on?"

She nodded.

"But the prime suspect is you-know-who." Eddie inclined his head toward a wooden door at the far end of the Russian Ops section. "The Ice Queen."

Talia wasn't ready to face that idea. She let it pass unchallenged. "You can't call your female boss the *Ice Queen,* Eddie. It's offensive."

"Don't be such a snowflake."

"I'm not a snowflake. You're a snowflake."

They locked eyes until their grim stares broke down into giggles, lightening the mood.

Eddie grinned. "If Jordan's the Ice Queen, doesn't that make *her* a snowflake?"

"Talia!" The wooden door was open. Jordan stood in the frame. "Get in here."

Talia went rigid. She whispered through clenched teeth, "How long was she watching us?"

"I don't know. But if you're not back in ten, I'm calling the Marines."

CHAPTER ELEVEN

CIA Headquarters
Langley, Virginia

The door banged closed the moment Talia walked through. Jordan stormed past her. "Just who do you think you are?"

Talia watched, dumbfounded, as her boss took up a post at the corner of her giant mahogany desk, arms crossed. She had no idea how to answer.

"You're an officer of the Directorate of Operations. You're part of a team, and I expect you to act like it." Her arms dropped. "How do you think I feel? One of my people—my own recruit—is ambushed and disappears in Volgograd. The next day, she turns up at Minsk Station long enough to grab a fresh passport and vanishes again. For how long?"

On foolish instinct Talia moved to check the date and time on her phone. She went so far as to touch her back pocket before thinking the better of it.

"Two days!" Jordan pounded the desk so hard a steel stickman on a tightwire—one of those perpetual motion desk toys—teetered near to the point of falling.

"I'm . . . sorry?"

"Two full days, Talia. Without a word. And then I come out this morning to find you laughing and joking with Gupta as if you'd been here the whole time."

"I checked in with Dulles Station. I turned in my IDs, my cash. I followed protocol."

"Yes. The cash. One hundred thousand dollars, earmarked for Zverev. All there. I found that detail particularly interesting."

"Interesting?" Why should returning all the Agency's money upset her boss?

"We'll circle back around to the money. My point, Talia, is the Directorate—this Clandestine Service you claim to love—is more than procedure. We are a team." The tightness in her features softened. "I'm your mentor, your friend. I would have thought you'd come to me the moment you set foot in the building."

The stiff-necked division chief had never used the word *mentor* with Talia, let alone *friend*. But now that the offense had been laid before her, rare and raw, Talia couldn't imagine it any other way. Maybe Tyler and Brennan were wrong about Jordan. "I'm sorry," she said. "I really am."

"I know. And I know I'm partly to blame. Listen, as a woman leading an intelligence division like REED, I *must* maintain a cold persona." She raised an eyebrow. "I have to be the Ice Queen."

"You heard us?"

"Yes, and I don't mind. I play the Ice Queen to keep my edge, to stay ahead. You'll have to do the same one day. But I'm not as calculating and heartless as I seem. The truth is, I was worried about you. I'm thrilled you made it home." She gestured to a chair. "Please. Sit. Regale me with the tale of your daring escape."

Talia did, hesitantly at first but with growing ease—until she came to the part where Oleg had betrayed her.

"Wait. *Who* knocked the gun away?"

"A . . . bystander. Someone trying to help. There were two in the bar." It wasn't a lie, but it sounded like one, even to Talia's ears. The next part made it worse. "Their friend was waiting with a truck."

"So, you're in a bar full of Russian killers when two bystanders decide to fight them. And they've even got a buddy out in the parking lot keeping the truck warm?"

"Some guys don't like smoky bars. The guy with the truck was very fit." That part was true.

"And these men, they never asked for payment. I know this because"—Jordan shrugged—"if you recall, you turned in all that cash. Every red cent."

The cash. Now she understood. She had been too honest for her own good. What was the alternative? Steal from the agency? Talia tried deflecting with humor. "Red cent. Russia. I see what you did there."

"Mmm. And this third helper"—Jordan flopped a hand—"the one so cautious about breathing secondhand smoke. He captures Oleg outside the bar and holds him long enough for a pack of new Russians to drive up and shoot him?"

The hairs on the back of her neck stood up. She hadn't told Jordan about the shooting. "Uh . . . Correct."

Jordan slapped a photo down between them. "This guy?" She pointed to a blurry form in the back of a Toyota HiLux. "Is he our health nut?"

There was Talia, in grainy glory, with Tyler and Finn holding Oleg up against the tailgate as a lifeless bullet sponge. The shot had come from an overhead traffic cam. Maybe they had run a red light. Maybe they had been speeding. Maybe both. Why hadn't she expected there to be pictures? There were always pictures. This wasn't a story shared between friends reunited. This was an interrogation. Jordan had played her. Like always.

Among the five in the truck, only Talia's and Oleg's faces were visible, and nowhere near recognizable with the blur. "No. Uh . . . The guy who caught Oleg is driving." Talia coughed. Her throat had gone dry. "Where'd that photo come from?"

"Speed cam. You didn't see it?"

"No."

"Not great for a field operative."

"I was getting shot at." Talia tapped the picture. "Shouldn't we be looking into the guys trying to kill me instead of the guys helping me?"

"You tell me. I see five targets in that truck, yet all the bullets wound up in poor Oleg." Jordan slid the picture away. "Talia. Is it possible these men who helped you are also the ones who sold you out? Is it possible the whole charade was just a way to make you trust them?"

"I . . . I don't know."

"Have they attempted to contact you since that night in Volgograd?"

"No. No they haven't." That, at least, was true.

"Good." Jordan walked around the desk to take Talia's elbow and help her up. "Look. I've been running you ragged for six months. You missed some tricks in Volgograd, leading to a dangerous situation. You certainly missed the camera. You're fatigued. Take some time off."

"What?" Talia stepped back from the chair. "No, I'm fine."

"This isn't an offer. It's an order. I don't want to see your face for two weeks." Jordan narrowed her eyes, studying her subordinate. "Better yet, three. Now get out of here. I have to prepare for a lunch with Senator Ramirez, the chair of the intelligence committee." She walked Talia to the door. "We'll keep on this. For my money, your good Samaritans and your attackers are more connected than you think. I'll have Gupta and Sue Lin work on tracing both groups."

"Without me?"

"I think we can handle it. The Directorate was, after all, the world's premier intelligence division long before you arrived."

By the time she finished the statement, Jordan had pushed Talia over the threshold. The door fell shut, and Talia heard her muted voice from the other side. "Don't just stand there. Go home."

CHAPTER TWELVE

State Route 123
Langley, Virginia

Jordan had played her. Talia's mind spun as her Civic clanked over the flattened hydraulic barriers of Langley's southern gate. How foolish she'd been. No conversation with Jordan was ever just a conversation.

"Leave them wondering how much you know," Jordan had told her moments before Talia walked into her first mock interrogation back at the Farm. "That's the key."

The Art of Interrogation—one of Talia's worst memories from her training despite a syllabus that included Arctic Survival and Sewer Navigation. The memory filled her with regret. "But how?" she had asked Jordan. "Scott won the toss and played interrogator first. He has the advantage." Talia watched him twiddle his thumbs on the other side of a two-way mirror. "The information is new, but the format is the same. The game favors Player One."

All Farm students spent time on both sides of the table in a two-player game. Each had to extract a set of unique, fictional information from the other. The more information extracted, the higher the score. Talia held up well under Scott's shouting, but he had gained enough points to take the lead in the class.

"Then think outside the game." Jordan laid a hand on her shoulder. "Find a pressure point. Don't dig. Poke it and let him stew for a while. Scott has a pressure point somewhere, right?"

Talia had seen Scott leaving a bar downtown a few nights earlier, and she had her suspicions about what he'd been doing there. "Yeah. I think so."

As Talia took the interrogator's seat, Scott gave her a wink. "Let me guess. You made me sit here alone for half an hour to soften me up. Good technique. I'm ready to talk just to hear my own voice."

"You're always ready to hear your own voice." Talia opened a manila folder in her lap. "Name?"

He grinned. "Klaus."

"Right. Klaus Karlson. But we both know that's incorrect."

"We do?"

"Mmm-hmm." The folder was a prop. Talia had Scott's file locked in her eidetic memory. Klaus Karlson was the sad alliteration name of a fictional Dutch-born American caught on the wrong side of a fence in the nonexistent state of Slapkovia—details created for the game. But she knew Scott. He wouldn't talk unless she moved the conversation outside the game.

"So . . . Klaus. You're married, right?"

The grin vanished. Scott looked past her to the mirrored glass.

"Don't look over there. And don't worry about answering. The tan line on your ring finger is enough for me."

He covered the mark with his other hand. "What are you doing?"

"My job." Talia lifted the folder into view, tapping its edge on her knee to make him wonder what else might be in there. The Farm was known for its tricks, not its fairness. She capitalized on the paranoia all of them felt. "You're a young man. Right out of college, I'd guess. Young man. Young bride. Must be difficult to be apart so early in the marriage."

"Where is this going, Talia?"

"Don't use that name. You don't know me." Point one. She'd opened the door and let Scott lead them outside the scenario. Now she'd run with it. "Tell me, how often do you visit the Ninth Street Lounge and"—she thumped her ring finger on the table, making a guess from what she knew of his preferences—"that blonde." Talia met his eyes. "What's her name?"

The color drained from Scott's cheeks. He leaned across the table. "Please. The cameras. They're recording this. The instructors are listening."

"You don't look well, *Klaus*. Why don't I step out and let you take a breather?" Talia walked to the door, waving at the glass. "The subject needs a break. Can we get a bottle of water in here?"

While Talia watched from the observation room, Scott fidgeted with the edge of the table, paced, sat again, and dropped his head into his hands. For nearly an hour, he looked everywhere but the mirror. When he finally did, with pleading eyes, Talia knew he was ready.

The instant she walked into the room, Scott started talking. He revealed line after line of the fake information he'd been tasked with protecting, anything to keep her from rehashing his visit to the Ninth Street Lounge. She stopped him before he gave up enough to get himself booted from the program.

Every word Scott spoke to Talia from then on was tainted with bitterness. In the end, the Agency washed him out of the program.

Pulling up to a stoplight behind an old hatchback more than a year later, Talia had no illusions as to whether Jordan had known about Scott and the blonde. She'd looked so proud when Talia left the interrogation room.

Leave them wondering how much you know.

Jordan was still the master.

How much did she know? If Jordan was on to Tyler and his merry band of thieves, she could have Talia drummed out of the Agency for working with them.

The worry as she waited for the red light to

change left her so distracted she didn't see the man approaching from behind until her passenger door opened.

Finn, with something akin to a blunderbuss under his arm, slid into the seat beside her. "G'day, princess."

Her Glock came out before his shoulders had settled into the seatback. "What are you doing here?"

Setting the blunderbuss in his lap, the Aussie pulled a short-bladed tool from his belt. He cupped one hand behind the other and started pounding the blade into her windshield.

Talia shook the Glock. "Stop that."

"Can't."

"You know this is loaded, right?"

"I'm doing this for your own good." The tool bounced repeatedly off the glass. "Tough windshield."

"It's Lexan."

"True blue? I thought they only gave that to important people."

"The special activities guys installed it after they hijacked my car last year, along with an armored hood."

Finn inclined his head toward the passenger window. "What about that one?"

"Standard auto glass."

"Right." He smashed it out with the back of the tool.

"Hey! You could have rolled that down!"

"Takes too long." Finn tossed the tool on the floor and snatched up the blunderbuss. "We're out of time. Look."

The light had turned green, but the car in front hadn't moved. A big guy with stark white hair climbed out of the driver's side, raised a cheap MAC-11 machine pistol, and opened fire.

Rounds pelted the hood. Talia threw the car into reverse and stepped on the gas. "What is happening?"

"Assassination attempt." Finn stuck half his body through the open window and blew the rear window of the hatchback to scattered bits. "Can't get the angle on our man. Little help?"

With a frustrated grunt, she switched into drive and gunned the engine. She hit the rear corner of the killer's car full force.

The hatchback skidded sideways and knocked the man down. He tried to rise as Talia continued past, but Finn dropped him with the blunderbuss.

"Did you just kill him?"

"Boss wouldn't like it." Finn pulled himself back into the car. One of his arms was bleeding, caked with chunks of broken glass. "But I'll wager that rubber ball Matilda planted in his chest shattered his sternum."

Talia could only assume Matilda was the

blunderbuss. She checked the rearview mirror. The attacker had dragged himself back into the vehicle. Two more cars drove through the intersection as if nothing had happened. Standard Washington, DC.

CHAPTER THIRTEEN

Great Falls Drive
Near Wolf Trap, Virginia

Finn directed Talia and her bullet-ridden Civic onto the Dulles Toll Road. She set the cruise control, thankful it still worked, and shot him a glare. She had to raise her voice over the wind blowing in through the broken window. "What's going on?"

"That guy had a scope fixed on Langley's southern gate all morning. He picked you up on your way out and pulled into traffic ahead of you. So I moved in."

There had to be more to the story. Talia waited for the rest. He didn't offer it. She ground her teeth. "I need more details. Who was the assassin? Better yet, why were you watching for him in the first place?"

He pointed to a sign over the highway. "Take exit 117. Two miles."

"I asked you a question."

"Did you? I must not have heard. Quite loud over here. Window's broken."

"Fine." She pulled out her phone. "If you won't work with me, I'm calling the Agency. Protocol dictates I call this in anyway."

"Nope." He snatched the phone away and tossed it out the window.

A semitruck crunched it under two of its tires. "Finn!"

The exit came up. He gestured at the sign with his gun.

Talia sighed and signaled for the lane change. "Please, talk to me."

The noise in the car quieted as Talia slowed on the feeder. "All right. Here it is. Tyler worries. With good reason. Did you really think the attempt in Volgograd would be a one-off? And by the way, a thank-you wouldn't kill you. I did just save your life. Again."

"Thanks. Okay? Thanks for Volgograd and thanks for today." She glanced at his arm. "You're bleeding."

"Nothing some Neosporin and a few Snoopy bandages won't cure. Take your next right."

She made the turn onto a long, tree-lined street and took a breath. "Tyler's still hovering—"

"Looking out for you."

"Hovering. And now he's using you as a proxy?"

"Not me. Mac. Our Scottish friend is following in the Jag." His eyes went to the rearview mirror, leading Talia's gaze. She saw a Jaguar F-Type turn onto the road to follow them. Finn gave her a little shrug, almost shy. "I . . . volunteered to ride along."

"Because you're *that* bored?"

There was a flash of heat in his eyes. His features hardened, and he looked out through the broken window. "Yeah. I'm *that* bored. Take your next right, your highness."

Her sarcasm had cut him more deeply than she intended. For the rest of the drive, she got nothing out of Finn but directions. One winding road turned to another until a gate swung wide and the trees gave way to a stone manor with a circular drive. Talia couldn't nail down the period of the house, but a long garage beside the drive showed signs of having once been a stable.

Finn got out. "Go in the house, out of sight. I'll park the car."

"Finn, your arm. It needs—"

"I said go."

Talia gave up on the argument and relinquished the driver's seat. Mossy steps led to the door and, thankfully, to a friendly face.

"Conrad." She took the older gentleman's hand. Officially Tyler's private chef, Conrad rarely traveled with the team, but he was Talia's favorite. The sight of him was like a warm hug. She moved in for a real one.

"Oh my," he said, patting her back. "There, there, child. I've missed you too. No one else in this band of misfits has a palate worthy of my creations."

She released him and passed a finger over the rich velvet breast of his waistcoat. "Plum. I like it. Branching out from the usual tweed, are we?"

"I'm feeling festive."

"Why?"

"You're home safe."

Home. What place qualified as home in their line of work? "What happened to Tyler's place on Chesapeake Bay?"

"He found it too ostentatious."

Talia glanced back at the Jag pulling into the drive. "Nothing is too ostentatious for Mr. Tyler."

"Touché. Perhaps, in truth, the other house was too far away from you."

Conrad led her inside, pausing beneath the walnut arch of a butler's pantry. "Can I get you something? Sweet? Savory?"

"Surprise me."

"I'll take some o' them wee sandwiches from last night if there's leftovers." Mac walked up behind them, waving a meaty hand. But Conrad had already disappeared into the kitchen.

Wolf Manor, as Mac called it, was a study in wood paneling and dim hallways. Sitting room, great room, dining room, atrium—the Scotsman gave her a tour while they both tried Conrad's sweet pea and risotto cakes.

"And where is Tyler?"

"Waitin' for ya in the library. Far end o' the western wing."

Mac directed her to a long hall, but he didn't go with her. Talia found Tyler in a hexagonal

81

room lined with bookshelves, each with a rolling ladder. As she walked through the door, he kept his gaze buried in the heavy text in his lap.

"So you're not dead."

"Thanks to you, I guess."

"You guess? Wait, I've heard this one before." He cracked a smile, eyes bright behind a pair of reading glasses. "You had it handled."

"Maybe. I didn't get the chance to try before Finn swooped in."

Tyler closed his book. "You mean Mac."

"No, I mean Finn."

His expression remained steady, as always, but Talia could see he hadn't known Finn had gone on the excursion. So, Finn had been serious about volunteering to look out for her. Weird. He'd never shown that much care for her before.

Tyler set the book on a cherrywood lamp table. "And now you've hunted me down to tell me off. Go ahead. Get it over with."

She opened her mouth, then closed it again. She couldn't think of anything to say.

The window behind the library's reading desk looked out over the Potomac. Tyler walked over, admiring the water, or perhaps scanning the shore for threats. "You can't go home, Talia. You know that, right?"

"Excuse me?"

"We've seen two attempts on your life in under a week. You're not safe out there."

Talia's apartment was one of her few refuges in an otherwise volatile life. She wouldn't let Tyler wrench it away so easily. "Mac and Finn caught the assassin watching the Agency, not my place. Ergo, whoever is behind this doesn't know my name or where I live. They only know my face and that I'm CIA. My apartment's clear."

He seemed to consider the argument, then rejected it outright. "Archangel is smart. She leaked enough intel to get you killed but not to point us to her position at the CIA. Plausible deniability." Tyler looked past her to the library's entryway. "Finn!"

"Yeah, boss?" The answering call came from the great room, followed by hurried footsteps.

"How do you feel about burglarizing Talia's place?"

"Brilliant." The Aussie appeared in the doorframe with a bandage on his arm—white gauze, no Snoopy. He spoke directly to Tyler, as if Talia weren't there. "Smash and grab or ghost work?"

"Ghost. Leave no trace. Get her some clothes. And what else, Talia? Hair dryer? Curling iron?"

She caved, turning to Finn. "Fine. You both win. Get me some jeans. Grab the red sweater and the three suits at the end of the closet." She hesitated, shot a glance at Tyler, and flattened her voice. "And my hair dryer, like he said. It's with the makeup bag under the bathroom counter. While you're at it, grab the makeup bag too."

Finn folded his arms and raised his eyebrows. "Please."

Some of the hostility faded. "And . . ."

"Thank you."

"You're welcome, your highness." He ducked into the hall. An instant later, he leaned his head back into view. "Are you sure there's nothing else?"

Talia winced. Why hadn't she thought of the rest? Worse, why had *he* thought of it first? "Top drawer of the dresser. Just close your eyes and dump the whole thing into a duffel bag."

"Right. Eyes closed." The hardness had vanished. He was trying not to grin.

"Promise me, Finn."

"Cross my heart." He set off down the hallway.

"Don't you need my key?"

Finn didn't answer.

Talia turned to Tyler. "He doesn't need a key."

"No, he doesn't need a key."

"This is totally unnecessary. You know that, right?"

Tyler guided her into the room and sat her in the chair beside his book. She noticed the title on the cover—*The Bishop of Myra*. He pulled a stool over from the bookshelves. "When are you going to face facts? Someone is trying to kill you."

"I am facing it. I *will* face it. Let me report this to the Agency. Jordan will bring in the FBI. We'll hunt this guy down and find out who hired him."

84

"Out of the question."

"Because Jordan is Archangel."

He nodded.

Talia wasn't ready to buy his theory. "If Jordan is Archangel, why did she let me take you along on the Ivanov job? The mission brief mentioned Lukon's involvement. And you're Lukon. Wouldn't Archangel know that?"

"Negative. You're forgetting the whole purpose of code names. I was the Agency's asset, not Archangel's. She was just the spy who requisitioned the . . . ," he stumbled over his next words, ". . . the job. She never knew my real identity."

The job in question had been the assassination of Talia's father, another CIA spy, falsely accused of being a threat to the US by Archangel. Talia had forgiven Tyler, but the cold she felt in her core now at the mention of the murder was the whole reason she hadn't wanted to get involved in the hunt for Archangel in the first place.

"Jordan might suspect I'm Lukon," Tyler said. "Especially now, for the same reasons I suspect she's Archangel. But she can't be sure."

"So in your mind, you and Jordan are playing this cat-and-mouse game and I'm caught in the middle. But you're wrong. Yes, Jordan is wary of you. She's suspicious of your vigilante activities and my involvement with them, but she's not Archangel."

"Then why"—Tyler checked his watch—"after you've been away from work less than an hour, is she calling?" He drew a phone from his pocket, an exact match to Talia's Agency device, which Finn had thrown under a speeding truck. "Eddie cloned a new one for you, sans the pesky CIA tracking chip." He held it out to show her.

The screen was active with an incoming call, ID masked, a sure sign the Agency was on the other end.

CHAPTER FOURTEEN

Wolf Manor
Wolf Trap, Virginia

"Answer." Tyler sat back against the reading desk. "But be cautious. Don't tell her anything about the attack."

Talia accepted the call and put it on speaker. "Inger."

"Are you all right?" Jordan's voice carried all the concern and fluster of a worried parent.

Tyler gave Talia an *I told you so* shrug.

She turned away from him. "Um . . . Sure. I'm fine. Why?"

"*Why?* The attack on Route 123. A witness saw a man we now know to be a Russian mobster shoot up a Civic. Your Civic."

"My Civic?" Talia cringed at her own reply. Repeating a question was the most obvious form of avoidance. Jordan would see right through it. She followed up by trying to redirect the focus away from her car. "Like I said, I'm fine—out here on the vacation you ordered."

Tyler touched her shoulder and waved a sticky note.

she'll ask location. say coffee shop.

Talia muted the phone. "She won't ask where I am. It's against protocol." When she unmuted it again, she took it off speaker.

"Talia, I'm worried about you. Tell me where you are."

Tyler jiggled the note. He was enjoying this too much.

"I'm in a coffee shop. Relaxing. You told me to take the day off, remember?" That earned her a thumbs-up. Tyler crumpled up the note and tossed it into the library wastebasket for two points. She wanted to punch him in the nose. "Um . . . What happened to your lunch with the senator?"

"I'll make it. But my people are my priority. You should know that."

The next note read, get intel.

Talia scrunched her nose at him in the universal sign for *No kidding*. "I'm fine. I promise. Tell me about this attack."

Silence. Now they were playing a game. "If you weren't involved, I probably shouldn't share details. This will become an FBI matter." Jordan had moved her next piece, an attempt to block.

"But I'm so bored out here on my mandatory vacation, and I'm only an hour in. Besides. If the Bratva are shooting up cars in McLean, I should be kept in the loop, right?"

More silence. "Okay. Route 123. The stoplight at Dolley Madison and Churchill. Our witness saw the suspect use his hatchback to block a late-model Honda Civic. He then stepped out of his car and let loose with a machine gun."

"Any cameras?" Talia remembered this time. She hoped Jordan was proud.

"The traffic cams on half the route were down for maintenance."

Whoa. "Quite a coincidence." Talia couldn't stop herself from saying it. They both knew coincidences like cameras going down right before a hit didn't exist, and the Bratva, the Russian mob, didn't have that kind of pull. "What about your suspect? Is he talking?"

"Our witness was fuzzy on the details, but she thought the would-be victim ran the suspect down during the escape. Seems she was right. The cops caught him doubled over in his vehicle two blocks away but failed to respect the severity of his internal injuries. He died in holding."

The blood drained from Talia's cheeks. Finn had used a nonlethal round. Talia had bounced the hitman with his own car, but she hadn't hit him hard enough to do lasting damage. Had Jordan or one of her people silenced the guy?

Tyler scribbled furiously on his notepad. suspect is dead, right?

She snatched the paper away, crumpled it, and threw it at the wastebasket. She missed.

He frowned and scribbled again. hang up.

She nodded. "Oops. Looks like my coffee's ready. I have to go."

"Okay, Talia." Jordan clearly wasn't buying it. She paused, so silent Talia could hear her own heartbeat. "I'll be in touch."

Smugness. Triumph. These were the things Talia expected from Tyler as she put the phone away. But he gave her none of those. He pushed himself off the desk and let out a long breath. "Usually I like being right, but not this time. I'm sorry, Talia. I know you looked up to Jordan. But I'm convinced. She's trying to kill you."

CHAPTER FIFTEEN

Ban Doi Henga Refugee Camp
Thai/Burma Border
Mae Hong Son Province, Thailand

Thet Ye had told no one about the uniformed men in the jungle. He couldn't say the same for Hla Meh.

"I warned you." Aung Thu slid close to Thet Ye on a bench beneath the school's pavilion. The older boy closed his mouth as the teacher neared. She handed each of them their graded assignments from the day, then moved on. "This is what comes of having a girl for a best friend." He poked Thet Ye in the arm with a bony elbow. "Hey, you hear me? She wanted to be your wife. You said no. Now she wants nothing to do with you."

Thet Ye refused to look at him. He watched Hla Meh, who sat with her gaze buried in her lap at the other corner of the pavilion, as far from him as possible. "You don't know anything."

"Then tell me why she's angry."

"I can't."

If Thet Ye told Aung Thu, by nightfall everyone in the camp would know of the men in the jungle—except Aung Thu would be at the center, confronting a whole platoon. No one would believe him, but Thet Ye could not take the risk. The teachers might get in trouble, and the school might close.

Hla Meh did not seem to care.

After confessing her fears to Thet Ye, Hla Meh had gone straight home and told her mother, who assured her that the uniformed men were part of the Thai military, there to keep them safe.

The following day, Hla Meh had dragged Thet Ye home with her. "Thet Ye saw the men too," Hla Meh told her mother. "He saw the militiamen." She grabbed him by the hand and jerked him forward. "Tell her!"

What was he supposed to do? Thet Ye kicked at the dusty floor of the hut, unable to meet the woman's eyes. "I saw uniforms. The men spoke Thai. That's all."

Hla Meh's mother ushered him out into the mud alleyway, apologizing for the tearful shouting that followed. Since that day, Hla Meh had not spoken to him.

Under the school pavilion with Aung Thu, Thet Ye finally tore his gaze from Hla Meh. "I guess I need a new best friend."

But Aung Thu was no longer paying him any attention. The bitter scent of scorched bamboo hit Thet Ye's nostrils.

His friend jumped up from the bench, waving his arms. "Fire!"

Teacher Rocha saw the flames too. "Everyone, move to the back of the pavilion. Form a line."

The flames spread quickly, leaping from hut to hut. Within seconds, the thatched roof of the pavilion ignited.

The teacher's calm crumpled. "Back, children." She spread her arms and moved the whole line sideways. "Into the yard. Quickly."

The girl beside Thet Ye tripped and fell. As he lifted her up, the thought occurred to him. He had forgotten about Hla Meh.

"Hla Meh!"

She didn't answer.

Embers swirled and spun on a growing wind of pure heat. Thet Ye shielded his face. "Hla Meh, where are you?"

The teacher shouted over the roar. Thet Ye did not understand her.

The little girl he had helped to her feet a moment before tugged at his elbow. "Teacher says run to the church."

The line broke. The students raced across the yard. Thet Ye and the girl were only a few paces from the church when the pastor burst through the door and tumbled down the steps, his shirt on fire. Smoke billowed out behind him.

The little girl screamed. The students gathered in a helpless circle while their pastor rolled in the grass at their feet. Teacher Rocha forced her way between them with a tarp and smothered the flames.

"I'm all right." The pastor, known in the camp as Pastor Nakor, pushed the tarp away. "Only a little singed."

He was not all right. Thet Ye could tell by the way he scrunched up his face as the teacher helped him to his feet. But Pastor Nakor took charge anyway. "We must go into the jungle. The trees will protect us."

Thet Ye understood. His father had told him the story. On the night of the last fire in Ban Doi Henga—the night Thet Ye was born—the jungle had saved many. The trees of the Thai rain forest were so wet they refused to burn.

Still, the students stood in the yard, hypnotized by the flames.

The pastor motioned them onward. "Go!"

Where was Hla Meh? A hand pressed Thet Ye toward the jungle. Teacher Rocha. He obeyed. He'd have to find his friend once the whole class was safe.

Once they were clear of the smoke, deep in the trees, the troop stopped, breathing hard and coughing. Black smudges masked every face, streaked with sweat and tears. The jungle muted all sound, so that the crackle of the fire and the shouts from the camp seemed miles away.

"Hla Meh?" Thet Ye spoke her name instead of shouting, hoping she was close by. She didn't answer, and he didn't get a second chance to call.

The *rat-a-tat-tat* of a machine gun broke the

quiet. Soldiers stepped from the surrounding trees. Pastor Nakor lurched toward the nearest of them and received a crack to the forehead with the butt of a weapon. Thet Ye recognized the attacker—the nice soldier from the day he and Hla Meh had run off into the jungle. He did not seem so nice now. Many of the children cried.

The soldier planted his boot in the small of the pastor's back. "Quiet down." He fired his weapon in the air. "Quiet! I want you to hear me. This hour—this second—is the start of your new lives. I am Soe Htun. And from now on, you all belong to me."

CHAPTER SIXTEEN

Wolf Manor
Wolf Trap, Virginia

Eddie didn't show up on Friday night. That upset Talia. She had needed a good cry, and Eddie was her go-to shoulder. But she awoke on Saturday to the sound of him arguing downstairs in the great room, in between sniffles and sneezes. Talia thought she recognized the other voice, although she hoped she was wrong.

A trip downstairs proved she wasn't.

"You called me for help, *mano*. Don't you think you should listen?" Franklin Perez, chief of Tech Ops and known in the Directorate as the Goblin King, raised his wheelchair to bring himself nose to nose with Eddie. "The fiber optic output goes *behind* the photon emitter."

"But that will cause EM field interference."

Franklin slapped a screwdriver down on a wood table beside a glossy black apparatus, a circle about a half meter in diameter. "Exactly."

Both men adjusted their glasses at the same time and stared each other down.

Mac, Finn, and Darcy lounged on dark leather couches and chairs while Conrad moved among them, pushing a cart of hot drinks and braided pastries. They looked like spectators at a ping-pong match.

"Eddie," Talia said upon reaching the inner rim of this peanut gallery, "what is Franklin doing here?"

Tyler appeared at her shoulder, a steaming mug hovering at his lips. "I know, right? An Agency tech officer, here on a Saturday, mixed in with our merry band of thieves? I feel like someone got peanut butter on my chocolate." He took a sip and swallowed, showing his teeth. "Or vice versa."

"I mean he works with Jordan. He could have led her here."

"Nah. You and Franklin aren't close."

Talia walked away from him.

"Hey, *chica*." Franklin ditched Eddie and rolled across the room's giant Persian rug to greet her. "Nice place you got here, but there's a big problem. The front door ain't wheelchair accessible. I had to come in through the kitchen." He lowered his voice, cupping a hand to his mouth. "The servant's entrance. I could sue."

Tyler sipped his coffee, several feet away. "That is not a servant's entrance, Franklin."

"Oh, I think it is, *jefe*. It's not like you called me here to watch football."

Eddie glanced up from his work on the black device. "No one ever invites you anywhere to watch football. You hate football."

Conrad had rolled his cart alongside Talia to cut her a slice of pastry. Franklin gave him a chin lift. "This guy knows what I mean, don't you?"

"Not in the slightest." The pleasant smile never left Conrad's face, but as he handed Talia her breakfast, she saw the knife turn and rest against his forearm, blade out.

She pressed the control pad of the high-tech wheelchair and steered Franklin back to Eddie and the device. A panel lay on the table beside it, with a spaghetti mess of wires sticking out. "What have you brought us?"

"New display system. Eddie convinced your boy Tyler to buy one, and now he can't set it up without me."

"I can too." Eddie pushed a pair of wires together. They sparked. He yelped and sucked on his finger.

"Sure. So, why'd you call me out on a Saturday, then? You wanted to see what a legless Marine looks like in short pants?"

The argument continued. Talia took a seat with the others to watch, suddenly grasping the appeal.

Finn claimed the seat next to her. "This is like the nerd version of *Real World*."

"That's not a thing anymore."

"Isn't it?"

"It shouldn't be. And they're geeks, not nerds. One is a social group. The other is an insult. I keep telling you."

"And I keep ignoring you."

Talia finished her last bite of maple butter twist and set the plate aside. "Well, the term is *geeks*."

As if to drive her point home, Eddie raised his hands and shouted, "Eureka!"

He and Franklin stuffed the wires back in and secured the panel to the black circle. The air above it shimmered like the air above a hot stretch of desert road.

"What is it?" Finn left the couch to get a closer look.

"New holographic briefing display." Eddie picked up a tablet computer and toyed with the screen. A 3D image of the earth and roving satellites appeared in the shimmering air.

The others gasped.

Eddie sniffled, either from his cold or raw emotion. "Better than *Star Wars*."

Darcy clapped her hands. "That is my Eddie. He is incredible, yes?"

"Yeah. *He's* amazing." Franklin backed his wheelchair away from the table. "I guess my work here is done."

Eddie took the screwdriver from his hand. "Okay. I admit, I couldn't have done it without you." He wiped his nose with his sleeve and offered a hand to shake.

"Ew, mano. No way. Keep your nasty virus-infested mitts to yourself. And while we're on the subject, don't bring that junk to work on Monday.

I'll tell the Directorate you're out sick." He said his goodbyes and made his way to the butler's pantry, spinning the wheelchair for a final wink at Talia. "See ya, chica." He held a pretend phone to his ear, mouthing *Call me*.

A carving knife embedded itself in the walnut an inch from his shoulder. Talia traced its path back to Conrad. The cook offered Franklin a congenial smile. "Drop that in the sink on your way out, will you? Good lad."

Franklin wrenched the knife from the wall and drove away. "You people got issues."

Once the Tech Ops guru was gone, Mac folded his arms. "How's that contraption work, Wee Man?"

Finn wiggled his fingers at the Scotsman. "It's magic."

"It's science," Eddie said, "the true heart of all magic. Ultrasonic vibrations disturb the air in a two-meter-diameter half-sphere. Nano-projectors build the image within the disturbance. This baby will help me show you what I've learned about Boyd's network. The field is interactive." As if he'd been using it as a prop the whole time, Eddie set the tablet on the table and rubbed his hands, pumping his eyebrows. With magician-like flare, he reached into the hologram field and expanded the globe until it burst into mist.

What remained was a busy city street. A

hustler weaved cards in and out of each other on a folding stand. A delivery boy rode past on a bicycle, ringing his bell. A taxi honked. And glowing purple lines rose from each, joining into a network of data balloons.

"Welcome"—Eddie turned to face the team— "to the world's first crowdsourced crime syndicate."

CHAPTER SEVENTEEN

Wolf Manor
Wolf Trap, Virginia

Talia watched as Eddie's briefing hit full steam, but she didn't take part. She kept herself at a distance, curled up and silent on the couch. This was not her mission.

Boyd. Archangel. They were Tyler's targets. Not hers. After the previous night's phone call from Jordan, he'd pressed her to join the hunt. But Talia refused. "I told you. I'm not going down that road again. I'll stay on the sidelines and let you and the team do your thing."

"Your choice. But 'on the sidelines' means you stay in the house with Conrad until this is over. Are you good with that?"

She was, except for one small engagement. "I promised Jenni I wouldn't cancel again."

"Your baptism? Talia, God understands. He'll wait."

But Talia had put her foot down, letting a touch of growl seep into her tone. "I am going to be baptized tomorrow, Tyler. No rogue spy and no hovering, helicopter-parent, wannabe-guardian-angel thief is going to stop me."

At the center of the great room, Eddie reached

into his holographic briefing display and zoomed out to a view of Europe. The network of purple lines joined city to city. "You've all heard of GoFundMe and Kickstarter? Now meet their dark cousin."

The geek walked before the image like a celebrity doing a TED talk. "The old business models are fading. Crowdfunding will pay for anything from a smart-bot startup to a high schooler's dream vacation. With competition crowdsourcing, a software conglomerate can buy expensive code for the price of a hundred-dollar gift card. This is the future, and our friend Livingston Boyd is already there, acting anonymously by his *nom de guerre*, the White Lion."

Tyler tapped a finger on his knee. "You're saying Boyd is outsourcing crime?"

"*Crowdsourcing.* As in simultaneously engaging multiple, unrelated participants from diverse sources to achieve a cumulative or a singular result. He's using crowd*funding* as well. Members pay their own way *plus* pay him a percentage of their earnings. Boyd calls his syndicate the Jungle. It is global, anonymous, and brilliant." Eddie snapped his fingers within the field and an organizational chart appeared. "He's a big gamer—openly references online massive-multiplayer gaming strategies in his business talks—so it's no surprise the Jungle's members are called players. Each player has their own invite code used for back-alley and Dark-Web recruiting. New players start as field mice and work their way up."

In the 3D organizational chart, animal names lit up as Eddie referenced each level. "Field mice, jackrabbits, hawks, cobras, and panthers—players level-up by increasing their take. A pickpocket might stay a field mouse forever. A dirty hedge-fund manager might be a panther within hours."

"What's the draw, eh?" Mac crossed the room to retrieve another pastry from Conrad's cart. "What do his players get fer their troubles?"

"The lower echelons get crowdfunding opportunities and contact with higher-order criminals. In return, the higher echelons get a crowdsourcing reach previously undreamed of."

Finn steepled his fingers to point at the chart. "And Boyd gets a percentage of every deal?"

"Not just Boyd. There are five top-tier animal positions. Each is an increasingly rare predatory species—Hyena, Snow Leopard, Clouded Leopard, Maltese Tiger, and White Lion."

Tyler got up from his chair and joined Eddie at the display. "Taking Boyd and his Jungle down comes back to Eddie's work on the network—that's our source for hard evidence—but we're a long way from cracking the whole thing." He gave Eddie a look that said, *Correct?*

"Exactly. I've got bits and pieces, rumors. To get more, we'll have to kick it old school."

"You mean infiltrate," Finn said. "That'll be dangerous, and time consuming. A lot of rungs on this particular ladder, by the look of Eddie's brief."

Tyler nodded. "I agree. So, we send in Val—go right after a top-tier mark and con him out of an invitation code. That way, Val enters as a jackrabbit or hawk with a high-level sponsor. She'll make a big splash at the Jungle watering hole, big enough to merit a face-to-face with Boyd."

The Aussie glanced from Eddie to Tyler and back again. "You said Boyd operates in the shadows as the White Lion. How is Val supposed to get a meeting?"

"Thanks. I almost forgot." Eddie snapped his fingers in the field. The image changed to a pair of twisted skyscrapers joined by five aerial walkways. "Remember, Boyd is a big gamer, and every game must have a boss level. The Jungle is no different." He paused, as if this was explanation enough.

"So . . . ," Tyler said, inclining his head toward the others, and prompted Eddie for more.

"So . . . each year, the Jungle's top players take their shot at the big boss, the White Lion. Dark Web rumors call it the Frenzy. Eight players, including the White Lion, make as many high-profit deals as they can in twenty-four hours, competing for the top five slots."

A time-lapse advanced the hologram from day to night. Thousands of windows within the twin towers glowed fluorescent blue. "Enter Bangkok's ultra-high Twin Tigers—Boyd's latest real-estate investment. My indicators predict the Frenzy will go down here, next week."

Mac snorted, waving his pastry. "Next week? Lots ta do. Little time. When do we leave? Tonight?"

"Monday." Tyler glanced Talia's way. "Our Sunday is spoken for."

CHAPTER EIGHTEEN

The Mission Church
The Heights, Oxon Hill, Maryland

"You're endangering The Mission. You shouldn't have come." Eddie maintained his poker face from the back seat of Tyler's Jag, and Talia could tell it took all his control.

She blinked. "How long have you been waiting to use that one?"

"Ever since you started coming here." He grinned. "The Mission. Great name for a church."

She climbed out and pulled the seat forward for him. "Don't joke. A top CIA spy is trying to kill me. I *really* am endangering this church with my presence."

"You're *really* not. The cell I cloned for you constantly spoofs all trace attempts. Digital Talia is halfway down the Virginia coast, heading to Newport News."

"Why Newport News?"

"Unlike the Real Talia, Digital Talia knows how to relax." He set off across the parking lot. "I'm going in to find Darcy. She came early for recon."

Tyler stood from the driver's seat and leaned his elbows on the roof. "We're going to keep you safe, and your church family. But you can still wave off, do this another day."

"Not on your life."

"I thought you'd say that." She caught a hint of a smile in his eyes. Tyler closed the driver's door and the locks automatically clicked. "Think of it this way. The desire to protect you has brought a band of thieves into a church to meet Jesus. God is at work."

"I'm also bringing them in to meet my poor foster mother." Talia shot him a frown. "That's on you."

Finn and Mac arrived in a rumbling Audi R8, drawing the wary eyes of parishioners arriving at the little satellite church in the Heights, an industrial district across the river from the wealthy suburbs of Arlington. Finn was dressed for the occasion in a blazer and jeans. Mac had done his best. Over his usual black muscle shirt, he wore a black leather jacket that might have used up the whole cow.

Talia smacked Finn in the arm as the two men caught up to her and Tyler on the way to the front doors. "Did you leave Matilda at home like I asked?"

"Against my better judgment, yes."

"Good. Nice car. Very low profile. Right now, half the church is wondering if you're a pair of drug dealers."

"What happened to 'Judge not'?"

108

Tyler chuckled at them both. "Easy to preach. Harder to execute."

Those three laughed. Mac didn't. The big Scotsman looked like an elephant about to enter a den of mice. "I'll watch the outside if ya don' mind. Churches make me nervous. I feel as if I'll be struck by lightnin' the moment I walk through the door."

"Interesting." Tyler checked the sky.

Mac looked up as well. "What? What is it?"

"I guess you didn't know. All God's creation is his church. Indoors, outdoors—doesn't matter. To be frank, I'm surprised you haven't been struck already."

The others walked on, leaving Mac standing in place and squinting at the gathering clouds.

Talia elbowed Tyler in the ribs. "That wasn't funny."

"Oh yes it was."

In the foyer, Finn jogged ahead to Eddie and Darcy, who were studying a bulletin board filled with pictures of the church's families. He tapped one of the photos. "Check out the earrings on this lady. Think those are real diamonds?"

"Hey." Tyler snapped his fingers.

The cat burglar withdrew the hand and shoved it in his pocket. "Sorry."

Before Tyler could say anything else, Talia pulled him aside and nodded at Mac, out in the parking lot. "You left our Scottish friend outside in Volgograd as well. I'm sensing a trend."

"His bulk and quickness makes him a good goal keep." Tyler cracked a smile. "What? Were you thinking I separated him from the team because of his history . . . because he almost sold us out to Ivanov a few months ago?"

"Why not? His loyalty was questionable then. Can we be certain of him now?"

"Absolutely."

"How?"

"Faith." Tyler guided Talia over to the coatracks. "The day will come," he said, helping her with her coat, "when that great big Highlander will no longer fear the front doors of a church— or the side doors, or the back entrance, or the cellar window. On that day, it will be all you can do to keep him from dragging strangers into God's kingdom by the scruffs of their necks."

She watched him hang up the coat, so totally at peace with the insanity coming out of his mouth. "Faith?"

"Correct. Now let's go make a declaration of yours."

The trip from the foyer to the pews was a gauntlet of family and acquaintances. Finn went straight to Jenni. "Finn. Michael Finn."

"Um . . ." Jenni leaned out to see Talia from the other side of the burglar, long blonde hair flopping to one side. "Who are your friends, Talia?"

"They're coworkers."

"We prefer the term *work family*." Finn took Jenni's hand, raising her fingers as if he might kiss them. But the man next to her pried his hand free and shook it, using the motion to tug him a short distance away.

"Bill Lewis. Jenni's father. Pleased to meet you."

After he let go, Finn winced and wiggled his fingers as if they'd been crushed.

Tyler's turn came next. "Hi, Bill. Call me Adam. Think of me as the weird uncle Talia never talks about."

"Apt." Bill cast a questioning glance at Talia. "Because she never does. Please, Uncle Adam, won't you and your friends sit with us?"

Tyler waved Eddie and Darcy into the pew past Wendy and her purse, but he stopped Finn with a backhand to the gut and inclined his head toward the rear of the sanctuary.

"Right," the thief grunted. "I prefer the back pew . . . It's an Australian Baptist thing."

The pastor spoke on Peter and the day he stepped out of the boat. Talia loved the imagery—the wind, the waves, the fear in Peter's eyes when he began to sink and the calming voice of Christ as he lifted him up again. When the music minister began strumming quiet chords, Talia took the cue and ducked out to change.

Passing Finn, she grabbed his shoulder and dug in with her nails. "While I'm gone, the offering

111

plates will come around." She bent to whisper in his ear. "If you take so much as a penny, I'll kill you in your sleep. You know I can." She started to walk on, then rocked back a step. "Also . . . Jesus loves you."

When she returned in her Georgetown Crew sweats, she saw Bill, not her pastor, standing in the Mission's rolling baptismal. He gave her an *Is this okay?* look as she walked up the steps. Talia answered with a smile.

"Today is—" Bill's voice caught in his throat. He coughed and started again. "Forgive me. Today is special, but I promise I'll be brief. The water's cold."

The congregation laughed.

Bill squeezed Talia's arm. "This is Talia. She came into our lives a while ago as a foster child, becoming a sister to Jenni and a daughter to Wendy and I. Since then she's achieved so much to make us proud—top of her class, captain of the rowing team, a post in the Foreign Service. Today we are proudest of all. Overjoyed. Not for her achievement, but for her choice."

He laid a hand at the small of her back and asked Talia to proclaim her decision to follow Christ. After doing so, she wrapped a hand over his, letting the strength of his arm support her for what came next.

"Talia Inger, upon your profession of faith, I baptize you my sister in the name of the Father, the Son, and the Holy Spirit, buried with him in death—" Gently, he let her fall back.

The water closed above her, turning the spotlights into waves of color. A hundred images passed through Talia's near-perfect memory. She saw a swimming pool rising to meet her, shards of glass splashing all around. She saw her father at the wheel of an old Ford on a misty road, the world tumbling, a man dragging her clear before the vehicle exploded. She saw her own gun pressed to that man's head and in the next instant her arms wrapping around him.

Forgiveness given.

Forgiveness accepted.

The water parted as Bill lifted her up into the free air. "—raised with him in newness of life. Our adopted daughter, now adopted by the Father."

The church cheered, even Darcy, though she looked a little bewildered.

Talia cried as she hugged Bill and let Wendy walk her back to the church's small kitchen, where the deacons had put up partitions to form a makeshift dressing room.

By the time Talia came out from behind the partitions, a second woman waited for her, chatting in a hushed voice with Wendy. She had her back to Talia, red hair turned inward to a bob below her collar.

For a split second, Talia mistook the woman for

Jordan and reached for a Glock that wasn't there. But the cant of the redhead's shoulders and the tapping of her foot spoke of someone else.

"Valkyrie?"

The grifter turned, laughing at the shock on Talia's face. "I've got to hand it to you, darling. That was quite a show."

CHAPTER NINETEEN

The Mission Church
The Heights, Oxon Hill, Maryland

"Wendy, could you give us a sec?"

Talia's foster mother waited for Talia to add a reassuring nod to the request, then started for the door. "I'll be outside. Your uncle Adam wanted to talk with me."

Once she had gone, Valkyrie pulled a stool over from the kitchen bar and sat down. She locked one spiked heel behind its bottom rung. "Let me get this straight. You get ritualistically dunked, and this buys you a ticket to the pearly gates? Why isn't everyone signing up?"

"It's good to see you too, Val."

The grifter sighed. "What did I teach you about deflection? Use it, but don't be so obvious."

"I'm not deflecting." Talia walked to a standing mirror to adjust her skirt and blouse. "I'm ignoring the question."

"Why?"

"It's beneath your intelligence. I've seen you cold-read a mark for gullibility, marital status"—Talia pointed at her with a hairbrush—"bank account password. We've been friends for months. You know I'd never believe such a thing."

"Papa had me christened as a baby."

"Okay . . ." Val had a point to make. Talia could see that. "Go on."

"Eleven years later, at our summer home in Capri, I heard a noise in the night. I crept down to the wine cellar and saw Papa standing over a bloodied man while our chauffeur beat him senseless."

The brush Talia had been running through her hair paused and came down to her side. "Why are you telling me this?"

"I assume the man who dedicated me to God was also christened as a child. And yet he became the devil himself. What does that say of me?"

All sense of teasing and sarcasm had fled Val's features. What remained was a skeptic struggling to face something that cut deep into her soul. "We all make our own choices, Val. You. Your father. This baptism was a symbol of my choice to accept the forgiveness and salvation bought with the blood of Christ."

"But you *are* going to heaven."

A portion of an unavoidable smile tipped up the corner of Talia's mouth. "Yes."

The smile did not help Val's mood. "And I'm not going to heaven, right? I mean, let's face it. That's what you and your church friends believe." Her arms were crossed, shoulders hunched. If Val could see herself, she would tell Talia that she— *the mark* in the language of thieves—was now seeking a reason to be offended, another defense mechanism.

Talia remembered a passage from 1 Peter she'd learned in the newcomer's class. For those who refused to believe, Christ the cornerstone would be a stumbling block and a rock of offense. A battle lay ahead. Was Talia up to fighting it? She put the brush in her purse, flattened her skirt, and opened the kitchen door for them both. "We believe heaven is open to everyone. It's simply a matter of accepting the gift."

The rest of the crew waited in the parking lot. As Talia came out with Val, the grifter and Tyler exchanged a glance, and only then did Talia realize Val had entered the changing area at his behest—for Talia's protection.

He never stopped hovering.

"You can go now," Talia told him, hurrying up to the Jag before Jenni or Bill came over and made frank conversation impossible. "I'm having lunch with my family. I'll ride with them."

Tyler scrunched his nose. "Why wouldn't you ride with us?"

"Because you're *not* having lunch with my family?" The implications of the statement hit her, and her stomach flipped. "Oh, Tyler. No."

"Wendy invited us. Sweet lady." He patted the roof of the car. "Hop in. I told her we'd pick up some fish on the way."

• • •

Lunch started at awkward and went downhill from there.

Wendy had bitten off more than she bargained for with Uncle Adam and his entourage. Talia could see it in her eyes as Mac ducked through the front door. Talia felt like Jack bringing the giant home for dinner.

Tyler caught her at the edge of the living room. "Stop looking so worried. Darcy left her explosives in the car." He shoved a bag of fresh cod into her hands. "Take these to your foster father. He's on the deck firing up the grill."

The dining room table did not fit all nine of them, so Bill set up a folding table at one end. He offered to sit there with Wendy, but Talia wouldn't have it. "Eddie and Darcy will take those places. Right, Eddie?"

"You're putting me at the kids' table?"

Tyler intervened. "Tell me you haven't read a comic book in the last twenty-four hours and you can sit with the grown-ups."

Eddie frowned and sat down.

A cat burglar in the kitchen and a grifter at the grill turned out to be the least of Talia's worries. Once everyone had gathered at the table, with platters of blackened cod and corn on the cob between them, Bill rang his glass with a spoon. "Excuse me, everyone."

They all looked up. Tyler swatted a roll out of Mac's hand.

"I didn't expect such a large audience, but I'm going to do this anyway. I have an announcement, or better yet, a presentation."

He was looking at Talia as he spoke. *What presentation?* she wanted to ask but couldn't find her tongue.

Her foster father produced a flat red box, wrapped with a silk ribbon. "Wendy and I prepared this a couple of weeks ago, but you can't imagine how hard it is to get Talia over for a meal."

Finn raised a fork. "Sure we can. Right, princess?"

Talia kicked him under the table.

Before she knew it, Bill was at her side, laying the box on her empty plate. "During the baptism, I referred to Talia as our adopted daughter, not our foster daughter." He squeezed her shoulder. "She may have noticed."

She had. For a foster kid, it was a sharp distinction.

"I should have remedied this disparity long ago. Go ahead, Talia. Open it."

Tingles shot through her arms, so strong that she struggled with the bow. When she finally pulled the top away, she found a short stack of papers inside. "These are . . . legal documents."

"They're adoption papers," Wendy said, hope in her voice.

"But I'm not a minor anymore."

"It doesn't matter to us."

"This is expensive."

Bill took his wife's hand, and they both smiled at Talia. "It's what we want."

Eddie sniffled, which might have been the cold, but Talia heard Mac sniffle too.

Bill kneeled beside her chair. "We understand. This is a big step. It's okay if you want to think about it. Right, Wendy?"

"Right." Wendy's hand slipped out of his, quivering a little. "You don't have to take our name, if that helps."

Everyone at the table watched her, none more intently than Bill and Wendy. Talia could feel their disappointment. They had expected a different reaction. But how could they have sprung this on her today, in front of people they hardly knew?

"I . . ." The truth rolled through her mind. *I have to check with the CIA first because legally tying myself to you puts you in danger. Oh, and by the way, the boss I have to ask is trying to have me killed.* "I do need a little time." She replaced the lid and set the box under her chair, out of sight. "Don't get me wrong. This is so generous. But like you said, it's a big step."

That was that. The numbness didn't go away for the rest of the meal.

Talia hardly ate and hardly spoke. Bill and Wendy went on with the meal, trying to act

120

as if nothing had changed, playing gracious and unwitting hosts to a reformed assassin, a mad bomber and her CIA hacker boyfriend, a wheelman with questionable loyalties, a cat burglar, and a con woman.

Through the fog, Talia heard snippets of conversation from all sides.

Tyler growled at Mac for taking too many helpings of fish.

Val, playing a role as ever, swapped cooking secrets with Wendy as if she had stepped off the pages of *Better Homes and Gardens*.

Eddie recounted his endangering-the-mission joke for Finn and received a pity laugh. "Heaps funny, mate. A real ripper."

Darcy clapped her hands. "Excellent, Eddie. You never tell jokes."

He pursed his lips. "I tell jokes all the time. You just never get them."

During the meal, Jenni spoke as little as Talia, and ate even less. After a while she excused herself, mumbling that she didn't feel well.

Talia pushed her chair back, glad for an excuse to leave the table. "I'll go see if she's okay."

She found Jenni in the room they had shared through high school and college.

Jenni sat cross-legged in the middle of her old bed, hugging a teddy bear dating back to the Build-a-Bear craze. "I'm okay, Talia. You didn't have to come up."

"Oh yes I did. I used you as an excuse to escape." She closed the door behind her, kicked off her shoes, and took up her old spot on the other bed, laying her box of legal papers on a conglomeration of pillows. "Is this about the adoption, because—"

"It's not the adoption."

"Okay . . ." Talia waited for her to clarify.

Jenni took the cue. "Remember I told you about the missing kids?"

"Sure. The refugee camps on the borders of Myanmar. You're still upset about that?"

Jenni shot her a frown.

Talia held up her hands. "You know what I meant. It's work. You can't bring it home with you."

"I can't help it. There was a fire at a camp in Thailand. More kids went missing—thirty-four in one night." Still clutching the bear with one arm, Jenni handed a folder to Talia. "This time we have names and faces."

An organization called Compassion International had put together a brief for the State Department. Talia flipped through the pages. Each child had a full profile: name, birthdate, parent information. There were handwriting samples for the older ones. "This is a lot of detail."

"Compassion is detail-oriented, especially when it comes to their kids. They helped the local pastor create a school and care program for the camp—something called a Child Development Center—and they were working to get these children registered in Thailand. Now they're putting pressure on State to find them."

"Pressure applied through you."

Jenni shrugged. "My boss gave me the same answer as always. State can only do so much. We're restricted by diplomatic barriers. But, Talia, you—"

Talia held up a hand. "Whoa. Hang on."

Too late. The request came flooding out. "I know about your work. You think I don't, but I do. Your posting reads Foreign Service, but you're never in the Foreign Service wing. And you're gone *all* the time."

Talia didn't answer.

Jenni seemed to take that as confirmation. "Find me some answers. Anything. Compassion's man on the ground, Ewan Ferguson, is worried the kids were taken by traffickers working out of Myanmar. He's heading up to the camp to investigate."

"Myanmar." Talia said the name for her own benefit, not Jenni's. A knot began unraveling in her brain. "Rangoon is in Myanmar."

"Yeah, sure. They call it Yangon these days, their commercial capital. So?"

Tyler had mentioned Rangoon right after Volgograd. *Boyd has his fingers in criminal operations in every major city, from London pickpockets to human traffickers in Rangoon to forgers in Volgograd.* Talia echoed his words out loud. "Human traffickers in Rangoon."

"It's Yangon. Talia, are you listening?"

Boyd had a human trafficking operation in Myanmar. He was about to hold his annual black-market deal-making extravaganza in Thailand's capital. And children from a camp on the Thai/Myanmar border had gone missing.

Too many coincidences.

Talia focused on the file in her hands. A little girl named Hla Meh looked up at her from the top page with an expression more grave than sad, as if she knew more of the world than a little girl should. Talia had worn a similar expression at that age.

"I've seen that look before. You know something about this. Can you talk to someone for me?"

She closed the folder, stealing a phrase from Tyler. "I think I'm experiencing what a colleague of mine calls *operational overlap*. And if I am, I'll do way more than talk."

CHAPTER TWENTY

Wolf Manor
Wolf Trap, Virginia

Talia lingered at Bill and Wendy's house after the others left. As she opened the front door with the box of adoption papers tucked under her arm, the evening sun poured into the family room. She clasped Wendy's hands. "I'll give you an answer soon. I want you to know this means the world to me."

Then why not go through with it? She could see the unspoken question on Bill's lips.

What could Talia say? Two of the people she cared for most in the world had thrown her a miracle curveball, and she had no idea how to swing.

As she reached the sidewalk, an Audi R8 rolled up, passenger window down. Finn revved the engine. "Need a ride, princess?"

"What if I say no?"

"You're the boss, but it's a long walk. And I'll be idling at your heels the whole way. Tyler's orders."

The walk was tempting, if only to put him through the long, slow drive. But her frustration was with Tyler more than Finn. "I'll save you the pain." She dropped into the bucket seat. "But only if you stop calling me 'princess.'"

He pressed the gas and let the acceleration close her door. "No problem, your highness."

"Why do you do that?"

"Do what?"

Talia wanted to smack him. "Your highness. Princess. What's it all supposed to mean?"

He gave her a one-shouldered shrug, and that was all she got for a couple of blocks. Then, when her mind had jumped back to the kids in Myanmar, he said, "I dunno. Maybe I'm pulling your pigtails."

"Pulling my—" She stopped as the meaning caught up to her. Flirting. Was Finn trying to say he'd been flirting with her, on some deeper level than his usual *Finn, Michael Finn* interactions with women? Before Talia could compose anything close to a suitable response, they came to the 267 feeder. "Take the U-turn under the next overpass," she said. "We need to run a surveillance detection route."

"I know how to run an SDR."

"Then run one."

"I am."

"No, you're heading straight for Wolf Manor. Take the U-turn."

Finn flipped on the hazards and slammed on the brakes. Cars whizzed by on either side.

Talia checked behind them. "What are you doing?"

He put the Audi in park. "I came to this team with skills of my own, Talia. I bring value. I'm not the chosen one like you, but I'm not support staff to be called up by the ring of a bell either."

A car swerved around them, horn blaring.

"You win, okay? You have value. Drive."

"Whatever you say, your highness." He punched the gas.

The chosen one. Your highness. She figured it out. "You're not flirting with me. You're mad because you're not the center of attention."

"Flirting?" He signaled left, heading for the same U-turn she'd indicated a few moments before. "Who said anything about flirting?"

"You did."

He took the corner at high speed, tires squealing through the curve. "You're unbelievable."

For the rest of the drive, Talia let Finn make the decisions, even when she would have taken a different road. Best not to provoke the man at the wheel. And by the time he pulled into the circle drive, he seemed like himself again.

"For the record," she said as they both got out, "I don't see you as support staff."

"Right. Then what am I?"

A crash and a tinkling saved her from having to answer. Darcy and Mac had been loading up a pair of cargo vans and dropped one of the crates. Silver discs like plug nickels lay strewn about the drive. Both had dropped to their knees to scoop them into piles.

Talia glanced at Finn across the roof of the Audi. "Should we ask?"

"Do you want to help pick those up?"

"No." She had important business to discuss with Tyler.

"Then let's go inside."

Finn went upstairs, but Talia headed straight for the great room and Tyler. "I'm in."

"You're not in." He lounged in a leather chair, playing with a novelty toy—a magnetic ball and a copper tube with a long slot cut out of the side.

"Why not? For the last week, you've practically begged me to join you."

"*Begged* is an overstatement. I'll admit, your involvement would greatly improve our odds of success"—he dropped the magnet into the tube and watched it slowly descend as if magically resisting gravity—"but you're not in."

"Who's not in?" Eddie emerged from the kitchen with a miniature tart in each hand—one lemon, one strawberry.

Talia's hands went to her hips. "We *literally* just ate at Bill and Wendy's place."

"But Conrad made them." The geek popped the strawberry tart into his mouth, chewing and repeating his question at the same time. "Who's not in?"

128

Tyler caught his magnet and dropped it into the tube again. "Talia."

"Talia's out?"

"She was never in."

"Hey." Talia glared at both men. They were doing this on purpose. She could tell by the smirk on Eddie's strawberry-stained lips.

The magnet dropped from the bottom of Tyler's pipe. He caught it and looked up. "Yesterday, you left no doubt you wanted nothing to do with this job. Now you want in. I need a good reason."

Talia opened her box of adoption paperwork and removed the file she had slipped inside— Jenni's file. She tossed it in his lap. The page with the picture of the little girl slid out a few inches.

Tyler drew the paper out and held it at arm's length, finding a focal point for the small print. "Missing children. In . . . Ban Doi Henga . . . Thailand." He lowered the page. "What's this?"

"Thirty-four children went missing during a fire on the Thai/Myanmar border. You said Boyd's crowdsourced crime syndicate has a hand in human trafficking through Rangoon. I think this is him."

"Could be coincidence."

Without looking, Talia pointed at the geek. "Eddie, what did we learn about coincidence at the Farm?"

Silence.

Tyler raised an eyebrow.

Talia dropped her shoulders and glanced back. "Anytime now, Eddie."

He was licking his fingers, still chewing his second tart. "You told me it was rude to talk with my mouth full. You can't have it both ways." He swallowed hard and wiped his lips. "The textbook answer is 'There are no coincidences in intelligence, only overlaps and intersections.'"

"See. Operational overlap." Talia flicked the paper in Tyler's hand. "Your favorite. Look at that report. On a per-deal basis, human trafficking is the most lucrative illicit trade in Asia."

"So?"

"So, this kidnapping is too close to Boyd's Frenzy—both in time and geography. It has to be one of his big players. The Hyena or the Liger or . . ." She signaled Eddie for a little help.

"The Hyena, the Snow Leopard, the Clouded Leopard, or the Maltese Tiger. But it could also be one of the three hungry panthers competing to supplant them, or the big boss himself—the White Lion."

Talia gave Tyler a *What he said* look. "You hate coincidences as much as I do. This kidnapping is connected to Boyd's Jungle. It has to be. So am I in?"

"Nothing that caused your earlier reservations has changed. You understand? I—" He glanced past her toward Eddie, as well as Finn, Mac,

Darcy, and Val, who had all walked in from the kitchen. "We will follow this rabbit hole wherever it leads. Even if that effort digs up past skeletons you don't want to see."

Talia took the file and showed him the picture of the little girl. "For her? I'll take the risk."

CHAPTER TWENTY-ONE

Ban Doi Henga Refugee Camp
Thai/Burma Border
Mae Hong Son Province, Thailand

Ewan Ferguson arrived on scene to find refugees tearing charred bamboo huts apart, salvaging what they could. A sea of cots lay outside an Order of Malta clinic tent. Doctors and nurses in masks and street clothes moved among them, treating burns and smoke injuries. Spellbound by the calm and care of the medical workers, Ewan bumped into one of four men dragging fresh bamboo out of the jungle. He reached out. "Sorry. So sorry."

The men never looked back.

Controlled chaos. The Thai way.

The child of a Scottish missionary and a Thai schoolteacher, Ewan understood both the Eastern and Western philosophies of time and order, and where the two clashed. That merger of language and culture had given him the advantage when he applied to become Compassion International's Director of Thailand Operations four years earlier. His mother had gone so far as to say God had purposed him for the position. While Ewan knew better than to argue with a Thai schoolteacher, let alone his own mother, inside he wondered whether the Lord created people for lifelong careers or for specific moments like this one.

"Excuse me." He caught the attention of a woman hurrying past. "Where is the church?" In his memory, the church building and the school pavilion rested at the top of the highest hill in the camp. All he saw now were ash and charred trees.

The woman pointed to the same spot.

His heart sank. "And Pastor Nakor? Where is he?"

Sadness joined the misery in her eyes.

"Teacher Rocha?"

She bowed her head and walked on toward the medical tent.

Dear Lord, help me discover what happened here.

God was with him. Ewan knew by the miracle which had brought him there so quickly—a perfect storm of circumstance. Travel and communications were difficult in Thailand, especially where the mountain borderlands were concerned. There were no phone lines, no cell towers. The dirt roads were muddy death traps from June to October.

By God's grace, this fire had hit the camp in December, when the roads were passable and the Order of Malta was on site for the season. The Order had a sat phone, and their Thai coordinator was a member of Ewan's Bangkok church. What should have taken a week or more between notification and safe travel had taken a day and a half.

"Pastor Nakor? Teacher Rocha?"

Each passerby continued on in post-disaster shock or sadly shook their heads. A few looked up to the charred hilltop. Ewan feared what he might find there. The Order of Malta always collected remains as quickly as possible, but the living took priority over the dead.

Remains. He didn't want to think about it. Ewan clutched the satchel at his side, feeling the binder full of profiles within. If Pastor Nakor and Teacher Rocha were gone, what had happened to the children? He had expressed his concern on that score to Jenni Lewis, his State Department contact.

There were thirty-four profiles in that binder— thirty-four children in this camp center, out of the more than forty-eight thousand spread across Compassion's Thailand facilities. Ewan's heart broke to think of even one of them in pain.

The fineness, the utter softness, of the ashes where the church had stood struck him as peaceful. Blackened cinder blocks showed him the four corners of the vanished structure. Across the yard, one charred and stubborn rosewood pylon spoke of the pavilion. These sights hurt his heart, but the scent of the place gave him hope.

The hilltop smelled of campfires, not death. Ewan had experienced the scent of deadly fires before. There were no bodies hidden in these soft ashes. The children were alive.

Someone touched his shoulder.

"Master Fer . . . Ferg-u-son." The woman, about his own age, struggled with his name, which had never fit well with the Thai tongue. "You are here."

They had been acquainted before. Obviously. For the woman had known him by the back of his head. But a name did not readily come to mind. "Forgive me, Mrs. . . ."

"I am Eh Taw. You were here when Pastor Nakor welcomed my daughter into the center program."

"Yes." Ewan took her hand. "I remember now. Your daughter is Hla Meh."

The remembered fact earned him a fleeting smile.

He clung to one last hope. "Can you take me to Hla Meh now?"

The woman's fingers tightened on his. She spoke with a voice broken and hard at the same time. "Come. The other parents have gathered in the yard at the center of the camp."

The parents mobbed Ewan at the edge of the yard.

Again, controlled chaos. The Thai way.

He could not blame them. Ewan had a daughter

135

of his own. Eleven going on twenty. How devastated and desperate he would feel if she disappeared in a fire.

Mothers cried. Fathers yelled. After a great deal of shouting for calm and listening to rapid accounts, Ewan gathered that the fire had taken place at the end of the school day. The flames had separated parents from children and spread into the huts. Eh Taw introduced him to Hsar, the woman who'd organized a bucket brigade from the river.

Hsar held her place at the front of the crowd with outstretched arms. "I was present at the last fire at Ban Doi Henga. My son, Thet Ye, was born that night."

"Thet Ye. I remember. Smart boy." He had been among the first from the camp to join the program. A sponsor family in the States had fallen in love with his profile, then him, and now sent him monthly letters to encourage his faith and studies. Hla Meh did not have sponsors yet, but there was still time. Perhaps.

Hsar told him how the refugees had worked the whole night to stop the fire, and Eh Taw made certain he understood Hsar herself had led the efforts. Hsar quieted her friend with a calming hand. "My husband only returned this morning from the rice fields in the next valley, hours after the fire went out. And still, the cinders burned his feet when he ran to the hill."

"And the children?"

"Tell him." Hsar placed her hands on Eh Taw's shoulders.

Eh Taw's face contorted with grief. "I should have listened. I should have trusted."

She struggled to continue.

Ewan pressed her. "Trusted who?"

"My daughter. Hla Meh warned me of men near the camp. She claimed they were militiamen from across the border." She began to sob. "I did not believe her. The militias are the reason we fled our homes—the reason my husband is dead. Fire is their favorite weapon."

So Eh Taw's husband was gone, but not Hsar's, Thet Ye's father. And according to Hsar, he had returned from the rice fields. Why wasn't he here, with his wife? "Hsar, you said your husband burned his feet in the cinders. Is he at the medical tent?"

"No, Mr. Ferg-u-son. Po left an hour before you arrived."

"To go where?"

"To track down the men who took our son."

CHAPTER TWENTY-TWO

Mae Surin Jungle
Mae Hong Son Province, Thailand

Thet Ye worried about his mother.

His parents had survived the fire. He had no doubt. They had survived the previous fire at Ban Doi Henga and brought him into the world at the same time. They were survivors. But his mother had once told him, after he had run off into the camp without permission, her heart would break if she ever lost him.

He believed her. He did not want to picture her crying.

The red light of the rising sun filtered through the jungle canopy, casting scattered rays on the marching column of children.

Thet Ye's third full day with his captors had started much like the first, with a lot of yelling and shoving in the dark as the soldiers herded the children into formation. There had been less crying that morning, except for Aung Thu. Thet Ye did not know how the older boy managed it. Thirst alone left Thet Ye's heart too dry for tears.

After the fire, the soldiers had marched the children through the night to a jungle camp, where they slept like sheep in a pen of barbed wire. By noon, the children were on the march again, and the first and second full day progressed much the same, with shoving, shouting, and tears. The column plodded along at a crawl. Children tripped and fell. Soldiers hauled them to their feet. And on they marched to another barbed-wire pen.

At each stop, two soldiers checked the children for burns and cuts, and treated them with balm and bandages. Teacher Rocha begged them to help the pastor too. The soldiers ignored her.

With no balm or bandages of her own, she had torn pieces of her sleeves and pant legs into strips. The soldiers passed a canteen around the group once every few hours. She used her ration to wet the strips and bind Pastor Nakor's burns. Three days in, after wetting and wrapping and re-wetting and re-wrapping, the strips looked like pieces of torn flesh clinging to his body.

Thet Ye worried about Pastor Nakor as much as he worried about his mother.

He worried about Hla Meh too. He could not get her to look at him. He'd tried to reach her during the nights in the pens, but the soldiers always forced him back to his place—once with a slap to the cheek. "Shut up, boy. Sit down!"

Now, in the growing heat of a new day, Hla Meh marched far ahead. The soldiers had put the girls up front to set the pace. Thet Ye plodded along at the back with Aung Thu, beside Pastor

Nakor and Teacher Rocha. She needed the boys' help to get him over trees and up steep hills.

As they struggled up the worst hill yet, Teacher Rocha mumbled prayers. Thet Ye heard her sob a little too.

At the top, Pastor Nakor whispered comfort. "We're going to make it. We stay with the children, and we see them through this. God will make a way."

The pastor's right leg crumpled on his very next step. The boys and the teacher lost their holds on his wounded body, and he fell into a depression hidden by the undergrowth.

"What is this?" The teenage soldier from the day Hla Meh had chased the butterfly stomped through underbrush. "Get up, old man. March or I will shoot you!"

Teacher Rocha could not get the pastor up fast enough. The young soldier dragged him to his feet, and Pastor Nakor cried out in pain from the strain on his wounds.

The soldier hit him with the stock of his gun. "Quit moaning and walk."

Thet Ye clenched his fists in anger. He wanted to rush the teen—not much bigger than himself— hit him, anything to punish him for hurting Pastor Nakor. Teacher Rocha must have felt the same way. When the teen stomped off, she took a step to follow.

The pastor caught her arm with a weak hand.

"No. Don't you see? He is a child, enslaved by these men like all the rest, and just as frightened. He knows no other way."

Could Thet Ye have heard him correctly? The boy who yelled and hurt the pastor. The boy who carried a machine gun. Could he be as frightened as Thet Ye and Aung Thu? Thet Ye could not imagine such a thing. But Pastor Nakor had never spoken anything but truth.

The light on the underbrush grew brighter. The trees were thinning. Not far beyond the girls, Thet Ye saw a dirt road. Soe Htun, their leader with the burn scars on his hands, barked orders, and the forward soldiers ran to the edge and kneeled, weapons ready. The rest quieted the children with shouted threats.

In the silence, Thet Ye heard a rumble. Soe Htun spoke into a radio. A voice answered back, and he signaled the men at the road to lower their guns. Two covered trucks drove into view, dust billowing around them.

"Go!" Soe Htun yelled. "Get them loaded!"

The soldiers bellowed in earnest. Some picked up the smaller girls, one under each arm. The trucks' tailgates dropped. Thet Ye found himself separated from Teacher Rocha and Pastor Nakor, hurrying through the brush in a cluster of his friends. He scrambled onto one of the tailgates. Aung Thu pulled him deeper into the bed, and the two huddled together in the grit.

The tailgate slammed closed. The canvas flaps dropped, leaving them in darkness. The engines growled. The floor shook. The tires ground over the gravel. They were moving.

Thet Ye imagined his parents wading through the underbrush to find him—following his trail. But he had never been in a truck before. How would they ever find him now? Sitting there with Aung Thu, he dropped his head into his hands. Thet Ye was lost. His mother would cry for sure.

CHAPTER TWENTY-THREE

Ronald Reagan National Airport
Arlington, Virginia

"What happened to the hangar at Stafford Regional?" Talia leaned forward between Mac and Tyler after an armed security guard waved their cargo van through the general aviation gate at Reagan. In the side-view mirror, she watched the guard wave Darcy through in the second van.

Tyler directed Mac toward a pair of hangars before answering. "New jet. New digs."

"New jet? You sold the Gulfstream?"

"I traded up."

Mac drove out from between the hangars, and Talia caught her breath. There, on the open ramp, sat a gleaming red-and-white blend of business jet and space fighter, with a fuselage like a needle and stubby wings set back near the tail. "What is that thing?"

"That's the Aerion AS2, lass." Mac eased the van to a stop near the rear of the craft. "They call her the boomless business jet."

"Boomless. As in a sonic boom? The AS2 is supersonic?"

Tyler helped her out of the van, then walked along the wing, running a finger over the metallic flake paint at the leading edge. "Up to Mach 1.6 over water. Over land, where there are noise restrictions, she can run up to Mach 1.2 without generating a boom. She's a revolution."

The other van pulled up next to them, and the team transferred the gear and crates to the cargo bay. Talia stayed close to Tyler while they worked. The two had argued extensively over his spending habits—the villas, the chalets, the jets. He claimed they were necessary for the circles the team worked in. She often reminded him how many children he could feed and clothe with that kind of money.

The Gulfstream had been a sharp point of contention. And now he had *traded up* to the first supersonic business jet? She didn't even want to guess at the price tag. She shouldered a black duffel from the second van and started toward the jet.

Tyler followed with a matching bag. "It's a lease, okay? More of a test project, really."

"Yeah. A test." Mac lifted a massive hard-shell crate as if it were full of balloons. "Come to think of it, the lads at Aerion should be payin' us."

She gave the Scotsman a skeptical look.

Tyler backed him up, tossing his duffel into the bay. "I'm paying half of what I recouped when I sold the Gulfstream." He paused to catch his breath. "More or less."

"How is that possible?" When his lips parted

144

to answer, Talia stopped him. "And if you say, 'I know a guy,' I'll drop this bag and shoot you where you stand."

His mouth snapped closed, and he headed to the vans for another load.

She dropped her bag in the bay. "Fine. Say it."

"I know a guy."

Talia was a fan of neither heights nor aircraft, especially after her experience earlier in the year on a doomed mesospheric airship. The takeoff in the new jet didn't help.

"Two hundred forty kilonewtons o' thrust, lassy," Mac shouted, glancing back at her from the flight deck, "at twice the ratio of yer average Richie-Rich jet!"

With all the G-forces, she had no idea how he'd managed to turn his head. "Eyes on the road, Mac!"

Seconds later, thanks to seamless, real-time projections of the outside air covering the cabin walls, Talia watched a cat's-eye vapor cone pass down the aircraft like an otherworld portal. She felt as if she could reach out and touch it—and be ripped right out of her seat. Five minutes later, they were over the Atlantic.

Not until Mac settled the jet into a high-altitude cruise did Talia release her white-knuckle grip on her armrests, leaving handprints in the leather. At the press of a button, her chair swiveled to face

Finn and Val. Darcy and Eddie were already up, exploring the high-tech cabin. "At—" She coughed and swallowed to gain control of her voice. "At this speed, when will we arrive in Bangkok?"

"We're not going to Bangkok." Tyler stepped out from the flight deck, leaving Mac to drive.

"But the kids—"

"Will have to wait." Val activated a table that rose from the floor between them. "You want to do this fast, or do it right?"

"Both."

Logic and the look on Val's face told her that wasn't an option. Tyler slid into the seat next to the grifter. "Sorry. They don't call it a long con for nothing."

"Exactly how long?"

"One week. If we play this right, we'll get an invite to Boyd's Frenzy and nail him there."

"And find the kids."

"Yes. Exactly. And find the kids. Eddie, show her the plan."

In the aisle, the geek bounced his favorite cobalt-and-copper fidget spinner from one pinky to the other, as if trying to decide if supersonic flight affected its balance. His cold seemed to be fading. Talia wondered if he'd faked it to come on the mission, until a giant sneeze made him drop the toy.

Darcy wiped a hand over her face. "*Merci, mon chou.* That was . . . quite disgusting, yes?"

"Sorry." He recovered the spinner and pressed a switch on the forward bulkhead.

The chairs on the left side of the aisle spread apart, and the real-time wall projection of the clouds outside faded to a black screen. A flowchart appeared. "The plan has three stages. Three progressive cons, each with similar elements but bigger and with more flourishes than the last. All different. All connected. Stage One gets us into the Jungle network. Stage Two earns us an invitation to Bangkok. And Stage Three—"

"Gets us into a room with the White Lion." Talia sat back and crossed her arms. "I get it. But if not Bangkok, where are we going right now?"

"Val?" Eddie gave her a *Take it away* wave.

The grifter rested an elbow on the glossy oak table. "Stage One is the attention getter, elegant enough to raise the right eyebrows but just a taste of things to come."

"I still say we can do Stage One with a good burglary," Finn said. "One night. In and out. Leaves us more time for the next two jobs."

Val rolled her head over like a big sister addressing an annoying little brother. "Did you not hear me say the first job has to be *elegant?*"

"What I do is elegant."

"What you do are smash-and-grabs with unnecessarily dangerous showmanship."

"Hey." Talia clapped her hands. "Finn, shut up. Val, get back on topic."

They both quieted down.

Tyler shot her a glance that said *Not bad*.

After a quick frown, Val tapped the screen's control tablet. The Stage One balloon in the flowchart expanded and became a picture of silver coins. "This gag is called German Silver."

"So we're going to Germany," Talia said.

"German Silver is not about the location, it's about the alloy—a cheap alloy used in industrial products."

Eddie zoomed in on the coins. "Low-level grifters pass these off on auction websites as"—he made air quotes—"100 percent German silver. It's a play on words. There's not an ounce of real silver in the coins."

The whole idea sounded sketchy. Before Talia could protest, Tyler read her mind and waved her off. "We're not planning to scam people on eBay. I promise."

Val gave him a *thank you* nod. "As I said. We have something more elegant in mind—and we're ramping up the price using gold." The pile of coins on the screen shrank away, replaced by a painting of an armored Cyrano de Bergerac look-alike, complete with curled mustache. "Meet Maximillian the Great, ruler of Bavaria."

"A German king," Talia said. "But we're not going to Germany."

Val rolled her eyes. "Would you let that go and listen? Maximillian the Great was a seventeenth-century duke. In the middle of the Thirty Years' War, he got hitched . . . to Maria, wife number two . . . his niece." She made a face and shrugged. "It was a different time. To legitimize this union, he had a horde of gold coins minted with her image at a Bohemian mine at the edge of his conquered territory."

"Let me guess. The coins went missing."

"Not just missing." Eddie waved his hanky. "They were wiped off the historical map. A hundred wooden boxes of newly minted coins left the mine in a mule train guarded by twelve hundred Bavarian knights and their soldiers. But this was the Thirty Years' War. The French and Swedes swept into the valley. Neither the knights nor the gold were ever seen again."

Lost treasure and lost artifact cons were something of a specialty for Valkyrie, like an old habit. Talia filled in the rest of the blanks. "So we pretend we found these missing gold coins—"

"The *Bavarian Thalers*," Eddie said. "The *thaler* is where the word dollar comes from."

"Whatever. We pretend we found these *thalers*, but in an inaccessible location. We throw out a coin or two as proof, and we con our first Jungle mark into helping us dig up the rest."

Val gave her a condescending smile. "Very good." She flicked a glittering coin across the table. It had the ring of gold.

Talia caught it and ran a thumb across a crude

149

and unconvincing face imprinted on one side—the Bavarian niece-slash-duchess. "And you expect an experienced criminal to fall for this?" She offered the coin back to Val.

The grifter pushed her hand away. "You go ahead and keep that one."

Talia did not miss the fact that Val failed to answer her last question. She hadn't answered the first one, for that matter. "We're running the German Silver con," Talia said, pocketing the coin, "using the lost gold of a Bavarian duke. So, if not some town in Germany, where are we going?"

They all answered at once, as if she were a complete and utter noob.

"Prague."

CHAPTER TWENTY-FOUR

Villa Václav River
Vltava Prague, Czech Republic

"Just once"—Talia followed Tyler down a spiral stair that must have dated back to the fourteenth or fifteenth century—"I'd like to see this crew bunk down in a warehouse or a back-alley basement like honest-to-goodness thieves."

Tyler paused on the bottom step to look up at her, scrunching his forehead. "Why on earth would we do that?" He strolled off into a low passage. "If it helps, we *are* in a basement."

"The basement of a castle."

"The term is *baronial hunting lodge*."

"The term is *castle*."

The lodge-slash-castle straddled a branch of the River Vltava, which passed through the Czech Republic from north to south. Thus, the passage from the stairs opened into a combination boat dock and garage, entirely covered by the main house. Iron boat gates allowed the river through from both sides.

Looking at the ancient stone dock, Talia imagined Bohemian barons and baronesses arriving under torchlight in unicorn-prowed boats or sneaking away in silent skiffs, depending on the century. But the garage portion had clearly been added in the last decade. The checkered epoxy floor gave it away, as did the halogen lights, electric doors, and aluminum worktables.

She and Tyler crossed an arched bridge, passing over a gray runabout.

Finn met them on the other side. He drew a red LED bulb from the cardboard box in his arms. "Hey, boss, you have any idea how to install these light globes?"

Tyler thrust his chin toward a Mercedes van, rocking on its tires, under the weight of an unseen force. "Ask Mac. Vehicular lighting is his department."

A hot, acrid scent filled Talia's nostrils. Near the dock's wrought-iron gate, Darcy had set up a mad alchemist's mini-lab. Bags of silver disks and gray powder lay open beside bubbling flasks. The chemist, wearing big orange gloves and a respiratory mask, poured molten metal into ceramic forms.

Talia poked Tyler's arm. "Is she transmuting lead into gold?"

"Close enough." He snapped his fingers, as if the joke had reminded him of some important task, and hurried off.

Everyone moved with a sense of urgency and purpose. Everyone seemed to know what to do. Except Talia.

"Yoo-hoo. Over here."

Talia heard Val's call but didn't see her.

"You look like you could use some direction." The grifter appeared at the door of a dressing room composed of cubicle panels. The red hair was gone, changed to a light golden brown, nowhere near her natural dark color—or what Talia assumed was her natural color. She wore jeans and a pink quilted biker jacket with leopard-print pumps and a matching belt.

"And you look like you could use some fashion sense."

"Funny. I'll admit I felt out of place at your little church. But this is a den of thieves. My domain. Better to save the jokes and put that eidetic mind in learning mode."

The new hair color and the Jersey Shore look were not the only things Talia found strange about Val's appearance. Her features had changed. Her eyes looked larger, her nose and chin a little smaller. She opened a makeup case and flipped on a lighted mirror, and without so much as a by-your-leave, sat Talia on a stool and dabbed her cheek with cleansing cream.

Talia caught her wrist. "What are you doing?"

"I thought you wanted in on this job."

She did. For the little girl and her friends. "Yeah. Okay." Talia let Val go to work.

In short order, Val had Talia's scant makeup removed and began applying a fresh coat. "We could be sisters, you and I."

That was a stretch. "Cousins, maybe. Or better yet, aunt and niece."

"What did I say about saving the jokes? Seriously, I think we could pull it off. You're an old soul." Val dropped a hand to her hip. "And I have a youthful face and figure. We could meet in the middle."

Talia would have nodded if Val hadn't caught her chin to run a brush across her cheekbones. After reviewing the exchange in her head, Talia drew back. "Wait. Are you saying I *don't* have a youthful face and figure?"

"Not at all, darling."

The makeup application continued, with pointers along the way. Val showed Talia how to change every feature of her face, even her eyes from almond-shaped to round. Satisfied—eventually—she dragged over a rack of clothes and held dresses up to Talia's shoulders, settling on a short velvety number. "Try this on."

"No."

Val sighed and returned the dress to the rack. "Well, we're going to have to do something. We can't stick with"—she gestured up and down at Talia's jeans and blouse—"practical and rugged."

"*Rugged?* Now you're just being mean. What's going on?"

"Eddie will explain. How's your Brooklyn accent?"

"Nonexistent."

"Then you'd better work on it. And then there's your hair." Val dug around in a box and brought out a light brown hair swatch. She held it next to Talia's head, crinkled her nose, and tossed it back. Her next attempt was a little darker but not much.

"I'll be wearing a wig?"

Val shook her head, trying a third swatch. "Wigs are a dead giveaway if the wind picks up. Dyes are better."

Talia had never dyed her hair, never in her whole life. "You're not changing my hair."

She'd been successful in staving off the dress, but Val stuck to her guns on the hair. "Open your mind, darling. Get into the spirit of the grift. Besides, if I'm not mistaken, Jordan put a target on your back. When you were Vera Novak, did you change your appearance?"

Talia's puffed-up stance deflated. "No, I didn't."

"Then guess what we have to do now."

CHAPTER TWENTY-FIVE

Villa Václav River
Vltava Prague, Czech Republic

The new hair color was nice. Val had done good work. But looking at herself in the standing mirror, Talia found it a level of different for which she was not prepared. She didn't know whether to laugh or cry. The Farm class on disguises had taken less than an afternoon. No one took it seriously, especially not the instructors. Voice changers and masks were a Hollywood joke, not a real thing. The Agency depended on clothing changes, camera evasion, and fake IDs.

With the addition of a skirt, blouse, and jacket combo Val called *academic-chic,* Talia didn't look like the same person. But after two assassination attempts, that was the whole point.

Out in the garage, Talia and Val found Eddie arranging keyboards and monitors atop a stack of cargo crates. He turned to see her coming and snapped the fingers of both hands. "Great. You're ready. Give me a victory pose."

"A what?" Talia asked.

"This." Val locked her fingers in Talia's and raised their hands together, tilting her hips and smiling at the camera in triumph. "Smile, darling."

Mac unfurled a green screen behind them, and Eddie snapped a picture with his phone. He checked the screen. "Not the best. But it'll do."

An instant later, the photo appeared on the largest of the monitors. Talia and Val stood in their odd pose—Val triumphant, Talia less so—with the Brooklyn Bridge behind them. Once she saw the two of them together, Talia understood Val's earlier comment.

The grifter gave her a friendly-but-a-little-too-forceful shake of the shoulders. "I told you we could be sisters."

The photo shrank to become the main image in a webzine article. Eddie added a tilted headline.

LOCAL TREASURE HUNTERS
FIND PIRATE GOLD

The geek made a *Ta-da!* gesture. "Meet the Macciano Sisters. Long Island's treasure-hunting queens. The sisters happen to have a meeting on the books with our first mark this evening."

Talia squinted at the article, reading the first few lines—something about William Kidd's lost gold. "Our first mark?"

Eddie tried to answer but sneezed into his hanky instead. He tapped the keyboard with his elbow. Another article appeared beside the first, a legitimate news release touting the rapid rise of an Albanian broker in the Czech Republic's financial sector. The photo was a power shot of a sharply dressed man in his thirties with green stock tickers flowing behind.

Eddie stuffed the hanky away. "Sorry. I have some lingering sniffles. Your appointment this evening is with Taner Atan—alleged mob ties, a few dead bodies, but nothing proven. This guy is the Bernie Madoff of Central Europe. Plus he dabbles in black-market commodities like arms and pharmaceuticals. He makes roughly twenty-five million a year for the syndicate with Ponzi schemes, insider trading, and penny-stock shell games, mostly based in the Far East markets. And according to Dark Web chatter, he nearly doubles that figure at the annual Frenzy."

Tyler joined them, pulling off a respirator that matched Darcy's. "Atan is the Jungle's Hyena, the lowest ranking of the top five, and one of only two top players we've been able to identify with near certainty."

"Who else have you identified?" Talia asked.

"Orien Jafet, the Maltese Tiger. He's a Greek underworld boss. We'll get to him in Stage Two."

"Tell me again why you can't ID the others, Eddie." Val sat on a couch Mac had brought down from the lodge and crossed her legs. "I thought you could move whole planets with those computers."

"Satellites. Not planets." Eddie shot the grifter a *get it right* frown. "The other two bigwigs—the Clouded Leopard and the Snow Leopard—are hard to nail down. All the top positions are fluid, up for grabs each year. Atan and Jafet fended off the competition the last three Frenzies, making them easier to track."

The grifter bobbled her head and looked away, as if grudgingly accepting the excuse.

Talia watched the interaction. Clearly she had missed a great deal of discussion. She was playing catch-up. She hated playing catch-up. "I'm having trouble connecting the dots between Atan and the German Silver gag."

Tyler had the answer, not a very helpful one. "Our mark is an avid numismatist."

"A what?" Talia asked.

"A numismatist," called Finn from a table laid out with an odd collection of items—a bowl of ice, a miniature slide, a radar gun. He beckoned them over. "A coin nerd. Or . . . coin *geek,* right, Eddie?"

A sniffle and a wiggling hanky muffled Eddie's reply. "Nope. Nerd is correct. Trust me."

Darcy brought Finn a tray of freshly minted gold coins, and the Aussie lifted one from the tray. "Geek, nerd, whatever. We're running a coin scam on a coin expert. No easy task. He's going to test our fake Bavarian Thalers. We're prepared for everything he can throw at us."

Tyler shook his head. "Never say that, Finn. It's unnecessary hubris. The mark can always throw you a curveball."

"Right. Okay." The burglar's cheeks reddened. Talia could see he wanted to argue, but he didn't and simply moved on. Finn rubbed the coin between his palms and set it on the bowl of ice. It sank like a hot stone. "Test one. Gold has a high thermal conductivity, so it melts through ice quickly, drawing heat from the air."

"But that's not gold," Talia said.

Darcy gave her a lips-parted *abracadabra* wink. "You are correct. But your chemist is *exceptionnel*, no?" She picked up a vial marked NITRIC ACID. "Test two—acid. Pure gold is corrosion proof, so most acids won't affect it. Other metals are not so fortunate." Using an eyedropper, she placed a dab of the acid on a copper penny. Fizz bubbled up and the acid turned green. She placed the next drop on one of her coins.

The acid remained clear. Talia let out a mystified huff. "Nothing." Again, the coin performed like gold.

"Wait, please." A few seconds later, the drop began to fizz, taking on the same green color as before. "The acid is a persistent foe, yes? A thin layer of epoxy protects these coins, but it will eventually fail. You must keep the mark moving if he tries an acid test."

"He won't. He'll love the idea of the thalers too much." A hint of a Brooklyn accent invaded Val's words. It grew stronger as she continued. "Not many men have the guts to pour acid on a two-million dollah coin. Know what I'm sayin'?"

The team turned to look at her. Even Tyler looked disturbed.

"What? You people got a problem?"

They all turned back to Darcy.

The chemist moved down the table to Finn's miniature slide. "Test three. A much less destructive test involving the magnetic properties of the gold."

Mac raised a hand. "Gold isn't magnetic."

"*Exactement.*" Darcy held a magnetic cube over the tray of coins, and none of them moved. "However, gold is diamagnetic, interacting in opposition to a magnetic field." She laid the coin on the miniature slide, and it slowly moved to the bottom, held back by an invisible force.

Talia had seen a similar effect a few days earlier when Tyler played with the magnetic disk and copper tube at Wolf Manor. And Darcy's coin had reacted to the acid with the same color change as the penny. "Copper," she said with a quiet chuckle. "You're using copper to mimic the conductive properties of the gold."

Darcy touched her nose. "You are like the Sherlock Holmes, no? But copper is much lighter than gold. Any dime-store scale will expose a copper alloy fake like ours. Yet . . ." She placed the coin on one plate of a balance scale and a lead cube marked 1 OZ on the other. The two teetered for a few heartbeats, then settled, perfectly level. Darcy grinned. "*Voilà*. A tungsten core brings us back into balance."

While Darcy worked the slide and scales, Finn had been playing with the radar gun at the end of the table. He waggled it in the air, and Darcy nodded. "This brings us to the last and most dangerous test—the XRF, or X-ray fluorescence, gun. Any wealthy numismatist worth his salt will own one."

"In fact," Eddie said, walking around the table to stand next to his girlfriend, "Atan's online purchases confirm he owns this particular make and model." He ended with a sniffle.

Darcy slid a half step away. "Are you going to do this snuffling, snotty thing the entire job?"

"It's a cold. What am I supposed to do?"

"Keep it away from me, yes?"

Finn whistled to get their attention and held the gun over the tray of coins. "Copper alloys. Tungsten cores. This baby can detect them all at the atomic level. No fake coin can beat it. True blue. No exceptions." He pressed the scanner's trigger. The device hummed and issued a pronounced *boop*. He showed Talia the readout.

GOLD 97.1%.

Talia scrunched up her nose. "But you said . . ."

Darcy gave her another *abracadabra* wink. "There are two variables in this equation, yes? The coin and the XRF gun. If you cannot fake the coin . . ."

"Fake the gun." Talia laughed. "I love it. Okay. We're meeting Atan in a couple of hours. How do we get the fake gun into his hands?"

Finn cracked his knuckles. "Leave that to me."

CHAPTER TWENTY-SIX

St. Vitus Cathedral
Prague, Czech Republic

The knight's eyes were all wrong.

Finn cocked his head, hoping a change of angle might make a difference. It didn't.

The life-size statue of St. Wenceslas hovered above a tomb in St. Vitus Cathedral, stepping out from a fresco as if stepping out of the past. He wore a knight's armor and carried a spear and shield, but his eyes did not match such warlike adornments.

A knight, in Finn's book, ought to be confident and hard. The eyes of this ancient Bohemian king were neither. The artist had given him a soulful look, generous and conciliatory, almost tearful. Those eyes said, *What's mine is yours. By all means, stab me in the heart and pillage my castle at your leisure.* According to a pamphlet, the king's brother had done exactly that.

Finn shook his head and dropped the pamphlet on the stack. A little past the table, however, his eyes fell on something more to his liking—a dark hall guarded by an iron-bar gate with a tempting sign.

THIS WAY TO
THE BOHEMIAN CROWN JEWELS

An invitation if ever Finn had seen one. Near closing time, few security personnel lingered in the cathedral. Most were out policing the surrounding compound—Prague Castle, among the largest hilltop fortresses in the world. Sure, the gate was locked, and Lexan cases and cameras would protect the jewels. Nothing he couldn't handle. He clenched and unclenched his fists. "Hmm."

"Finn." Tyler came in clear over the SATCOM link. "Your GPS tracker is stationary. What's the holdup?"

"Just . . . taking in the sights."

"I see. Since you've got time to kill, pick me up a few souvenirs."

"I was just thinking about that." Finn took one last look at the Crown Jewel sign and walked off. "But you'd only give 'em away, like that dewy-eyed King Wenceslas."

"Say again?"

"Nothing."

A thigh-crippling two hundred eighty-seven steps brought Finn to the top of the cathedral's southern bell tower, where the giant Zikmund Bell and its lesser cousins looked out over Prague. A young boy pressed himself back against the wall beneath one of the windows as Finn arrived.

Children never shrank away from Finn. But he remembered the business suit he wore—not among his usual fashion choices. To a kid in jeans too short for growing legs and a grease-stained flannel shirt, a guy in an expensive suit must look like a mobster or a stockbroker. In Prague the two were interchangeable.

"Relax, kid. The suit's just a costume." He glanced around. "You lose your parents or something?"

The boy gave him a blank stare.

"Where is your papa?" Finn held up a hand, palm down, even with his own head. "You know. Papa?" He moved the hand a little lower. "Mama?"

The kid shook his head.

"Right. You went walkabout on your own. I get that. My mom preferred it when I made myself scarce during the day, too, especially when her boyfriends came around."

The kid seemed to accept this, or at least the idea that Finn was not some authority figure there to drag him out of the cathedral. He turned to the window, trying—and failing—to pull himself up by the limestone sill.

"You want to see out?"

That question got through loud and clear. The kid nodded and held up his arms. He was light, even for his size. Finn set him on the sill and guarded his waist. "Nice view, huh?"

The kid said nothing, eyes roaming the fortress below and the city of Prague beyond.

"Finn." It was Tyler again. "The girls are approaching the dock. Time to move."

"Yeah. I see them."

The Vltava River split the city. Val and Talia had taken the runabout rather than brave the traffic on the winding, medieval streets. A municipal dock put them within walking distance of Atan's brokerage, occupying the top floor of a seventeenth-century building at the base of the fortress hill. The building's red tile roof looked a little close for Finn's comfort.

"Darcy, are you sure about this jump?"

"*Naturellement*. The tower is fifty meters above the courtyard—almost two hundred above Atan's office, yes? That is six times higher than Russell Powell's jump from the dome of Paul's." After a pause, she added, "And Powell was *inside* the church."

"But Powell didn't have to cover a hundred fifty meters of horizontal distance." Finn lifted the kid down from the sill and pulled a matte gray wingsuit from his backpack. The kid watched him put it on with mild interest. "Darcy, you didn't answer the question. Am I going to make this?"

"You will accelerate at nine point eight meters per second, reaching a velocity of thirty-one meters per second in the first fifty meters, generating enough lift to glide and enough force to properly open the chute."

"I give you a yes or no question, and you spout a bunch of maths. Thanks."

Finn climbed up into the window, which bought him a great deal more interest from the kid than the wingsuit had. He mustered his sternest schoolmarm look. "Don't try this at home, kid. Don't try it here, either. Especially here."

As he began scaling the aged copper roof to the tower's peak, Darcy interrupted. "You did not lie to me about your weight, did you?"

"Guys don't lie about bodyweight."

"Good. Okay. Safe flight."

Bodyweight. A chill went down his spine. Finn never lied about his weight. Why would he? His abs were like a riverbed. But he did have a habit of removing the contents of his pockets whenever he stepped on a scale.

Finn crawled back down to the window. Using the Velcro access panels in the legs of his wingsuit, he dug every bit of spare change out of his pockets and slapped two fistfuls down on the sill. "Hey, kid. These are for you."

The kid scooped up the money and scampered off before the strange suicidal man changed his mind.

CHAPTER TWENTY-SEVEN

St. Vitus Cathedral
Prague, Czech Republic

Finn muttered a quick prayer to the God Tyler claimed was watching over them all and jumped.

The fortress courtyard came on fast.

Years of daredevil stunts for big shows and burglaries had acclimated Finn to the terror of ground rush. This stunt, however, came with the unsettling knowledge that he would have to generate enough forward velocity to clear the battlements.

He snapped into the spread-eagle position and arched, begging the air to grant him lift. The toes of his Italian wing tips came so close to the battlements, they drew dust from the bricks. The worst was over. Beyond the wall, the steep descent of the fortress hill gave him an additional hundred twenty-five meters of free fall to play with. Finn breathed a sigh of relief and adjusted his path for a late-opening landing on the roof.

Talia heard Finn's jump call through her earpiece, but she didn't look. The last thing she wanted was to draw some pedestrian's attention to Finn's covert entrance. The gray wingsuit against the gray dusk sky made him nearly invisible, but she knew better than to take chances.

As a doorman waved them through the entrance, Val whispered in Talia's ear. "Your name on this one is Natalia Macciano. In character, I'll call you Nat."

"I hate that nickname. Call me Natalie."

"I wasn't giving you a choice."

Talia had put a stop to the *Nat* thing on day one in kindergarten. Why would anyone think a little girl wanted a nickname homonymous with an annoying bug? "Do it, and I'll make you pay."

"Go ahead. I have lots of money." Val fell into her Brooklyn accent, signaling the desk guard. "Hellooo-ooo. We're *Nat* and Val Macciano, here to see Mr. Taner Atan."

A deer-in-the-headlights response told them all they needed to know about the guard's command of English.

Val tried again. *"Ma-see-ah-no.* Here to see Mr. *Atan. Capiche?"*

The guard held up a finger and flicked a switch below a panel of monitors. They showed the main hallways and the elevators, but not the interior offices. Good news for Finn. A moment later, the guard touched the headset cup at his ear, murmured a response in Czech, and nodded to Val. *"Šesté patro.* In English, eh . . . Floor 6."

Three-foot copper letters, illuminated by warm spotlights and spelling out ATAN INVESTMENTS, greeted Talia and Val as they stepped off the elevator. As if that much copper wasn't striking enough, Atan's receptionist sat dwarfed behind an oversize copper reception desk, lacquered with clear coat to make it shine. Eddie had mentioned their mark had a thing for the stuff. Funny, given the true content of their fake Bavarian Thalers.

"Copper is the lowest of the currency metals," Atan explained when he came out to meet them. "It reminds me of where I started—the son of a penniless mechanic in an Albanian slum. As you can see, I have come up in the world. How may I help you ladies to do the same?"

Tyler coached them through the comm link. "Keep him away from his office. It sits too close to the coin vault where he keeps the XRF gun. Get him to the conference room."

Val kept her Brooklyn accent running at full steam. "Don't ask what you can do for us, Mr. Atan. Ask what we can do for you." She pressed her thumb and forefinger together. "A unique opportunity has popped up in your little neck of the woods. We're here to give you first crack."

"Crack?" Atan's smile flattened. "If I understand correctly, you are here with a proposal. But I am a busy man. You have thirty seconds to pique my interest."

Val flung a hand over her shoulder. "I'll do it in five. You're a coin collector, right?"

"The term is *numismatist*."

"Sure, honey. Whatever. Then maybe you've heard of the Bavarian Thalers."

The sudden shift in Atan's expression told Talia the hook was in.

"You see, Nat." Val smacked Talia's arm. "We came to the right man."

To the right. Talia recognized the method in Val's Brooklyn madness. The flamboyant accent kept Atan's conscious mind distracted while key words and hand signals told his subconscious where to go—the conference room, to the right.

Val finished her play with a more obvious push. She ran a finger along the reception desk. "I've never seen so much copper. So gorgeous. I bet your conference table is made of the same stuff too, yeah? It's gotta be 'uge."

"Enormous." The smile returned to Atan's face. "Let me show you."

"They've got him, Finn," Tyler said through the comm link. "You're on."

CHAPTER TWENTY-EIGHT

Atan Investments
Prague, Czech Republic

A red tile cracked under the press of Finn's knee as he low-crawled across the roof. A piece slid away, threatening to bounce over the gutters and crash onto the street below. He caught it with a toe and held it steady until he was sure it would stay put.

If they had come a day earlier—skipped princess Talia's church service and Sunday lunch—Finn could have done the job at night, properly. Instead, the rushed timing had made it an evening swap, still during business hours.

Risky.

On the plus side, daytime burglary took the *break* out of *breaking and entering*. Alarms were shut down for employee movement, especially the alarms on roof access doors in a country like the Czech Republic, where smoking was the national pastime.

The door opened with the tap and turn of a bump key. Finn adjusted his tie and walked down the steps as if he owned the place. He carried his backpack in plain sight—a young stockbroker with a twenty-first-century briefcase. "I'm in."

. . .

Val went on about the gorgeous copper conference table, but Atan fixed his gaze on Talia.

"Your sister," he said when Val allowed him to get a word in, "does not say much."

"Nat's the introspective one. Know what I mean?" Val gave her an accusing look. "Ditched me after high school and ran off to a fancy Ivy League school in DC. Got so *edumacated* she don't even talk right anymore." The *anymore* sounded like *any-mo-ah*. "But Nat's my research queen. She traced Kidd's treasure to that cemetery in Flatbush. And she's the one who traced the Bavarian Thalers to the Czech Republic." Val slapped Talia's arm again. "Nat. Say somethin'. Don't be rude."

Talia swallowed. "I—"

"See. Introspective. That's my little Nattie-pie."

A second mention of the Bavarian Thalers shifted Atan's focus. "So, you think you have found Maximillian's gold."

"We don't think. We know." Val nudged Talia. "Show him, Nat."

The nickname didn't bother Talia all that much. She had been ribbing Val, but all this nudging and slapping scraped at her patience, character or not. She tried not to growl. "Show him what, Valerie?"

Val lowered her chin. "The coin, Sis. You know, the one I gave you for safekeeping?"

Maybe Val's mind worked on a different level. Or maybe she'd purposely failed to tell Talia the coin she'd flipped across the table on the jet would play a principal role in the con.

Talia dug the coin out of her purse, grateful she still carried it. The fake gold made a lovely *tink* as she set it on the copper table.

Atan's nostrils flared. "The Duchess Maria?" However ugly and malformed the engraving of the Bohemian duke's niece-wife looked to Talia, Atan treated it like the image of a beauty queen. He drew a monocle from his breast pocket and held the coin to his eye. "It cannot be."

"Oh, it is, sweetums," Val said. "It most certainly is."

He let the monocle fall. "And there are more?"

"Thousands, Mr. Atan." Talia kept her diction slow and precise to cover the Ivy League New Yorker backstory Val had given her. "Perhaps tens of thousands, depending on how many coins history and the elements have stripped away. My research confirms Maximillian the Great had at least forty thousand minted."

A notion—perhaps a suspicion—seemed to strike the Albanian. He placed the coin on the table. "If you have the location, why do you need my help?"

"We don't," Val said.

"But . . . you need me to move them, correct?"

"*Ver-ry* good. This guy don't miss a trick, right, Nat."

Talia conjured up a smile. "No, he doesn't."

"But, ladies, you could simply report this find—enlist the help of the Czech authorities."

Val laughed, ending it with a snort. "Okay, maybe he's not such a smart cookie after all. Treasure hunters and governments don't get along, Mr. Atan. Everyone knows this. Take the South African kayaker who found the Boer Krugerrands, for instance. This law-abiding *zero* finds billions in gold and dutifully reports every penny to the authorities." She smacked Talia's arm again. "Nat, tell the man how much the kayaker paddled away with."

Talia had never heard of the Boer Krugerrands, but Val had given her a clue—the same way a fortune-teller's shill passed information. *Law-abiding zero.* "Nothing," she said with absolute confidence.

Atan nodded. "Yes, I followed this affair. A shame."

"Same thing happened to us," Val said. "The press got wind of it, and once the cat was out the bag, the government pounced. State, local, federal. Taxes, fees, tariffs. The Historic Preservation Act. We barely got outta there with our Louis Vuittons."

Talia glanced at her, beginning to find the

rhythm of her academic-sister-to-the-flamboyant-Brooklyn-girl character. "I don't wear Louis Vuitton."

"Ain't that the truth." Val touched Atan's hand. "The Boer Krugerrands, the Odyssey Pieces of Eight, Kidd's Gold—when governments get involved, treasure hunters lose. We're looking to move these coins quietly on multiple continents. You're our guy for Eastern Europe and Asia."

Atan scratched his chin, eyes on the coin.

Val tapped his hand twice with her finger before drawing back. "You'll be paid, of course."

The hard set of Atan's jaw worried Talia. Val liked to flirt with the edge of believability to throw off a mark. She might have flirted too much.

"I keep my collection here in the office," Atan said, "along with a few tools for authentication. May I take a closer look at your sample?"

Talia pushed back from the table. "By all means." Finn had told them he needed less than three minutes to breach the keypad lock on the coin room door. She and Val had given him five. She threw Finn a hint over the comms. "Your coin collection is one of the reasons we came to you. We'd love to see it."

Before she finished the statement, her earpiece buzzed with a desperate whisper from the thief. "Negative. Negative. Stall him. I haven't made the switch."

CHAPTER TWENTY-NINE

Atan Investments
Prague, Czech Republic

To Finn's knowledge, no real thief had ever used a Hollywood hacker box—the kind with analog numbers rolling through pass codes at a thousand numbers a second to defeat keypad locks. Sure, a few YouTubers had built working replicas, but such boxes were overkill.

The keypad lock was the biggest con in the security industry, including its prettier cousin—the biometric lock. Experts called them *security theater*. Thieves adored them. High-end tumbler and bolt locks were bump key–proof and unpickable. Defeating mechanical cipher locks required a cutting torch. But keypad locks were electric, and therefore vulnerable. To defeat them, a pro need only carry a multi-tool and a stun gun.

Or so Finn had thought. Atan's lock shattered this illusion.

The keypad lock on the coin room door looked like a medium-range model—decent internal shielding but nothing more than a sixty-second job. The hardest part should have been popping off the cover and removing the shielding to get a better hit with the stun gun.

All keypads appeared inaccessible from the outside. But Finn knew where to look for the hidden screws. He found them behind a piece of aluminum trim, easily pried loose with his flathead. Thirty seconds later, the cover was off and the guts exposed. He checked the hall, pulled the rubber shielding free, and zapped the lock with his stun gun.

The overload should have triggered the electric motor to throw the bolt, mimicking the result of an electric pulse from the keypad.

It didn't.

The motor whirred and whined, but the bolt never clicked back. Finn tried again. Another whir. More whining. No click. The steel door wouldn't budge.

"Huh."

Finn knew other ways to defeat a keypad lock or a vault door. None were quiet or left no trace. This job required both. In moments, Atan had to open that door with his own code, believing no one had tampered with it.

When Talia hinted they were coming, panic set in.

"I can't do it."

"Talk to me, Finn," Tyler said. "Is someone in the hall, blocking the way to the door?"

"Negative. I'm *at* the door. I can't beat the lock."

A moment of silence. "You . . . what?"

"This lock has some secondary defense mechanism I've never seen. I don't know the trick." Voices drifted down the hall from the reception desk. Val, in her loud Brooklyn persona, admired the furnishings in Atan's foyer. She was stalling, clearly tracking Finn's struggles through the comm chatter. She couldn't keep it up for long.

Tyler pulled the plug on him. "Get out of there."

"But—"

"Now, Finn."

"Right." He scrambled to replace the shielding and cover. In the process, he dropped a screw. It vanished into the carpet.

Talia heard Finn's frantic breathing, followed by a *Got it!* and the *kerchunk* of a door closing.

Trailing Val and Atan, she rounded the corner past the reception desk and walked by his office—which included a king-size bed, complete with zebra-striped duvet.

Atan winked at Val when she commented on his choice in decor. "What can I say. I am one with my animal instincts." His leer dropped to her leopard-print pumps.

Talia wanted to be sick.

Val laughed and snorted. "Oh, Mr. Atan. You're so funny."

The hallway ahead was empty. Had Finn gone inside the vault?

Tyler must have had the same thought. "Got what, Finn? Did you beat the lock? Finn, answer me."

"Sorry. I'm at the roof. I couldn't talk in the stairwell. Atan might've heard."

"Fine. What about the XRF?"

"Never made the switch. The one he'll be using is real."

As Atan and the girls reached the coin room door, Talia tried another delay tactic. Tyler had insisted the team set the hook tonight, but if Atan spied their fake, they'd lose this whole game in the first round. No Boyd. No Archangel. No Hla Meh. "It's late, Mr. Atan. I'm sure a man like you has plans for the evening. We can come back in the morning."

"Nonsense. You are here now. Let me test the coin. Otherwise, the curiosity will deny me my beauty sleep."

His next motion caught her off guard. Atan rested a shoulder against the door and offered an embarrassed smile. "Forgive me. My coin vault is all steel construction, and I made the error of choosing the lowest bidder." He entered his pass code. The lock whirred and whined until he gave the door a shoulder-check worthy of a hockey team enforcer. The bolt clicked back. "My installer set the door out of plumb. Since the steel wall is a seamless unit, this will cost me thousands to fix."

If not for the danger of exposure, Talia might have laughed. Finn, despite all his skill and cockiness, had been defeated by a sticky door.

The vault was an Aladdin's cave of silver, copper, and gold. Mostly gold. Val whistled. "Niiiiiice." Talia could hear real interest in her voice. "Not to tell you your business, Mr. Atan, but one lock and a sketchy vault door ain't enough to protect a trove like this. You need lasers and such. I've got a guy in town right now for this Bavarian Thaler hunt. Australian. Really knows his stuff." She shot a sidelong glance at Talia. "Most of the time."

"I can still hear you," Finn said over the link. "I'm not laughing."

Atan would not be distracted so easily. He brandished the coin. "Let us focus on the task at hand and worry about my security later."

The center display case served as Atan's worktable. Worn coins labeled with dates in the early Roman period sat on velvet pillows inside. But on top, on polished wood trays, were instruments and tools similar to those Darcy and Finn had used in their demonstration.

"I am a discerning, if not neurotic, collector." Using a ruler and calipers, Atan took width and diameter measurements. He jotted down his findings on a notepad, then set the thaler on a digital scale and punched in a few numbers, eyeing the readout. "Mmm-hmm. Good." With casual flair, he let the coin fall down a magnetic slide. "Yes. Very good. But only one test will tell if this gold came from the old Bohemian mines."

The XRF gun sat unmolested on its own swiveling stand. Atan waved Val away from the business end. "Step over there, please." He patted the gun. "The XRF works by displacing electrons at the atomic level. I'd hate to scramble yours. They are so beautifully placed."

A quick pull of the trigger, a hum from the XRF, and it was over.

Atan frowned at the screen. He lifted his gaze to meet Val's. "*Now* you have my full attention, Miss Macciano." He swiveled the XRF so his guests could see the readout.

GOLD 97.1%.

If Val was fazed at all by the real analyzer's positive result, she didn't show it. "Ninety-seven point one. The percentage found in most Bohemian gold of the period, right, Nat?"

When Talia didn't answer, Val prodded her with an elbow. "Earth to Nat. You with us?"

"Uh . . . Right." Val had done something—some sleight of hand. How had Talia missed it?

The conversation went on without her.

Atan set the XRF on its stand. "I am happy to move these coins for you. Honored, in fact."

"Good. Use your contacts here, and in the Far East. Private auctions, quiet and simultaneous so the buyers won't know there are others on the market. Rarity drives up the price. We play this right and we can pull in more than a million per coin. Your commission is 20 percent, plus one coin for your very own."

"Perhaps I misunderstood." The Albanian gave her a flat and fleeting smile. "I believe you meant to say my commission is 50 percent . . . plus five coins." He raised a finger. "*And* I will be present at the dig site when you unearth the duke's treasure."

"Whoa there, horsey." Val waved her hands. "Nat and I weren't born yesterday. We give you the dig site, what's to stop you from sweeping in with a small army and cutting us out?"

"You have my word."

"Your word ain't enough. But money talks. Our other fences paid well for dig site privileges."

"*Other* fences?" He glanced at Talia. "What other fences?"

Talia wanted to ask the same question. "Er . . . moving the coins is my sister's department. She'll tell you about our other arrangements."

Val picked up the coin. "Mr. Atan, we're moving these babies on a *global* scale. A guy named Tyler is covering the American end, and we've got a Brit covering the UK and Western Europe—last name Smythe."

"Malcom Smythe?"

"Oh good. You know him."

"I know *of* him. Mr. Smythe is a show-off, a

press hound in a gaudy waistcoat." Atan pressed his lips together in distaste. "You are bringing this Willy Wonka of coins to your dig site?"

"He and Tyler paid half a mil each for the privilege."

"Done."

Val placed the coin in Talia's hand, signaling her to put it away, a method of pushing a mark to pursue his goal. "What's done, Mr. Atan?"

"Five hundred thousand US. I will wire the money on the way to the site." But when Val went to shake on the deal, he pulled his hand back. "You have presented one coin while claiming to know the location of thousands. You must have more. Show me."

"No problem." She slapped a fistful of matching coins on the display case.

The Albanian drew a breath. "Deal. I will prepare your money and make the transfer en route to the dig site." He pulled out his phone. "All I require is the when and where."

Val took the phone, Atan's hand included, and typed an address into a time slot on his calendar. "Meet us here tomorrow at nine a.m. sharp. We'll take you to the spot."

"That's it," Tyler said into the comms. "Good work, team. All of you."

All of you. Talia knew that last part was for Finn. She hoped it would help.

CHAPTER THIRTY

River Vltava
Prague, Czech Republic

Mac piloted the runabout for the return trip to the castle-slash-baronial-hunting-lodge. The moment he silenced the engines to drift through the stone arch beneath the lodge, Talia lit into Val. "You jeopardized the mission."

"You got it all wrong, sweetums. I *saved* the mission after Finn blew it."

"You threw me a curveball in front of the mark."

"You're overreacting." The grifter let Mac lift her up to the dock like a stage trapeze, smirking as her leopard-skin pumps alighted on the stones. "I like to keep you on your toes."

"The gold coin," Talia said, climbing out on her own. "You gave it to me fully intending to use it to fool the XRF."

"I gave it to you as a plan B, in case Finn dropped the ball." She pronounced *ball* as *boowall*.

"Would you quit with the accent, Val?"

"She can't." Tyler, seated on a stool beside the van, folded a Czech newspaper. "Val's maintaining her character for the con. To be honest, you should do the same."

Val gave him a wink. "I think she is."

"Whatever. She still could've told me about Plan B." Talia walked to the dressing area and checked her hair in the mirror. She no longer liked the new look Val had given her. She preferred the Agency's way of running games on a mark. Simple. Straightforward. CIA officers coerced, stole, lied, and paid. But they didn't do drama.

Val appeared behind her in the reflection. "Fun's over, sweetums. I'll take the coin back."

"Yeah, okay." Talia dug the coin out of her pocket, went to place it in the grifter's waiting palm, then stopped and drew it back. "On second thought, no."

"Excuse me?"

"You called me Nat."

"So."

Talia rolled the coin between her thumb and forefinger, watching how the scalloped edges caught the glow of the mirror's ring light. She had a new respect for the ugly image of Duchess Maria, knowing her face was real gold with a dash of silver. "You had this thing minted to mimic seventeenth-century Bohemian gold, right?"

Val canted a hip, maintaining the affectations of a Jersey Shore darling. "Maybe. Why?" Her eyes darted to the thaler. Her shoulder twitched.

She obviously wanted the coin back for reasons

more than she was saying, and Talia wanted to make a point. The whole Nat argument gave her an excuse. Talia dropped the thaler into her purse. "I said you'd pay. Now you have."

Val's hard expression cracked. Her lips parted, speechless. She spun around and stormed off to the clothing racks.

On the sidelines, Tyler raised his newspaper. Talia felt sure he was using it to hide a grin. "And you," she said, pointing. "How much of this did you know before I walked unprepared into an Albanian mobster's office?"

"Do you really have to ask?"

She took a breath to fire off a rebuke. "Wait. Where's Finn?"

"Off comms." Eddie glanced back from his bank of computers. "He went dark after he botched the switch."

The look Talia gave Tyler was a question and an accusation rolled into one.

He raised his hands. "I'm giving him space. Finn is a big boy. He can take care of himself."

"Send Mac out to look for him."

"To what end?"

He had a point. If Finn didn't want to be found, Mac stood no chance. Talia returned to the problem of being left in the dark. "You could have told me you and Val had a plan B. Since when did keeping crew members in the dark become a good idea?"

"Depends on the job."

He was up to something, teaching her some unwelcome lesson. "I don't follow."

"You keep claiming you can handle things on your own." Tyler inclined his head toward the clothing racks, where Mac was helping Val select another Jersey Shore outfit.

When Talia looked their way, Val crossed her arms and raised an eyebrow. No surprise there. But Mac crossed his arms as well.

She let out a breath. She wished Finn were there. After all the *princess* and *your highness* talk, he'd have wanted to see Talia eat a little humble pie. "I get it. I need you all. And I know a large part of this is about stopping the person trying to kill me. I'm grateful for the help."

Mac nodded.

So did Tyler. "Good. The occasional tête-à-tête is healthy for a team—a set of checks and balances."

Val kept her expression hard, unmoved, and Talia narrowed her eyes. "I'm still keeping the coin."

The grifter huffed and turned back to the clothes.

The gold coin was only part of the whole keep-Talia-in-the-dark game Tyler had been playing. She fell in step behind him on the way to Eddie's computer bank. "What about this second mark, Malcom Smythe? Is he some kind of collateral damage?"

"Does it matter?" Val held a gold blouse and a rhinestone-studded jacket up to her shoulders. "A mark is a mark. As long as we get the job done, right?"

"Wrong." Talia caught up to Tyler. "Tell her she's wrong."

"I never tell Val she's wrong. It's counter-productive. But don't worry. I think you'll like our Mr. Smythe." Tyler thrust his chin toward the main screen. "Go ahead, Eddie. Call him."

A blue globe spun at the center of the screen, and a ringtone pulsed in the speakers. When the call went through, a white-haired man materialized. He wore a waxy mustache and goatee. Talia recognized him anyway. "Conrad?"

"Mr. Smythe, thank you very much." The cook added more pretension than usual to his accent.

Talia had trouble taking her focus off the plum waistcoat. Atan had mentioned Smythe's preference for outlandish colors. "You told me you wore that to celebrate my homecoming."

"As I did, child. But I was also trying it out, getting comfortable. I am . . . unused to pushing the boundaries of fashion." He held a royal blue bow tie to his neck and wiggled it.

Talia giggled.

Tyler brought conversation back to business. "Are you all set, Mr. Smythe?"

"Set and ready. We'll see you at the dig site tomorrow morning."

"Good. Until then." The screen returned to the blue globe. Tyler glanced at Talia. "Happy?"

"Not until we find those kids."

The groan of the garage door stopped Talia from asking why Conrad was bunking apart from the rest of the team, or what he had meant by the *we* in *We'll see you tomorrow*. Finn ducked in. He pressed the button to send the door down again the moment his head was clear.

Mac shoved the clothes he'd been holding into Val's arms and strode off to greet his friend. The two had grown closer in the months following the Gryphon heist. He clasped Finn's hand and bent close to his ear, muttering. The thief nodded and gave him a sad smile.

Talia wanted to do the same—to go to him and say something encouraging. But what?

Eddie made an attempt of his own. When Finn sank into the couch beside his computer bank, the geek swiveled around and laid a hand on his arm. "Next time I'll build you one of those boxes that hacks the code."

Finn gave him a *you can't be serious* stare.

"No. Really. I built one last year for fun. Worked great."

"*Psst.*" Talia leaned into Eddie's line of sight, running a hand across her throat.

He didn't notice. "I learned how to build it from this guy on YouTube."

Finn dropped his forehead into his palm. "Someone shoot me."

Val sat on the couch beside the thief. "Are we feeling sad because we couldn't get the job done?"

"Valkyrie," Tyler said.

She ignored the warning. "A cat burglar defeated by a stuck door—as if you have no clue what you're doing. Don't worry. I covered your slack. Come to think of it, you only got in the way."

No one breathed. The only sound in the garage was the hum of halogen lights. After a few heartbeats, Finn got up and walked out, slamming the old iron dock gate behind him.

Misguided helpfulness was one thing. A direct attack was another. Talia gave Val a death stare. "You don't care who you hurt, do you?" She hurried after Finn.

CHAPTER THIRTY-ONE

Villa Václav
River Vltava
Prague, Czech Republic

Finn couldn't brood like a normal guy, by moping on the mossy steps cut into the riverbank. Talia had to search for several seconds before she found him, perched on a decorative ledge between the second and third stories, a good twenty feet above the basement dock.

To the best she could figure, he'd climbed a tree, balance-walked across a branch to the wall, and scaled the rest using cracks and uneven stones. "You wouldn't want to come down and talk, would you?"

Silence.

"Right. Of course not." Talia hated heights, and she hated climbing. She gave it a shot anyway.

The old oak proved no challenge. But to reach the wall, she had to walk across a gnarled branch with no suitable handholds for balance. "I'm doing this." She stepped out from the root of the branch, wobbling the moment she let go of the trunk. "I'll probably fall and break my collarbone. Not that you care."

After three terrifying steps, she flattened her

body against the wall, cheek pressed into the cold, wet stone. "I'm not dead. I didn't fall. Feel free to stop me at any time . . . Please."

"Don't come up. I came out here to be alone, not to watch you embarrass yourself."

Progress. He'd spoken. She dug her fingers into the first handhold, a fissure running through a stone.

Urgency banished the sarcasm from Finn's tone. "Oi. I said don't come up, yeah? I'm serious. You'll fall."

"I'm serious too. Either I'm coming up or you're coming down. Your choice." Her foot found purchase on the eyebrow of a first-floor window, and she pushed upward. Her fingertips barely fit the second handhold, an uneven block. It hurt to let them take her bodyweight.

"Don't do this to me, Talia. Tyler will blame me if you fall, fair dinkum."

"Yes, he will. *Fair dinkum.*" She let out an indelicate grunt and kicked a toe into another crack. "And then the team will have two funerals on their hands."

She heard him moving above, grumbling to himself as he worked closer. "Of all the pigheaded, obstinate little dingbat . . ." He stopped complaining and started coaching. "Right. Here we go. Move your right inward. No. Farther inward. Up a little. There. That's the one."

So it went. Talia navigated two more handholds

and two more footholds before the ledge and Finn were within arm's reach. Except they weren't. Her fingernails scraped the stone a full inch below her goal.

"Close. Give it another go. You've gotta really commit."

"Like I'm not fully committed already." She tried again, and in the effort, her right foot slipped. "Finn!"

He caught her wrist. "Gotcha."

His strength surprised her, despite everything she'd seen him do in the past. Kneeling on a lip of stone less than twice the width of his knee, the thief lifted Talia to the ledge. She sat beside him, back pressed into the wall, breathing hard.

"That was stupid." Finn turned to sit beside her.

"No argument here."

"Then why take the risk?"

"You looked like you needed some company."

Neither spoke for a long while. Finn seemed to have no inclination. Talia needed the time to lower her heart rate. Frogs chirped in the reeds below. A fish splashed in the river.

When she finally spoke, Talia kept her eyes forward. Any movement might spoil her balance. "It could have happened to any of us."

"But it happened to me. I should've listened to Tyler's warning. I wasn't prepared for everything the job could throw at me."

"None of us are ever fully prepared. Wasn't that

his point? That's why we have each other. And don't listen to Val. She's only trying to get under your skin—the whole grifter–cat-burglar rivalry. You'll have the next laugh."

Finn laid his head back. *"You only got in the way.* Those words. They . . ."

"They what?"

"Nothing. Never mind."

Men. The Farm had given Talia the world's best training in information extraction, whether through coercion or conversation. Yet here, she was at a loss. "Look. I almost fell to my death getting up to this ledge. The least you can do is tell me why you're taking this so hard."

"The problem isn't Val, okay? It's Tyler and this whole do-gooder plan of his."

Talia took the risk of rolling her head to look at him. "You don't like doing good?"

"No . . . Yes." Finn sighed. "You don't understand."

"Then help me get there. Draw me a map."

He closed his eyes. "I'm afraid."

What an insane thing to say while sitting two stories up on a ten-inch ledge. "A week ago you fought a bar full of Russians. A few days after we met, you jumped from a weather balloon in the middle of a mesospheric electrical storm with rockets strapped to your legs." *Both to keep me safe,* she didn't say. "You're not afraid of anything."

"Heights and explosions become commonplace with enough practice. Other fears aren't so easy to bury." He paused for a few heartbeats. "My dad died when I was young, like yours. I never told you. Know what he died of?"

She expected him to say a parachuting accident or in a shootout with the police.

"Shame, Talia. My old man died of shame. Night guard. Janitor. Bricklayer. He couldn't hold a job. We wound up in a trailer park on the south side of Melbourne. He drank. So did Mom. At ten years old I started shoplifting to help put food and booze on the table."

Ouch. "I'm sorry, Finn."

"The cops came to the house once a week. Dad and Mom fought like tazzies about it, until one night she didn't come home. I ran off too. Did my first B'n'E. A condo in a rich beach neighborhood." Finn lowered his head, bending so far forward Talia worried he might fall. "I filled my pockets with every scrap of coin, cash, and ice I could lay my hands on and brought it home to Dad the next night to show him my big score."

"What did he say?"

"Mom was still gone, out with the super, I think. The lights wouldn't come on, so I grabbed the electric torch from the kitchen drawer . . ."

"And your dad?"

"I found him in the tub, wearing his bathrobe

and holding the toaster in his lap." Finn sat back again. "I can still smell the burning hair. The man couldn't keep his job or his wife. He'd fathered a little thief. Like I said, he died of shame. I'm the one who pushed him over the edge."

"You can't blame yourself, Finn."

He didn't answer, and Talia bit her lip. She sensed there was more he needed to get out. "Help me understand. What does your dad's suicide have to do with Tyler?"

"Don't you get it? Dad gave up. Mom had her boyfriends. I was on my own." He pounded his chest. "Just me. If I died jumping from a mountainside, I died. If I went to prison for a heist, no big deal. No one would care. No one would be hurt."

"Until Tyler made you part of a family again."

His eyes were glossy in the moonlight. "Tyler is a new kind of father, in this Fabian-became-a-preacher-man sort of way. But I'm afraid of failing him like I failed my dad. And if I'm honest, I'm afraid of failing you too. That's what all the princess and your highness stuff is really about." Finn shook his head. "Today I failed you both."

Her mind spun. For months, from the moment she'd first seen him signing autographs for snow bunnies, Finn had been this two-dimensional person—always cocky, wearing his *You must be thrilled to be in my presence* smirk. But in the last week Talia had met a new version of him.

198

Trembling, mostly from her fear of falling, Talia let go of the ledge and touched his knee. "You didn't fail Tyler . . . or me. You stumbled. And the team was there to catch you, just like you were there to catch me in Russia. That's—" Talia blinked at her own words. Was she preaching the very lesson Tyler had been trying to teach her? She smiled. "That's what families do. They catch each other, and they keep going, no matter what."

The two watched the clouds move over the trees for a while, until Talia shivered from the cold. Her right arm was going numb from holding herself up on that ledge. "Finn?"

"Yeah?"

"How am I going to get down from here?"

He laughed. "I have no idea."

CHAPTER THIRTY-TWO

Mare's Orbit Forest Preserve
River Vltava
24 km South of Prague, Czech Republic

Site preparations began at sunrise and continued through the last hour before the rendezvous with Atan.

"If you have the time," Tyler said, chest deep in the river and holding a shovelful of silt, "nothing sells a con like proper staging."

Val and Talia had been relegated to simple lift-and-carry tasks, since they had to dress nice later on. Tyler would join them for the rendezvous with Atan, but he claimed men—even con men—didn't take near as long to clean up. Talia couldn't argue with his logic.

With a grunt, she set a remote-control submarine on a crate beside Eddie's fake monitoring station. "Is this ROV as capable as we're claiming?"

"Are you kidding? I bought that thing on Amazon." Eddie twirled his fidget spinner. "She'll dive and send video. The rest is illusion. I stole the sonar feeds from a marine biology site and put them on a loop." He thrust his chin at his biggest screen. "That's a school of mackerel off the Florida coast."

Finn and Tyler had taken on the hardest job—making a slow and shallow river appear deep and dangerous. Tyler had stretched a net supported by floats twenty meters out and was now digging a hole in the riverbed. Finn, wearing a wetsuit pulled up to his waist with the sleeves tied around his midsection, kneeled at the bank to attach a coil of five-inch-diameter hose to an air compressor.

The thief had regained some of his swagger. He nodded to Eddie and Talia. "This compressor looks like one of those blowers treasure hunters use to blow silt off a wreck, right?"

She sensed a *but* coming and threw it out there. "But . . ."

"Its real purpose is to muddy the water so the mark can't see what we're doing. Mac loosened a few bolts to make it rattle. The noise will keep Atan from collecting his thoughts."

A hundred meters of woods separated the road from the river, which meant long trips to and from the van. Val walked out of the trees, pushing a dolly with oversize tires. She'd saved the worst load for last—a fifty-gallon drum.

Talia put a hand on the front end to take some of the weight. "This thing is heavy. What's inside?"

"You're smart, darling. Why don't you tell me?" The question carried some bite.

Val was clearly still miffed about the gold coin,

but Talia wasn't ready to let her off the hook. She ignored the grifter's sharpness and assessed the drum. "You filled this with the fake coins from Darcy's copper-tungsten mint."

"Good analysis. Several hundred. Enough to wow Atan with the big reveal."

Once they had the drum in the shallows, Finn attached a pair of inflatable tubes. He pulled on the remainder of his wetsuit and dragged it out to Tyler. Talia watched the two of them position it over the underwater hole Tyler had been digging.

"And what happens after the big reveal?" she asked Val.

"Darcy's Keystone bit, and then it's all up to the mark. This con only works if Atan takes control. He has to drive the brushoff and the mulligan."

"Brush-off. Mulligan. Right." Talia was still learning grifter jargon. "What if he doesn't?"

Out in the river, Tyler drew a knife from an ankle sheath and stabbed the floats. The drum vanished into the gloom.

Val shrugged. "Then we're sunk."

CHAPTER THIRTY-THREE

En Route to an Industrial Park
District Twelve
Prague, Czech Republic

The mysterious *we* from Conrad's brief video call nettled Talia's brain as Val drove her and Tyler to the rendezvous. "Who else did you bring in on this?"

"Sorry." Tyler, seated on the bench behind her, wore a smug mastermind grin. He'd traded his muddy wetsuit for a Ralph Lauren overcoat and flatcap. "I like a mark to see honest reactions whenever possible."

"You mean you want to surprise me."

Val added her own interpretation. "He means he wants you to do your annoyed-frustrated-goody-two-shoes look." She framed Talia's face with one hand as she drove. "The one you do so well."

Talia swatted her hand away. "You have to give me something. I hate going in unprepared."

"How about this?" Tyler said. "Smythe is bringing a guest to the dig site. I want you to object to his presence."

"Why would I do that?"

"You'll know when you see him."

• • •

Atan brought his own uninvited guest, giving Talia the opportunity to practice the annoyed-frustrated face Val had mentioned.

Val made a face of her own, nodding at the minor giant who followed their mark across the gravel parking lot. "Who's the beefcake?"

Atan slapped the giant in the chest with the back of his hand. "This is my cousin Janos. He is quite interested in starting a coin collection, so I told him he could come along."

Cousin. Right. The bulges at Janos's biceps told Talia he was proud enough of his muscles to wear a suit jacket one size too small. The bulge at his hip told her he was packing a large-caliber handgun—a .45, most likely. The plan didn't account for a tagalong bodyguard. Extra firepower at the phony dig site would spawn too many variables.

Val seemed to agree. "I don't remember a plus-one on your RSVP, sweetums. A bodyguard wasn't part of the deal."

"Then let us make a new deal, eh? Either Janos joins me, or I walk and you find another broker to move the coins."

Val and the Albanian stared one another down for a long moment.

Atan shrugged. "Okay. I walk." He and the giant turned to go.

"Wait." Talia broke first, buying a hard look from Val.

The van's sliding door opened behind her, and Tyler stepped out. "Let him go, girls. I told you before. We don't need this guy. I can move the coins in Russia and Asia."

The challenge in his voice had the desired effect. Atan turned. "You must be the American broker. And how do you propose to move these thalers in Asia, hmm? Who are your contacts?"

"That's my business. I thought you were bowing out."

Atan's gaze shifted to Val. "Miss Macciano, this is your call. But I guarantee he cannot get you the prices I will."

None of the contingencies Tyler had discussed with the crew included a heat-packing, six-foot-five behemoth attached to Atan's hip. The broker had called an audible. But what choice did they have? If they wanted to infiltrate the Jungle and find the missing children, they had to keep Atan on the hook. There wasn't time to find a new mark.

Talia wanted to poke Val, cough, whisper—anything to tell her to make sure Atan didn't get away. She could only pray and try to breathe.

Val played along. "Okay. Beefcake can come. But that cannon under his jacket stays in its holster. So does the spare on his ankle, *capiche*?"

The giant glanced down at his right leg. Val couldn't have seen the spare gun, but she had Jedimind-tricked him into confirming both its presence and location. Talia had to suppress a chuckle.

Mac had configured the van for cargo, with only one bench seat. Val drove, and Talia took the front passenger seat, leaving the bench for Tyler, Atan, and Janos, who sat in the middle.

"I looked you up." Atan bent forward to speak to Tyler around the giant. "I thought I had never heard of you until Miss Macciano brought your name up in my office, but it seems our paths have crossed before. Do you recall a piece of Arabian silver known as Scheherazade's Phoenix?"

Eddie had built a history for Tyler as a coin collector and broker, but Talia didn't know how deep it went, or whether Tyler had found the time to study the details. In the rearview mirror, she saw Janos slip a hand beneath his jacket. She inched forward a hair in her seat, ready to grab the Glock 26 at the small of her back.

Tyler stared out the windshield, saying nothing.

"What about it, Mr. Tyler? You were a buyer at the auction—a small affair in Dubai. Did you take Scheherazade's Phoenix home?"

He finally locked eyes with Atan. "I never made it to Dubai. But neither did you. We both bid by proxy. And if I remember correctly, you were the one to claim the prize. The Phoenix is in your collection."

Atan's frown melted into a smile. "Ah, silly

me. I must have forgotten. But then again, I own so many treasures."

The bodyguard's hand reappeared from under the jacket.

Talia relaxed.

Tyler went back to looking out the window. "This time there's plenty of treasure to share. I ponied up my dough, Atan. Now it's your turn. A half million US to see the Bavarian Thalers resurrected."

"Too right." Atan unlocked the screen of his phone. A few taps later, he tucked it away again. "It is done. The money is in Miss Macciano's account."

Eddie confirmed the transfer over the comm link. "I see it. Five hundred thousand US, coming in from a bank in Zurich. We have his money."

The van rolled to a stop. Val turned in her seat. "Just in time, sweetums. We're here."

CHAPTER THIRTY-FOUR

Mare's Orbit Forest Preserve
River Vltava

The distant rattle of Finn's modified air compressor reached the road through the trees. Val slipped the keys under the visor and climbed out with the rest, but neither she nor Talia made any move to lead them to the dig site.

Atan looked toward the sound. "What are we waiting for?"

Val yawned. "Our other guest." She checked her watch and glanced at Talia. "We should have stopped for coffee."

"By 'other guest,' you mean Malcom Smythe." Atan spoke the name like a curse.

Tyler joined him, feigning anger. "Atan and I had to be driven here, kept in the dark, but you gave that British peacock the location?"

"First money in, boys. Smythe got the ball rolling, so he gets the VIP treatment. He's been here every day to keep tabs on his investment. But I wouldn't worry about him having the location. He's not the sharpest . . . Oops. Speak of the devil."

A Land Rover bounced down the road and skidded to a stop mere feet from the van, sending up a cloud of dust. Tyler coughed and waved a hand in front of his face. Talia heard him sneak an admonishment over the comms. "About time you showed up. You were supposed to be here when we arrived."

"My apologies," Conrad said. "Traffic was murder."

On the comms, he spoke like a grandfatherly statesman. Stepping out of the Land Rover, he became Malcom Smythe, a pretentious Brit. "Ladies! I'm here. Let's go unearth my treasure."

Atan crossed his arms. "Your treasure?"

Conrad ignored him. "Winston, hurry it up. Time's a wasting."

The driver, who had gone to the back of the Land Rover, reappeared with a large, black apparatus.

I want you to object to his presence.

Why would I do that?

You'll know when you see him.

Talia did. Conrad's guest had brought a camera rig. "You!" she shouted. "Put that away!"

The driver hefted the rig onto his shoulders and gave her a *Who, me?* look.

Talia could swear she recognized him. But from where? Her eidetic memory rarely left her drawing such a blank. The result was annoyance and frustration, exactly what Tyler wanted. "A cameraman?" she said to the fake Smythe. "Are you insane! We said no press."

Atan strode over, with Janos close at his heels. "I warned you, did I not? This man is . . . How do you Americans say it? A glory hound."

Conrad raised a dismissive hand. "Relax. Winston is not 'the press.' He's here to get a few jittery shots for my blog. No identifying landmarks. Follow me, everyone. Onward." He passed them by, leading the way into the trees—in completely the wrong direction.

Val caught up to him and corrected his heading. "This way, Malcom. Same as yesterday. Same as every day this week."

Nearer to the site, a shouting match overpowered the compressor's rattle. Finn and Eddie looked like they might come to blows. The geek crossed his arms and shook his head. "I'm telling you, it's too dangerous."

"And I'm telling you, this is what subs are for, mate. They go where divers can't." Finn flicked the rounded metal frame of the ROV. "Now send this little Sheila down, or I'll toss her in myself." He pushed his face closer to Eddie's. "And maybe I'll toss you in too."

The geek didn't back down. "Go easy, *mate*. That's a quarter-million-dollar rig you're smacking around. And she's a rental."

"Hey," Val said. "What's the problem here?"

"You want to show her?" Finn thrust his chin at the screens. "Or shall I?"

"Like you could." Eddie fiddled with a

keyboard and mouse to bring up a sonar image—the one he'd told Talia was a school of mackerel. "This right here. This is the problem."

By appearances, the fake Smythe and Winston could not have cared less. They busied themselves looking for good camera angles. But Atan took an instant interest. "What is this we are looking at?"

"*I'll* tell you"—Eddie shot a look at Finn—"because he can't tell a marine sonar from a sonogram. This is a river cave, with a big metallic signature deep inside."

Val made some late introductions. "Taner Atan, meet Edward Fyers and Phineas Scrug." She didn't specify which was which.

Eddie pointed to himself, then the thief. "Eddie . . . Finn. In case it wasn't obvious."

"So, Mr. Scrug." Atan narrowed one eye at Finn and his scuba gear. "I take it you are the Australian Miss Macciano mentioned in my coin vault. I thought you said he worked in security."

"I'm something of a jack-of-all-trades."

"And master of none." Eddie reclaimed the group's attention. "I'm glad you're here, Miss Macciano. As I was just explaining to your diver, we can't proceed. The cave is too dangerous, even for the ROV." He launched into a drawn-out explanation of deep river topography and current variations, so animated he had to continually reset his glasses. Atan, reduced from mobster to schoolboy by his desire for the Bavarian Thalers, hung on every word.

Talia fought back a cringe as he finished the monologue with a honking blow of his nose. He stuffed the handkerchief away and tapped his screen. "River caves are nature's time capsules, Mr. Atan. The current drives debris in, like the wreckage from a crashed vessel."

"Or a lost treasure"—Atan's smile grew—"perhaps barrels of Bavarian coins."

"Sure. The problem is, whatever or whoever goes in"—Eddie glanced at Finn—"stays there forever. The current is too strong for a scuba diver and way too strong for a remote sub."

Talia caught Atan holding his breath, enraptured by all their theater. At the riverbank, Finn dropped his vest and tank in the tall grass and sat on a rock overhanging the water. He strapped on his fins. "Maybe I can't make it out of that cave weighed down with scuba gear, but I can do it freediving."

"Finn, don't," Val said. "That's suicide."

"Then say goodbye to my mum for me. Her flat's on Baker Street. South Melbourne." He dropped into the water.

CHAPTER THIRTY-FIVE

Mare's Orbit Forest Preserve
River Vltava

Tyler stared at the river's surface from the ROV station. "Your diver's been down too long. I don't like it."

Atan regarded him with a raised eyebrow. "Why, Mr. Tyler, how compassionate of you."

"Don't be ridiculous. I couldn't care less about Mr. Scrug. But I'd rather not answer questions from the Czech authorities if he dies."

This wiped the grin from Atan's lips. He turned to Eddie. "Get him back. Now."

A few feet away, on the riverbank, the fake Smythe played to his camera, talking over the rattling compressor. "Will our intrepid diver return with the gold? Will he return at all?"

Atan spun Eddie around by the shoulder. "I said, get him back."

"How? We have no communication."

"The sub. Send it down."

"And do what? Video the drowning?"

The Albanian was done arguing. He nudged Tyler and nodded at the sub. "Help me get this into the water."

"Why? You heard the kid. The sub can't pull him out."

"Perhaps not. But I have a plan." Atan snatched up one end of a nylon rope coil lying atop a pile of crates and gear. "We use this."

"A lifeline." Tyler held the sub while Atan secured the rope. "It's worth a try."

This con only works if the mark drives. Val had written the play. Tyler had directed. And now Atan had made himself the hero. With Tyler's help, he put the ROV in the water and secured the other end of the rope to the steel post of Eddie's satellite dish. "Drive, Mr. Fyers. Find our man."

The whole group gathered around the monitors, except for Smythe, who stayed at the bank, pontificating about the eternal war between the fragility of life and man's lust for gold. The signal from the rig's 4K camera popped up on Eddie's left screen. The murk lessened for a fleeting moment. "There." Atan pointed. "Go back. I saw a light."

"I saw it too," Val said. "The dive light on Finn's mask. He's still alive."

But Tyler shook his head. "A light only tells us his battery hasn't died. I don't care how good Mr. Finn is. No one can hold their breath this long."

The silt flowing past the camera parted like curtains on endless gold half buried in the muck. Atan seemed to forget all about poor Mr. Scrug. He gasped. "Maximillian's gold. After all these centuries. It's ours for the—"

The rope went taut. A light washed out the coins.

Atan looked from the screen to the water and back. "What is happening?"

"It's him." Val clasped her hands together. "Finn has grabbed the rope."

Tyler's jaw dropped. "It can't be."

"He's alive," the fake Smythe declared for his camera. "Man triumphs once again!"

All eyes watched as the rope slackened, jerked, and jerked again. A gloved hand broke the surface. Finn thrust his head out of the water, sucking in air.

Atan led the charge as the whole group ran to meet him. Using only one hand, the Aussie dragged himself closer to the bank.

"But what of the gold?" Atan asked. "We saw it on the camera."

Finn lifted a mesh bag heavy-laden with gold and heaved it onto the bank.

It fell open at Atan's feet. He scooped up a handful of coins and let them fall between his fingers.

Smythe moved in with Winston and kneeled at the water's edge. "Tell us, brave . . . Mr. . . . ."

Finn managed a frown between breaths. "Phineas Scrug. You've worked with me every day for a week."

"And what a week it's been. Tell us, Mr. Scrub—"

"Scrug. With a *g*."

"Of course it is. Tell us, how did you manage to survive that deadly river cave? We all thought you were done for."

"Survival's in my nature, mate." Finn looked past him and gave the camera a smolder. "Even so, I thought my life was over until the ROV arrived. I had no air, but I still had my wits, right? I shoved Eddie's rig into the silt as a marker for the treasure and clawed my way back to the light." He gave the line a sharp tug. "This rope saved my—"

In his effort to get a moving shot, Winston the cameraman tripped over the rope, pulled taut by Finn's untimely tug. The added force jerked the post supporting the other end free of the soil. Winston jumped out of the way. The satellite dish bounced down the bank and splashed into the water. The rope, the dish, and Finn all went under.

The air compressor ran out of fuel, ending the rattle, leaving the bank quiet until Val let out a dismayed cry. "He's gone."

"Again," Eddie added.

A wail of sirens left Atan no time to process Finn's second disappearance. A moment later, a green police boat appeared at the river bend less than a quarter mile away.

The fake Smythe stuffed two fistfuls of coins into his vest. "Time to go, Winston." The two ran off, with the cameraman correcting Smythe's heading as they hit the trees.

As the police boat closed the distance, Janos took cover behind a cluster of boulders and drew his gun. Talia picked up a dive tank and smashed it down on his arm. The .45 dropped into the water.

Janos turned on her, but Tyler bodychecked him and the three tumbled into the mud.

Tyler pushed himself away from the bodyguard. "Are you crazy? This is bad enough without you shooting at the cops." He grabbed a handful of coins and shook them at Val. "Consider my five hundred thousand your payment for these. I'm out of here. Malcom, wait up!"

Cued by Smythe and Tyler, Atan grabbed the mesh bag with the rest of the coins. "And you may consider my half million payment for these." In the distance, the Land Rover started up and roared away. The other two had left him behind. Atan shrugged. "Apparently, it is also payment for your van."

"Our van?" Val asked.

He ran off with Janos. "You should not have left the keys in the visor."

By the time Talia heard the van motor rumble to life, the boat had coasted up to the shore. A black woman standing on the bow held a rifle pressed to her shoulder.

"*Ruce vzhůru! Nehýbejte se!*" she said in Czech, then repeated herself in English. "Hands up! Don't move!"

CHAPTER THIRTY-SIX

RabynĔ Hydrodam Complex
River Vltava
28 km South of Prague, Czech Republic

"I should win an Academy Award for that performance." Finn piloted the boat while Darcy, still in her Czech police uniform, washed the *policie české republiky* seals and stenciling from the hull. White water-based paint ran down the sides into the river.

Val snorted. "No. You were amateurish and melodramatic. Conrad deserves the award. He played a real and very public figure in the numismatist community, and Atan bought every word."

The last of the white drippings faded into their wake. A few fiberglass panels, some forest-green paint, and Darcy's special white stenciling had turned the lodge's gray runabout into a police boat long enough for the brush-off with the Albanians. But with a major hydroelectric dam coming into view, the boat had to become civilian again. So did Darcy. She finished her work and flipped her police coat inside out, turning it into a plain denim jacket.

As soon as Atan and Janos had stolen the van,

Finn had surfaced, bringing with him the scuba tank and regulator he used to fake his death. The site breakdown took less than an hour, and the crew fled south, away from Prague. They could go no farther than the dam, four kilometers away, but Mac had positioned a second van there to take them to Příbram Airport.

"Keep it moving, everyone." Val hopped to the concrete dock with the boat still moving. She tied the mooring line to a post. "There's no telling how much time we have before Atan gets wise."

"Not long, I am afraid." Atan came walking down the dock with Janos. He held a 9mm close to his body, out of view of the dam's control station. "Please. All of you. Step out of the boat and keep your hands where I can see them."

Talia was the first onto the dock beside Val. "How did you find us?"

"I had a fifty-fifty choice, and thieves run away from their victims, not toward them." Talia's arm twitched, and he twisted his gun. "Ah, ah, ah. I said show me your hands."

Val gave her a nod.

Talia moved the hand into view, holding a .38 Ruger, barrel down.

Scowling, Janos quick-stepped forward and snatched it away, leveling it at the group. The gun was his spare, stolen by Talia when Tyler knocked the brute to the ground.

"I am impressed, Miss Macciano." Atan's eyes

tracked Finn and then Mac as they stepped off the boat behind Talia. "Very few have battled Janos and lived to tell about it. None were women, and none have ever taken both his guns."

Talia only shrugged.

"There was one more. The policewoman. Where is she?"

The chemist peeked out from behind the fiberglass wall of the pilothouse.

Atan shifted his aim. "You had a rifle. Come here, slowly, and lay it on the dock."

Darcy did as commanded, and Atan nodded. "Good. Now. We will retire to your van, where you will return my money."

"That's it?" Finn asked. "And then you'll let us go?"

"We shall see."

Atan had parked the other van behind a utility shed, out of view of the control station. He and Janos kept their guns trained on their captives. Talia still had her Glock, and she knew Mac always kept a blade available, but neither of them made a move. The Albanians positioned them all with their backs against the shed.

"How did you know?" Val asked.

"How does the fox know to be wary of the snake? Or the wolf, the sable? Instinct."

That was a stretch. Atan had stayed on the hook through 90 percent of the con. Talia would have

220

laughed at his drama if not for the guns pointed at her teammates. "So what gave us away?"

"The more I thought about it as we drove away, the more I worried the coins were too good to be true. And the timing of the police boat's arrival was . . . suspicious." He raised an eyebrow. "But most of all, you lost me with the ridiculous accent."

Before Talia could say *I told you so,* the Albanian continued. "I pride myself on my ear for authenticity." He pointed his gun at Val and then Finn. "Real New Yorker. Fake Australian."

Finn's eyes went wide. "You can't be serious."

"Give it up, Mr. Scrug, or whatever your name is. Your true origins are obvious. I'm guessing"— the Albanian tilted his gun to the side— "American Midwest? Iowa? Perhaps Illinois?"

After a long pause, the Aussie tensed his jaw, apparently deciding there was no point in arguing with the mark. "Nebraska."

"Do not despair." Atan lowered his gun, letting Janos keep them covered. "As I said before, I am impressed. You had me until the end, and you stole from Malcom Smythe, which endears you to me. Simply make reparations, and all will be forgiven."

Val leaned against the shed and crossed one ankle over the other. "What reparations?"

"Return my half million, and add to it everything you stole from Tyler and Smythe."

Mac rocked forward. "That's our entire take, you greedy—" A stab of Janos's revolver pressed him back, shutting him up.

"Not all the money is for me. Consider the extra million a buy-in."

Val's mulligan, the encore to the brush-off, had worked. Talia made sure. "A buy-in to what, exactly?"

"To a special organization, Miss Macciano. Anonymous. Global. Ruthless. I am your ticket in, and until you advance to the next level, a portion of all you and your sister provide will go to me. In return, the organization will offer your crew opportunities beyond anything you ever imagined."

As Val had hinted on the jet two days before, the plan hinged on Atan *not* falling for the German Silver con. Instead, he'd fallen for the larger play—offering the team a personal invite into Boyd's organization.

Atan tucked his gun away and gave them all a crooked smile. "Welcome to the Jungle. Take care you are not eaten."

CHAPTER THIRTY-SEVEN

Villa Václav
River Vltava
Prague, Czech Republic

"Okay." Tyler folded his hands on the lodge's gothic dining table. "Where do we stand with Boyd's syndicate?"

The blaze in the two-story fireplace at his back seemed a bit much, not to mention the coats of arms above the mantel—stags, lions, eagles, and all manner of manly creatures. Talia had warned him months before that the whole leader-at-the-head-of-the-table thing was an archaic tradition best left to wedding parties and *Mad Men* reruns. "It makes you intimidating and unapproachable."

Tyler had answered with a nod. "I know."

Eddie fielded his question. "Atan supplied Talia and Val each with a digital entry code. They're in the Jungle now."

"As panthers?"

"No," Val said, seated to his right. "But not as field mice either." In the poor lighting of the electric candles set in an antler chandelier, Talia found it harder than usual to read the grifter's expression. "The extra million Atan used as our buy-in took us straight to the hawk level. As of now, you're looking at Hawk Four One Eight and Hawk Four One Nine—probationary members."

"Probation'ry," Mac asked. "What's that s'pposed to mean?"

"I guess we'll find out, won't we?"

Cowed by her tone, he looked down at his empty place mat, but Mac's dejection did not last long. Conrad, aided by the fake Winston, arrived with the food. They each pushed a cart, starting at either end of the table.

"Dinner is served." Conrad set a plate and bowl in front of Talia. "Braised sirloin in white sauce with minced pork dumplings and a side of rabbit goulash."

She inspected the offering. "That is . . . a lot of meat."

"Welcome to Bohemia, my dear."

The fake Winston took the seat across from her. He looked so familiar, yet he did not introduce himself even as the meal wore on, as if taunting her to figure out his identity for herself.

"Give up yet, do ya?" he asked twenty minutes later, pushing a touch of Cockney into the question.

Talia dabbed her lips with her napkin and sat back. "So I *do* know you."

"We've met, if that's what ya mean. But ya don't remember where, I can tell."

He had strawberry-blond hair. Freckles. But those details seemed wrong. "You have a name?"

"Pell."

She felt Tyler watching them, enjoying the show. The phrase *You don't remember* rarely applied to Talia. It unnerved her. "How about a hint."

"Awright. How 'bout this." The Cockney manner vanished, replaced by a drab expression and an equally drab Eastern European accent. "Yeah. Okay. No problem."

Sunglasses. A driver's cap. Blond hair. The images flashed in Talia's mind. She caught her breath. "Davian. Tyler's Moldovan driver."

Pell offered a short bow over his plate. "At your service."

A golf clap from Tyler interrupted them. "Well done. Both of you. I love good dinner theater."

Talia failed to suppress a chagrined smile. "You've been waiting six months for this, haven't you?"

"Correct. I didn't have another position for him after Moldova, until today." Tyler gestured at each of them. "Pell, Talia. Talia, Pell."

"So he's another grifter."

Talia heard a snort from the far end of the table. She looked, but Val had already turned her attention to Conrad, who had brought out a tray of tortes.

"Pell is a chameleon," Tyler said. "In any given setup he might be the moving eyes in the painting, the needle in the haystack, the fly on the wall—"

"Or in zee ointment, yes?" Pell took on the

affectations of a pretentious Frenchman, earning a quizzical look from Darcy.

Finn, accepting a torte from Conrad, took an interest in the conversation. "So is Pell a first name or a last?"

"Can't say as I remember." The chameleon matched Finn's voice to a tee. "I hardly ever use it anyway."

"Don't do that."

"Do what, mate?"

Finn's expression went flat. "That *put another shrimp on the barbie* accent."

"My Australian's better than yours."

"Don't be daft. I'm from Melbourne, born and raised."

"Not bad, mate. Not bad." Pell didn't miss a beat. "But next time, try sinking your glottis into the schwa." He stuck his chin out, holding his Adam's apple. "Mel-*buhrn.*"

Finn took his plate of tortes to Mac's end of the table, muttering to himself. "Twice in one day. What's the matter with people?"

Pell became the Moldovan driver again. "What is the thing that is eating your friend, Miss Talia? Was it something I said?"

A fit of giggles buried her answer. She turned to Tyler. "Okay. Stage One is complete. Where to next?"

"The Isle of Milos. I'm getting back into gun-running. Special appearance. One night only."

CHAPTER THIRTY-EIGHT

Hangar 13
Linz Airfield
Prague, Czech Republic

Conrad would not be accompanying the crew to the Greek Isles. He saw them off at the hangar with a basket of donut-like cinnamon-sugar pastries he called *trdlenik*, and which Mac called turtlenecks.

He took Talia aside while the others loaded the aircraft and pressed one of the pastries into her hand. "I want you to be careful from this point forward. Boyd and his people. They are no joke, and they may have connections we have yet to trace."

She could read between the lines. "You mean Jordan. Did Tyler put you up to this?" Talia gave him her *for shame* look. "Don't feed his hover-mom syndrome, Conrad."

"I wish you would learn to lean on him."

"Maybe I'm not ready. You know our history."

"Then learn to lean in general. This new life you've found is not solitary. The children of God have each other, and most of all we have him." Conrad set his basket aside and took her hands. "You are strong and courageous, my child. So strong, and so courageous. But remember what follows those words from Moses to Joshua."

An eidetic memory, and everyone expected her to have the Bible memorized. "I . . . haven't read that part yet, Conrad."

He smiled. "Give it a look. Joshua, like you, was strong and courageous—not on his own, but because God was with him."

Twenty minutes later, the stars above the cloud layer twinkled in the morning sky, projected in real time on the walls and ceiling of the jet cabin. Fortunately, Tyler's supersonic AS2 came well-equipped with an espresso machine.

Val, knees tucked into a long knit sweater, clutched an oversize mug topped with milk foam. "Why did we leave so early, Tyler? You know my rule about never being up before the sun."

"Except when there's money to be made. And there's a great big pile waiting at the end of this particular rainbow." He threw a *roll it* motion at Eddie.

"You do realize I'm a human being, right?" Eddie stepped out in front of the whole-wall video display with his tablet. "Not a remote control?"

Darcy poked his calf with a bare toe. "Don't be so sensitive, *mon chou*. Tyler's hand is the remote, no? That makes you the computer."

This seemed almost enough to satisfy his ego. He glanced at Tyler. "A supercomputer?"

"Sure. Okay. A supercomputer."

"Like maybe a neuromorphic, quantum array with—"

"Hey!" Talia clapped her hands together. "Quit being such a snowflake and get on with it." The whole outburst came out louder than she intended.

Finn passed her his coffee. "Take this. Sounds like you need it more than I do."

The wall switched from the passing twilight sky to a simple chart with animal pictures and dollar figures. "What the boss was getting at when he snapped his fingers at me—"

"I didn't snap them. I rolled one in the air."

"—like the man in the yellow hat with Curious George, is that an enormous challenge still lies before us. We're in the Jungle, but now we have to work our way to the top of the food chain."

The chart listed Val and Talia's current level of hawk at three hundred thousand each in annual earnings for the syndicate. To reach cobra, they'd have to hit one million each.

Eddie gestured to the next rung up. "Our goal is panther. That's ten million in annual earnings. Each."

Finn let out a low whistle.

"And I'm just getting started." Eddie switched to a picture of the Bangkok towers. The text in the sky above them listed the three panthers who had earned invitations to the previous year's Frenzy. Their dollar figures were higher.

Talia read the lowest out loud. "Fifteen million buys one seat. We want two. That's thirty million US, assuming the numbers play out like last year."

"And that's where our next stage comes in. Stage One was Val's. The plan for Stage Two is Tyler's brainchild." He gave Tyler a nod. "Boss?"

"We need a minimum of thirty million. My plan gets us forty-five."

Tyler had mentioned something at dinner about running guns. Forty-five million dollars could buy a whole lot of guns, an idea that didn't sit well with Talia. She knew Tyler financed his lifestyle by buying up confiscated weapons and ammunition from national governments, usually to recycle them and sell the materials. What was he playing at? "We're selling a massive load of your secondhand guns to some black-market buyer?"

"Not my guns." Tyler flashed a grin. "Someone else's guns. We're going to hijack an arms deal, and it's going to be so much fun."

CHAPTER THIRTY-NINE

Western Tower Penthouse
Twin Tigers Complex
Bangkok, Thailand

"How long have you been here?"

Standing in Boyd's penthouse office, Gorev shifted from one foot to the other, praying the glass floor didn't crack under his weight. He did not relish a fifty-foot free fall into the jungle atrium below, or a visit from the beast lying hidden in the foliage. "One week."

"One week." Boyd stormed out from behind a crescent-shaped desk, unafraid to cross the glass. The young Englishman had more confidence than Gorev in their Thai contractors. "You had one full week to finalize negotiations with Panther Five One and oversee the final construction of the maze floors for the Frenzy." Gorev had lowered his eyes, but Boyd, the shorter man, stepped into his vision, hand on his hips. "Is either job complete?"

Gorev could have crushed him where he stood—pounded him through the floor as food for the big cats. "I did order the place cards. They will be here on Friday. The font is Goudy Old Style. Very nice."

"You disgust me."

The former Spetsnaz reined in his instincts until Boyd left the kill zone and returned to his desk. Gorev let out a long breath through his nose. "I complete Panther Five One job tomorrow."

"Wrong." Boyd's eyes followed the stock tickers running across the giant picture window behind his desk. "*We* will complete the job. I'll go with you and finalize the deal in person. Panther Five One can wait an extra day or two until my schedule allows. Meanwhile, you babysit the contractors. If they keep dragging their feet, throw one from the helipad."

"Yes, sir."

"Better yet, feed one to Lionel. We can't have bodies landing in the plaza."

"Yes, sir."

Boyd chuckled at his own joke and turned from his window, with the sprawling Bangkok metropolis behind him, smothered in haze. "Do you know why I live in penthouses, Anton?"

"The view, I assume."

"Wrong again. Down on the street, where those contractors live and where I found you, the air is oppressive, filthy and toxic—quite literally here in Bangkok. Like the gods of Olympus, I was meant to rise above and breathe freely." He went quiet.

Gorev shifted his weight again as a monkeypod tree wavered in the atrium directly beneath him.

He cleared his throat. "There is second reason I come to see you."

"Spit it out. I'm busy."

"We have two new hawks. Sisters. They bought positions at hawk level, under sponsorship of Panther Four Nine."

This captured Boyd's attention. "Aggressive. Do they know the price of earning their wings?"

"*Nyet*. I was suspicious. I ask your approval first."

The Englishman drummed his fingers on his desk, then nodded. "Go ahead. Send the usual invitation. Let's see if they have the stomach for Jungle life."

"And if they do not?"

"Kill them. Send one of the cobras. We don't have time."

CHAPTER FORTY

Aerion AS2 Adriatic Sea
Forty-Eight Thousand Feet
En Route to Milos, Greek Isles

Tyler could play semantics all he wanted, but forty-five million in blood money paid for guns heading off to who-knows-where raised all kinds of red flags for Talia. "What are we compromising here?"

Her question brought more ire from Val than Tyler. The grifter set her coffee down for the first time since takeoff. "You're the one who demanded to be part of this job. You're the one on a crusade. Why should you care where the money comes from?"

"I care because I *am* on a crusade. I won't trade lives on one continent for lives on another. That's not how this works."

"Talia." Tyler put enough sharpness in the interruption to command her attention. "Remember what I told you at The Mission."

The conversation near the windows of the church, watching Mac outside, came to her mind unbidden. "Faith. You told me to have faith."

"And now I'm asking you to place some in me." He rolled another finger at Eddie. "Nano-quantum

Supercomputer Guy, you're up. Keep it moving."

"Neuromorphic."

"Whatever."

Eddie wiped his nose, giving the hanky an annoyed flick, and tapped his tablet. A video ad for a defense tech company called TACRON Systems played. The logo faded to black, replaced by a micro-drone in flight over a desert road. Eight fans on struts supported a bulbous glass payload, like the abdomen of a flying tarantula. Talia mentally dubbed it a *spider drone*. The creature drifted left and right, then zeroed in on an approaching SUV and tilted forward.

"That's not disturbing at all," Finn said.

"Shhh." Darcy hushed him as if they were watching a blockbuster movie. "Quiet. I want to hear, no?"

The camera view switched to the spider drone's sensor package, a three-hundred-sixty-degree camera blending optical and infrared. The perspective narrowed and penetrated the front windscreen. Green boxes appeared all over the driver's face. Text faded in and out.

FLAWLESS FACIAL RECOGNITION

Again, the camera switched to a follow view on the spider, but not for long. A midsize quadcopter drone with a brawny fuselage blew past. The camera gave chase. Fire spat from the front of the quad. Bullets sparked off the SUV, unable to penetrate the hood or the windshield. The driver swerved into the desert. The drone peeled off. More text faded in and out.

GRADUATED RESPONSE OPTIONS

The camera ditched the gun drone and rose higher until it passed a spherical drone with a large central fan. Rockets hung vertically from the outer shell. Three of them launched, trailing smoke, and nailed the armored vehicle. Every window blew out in bursts of flame. The camera returned to the spider drone as it flew past, recording the burning bodies inside.

MISSION ACCOMPLISHED

The screen went black, and the TACRON logo faded into view. A deep voice read the tagline. "Networked. Autonomous. Lethal. TACRON Swarm. Tomorrow's battlefield solution, today."

Darcy applauded.

Talia rotated her chair to face Tyler. "Tell me that wasn't a DoD pitch reel."

"It was. TACRON made their bid last spring. Each squadron comes with thirty-two drones. TACRON asked the US government to buy a minimum of two squadrons at two hundred million a pop."

"And?"

"And they were laughed out of the Pentagon."

"Why?" Finn asked. "Doesn't the US already use Predators and Reapers to kill people?"

Eddie fielded the question, putting on his *geeksplaining* face. "Actually, Predators and Reapers aren't drones at all. They're Remotely Piloted Aircraft with whole crews of professionals at the wheel. True drones are autonomous, part of a collective." He tilted his head toward the screen. "Like those. They take humans and common sense out of the kill chain. The public relations optics are untenable for any democratic . . ."

Something on Eddie's tablet drew his attention, and Tyler took over. "The point is, TACRON built three complete squadrons, each designed to fit into a standard shipping container, and nobody bought them. Last month, all three containers turned up on the black market with a 90 percent markdown. TACRON is trying to cut their losses."

"And that's where we come in," Talia said.

He nodded. "TACRON's top negotiator, Emma Knight, has been courting the latest and nastiest warlord to come out of the Kongara Republic of Central Africa—a real piece of work named Martin Iwela. Knight and Iwela's lieutenant, Mr. Aku, will meet for the final deal in an underworld sanctuary on the Greek Isle of Milos." He paused, clearly waiting for Eddie to continue,

237

then cleared his throat and slapped his armrest. "Eddie."

"Hmm? Oh, right. The briefing." A satellite graphic of the Isle of Milos appeared on the cabin wall, zooming in on a dormant volcano on its western point. "The locals call this Profitis Ilias, or the mountain of the Prophet Elijah. But don't be fooled. This mountain is sacred only to criminals."

A graphic overlay showed natural formations inside, like an ant hill. "Many moons ago, a silver miner bought the land, only to discover the mountain was hollow—full of defunct magma tubes and chambers, coated with obsidian and flooded with seawater. Fortunately for his struggling bank account, our intrepid miner was born without a conscience. He made seriously evil lemonade out of his lemons."

Eddie replaced the volcano with a glamor shot of an older Greek gentleman, holding a pose Talia might expect to see in a painting above a rich man's mantel. "Meet Orien Jafet, the owner of Club Styx, serving all your underworld needs since 1975. Club Styx is the criminal Switzerland of the Mediterranean. Neutral ground. A criminal sanctuary. Deals go down in the club without the worry of murder or cops, and Jafet takes a cut of every one."

"As I'm sure you've guessed," Tyler added, "Jafet is also part of the Jungle syndicate. He is

Boyd's top player, the Maltese Tiger—one step away from the White Lion title."

The moment Tyler spoke, Eddie's attention returned to his tablet. He scrunched his nose. "Guys, I have a message here. It's—"

Talia held up a hand to quiet him. She had heard everything she needed to hear, with one glaring question. "So, we waylay TACRON's negotiator, Emma Knight. Val and I replace her at the meeting with Mr. Aku in Club Styx. And then Aku wires the money to our accounts instead of TACRON's."

Tyler touched his nose, then waggled the finger. "Close enough. We get our forty-five million from the drone sale and send a big chunk of it to the Jungle. With Atan and Jafet—the Jungle's Hyena and Maltese Tiger—both watching, we should earn our seat at the Frenzy table."

"But how will we ensure the weapons don't fall into the wrong hands?"

"You're going to love this." Holding her gaze, Tyler made a beckoning motion to Eddie. "Show them my favorite part."

But they had completely lost the geek, still absorbed in whatever he'd found on his tablet. He scratched his chin. "Seriously, guys, this is weird. I'm putting it on the big screen."

The picture of Jafet on the cabin wall vanished, replaced with a gray message box labeled A MESSAGE FROM THE JUNGLE. A little white hand icon hovered over the OPEN button. Eddie shook his head, perplexed. "This shouldn't be possible. When I hook up the tablet to the aircraft display system, it becomes isolated from all networks—behind a curtain of *my* custom firewalls. This message shouldn't have come through until we landed and the tablet left the plane."

"Yet there it is." Tyler narrowed his eyes. "Is it safe?"

Eddie shot a glance toward the flight deck. "Probably snuck in through the aircraft SATCOM—text and voice only. That data stream doesn't have the bandwidth to carry files, viruses or otherwise."

They all blinked at him.

"Meaning yes, the message is safe. Has to be. I'm opening it."

The *click* resonated through the cabin. For a split second, Talia thought she saw the big blue eyes of a white lion on the walls, ceiling, and bulkhead, until a flash of sparks from air vents blinded her. The cabin went dark. The AS2's three supersonic engines spooled down to silence.

CHAPTER FORTY-ONE

Adriatic Sea
Forty-Seven Thousand Feet and Falling
En Route to Milos, Greek Isles

"Masks!" Tyler bolted from his seat, heading for the flight deck. "Mac, we're losing pressure. Drop the masks. Get us down!"

"Copy!"

In the red flash of the flight deck warning lights—the only lights in the aircraft still operating—Talia saw Mac flip a toggle on the overhead control panel. Oxygen masks dropped from the ceiling above every seat.

Tubes with yellow cups hung like flowered vines from the ceiling. Eddie had pulled his mask on but seemed to be hyperventilating. Finn unbuckled and yanked on the geek's tube to get the oxygen flowing. Eddie took a deep breath and gave him a thumbs-up.

Like Finn, Talia did not immediately put on her mask. Her delay was not born of calm, but of the one fear she'd never been able to master. Heights. And by extension—flying.

Hidden behind the fear, she found intellect, and clung to it. She didn't see any holes blown in the fuselage. Farm training and life experience had taught her the aircraft would take a while to lose residual cabin pressure. The masks were a precaution. Mac should get them down to breathable air before they became necessary.

He was sure taking his time, though.

She released her death grip on the armrest long enough to signal Finn. "Why isn't Mac diving for better air?"

"The engines. They won't start at high altitude, but they won't start at supersonic speed either. We're in a catch-22. Mac's gotta slow below Mach 1 while tobogganing downhill." The Aussie left his seat and plopped down next to Eddie. "What did you do?"

Eddie answered with a series of unintelligible mumbles behind the mask.

Finn pulled it away from his face and let it snap back into place. "Take that off. You look like a nerdy duck."

The geek pulled the cup down to his neck and shrugged. "I opened a message. It shouldn't have killed the engines or sent sparks flying from the ceiling." At the word *sparks,* he glanced at Darcy.

She shook her head. "It was not me this time. I left all my toys in the cargo hold."

Through the open flight deck door, Talia watched Mac fight the controls while Tyler jammed a finger into a button on the overhead panel. She heard a *thump* and a long whine. Lights flickered on. Fog poured from the vents. "Was that an engine?"

"Negative." Finn said. "We're still too high to crank the motors. That was the auxiliary power unit. We have air and electricity, but no thrust."

"So, we can see and breathe . . ."

"But we're still falling to our deaths."

As if to emphasize Finn's point, the nose pitched over, steepening the dive. One by one, lights and systems came back on.

The restored power also brought Boyd's message back to life. A distorted laugh echoed through the cabin. The blue eyes Talia had seen before—a close-up of the eyes of a white lion—filled every display surface. "The law of the Jungle," the voice repeated after every laugh. "Kill or be killed."

Tyler scowled back at them through the open flight deck door. "Shut that racket down!"

"Working on it!" Eddie's fingers flew across the tablet. "I'm isolating the message source. Cutting off the data flow. That should disable the virus . . . I hope."

From behind the laughing came another *thump* and another whine, bigger and louder this time. "Engine one is up," Tyler yelled at Mac. "Pull out of the dive."

"Can't." There was strain behind the Scotsman's voice. "Now that the laughing is back, my controls are locked."

Talia's gaze fell on the windscreen. Clouds rushed up at them, and beyond she saw a hint of dark blue. The sea. She cringed and looked to

Eddie. "How can a message take down an aircraft?"

Another *thump*. Another whine. Engine two was up, but the dive continued.

The lion's image dominated the cabin. "The law of the Jungle. Kill or be killed."

Tyler fought the controls with Mac. "Anytime now, Eddie!"

"Got it!"

The lion disappeared. The laughing stopped.

"Controls are live," Mac said.

Tyler threw a lever forward and the third engine spooled to life. "Full power is available. We're at the edge of the Mach. Watch the pull or we'll rip her in half."

Blue water glinted with the morning sun, growing in the windscreen as the nose began to track. Talia held her breath. She could swear she saw a wave crest above the horizon before Mac and Tyler had them climbing again. The whole group let out a collective sigh.

"When we catch Boyd, I'm going to kill him." The statement came from Val, a little behind Talia and across the aisle, red-faced and angry. She had not said a word through the whole ordeal. Her coffee mug hung limp from her fingers, with most of its contents staining her front. "This was my favorite sweater."

Tyler banned Eddie from any and all digital mischief until Mac had the AS2 safely on the ground.

"You do realize I'm the one who saved us, right?" Eddie asked in his own defense. "I stopped the virus, restoring control. Any monkey can pull back on a stick."

The look he got shut him up until well after landing.

They parked in a hangar looking out over the tarmac, beach, and blue water. Mac, Darcy, and a couple of Greek mechanics pored over schematics to fix the AS2, while the rest of the team gathered around a monitor on a folding table.

Val placed a hand on the back of Eddie's chair. "Can you play the full message without bringing the hangar down on top of us?"

"Funny. But I don't think Boyd intended to crash our plane. This is a canned message, designed to be opened on a regular computer and demonstrate the sender's power. The virus shuts the computer down in a pseudo-infinite loop to freak out the user without doing real harm."

"It did plenty of harm to the AS2," Tyler said.

"Because my tablet was hooked into the aircraft mainframe." Eddie turned in his seat to face the boss. "Look, this thing is entirely text based, like nothing I've ever seen, completely integrated into the message title."

"Is that how it got into my jet's comm system?"

"Correct. There are several ground-based SATCOM repeaters, all tethered to the internet.

When we pinged one, the message spotted the Dark Web address I created for the Macciano Sisters and jumped on board. Only one frame of the video made it through, but the text, the audio, and the embedded virus kept going." He waited, perhaps for an attaboy at figuring the whole thing out, but he received none.

Tyler folded his arms. "You're saying Boyd sent the equivalent of a heat-seeking missile straight through an airplane's text-and-voice-only SATCOM receiver?"

"That's one way to put it, and the possibility poses a serious threat to air traffic. But I think it was accidental. Neither the virus nor the AS2 knew what to do when they found each other." The geek held up both hands like puppets. "Imagine two cats meeting unexpectedly in an alley. They both hissed, batted each other's faces for a while, then ran yowling into the night, leaving me to unscramble the mess."

"Can you reverse engineer the malware?"

"Yeah, but—"

"Do it. We may have a use for something like this in the future."

"Sure, boss." Eddie seemed to wait one more second for his attaboy, then gave up and went back to the keyboard. "For now, I've recovered and isolated the video portion, so we can skip the drama."

He was wrong. The message was full of drama, all based in Boyd's megalomania.

The white lion paced on the monitor amid a final laugh and an echoing *Kill or be killed.* "So, you want to be a hawk. Good. I approve. But even those who fly above the Jungle are not free of its law." The echo returned. *The law of the Jungle. Kill or be killed.* "You have one month to earn your wings or I will rip them from their sockets and leave you in a pool of blood."

"What does he mean, 'earn your wings'?" Val asked during the pause that followed.

The white lion answered. "The hawk preys upon the smaller beasts. To earn your wings, you must eat a field mouse or jackrabbit. Remove your target from the Earth, consolidate operations, and improve the overall take for the syndicate. That is the circle of life."

The law of the Jungle. Kill or be killed.

"If you fail to comply, I will remove *you* from the Earth. That is all."

The lion walked off the screen, and a short list of field mouse and jackrabbit members came up, along with names and addresses.

Eddie had gone pale. "That is so not right."

Finn looked just as stunned. "We've got to murder someone to reach the next level?"

"And if we don't," Talia said, "we'll never get Boyd, and we'll never save those missing children."

CHAPTER FORTY-TWO

Adamantas Marina
Milos Caldera
Milos, Greek Isles

It shamed Talia to recognize her own disappointment when Tyler didn't put them all up in some luxury chateau overlooking the marina. He put them *in* the marina—in a houseboat.

She took a few minutes to clean up after the drive from the airport and emerged from the stateroom she would share with Darcy, wearing white shorts and a tank top. She found Tyler lounging on the boat's rear deck with a frosty pink drink. He looked unnervingly calm, given the bomb Boyd had dropped on their plans.

She stood over him, making sure her shadow blocked out his sun. "What happened to your usual virgin piña colada?"

"Normally my favorite. But this is a local concoction, a virgin Santorini Sunrise." He took a sip and smacked his lips. "You know. When in Rome."

"We're in Greece. And we're in trouble." Talia glanced around. "Where is everyone?" The lower deck, the living room complete with ethanol fireplace, and the kitchen and bar were all empty.

"Eddie's in his room, working on a project. I sent Darcy and the other boys off to run some errands. And I assume Val is off pouting somewhere because the bathrooms on this boat don't meet her standard."

"Which is?"

"*Not* being on a boat."

"Errands." Talia sank into a deck lounger whose overstuffed cushion threatened to swallow her whole. "You're pressing forward with the weapons heist?"

"We don't have to scrap the whole plan. We just have to explore new alternatives."

The cushion added an extra level of difficulty to the conversation. Talia wanted to sit sideways so she could frown at him if necessary, but she was struggling to keep her feet on the deck. "We're not murdering one of Boyd's field mice to move up the list."

"Why not?" Val came down the steps from the upper deck in a black one-piece and sarong. "They're all criminals."

"Like you?"

"Cute. This is all part of Boyd's game."

"I don't care about Boyd's game." Talia gave up searching for the deck with her toes and let her body fall back into the lounger, trying and failing to make the movement look natural. "We're not playing by his rules."

"Speaking of . . ." Val pointed at Tyler as she

reached the bottom step. "You know I don't do accommodations that store waste in a tank."

"Why do you think I chose it?"

She scrunched her eyes at him.

Tyler smiled and sipped his drink.

Talia rolled her eyes. "We were talking about the merits of murder?"

"Relax." Tyler set his drink down on the glass table between them and laid his head back. "I'm not planning to kill any of Boyd's small woodland creatures."

"That's good to hear."

"We're hunting bigger game. Jafet himself."

"Tyler—"

"He's right." Val sat on the edge of Tyler's lounger. "Jafet is Boyd's top earner. If we kill him, we're guaranteed a seat at the Frenzy."

"We're *not* killing anybody."

Tyler waved her off, gazing up at the sky as if the clouds held all the answers. "Table the murder part for later and carry the idea forward. What will it take to bring Jafet down?"

Murder didn't seem like the sort of thing they should *table for later*, but Talia humored him. "You'd need a small army. From what Eddie told me, his place is well stocked with security."

"Done." Tyler rolled his head over, eyes perfectly serious. "We have a small army ready to go and close by. Think about it. We've used them before."

It took her only a moment to catch his drift. "That . . . might work. Okay, but we can't storm Club Styx SWAT style. Word would get back to Boyd, tipping our hand."

"True. We need to subdue his people quietly."

"And you'll need to draw him out," Val said. "Jafet doesn't leave the safety of his office for just anyone." The confidence in her tone told Talia that Val knew more about Jafet than the rest of them. Val had started her grifter career in the Mediterranean region. Maybe she had crossed paths with the man before.

Tyler agreed with her. "Not just anyone. I have a specific someone in mind. Don Marco."

An image of the mafia-don-esque gentleman who had helped her and Tyler locate Valkyrie on their first mission appeared in Talia's mind. "What does Don Marco have to do with this?"

The other two ignored her. Val walked away from Tyler. "Don Marco won't leave Campione for the same reasons Jafet won't leave his office."

"He'll come," Tyler said.

"He'll want to, because you're the one who's asking, but I'm afraid he'll still say no."

"I won't be asking. You will. Don Marco won't leave Campione d'Italia for me. But he'll do it for his only daughter."

CHAPTER FORTY-THREE

Adamantas Marina
Milos Caldera
Milos, Greek Isles

Finn, Mac, and Darcy did not return until dusk, cutting across the caldera in a pair of rented powerboats. And they did not return empty-handed. Black canvas bags bulging with their purchases filled up a quarter of the houseboat's living room. When Talia tried to unzip one, Darcy slapped her hand away. "What are you trying to do, blow up the boat?"

"I just wanted to see," she said, rubbing her smarting fingers.

"So did the curious cat, yes? And look what happened to her."

Bunking with the chemist that night had charms of its own. Eddie stayed well past his welcome, and something in the way he and Darcy talked science made Talia want to put her earbuds in. There were passionate undertones hidden in all the technical jargon. "Time for you to go, Eddie. It's late."

"Am I being too loud?"

"No." Talia caught his elbow and led him to the door, all of two steps from the edge of Darcy's bunk. "You're being too . . . *here*. I need to sleep."

"We'll be quiet. We can talk with the lights off."

"Not a chance. Out."

They both glanced at Darcy, who had lost interest and started digging in her purse. Eddie lowered his voice. "But we were connecting."

"Connect tomorrow, when I'm not around. Good night, Eddie." She pushed him out and closed the door.

With Eddie gone, Talia began a nighttime ritual she had started many years before, after losing her father. Any first night in a new bed, she read a worn copy of *The Cat in the Hat*.

She had barely passed the title page when Darcy set her purse down and propped herself up on her pillows, playing with what Talia took to be a ball of clay. "He is sweet, no?"

Talia lowered the book to her lap. "Always has been." To her, Eddie was like a little brother—not the annoying kind, but the kind who needed protecting. "Darcy . . ."

"Yes, *mon amie*?"

"Where do you see things going? With you and Eddie, I mean."

Darcy kept playing with her clay, molding it into a little man. "Nowhere. Anywhere." She shrugged, and in the process, tore one of the clay man's spindly little arms off. She frowned and tried to stick it back on. "We are having fun, and for me, that is enough, yes?"

"Does he know that?"

Darcy let go of the repaired arm, and it stayed in place, now shorter and grossly uneven with the other. "Does he know what, *mon amie*?"

"That you—" In that instant, the clay's yellow tone and glossy sheen registered in Talia's mind. "Darcy, is that . . . ?"

"X-dough. Swedish plastique."

"And you thought *I* would blow up the boat?"

"Don't be silly. X-dough has the stability of C4, with improved plasticity. Watch." Darcy smacked her hands together, squishing her art. "See? Safe. You cannot set it off without detonators." She held the little man, now as flat as a pancake, in her palm and placed two tiny black discs where his eyes would go.

"What are those?" Talia asked.

"Detonators."

"Darcy!"

She showed Talia another one, holding it between her thumb and forefinger. "Look how small they are—the latest advance from Singapore."

The Cat in the Hat could wait until their next location. At the moment, she needed to keep Darcy from playing with bombs in bed. Talia slapped the light switch. "Go to sleep, Darcy. Let's hope we both live to see the morning."

She rolled over against the bulkhead side of her bunk, and the moment she closed her eyes, trying not to picture Darcy playing with plastique, her phone rang. Talia nearly jumped out of her skin. "Yes?"

"There you are."

The caller's voice rose from the bottom of a well of static, but Talia recognized it. "Jenni?"

"Were you in the bathroom? You let it ring for like two full minutes."

"No. The call has to . . . Let's just say it has to pass through a lot of junctions before it reaches me. What's going on?"

"Mom tried to call yesterday. She never got through."

"Wendy's number is not on the list."

A long pause. "You can call her Mom too, you know. Even if you don't sign the adoption papers."

"Jenni, it's nighttime here. Are you calling to catch up or—"

"Two things. The police came to the house. Except, I don't think they were police. They said you didn't show up at work. I told them they were mistaken. You're on vacation. But Mom's worried."

The police. Unlikely. Jordan hadn't taken long to make her next move, escalating the game. "Did they ask where?"

"I told them I didn't know."

Smart. But Jenni had always been quick on the uptake. "Thanks. I'm okay. And I'm sorry it upset . . . Mom."

She could almost hear Jenni smiling at her use of the word. "That's okay. I'll handle it."

"You said there were two things. What was the other one?"

"I got a call from Ewan Ferguson."

Talia sat up in bed. "The guy from Compassion International—the one on the ground in Thailand."

"He has a lead on the missing kids."

CHAPTER FORTY-FOUR

Milos National Airport
Milos, Greek Isles

Moonlight pooled on the hangar floor beside Tyler's AS2. He kept the overhead halogens off, in case Jafet had eyes watching the airfield. While the others slept, he and Val had driven out there to await Don Marco's arrival.

Val walked the threshold between the polished concrete and the airfield's cracked asphalt—agitated, unwilling to sit down at the folding table Tyler had pulled out for them. She still wore the black one-piece, but she had added a thin white shirt and a matching skirt that fell to her ankles. Both billowed in the breeze coming off the water. He watched her for a time, then disappeared into his jet to raid the coffee bar.

"You want any?" Tyler asked, coming down the hatch stairs a few minutes later with a full pot and stack of paper cups.

Val shook her head, still placing one foot at a time on the threshold like a tightrope walker.

"Suit yourself." He sat down and poured himself a cup. He dumped a packet of sugar into the coffee, swirled the liquid with the empty packet, and rolled it up into a little ball. Three of the four other cups he lined up one by one, upside down.

The runway outside remained quiet. Depending on winds, Marco might be anywhere from ten minutes to half an hour away. He hadn't exactly filed a flight plan.

Val made a hundred-eighty-degree turn at the end of the threshold. "You never did tell your little protégé how you plan to deal with those containers full of weaponized drones."

"I thought you didn't care what happened to the drones, as long as we get the money."

"I don't. But she does." The grifter took two quick steps, holding her arms out for balance. "You shouldn't keep her in the dark all the time."

"I like to surprise her. Builds trust."

"Not always." She abandoned her tightrope walk, taking interest in Tyler's upturned cups. "Shell game?"

"Mmm-hmm." He slipped the paper ball under the first and began weaving all three in figure eights.

"Keep the ball cup back. Otherwise the mark will see the transfer." Val waited for him to stop and tapped the center cup. As predicted, the paper ball was there.

Tyler sighed and started over. "I always loved this game, but I never mastered it."

She pulled over a chair and sat down. "Move the cups a little faster, not enough to make it hard, but enough to make them wonder."

He stopped. She tapped a cup. The ball was there.

He started again, slower this time, instead of faster as she suggested. After a few seconds, he paused, squinted at the cups as if he had lost track of the ball himself, then kept going.

"The weapons, Tyler. What's the plan?"

All that maneuvering and weaving in and out had left the cups in relative disarray. Tyler lined them all up at the edge of the table and lifted his hands, giving Val a nod.

She rolled her eyes and lifted the center cup.

The ball wasn't there.

She lifted the left, then the right. No paper ball. She frowned. "Okay. Good transfer. You're wearing a T-shirt, so it's not up your sleeves. Show me your hands."

He did, rippling his fingers. Both hands were empty. Tyler lifted a fourth cup at the far corner of the table—the extra cup he had offered to fill with coffee for her when he first emerged from the AS2. The paper ball rocked back and forth in the breeze.

Val sat back, perplexed. "How did you—?"

"I like to surprise you too."

The sound of a light jet on final approach drew both of their gazes to the runway. Tyler left her sitting at the table and walked out into the moonlight. "Here comes Don Marco."

An observer might have thought Tyler and Val looked like a miniature welcoming party, waiting on the tarmac as the jet pulled in before the next hangar over. But Tyler couldn't banish the feeling they were two teens—a boy and his date, out past curfew and now waiting to face her angry father.

Don Marco seemed to share Tyler's thoughts. "You two," he said, coming down the steps after four young handlers took defensive positions at the nose, tail, and wingtips. "Did I not say once the Gryphon job was done, you were to sit down with me in Campione? Together?" He gave Val a kiss on each cheek, earning a dutiful but cold kiss on each of his, then stepped in front of Tyler. The old Italian's bushy white eyebrows pressed together in a scowl. "We made a deal, Adam. Yet here we all are, six months later. What have the two of you been doing all this time."

"Working." Tyler cleared his throat, which had suddenly gone dry. "Val's been working for me. That's all."

"With him," Val said. "I've been working *with* him, not for him."

"Right. With me." Tyler couldn't stop himself from giving Marco a subtle head bobble that said *With me means for me.*

Val smacked his arm. "I saw that."

"Your pilot can stow the jet in there." Tyler gestured at the empty hangar. "And I made arrangements for you and your men at a house near the marina. We can still have that sit-down you wanted, tonight or tomorrow morning. By noon, things will get busy."

"No." Marco turned away from him to scan the airfield.

When he didn't elaborate, Tyler cocked his head. "No sit-down? No, your pilot isn't staying?"

"Both. You two need to leave."

Something in his tone—something Tyler hadn't picked up—seemed to affect Val. She touched her father's arm. "Why would we leave? You don't have a vehicle."

He stopped scanning the airfield long enough to look her in the eye. "There was a time when you called me Papa."

"That time is long past, but it doesn't mean I don't care what happens to you. Why do you want us to leave?"

"Jafet's people are coming. They can't see us together."

The hair on the back of Tyler's neck stood up. Marco wasn't scanning the airfield out of routine paranoia. He was expecting Jafet's men— dangerous men. How much time did they have? "You spoke to Jafet without me."

The Italian nodded. "I'm staying with him at Club Styx. It was the only way he'd agree to the meeting. An escort is coming for me now. My men and my pilot will return to Campione."

Concern choked Val's voice. "If you go into

261

that mountain alone, you'll never come out again."

"You don't know him as I do. Jafet will want to gloat—to lord his hospitality over me for a night and a day." Don Marco shifted his gaze from Val to Tyler. "After that, my survival depends entirely on you."

CHAPTER FORTY-FIVE

Adamantas Marina Milos Caldera
Milos, Greek Isles

Sleep eluded Talia. How could she close her eyes when every minute counted?

With the help of one of the refugee parents, Jenni's contact in Thailand had discovered a pen of barbed wire strung between trees in the jungle. There were medical scraps, cigarette butts, and a ball made of rubber bands that one of the little boys always carried. Ewan Ferguson had given Jenni the GPS coordinates for the first stop in a trail that might lead directly to those kids.

Tyler had nothing more than a teetering stack of assumptions. If his thieves could navigate three complicated cons, and if those cons led to the capture of Livingston Boyd, Talia might be able to pull the location of the kids straight from the kingpin's mouth. But that hope was built on the assumption the kidnappers were truly part of Boyd's global organization.

She and Tyler had different goals. Talia was in this job for the little girl, Hla Meh, and the others. Tyler was in this for Boyd and Archangel.

She lit a fire in the boat's fireplace, curled up on the couch, and when Tyler and Val stepped in off the dock and turned on the light, Talia was there waiting for them. She had her speech all ready, but the worry in their faces stopped her. "What happened with Don Marco? Did you take him to the house?"

Tyler pushed the door closed behind him, locked it, and closed the blinds on its window. "Jafet has him. Part of the deal. Nothing's changed."

But something had changed. She could hear it in his denial. And with Don Marco in Jafet's clutches, Talia's decision would hurt Tyler all the more. "I . . . I have to leave."

Val tossed the van keys on the bar and threw up her hands. "Oh, here we go."

"I'm sorry, but the child advocacy group that told us about the missing kids has a lead. We could walk this long meandering trail of cons to Boyd, or we could cut a path directly to the kidnappers."

Tyler walked past her to the sliding door of the lower deck and cracked it open, letting in the cool sea air. "That's an ethanol fireplace. You should always ventilate the room when you use one."

"Tyler, I'm serious. I'm going. And I'd like to take Finn and Mac with me."

He didn't answer.

Val gave her a long look that told Talia exactly what she was thinking, then descended a short stair to her bunk. The door slammed shut. Two beats later, Talia heard a muted shout from beyond.

"Flip . . . flop!"

Tyler lowered himself into a recliner across the living room, facing the sliding door. The way his mind worked was not lost on Talia. Hers worked the same way. Tyler had secured one point of entry, and when prudence necessitated the opening of another, he positioned himself to keep tabs on it. "We talked about this. One hundred percent committed. That's what we agreed upon."

"Those were your words, not mine. And that was before I had a set of coordinates."

He raised an eyebrow, looking her way. "For the kids?"

"For a spot in the jungle where we know they were held."

"That's a huge distinction."

Talia hugged a pillow to her chest and fell back against the cushions. "Yeah. I know."

They both sat there, with only the hiss of the fireplace and the soft splashing of the waves.

After a while, Talia broke the silence. "You never told me the story."

"Which story."

"You know the one."

In an airport in Italy, a lifetime ago, Tyler had hinted at the history between him and Don Marco. *That's a story for another day.* So far, *another day* hadn't come.

"Humor me," she said. "I've waited six months to hear this tale, and now Don Marco's life is at stake."

He sighed, and for a few long heartbeats, Talia thought he wouldn't cave. But then the story began. "Don Marco is Val's father. That much, you know from recent events. And if she's spoken of him, you also know he was once a brutal crime boss."

"Orien Jafet's rival in the Mediterranean region," Talia said.

Tyler nodded. "Back then, he was simply Marco. I wasn't lying when I told you the locals in Campione d'Italia gave him that title for all his praying. And Marco the crime boss was my final assignment as an assassin."

Talia sat up. "But my dad—"

"Came first in the timeline. Think of the contract on Marco as an outsourcing job, brokered by the Agency on behalf of elements within the Italian government. But after what I'd learned—after I realized Archangel had betrayed both your father and me—I wanted out."

"So you refused the assignment."

"Not quite." Tyler offered a thin smile. "I changed the terms. I hunted Marco down at a castle in the hills above Salerno, dragged him into the woods, and gave him a choice. Repent or die."

Ultimatums weren't Tyler's style. "You're

266

saying you threatened to kill Marco if he didn't convert?"

"I was a new Christian, but not so ignorant. No, I chose utter honesty. I admitted leaving the game and promised to let him live. But I told him another assassin would come calling. Instead of demanding his conversion, I offered to become his advocate." Tyler left his seat and walked to the fire, kneeling to warm his hands. "I asked him to renounce his ways and retire. Faith was not a requirement. But God had prepared the way. Marco's demons had caught up to him long before I arrived. He was ready."

"And after his repentance, you ran interference for him with the powers that be."

Tyler nodded. "I fended off two more assassins before the Italians came to the table. I convinced them Marco's permanent retirement accomplished the same operational goals as his death. With additional benefits."

Talia could see what he meant—any case officer could. A man like Marco was a treasure trove of intelligence. "What happened then?"

"I set him up with some friends in Campione d'Italia, and he never left." Tyler let out a sorrowful laugh. "Until today, when I still managed to become his grim reaper. May God and Val both forgive me."

She didn't know what else to say. Talia hadn't known how much of Tyler's spiritual blood he

267

had staked on this one job, intermediate to his ultimate goal of catching Archangel. How could she abandon him now?

Tyler let out a long breath. "I know you want to go after those kids, Talia, but you're central to every piece of this con. I need you here. Finn or Mac, I could spare. Maybe."

Finn or Mac. The thought hadn't occurred to Talia. *Faith. Lean.* Isn't that what Tyler was trying to teach her? She didn't have to be the one to go. "Okay. What about both?"

Prayer—deep prayer—became sleep, which became waking again, all before the sun rose. Talia did not wait for the others to get up. She left Darcy lying as still as a corpse and crossed the hall to the opposite berth.

A single bunk was set against the bulkhead on one side, and a pair stacked on the other. Mac lay facedown on the single, with one arm hanging to the floor and one big foot sticking out from beneath the covers. Talia turned to the pair and recognized Eddie's steady snore from the top bunk. That left the lower bunk for Finn.

She gently shook his shoulder. "Finn. Finn, wake up."

The thief sat up, ducking to avoid banging his head on the upper bunk. "What? Who?"

"It's me, Talia. We need to talk."

He yawned and rubbed his eyes. "What about?"

"Not here." She grabbed his hand to help him out of the bunk, but for a reason she couldn't explain, she didn't let go until she had him out on the upper deck.

Finn left her side and walked to the stern rail. "What's so pressing it couldn't wait until morning?"

She told him about Ferguson—about his lead on the children. "I want you to head out to Thailand early and rendezvous with Compassion's man on the ground. Try and get to the children now, in case we never make it to the Frenzy."

"A shortcut," he said, looking out at the water.

"If that's what you want to call it, sure."

"Shortcuts never work out like you hope." He turned, resting his hips against the rail. "Why me? Why don't you go?"

"Tyler made a good case for keeping me on task with Club Styx. And . . ." Talia dropped her eyes to her bare toes. "I prayed about it. I think God wants me here."

"Which means he wants me to drop into a Thai mountain jungle?"

She shrugged.

"Great."

The moon had set, and with no big-city lights to wash them out, the stars were bright in the predawn sky. Before Talia could come up with more reasons for him to go, Finn spoke again. "You're needed here, but I'm not. That's what you're saying. Like Val said when I messed up in Prague, the team doesn't need me."

Her hand was on his again. Talia didn't remember putting it there. Finn rolled his over and held her fingers. Even with pillow hair and reddened eyes, he had the looks to melt a woman's heart. Talia had seen those looks in action with fan girls and snow bunnies at his daredevil events. So often, a haughtiness came with them, but not now. Looking up at him, she saw only Finn's vulnerability—his need to be wanted.

"I'm . . . I'm not saying that at all. I'm saying those kids need you more. Will you go?" She squeezed his hand and pressed closer. "For me?" Maybe it was the sea breeze. Maybe it was the electricity in the starlight. Every romantic experience of Talia's lifetime told her that was the moment to kiss him. Yet a small voice said, *Not yet.* She let go and backed away.

Finn did the same. "Right. Yeah. I'll go." He walked to the stairs to head below. "For the kids. And I'll see if I can get Mac to go with me. We'll fly commercial, first flight out."

She watched him go, not sure what to say. "Um . . . Thank you. And Finn?"

He glanced over his shoulder from the top step. "Yeah?"

"Be careful."

CHAPTER FORTY-SIX

The Catacombs
Milos, Greek Isles

The team spent the final minutes before go time—what Tyler called zero hour—in a Mercedes van, surveilling the entrance to an ancient Christian crypt known locally as the Catacombs. Spotlights illuminated a church façade carved into the hillside bedrock.

"Incoming." Talia raised a set of binoculars as a town car eased to a stop. The door opened and closed. "Single male. African. Maybe. This might be our warlord's negotiator."

Without speaking, Eddie held out a tablet with a photo of two men in the African bush, sporting AK-47s.

She pointed to the man she'd seen.

Tyler gave the photo a glance. "Confirmed. Mr. Aku has arrived. Say a prayer, folks. We're on in five."

The usual butterflies played in Talia's gut, but she felt better about Jafet and Club Styx than she had about Atan and the German Silver gag. A day of planning at the boat and a video chat with some old friends had left her feeling prepared. Still, she prayed for help with the dangers and the unknowns, for comfort for the children in Thailand, and for Finn and Mac. By now the boys were flying low over some of the densest foliage on the planet.

"Did you have to send Finn *and* Mac?" Tyler asked when Talia opened her eyes, as if he'd been listening in on her conversation with God. "I was only spitballing when I said I could spare them. Now I have to take Mac's piece of the job, and we still haven't heard from Pell about covering for Finn since offering him the job this morning." He stared her down for a couple of heartbeats, then cranked the motor and put the van into gear. "This is not optimal."

Eddie's tablet buzzed. "Uh oh."

"Uh oh, what?"

"You know that whole bit about not hearing from Pell?"

Tyler stepped on the brake and turned in his seat. "Spit it out, Eddie."

"I . . . just heard from Pell. A blizzard in Vienna delayed his flight. He landed in Athens five minutes ago, three hours late."

"We're done, then. Without Pell, we don't have the numbers."

Val grabbed the back of his seat. "What? You can't call this off. You'll be signing Marco's death warrant."

"And we do have the numbers," Talia said. "I can cover Finn's role. I have the time."

Darcy raised her hand. "Or I could do it, yes?"

"No." Talia gently pushed the chemist's hand down. "You're throwing the locks and setting the detonators. It has to be me. I have the skills. I learned B&E at the Farm."

Tyler lowered his chin and gave her his *Really?* look. "You're talking about the equivalent of a weekend learning annex course versus Finn's PhD."

"It'll be enough."

He closed his eyes, either thinking or praying. When he opened them again, he put the van into drive. "Eddie, tell Pell to hurry up as best he can. We're pressing forward."

Tyler and Eddie dropped Talia, Val, and Darcy off at the church façade. As the boys drove away, the girls took the worn limestone steps down into the Catacombs.

Darcy had chosen a white satin evening gown, while Talia had gone with black. Both dresses were simple and elegant. Val shimmered between them in red sequins. At the shops, she had justified her selection with psychobabble about shallow hypnosis and color associations.

"I don't believe you," Talia had countered. "I saw the grin on your face when you tried it on."

Val hadn't argued.

Their clutches were red, white, and black as well, but of the same style and material—slightly

273

large for a fancy evening out and completely interchangeable.

A raised walkway passed above the flooded limestone deep in the tombs. Red lights below the waterline cast a wavering glow on rows of columns on either side. Silhouettes watched from the darkness beyond, skeletons in the alcoves. Talia pulled her wrap about her shoulders. The air had grown cold.

"With a little help from yours truly," Eddie said, offering a final briefing over the comm link, "the TACRON team found their way onto the Terrorist Watchlist. The *top* of the Terrorist Watchlist. They never left the States. And they won't be talking to anyone for quite a while."

Like any five-star establishment, no one entered Club Styx without a reservation. Jafet's neutral sanctuary worked via tight access control. Earlier in the day, Eddie had stolen TACRON's digital reservation package, and Val had passed the confirmation number to a fishmonger at the Milos street market. In exchange, she received a greasy paper bag with four tokens. Talia could feel her token burning like a coal in her clutch—not a pretty picture considering the rest of its contents.

The deeper they walked into the Catacombs, the worse the comm signal became. "Remember," Tyler said through the static. "You're heading into an extinct magma dome, a natural EM barrier. The only sig . . . going i . . . r out must pass thr . . . Jafet's monitored network. We can't talk . . . one . . . nother. We . . . an't coordin . . ."

The static took over.

Talia removed her earpiece and tucked it away. "That's it for SATCOM coordination. From this moment forward, every action we take is on a schedule. Our lives and Don Marco's life all hang on the ticking of the clock."

She fell silent. Up ahead, a wooden boat drifted up to the path, punted by a stolid figure in a leather overcoat and fingerless gloves.

"Those are the most sunken eyes I have ever seen," Talia whispered to Val.

"Makeup," the grifter whispered back. "Jafet has a flare for the dramatic."

Talia spoke for the group, using a code phrase from the reservation package. "Mr. Charon, I presume?"

The ferryman kept his gaze fixed on oblivion and held out an open palm.

She dug out the token, a golden drachma, and placed it in his hand. He offered a slow, deliberate nod, and she stepped into the boat, taking a seat on a bench of quilted black velvet. Val and Darcy gave up their drachmas and did the same.

The boat drifted through the columns, well off the tourist path. The red lights faded behind. And as Talia's eyes adjusted, the skeletons in the alcoves took on more definition. A few were complete, set into the plaster, bone fingers splayed as if reaching for the passing souls. Most were not so well put together. Skulls, lying askew on piles of shanks and femurs, stared at her with empty eye sockets.

Val shivered. "Nice place. Lovely decor."

The cold had not affected Darcy. She glanced in every direction like a child on an amusement ride. "I like it."

Presently, they passed into a tunnel, and the air grew warm again, as if a furnace waited at the far end. The darkness became complete. Talia had to clutch Val's arm to counter the vertigo. More to settle her nerves than to correct his dramatic detail, Talia thrust her chin at the ferryman. "Not to be a stickler for detail, but the ferryman's price was an *obolus*, one sixth of a drachma."

To her surprise, he answered. "I get that a lot. Blame it on two thousand years of inflation."

"He speaks," Darcy said.

"I do now, for we have crossed into my domain."

Light returned to the tunnel, orange and flickering, and the black walls gave way to a huge domed chamber. Sporadic flames burst from torches on carved arches and lava-rock bridges, and occasionally from the water itself. Guests sat at tables along seven stories of obsidian balconies. And at the center of it all, on an island of gaming tables, the most adventurous and foolhardy among them drank and gambled.

The ferryman punted past the island toward a half-moon dock. "Enjoy Club Styx, wandering souls. Seek me out when you are ready to return to living lands." A smile touched his thin lips. "Should that time ever come."

Hard to say at this point, Talia thought. She palmed her phone and glanced at the clock. The readout switched from 10:29 p.m. to 10:30. Zero hour for this mission. At midnight, or *zero plus ninety* to use Agency terminology, Stage Two would be over, one way or another. Ninety minutes. The team had ninety minutes to draw out the ruler of this thematic underworld and kill him.

CHAPTER FORTY-SEVEN

Ten Thousand Feet
Mae Surin Jungle
Mae Hong Son Province, Thailand

A speed bump of wet air bounced Finn, chute pack and all, up from the floor of the rickety prop plane he and Mac had rented for the night. Flying in the wee hours over Thai mountain ridges was no better than driving up a rocky jeep trail. "Any chance of finding smooth air?"

"No."

Finn waited through two more bumps for the Scotsman to offer any form of elaboration. None followed. Mac had never been a verbose man, but the terse answer likely had to do with the level of concentration required to keep the little T-41 Mescalero upright in the rough air, so Finn didn't press. "Alright, then."

They had found the plane at a fly-by-night skydiving operation in Chiang Mai. It met their requirements—copilot and passenger seats ripped out and door widened for jump operations. Airworthiness was a secondary concern. The souped-up Cessna 172 had started life as a Royal Thai Air Force trainer and still sported the original olive drab paint job. Looking out at the

278

wings and struts, Finn could see several poorly matched spots where the owner had painted over fifty years of corrosion. He made it halfway through a sigh, only to be bounced off the floor again. "Okay, now you're doing it on purpose."

Mac pointed at a portable GPS display suction-cupped to the dash. "We're approachin' the drop zone, lad. Yer up."

"Roger. I'm off comms." Finn pulled his headset cord from the aircraft jack and plugged it into a Motorola handset. He dialed the UHF frequency Talia had given him. "Ewan Ferguson, this is Nightflyer. Come in, please." *Ewan Ferguson.* Another Scotsman. What sort of purgatory had Talia thrown him into? "Ewan, this is Nightflyer. How do you read?"

The radio crackled. "Nightflyer, I read you." He didn't sound Scottish, although the aircraft noise and the weak signal made it hard to say for sure. "I am at the drop zone."

By drop zone, he meant a twenty-meter clearing Finn and Mac had identified via satellite imagery before leaving Milos. Sixteen hours had passed since then, added to the hundred or more that had passed since the children first disappeared. Needles and haystacks came to mind.

Rising to his knees, Finn peered out through the prop at the fog-lined ridges. A moonlight jump into a jungle forest. Timing and coordination were everything. "Ewan, do you have the flare gun?"

An orange star, trailing flame, rose from the trees dead ahead, lighting up the wisps of cloud.

"I asked if you had it," Finn grumbled to himself. "I didn't tell you to shoot it off." He keyed the radio. "Load another round, and when I give you the signal, count to thirty and fire it off."

No answer.

"Ewan, do you copy?"

"Yes. I copy."

Amateurs. He tapped Mac's shoulder and shouted over the engine. "Speed?"

"Aboot eighty knots!"

"Aboot?" The calculations Eddie and Darcy had made for them required a precise heading and speed. Finn would have time to make a few adjustments under canopy, but if he fell outside his margin for error, he might wind up with a tree branch in his gut. "Right now, I'm not too fond of *aboot,* mate. *Exactly* would be better."

"Ya get what ya get. Now quit yer whingin' and get ready to jump." The aircraft bucked and shimmied. Mac tightened his grip on the yoke. "Two thousand meters from the target."

"Ewan, this is Nightflyer. Start your count in three, two, one . . . now!" Finn didn't wait for a reply. Headset off and goggles in place, he slid the door open to the roar of the slipstream and climbed out onto a one-meter-wide platform welded to the wing strut. Mac held three fingers in the air. In tick-tock rhythm, he lowered them to a balled fist and then pointed straight ahead.

Finn let go and dropped.

Two seconds into the free fall, a cloud the size of a house slapped him in the face. The thing had weight—and depth. His first jungle cloud and all Finn could think was, *Ow,* and *Smells like fish.* He flew out the other side with a soaked wingsuit and blurry goggles. He sacrificed altitude to keep stable while wiping the goggles clean, and when he spread his arms again, Ewan's flare had already lit the sky ahead.

Finn never saw where it came from.

The first flare—the one he hadn't asked for—had drifted left over the trees. This one drifted left as well. Finn traced an imaginary line down and to the right from the falling orange ball and thought he saw a break in the foliage. He shifted his track and hoped for the best. Talia would have told him to pray, but pride prevented him from starting now. The whole atheist-in-a-foxhole line seemed like a cowardly out. But maybe if she was praying for him, that would be enough.

The behavior of the flares told Finn to line up right of his target, and the experience of more than two hundred night jumps told him when to pull his chute. Opening shock jerked him back. He checked his canopy and snapped both steering toggles free of their stowage. When his eyes returned to his mark, he saw a faint white spot flashing across the trees. An electric torch. Ewan.

With renewed confidence, Finn set his aim. The air chop off the treetops whipped his chute, but he kept things under control. His man on the ground did not. The torch dropped to the ground and rolled. In its wash, he saw Ewan running into the jungle. Was he getting clear of the landing zone or fleeing a threat? Two flares and a swinging torch might easily have drawn the attention of the very kidnappers they were after.

Finn scanned the tree line. He had one of Tyler's modified machine guns strapped to his chest, but he only had two hands, and he needed those to manage his toggles for the landing, coming up fast. If armed men waited for him in the trees, he was at their mercy.

CHAPTER FORTY-EIGHT

Club Styx
Milos, Greek Isles
10:31 pm

As the ferryman punted up to the dock, Valkyrie saw Darcy slip a gray ball into the water. She had missed her teammate's other drops. Good. Darcy's sleight-of-hand skills were coming along. If she managed to dodge a fiery death at the hands of her own creations, she might make an excellent grifter. The French accent helped. Half the men in the world were suckers for a French accent. But for Club Styx, Val put on her Southern Belle.

Emma Knight, TACRON's negotiator, had graduated *summa cum laude* from Auburn. *Emma Knight.* Val liked the name. After this job was done, and with the real Emma locked away for weapons trafficking, Val might take on her persona for a while.

The ferryman sailed off to collect more souls, and the girls got to work. They merged into the crowd at the periphery of the cavern, then split off one by one. Val went first. She glanced back to see Talia and Darcy, arm in arm, giggling as they walked. Their antics drew eyes, but Val doubted that any of the onlookers noticed them swap clutches. The two parted, fingers touching until the last moment. Darcy went left. Talia went right.

"Drink, madame?" A waiter offered Val a tray of selections.

She lifted a champagne glass with two fingers. "Thank you. How kind." Val wasn't drinking, not on this job. Tyler had made her promise. But she held the glass, a prop to complete the picture the Kongaran warlord's buyer expected.

She spotted the buyer on the fourth level, sitting alone at a table, and took an open lift to meet him. On the way, she searched the cavern for Marco but didn't see him. Jafet's private poker table, on a platform extending from the eighth-level balcony, remained empty.

Val hated the monster Marco had become early in her youth, and despised him even more for pretending to reform after Tyler spared his life. Yet, try as she might suppress it, she cared what happened to him. If the team failed tonight, after dragging Marco out of hiding, she might never forgive herself. She'd certainly never forgive Tyler.

Val sauntered up to the mark's table, champagne held slightly above her navel, a smile—barely there—on her lips. "You must be Mr. Aku."

"Yes. Who is asking?" The warlord's man had his nose buried in a smartphone, brand new and too large to fit in any reasonable pocket. His eyes came up first and widened. The rest of his head followed. "Oh."

"Emma Knight." She pushed the accent. Alabaman. Not Texan or Georgia peach. Aku likely wouldn't know the difference, but Val was a perfectionist.

When he got up to take her hand, almost knocking over his chair, she made her assessment.

Eager to please—a result of physical and psychological abuse in his present superior-subordinate relationship.

Eyes flitting all over the place—doesn't know where to look when talking to an attractive woman in an evening gown. Makes him distracted, nervous, vulnerable.

New phone. Silk tailored suit, also new—Aku had laid down some cash since arriving in the Greek Isles, hopefully some of his abusive boss's cash.

Val broadened her Alabama smile. "I'm so pleased to make your acquaintance. Shall we sit?"

The obsidian tables were etched with games designed for guests to enjoy and gamble among themselves. Aku's table boasted a black felt dice tray and a board of squares with castles carved into the corners, a red dragon at the center. The dice, most of all, caught Val's eye. There were five, one in the tray and the other four placed on the castle squares, but all were ten-sided gems—sapphire, ruby, amethyst, amber, and emerald, inlaid with gold and silver numbers. The jewels were lab-created, to be sure, but gorgeous nonetheless.

"It is called Dragon's Domain," Aku said. "What shall we play for? Pride or greed?"

"How about five million?"

"US dollars?"

"Is there really any other currency worth mentioning?"

"Uh . . . I . . ." The warlord's lieutenant pressed his lips together and swallowed.

Val already knew he didn't have that kind of cash. "If I win, your boss, Mr. Iwela, pays TACRON's asking price for the three squadrons of drones. Fifty million. That's a respectable bulk discount off our original twenty-million-per-squadron ask."

"And if I win?"

"If you win, darlin', your boss still pays fifty, but I divert five million into the account of your choosing."

Aku's eyes widened. "You mean—"

Val lifted the amber die from the tray, rolled it between her thumb and forefinger, and winked. "What happens to the extra five million is entirely up to you."

She didn't have to ask twice. Aku nodded. "This arrangement is acceptable. Quite acceptable."

"Excellent." Val flicked the die into the tray,

watching the yellow facets catch the torchlight. She set her champagne glass beside the board. "How do we play?"

"You do not know?"

"Darlin', I've never seen this game in my life."

The Kongaran could hardly contain his grin. "I will teach you."

The game had something to do with moving Val's ruby and sapphire pieces to reach the opposite castles or forcing Aku's gems into the center, which he called the Dragon's Domain. Aku was no genius, and despite Val's best efforts at losing, his emerald and amethyst pieces were soon sitting at the clawed feet of the dragon.

She clapped a hand to her mouth. "Oh my. Did I win?" She wanted to smack him.

The Kongaran stared at his pieces in disbelief. "Best two out of three?"

"I'll tell you what. I'm all about makin' friends. So, let's you and I pretend you won, and if you don't tell your boss, neither will I."

"Really?"

She ran a finger along the back of his hand. "Really. Now, shall we make this official so we can enjoy the rest of the evening?"

His eyes were dazed, mesmerized. Five million dollars and a glittering red dress had that effect on a man like Aku.

"I'll take your silence as a yes." Val sat back, taking his smartphone with her.

"Hey!"

"Oops, you left your screen unlocked. Not wise in a place like this."

"No, I—"

She turned the phone around to show him.

He smiled, embarrassed. "I suppose I did."

Val yawned, typed a number into his banking application, and returned the phone, letting her fingers linger. "Make the transfer, and our grunts at the dock will do the rest."

He started typing, then stopped. "Weapons first. You have been generous, but you will get paid only when I know the containers are on board my ship."

"Ooh. Aren't we feisty?" Val could feel Aku grasping for some smidgeon of self-respect. Her mock charity had pushed him as far as his pride would allow. The clock in her head ticked on. She needed to close the deal. "All right, darlin'. You win. What choice do I have?"

"Exactly my point."

With a demure smile and a slight turn in her seat, she dialed Eddie. "Matthew? Hand over the merchandise . . . No, I don't have the money—not yet." She glanced sidelong at Aku and winked. "Their position is strong. I'm authorizing you to move the containers."

Val set the phone on the game board beside his fallen pieces and switched to a video display, a wide view routed directly from the dock security cameras. "There they are, the three green shipping containers. We'll watch the transfer from here."

Aku nodded his agreement, and Val drew a subtle breath. The rest was up to Eddie, who rarely left his computer during the team's cons, and a crane operator who hadn't run heavy equipment in years.

CHAPTER FORTY-NINE

Eddie hung up the phone, looking up at a pair of big Kongarans. "My boss says the deal is on. The merchandise is yours. You want to see it?"

Waiting around with these guys had almost been more than Eddie could take. The bigger of the two carried a machete slung at his back. Eddie figured the only thing keeping the man from slicing him into bits for sport was the occasional sniffle. The guy probably didn't want virus-infested blood fouling up his blade.

One of the men said something to the other in their native tongue that sounded like, "What did he say?" It might also have been, "Shall we crush this little Indian geek like the bug he is?"

The other one shrugged. They looked at him and frowned.

"The drones." Eddie flattened his hand and flew it around like an aircraft, then pointed to his eyes. *"Do you want to see them?"*

The bigger one thrust his chin at the container. "Yes. We see weapons now."

Communication lines established. Good. Eddie

pressed a key fob, and the container's electric lock disengaged with a hefty *clank*. He heaved open the door.

The bigger Kongaran pulled a hard-shell case from the stacks inside and set it on the wet pavement. He lifted a gunship drone from the foam packing.

"Careful, please."

The Kongaran glowered at him.

Eddie shrank back, adding a preemptive sniffle to remind the man of his cold. "It's just . . . the magazines come pre-loaded, okay?"

After a long exchange in their own language, the Kongarans seemed satisfied.

"All good?" Eddie gave the bigger one a thumbs-up.

As Val predicted during her coaching earlier in the day, his mark answered with a matching thumbs-up, visible to Aku via the dock security camera.

"Good." Eddie shoved the case into the container and shut the door. "Tell your pilot to dock the boat at Berth E-Four and I'll have my crane operator load you up."

Once again, they both frowned.

Using his tablet, he showed them a map of the docks. "E-Four." He pointed at the berth in the picture and then pointed at the actual berth across the yard. "Your boat. E-Four."

The big one shook his head. "No E-Four." He

dug a crumpled printout from the pocket of his cargo pants. "Look. Look here. Your message say *G*-Four."

Eddie slapped his forehead. "Sure enough. Autocorrect. Gets us every time."

"Move boat cost fuel." The Kongaran shook the printout and poked Eddie in the chest. It hurt. "No move. You did this. You fix."

Eddie could see the guy's blood beginning to boil. Val had told him to press the Kongarans to the limit, but she hadn't seen the size of these guys. "Okay, okay." He let them off the hook. "There's another solution. The dock crane is on rails. I think my operator can work this out." He raised a handheld radio to his lips and looked up at the crane cab. "Santini, you awake up there?"

The answer came in garbled, staticky Greek.

Eddie didn't speak a lick of Greek. "Good. Good. Hey, can you run that baby down the dock—move these containers all the way to G-Four?"

More garbled Greek, with a little annoyance thrown in.

"Yeah. That's right. *G*-Four. There was a mix-up with the paperwork."

The final answer came in short and angry.

Eddie clipped the radio to his belt and clapped his hands. "We're good."

"You load containers now?"

"One more thing." Eddie unzipped a duffel and

drew out two cans of red spray paint. "We can't have containers with TACRON's logo showing up in the Kongaran Republic." He walked down the line, working the cans to cover each logo with a large, dripping blotch.

The Kongarans didn't interfere. The smaller one said something in Kongaran. The big one laughed. They seemed to understand.

With his artwork complete, Eddie gave the crane operator an exaggerated wave. The machine swung into action, lifting the containers one by one over the stacks of cargo on the docks and setting them down out of sight on the other side.

As the third container disappeared, the big Kongaran lost faith. "What you pull? Where your man take weapons?"

"It's all right. It's all right." Eddie took the significant risk of touching the man's arm—another piece of Val's coaching. "My operator has to reposition the crane before he can move them all the way down to G-Four."

Milos was not exactly a bustling port. Eddie had to wonder how long it had been since the roving crane had moved down the rails. He cringed as a horrible ratchet and clank emanated from the machine's massive base, as if the whole thing might topple over and crush them all. And then it began the slow crawl to the other end.

Ten minutes later, the operator lifted the first

container into view. Eddie pointed. "See the red blotch? Still dripping. There are your weapons. My operator will now load them onto your ship at *G*-Four."

Once all three containers were on the ship, Eddie sent his new friends off with a sniffle and a hardy handshake, making sure the dock cameras caught the whole pantomime. He activated his earpiece. "It's done, boss. You think they bought it?"

"I hope so." Tyler had abandoned the garbled Greek of his Santini-the-Crane-Operator role. "Check the accounts."

Eddie unlocked his tablet in time to see the warlord's funds coming in. Fifty million dollars to a fake TACRON Cayman fund Eddie had created, with five million immediately rerouted into a separate numbered account at a bank in Djibouti, all for Aku. "Yeah. They bought it."

CHAPTER FIFTY

Mae Surin Jungle
Mae Hong Son Province, Thailand

Finn plowed his heels into the wet grass and let his rear end fall into the mud, the only way to stop in a clearing no wider than the height of the surrounding trees.

No one shot him. Good deal.

He jerked his quick-release rip cord and rose to a knee, leveling his gun. The TacLiTe torch fixed to the barrel illuminated the trees. He panned it along the perimeter.

No one.

Ninety degrees to his right, Finn heard a rustling in the underbrush. He swung the weapon and its light toward the sound. "Hands! Let me see them!"

A pair of Thai men stepped out of the trees, hands high, squinting against the beam. One wore a blue T-shirt and tattered gray slacks. The other wore western jeans and a mud-stained button-down. They were unarmed. The man in jeans held a radio.

Finn put two and two together. "Ewan . . . Ferguson?"

The man lowered the radio far enough to shield

his eyes from the light. "Yes. It's confusing. Little Thai guy with a big Scottish name. My dad was a missionary. Would you mind lowering that gun?"

The other man muttered something, eyeing the weapon.

Ewan translated. "This is Po, the father of one of the missing boys. He says he's glad to see an American commando, but he doesn't want a firefight when we find the children."

"I'm Australian, not American. And I'm no commando." Finn let the weapon hang from its sling. "This gun is nonlethal. Without getting too technical, the rounds are mini flashbangs filled with pepper spray. All the same, mate, it's best to be prepared." He reached to his back and drew Matilda from his pack. "Sometimes firefights come along whether we want them or not."

Ewan translated. The other nodded in understanding. The man had seen his share of war and ugliness, Finn could tell. The three converged in the clearing and shook hands. "If you're not a commando, what are you?"

"I'm a thief."

Ewan stared at him for a long moment, then started for the trees. "Great. Follow us."

The jungle turned thick a few meters into the trees. Ewan stumbled along with his torch, a step ahead of Finn. Occasionally, he let a branch snap back to hit the thief in the chest or face. "Sorry," he said every time. "Sorry about that."

In contrast, Po moved through the vines and foliage like a ghost, rarely raising a hand to fend off a branch—rarely needing to.

"Is this area dangerous?" Finn asked, blocking a flying branch with his gun.

"You mean in terms of animals or militia?"

"Take your pick."

"A few of the snakes can kill you, so watch your step."

Finn shined his light directly at his own boots. He couldn't see the soil beneath them, let alone any snakes. "Smashing."

"Militia shouldn't be a problem other than the kidnappers. In this region our biggest danger is bandits." Ewan looked back over his shoulder. "You know. Thieves."

Finn didn't laugh. "How much farther?"

"At least another half kilometer." As he spoke, Ewan bumped into Po. The refugee grumbled and said something harsh in Thai.

"What did he say?" Finn asked. "Why did he stop?"

"Um . . . We're here."

Po led them in a wide misshapen circle, tracking a five-foot-tall fence of barbed wire strung from tree to tree. He spoke in a low monotone, detached, as if all his emotion were already spent.

"Po believes this is a pen. Not for animals, but for people."

"You mean children." Finn found a loose wire and lifted it with the barrel of his weapon.

Po met his eye as he ducked under. "Yes, Thief. Children." That bit of English, he knew.

They spread out, each with a light, and searched the area. Po held up a foil wrapper with a green and yellow logo—packaging from some kind of junk food. Finn gave him a nod and continued tromping through bushes. Most were tamped down, possibly by animals.

Finn needed better evidence. "Po thinks this was the kidnappers' first stop with the kids, right?"

"No. The second stop." Ewan seemed confused that Finn did not already know this information, a hazard of dealing with a communication chain that crossed multiple groups, continents, and languages. "Po found the first one a few days ago. From there he searched in a wide arc and discovered this one."

"Rightio. You've made more progress than I thought." Finn blinked at the light shining in his eyes. "Lower your torch a bit, would you?" As Ewan complied, he threw out a hand. "Wait. Stop there."

"What is it? What did you find?"

Finn plucked a brass cylinder from a clump of grass. "Shell casing." He searched the immediate area for more, but found something else— something that made his stomach turn. "And blood, mate. Smears of blood."

CHAPTER FIFTY-ONE

Talia watched Val and Aku shake hands, then searched for Darcy. She found her a quarter of the way around the third-level balcony, moving in on their mark.

On all nine levels of Club Styx, Jafet's men stood watch. Those who worked the main chamber, standing in obsidian alcoves, wore black suits trimmed with red. Those who worked the guest room hallways and utility tunnels wore black trimmed with yellow. Both blended into the décor like creatures in Dante's circles. But these were not mythical beasts.

They were employees. On a schedule.

Shift change came at eleven, three minutes away. Replacements were already turning up. Darcy bumped into one of the new arrivals stepping off the lift. She poked his chest and made an accusation.

He emphatically shook his head.

Talia got moving.

With an easy pace, she made her way around the circle toward the arguing pair. Darcy saw her coming and advanced a step. The guard, unable to counter his own instincts regarding personal space, backed into Talia as she passed. He muttered an apology. She waved him off and kept walking, with his keycard palmed in her other hand.

Finn would be proud. And the idea that she *wanted* to make him proud caused Talia to crack a half smile.

The guest halls, founded on magma tubes, had no predictable organization or arrangement. They snaked and wound through the mountainside, branching off at odd angles. Obsidian sections poked through creepy wood wainscoting and silk wallpaper. Talia hoped the map Eddie had shown her was accurate; otherwise, she might walk in endless circles seeking her target room. Darcy couldn't stall that guard forever.

The intersection ahead matched the map in her mind. She peeked around the corner, and there it was, a door like all the others but with a scan pad. A camera dome hung above the door. Jafet was no fool. Had Finn or Pell done this part of the job, they would have worn a guard uniform easily adapted into evening wear. Gowns didn't work that way. Talia would have to move in and out of the camera's view as quickly as possible.

"Come on," she hissed at the guard behind the door. "Where's your relief, huh? Go find him. You know you want to."

As if by telepathic prompting, the guard waiting

on the other side opened the secure door and stuck his head out. Talia jerked back. Footsteps. She jiggled the knob on a guest room door, offering a fleeting smile as the guard passed. He paid her no mind, and when he turned at the next intersection, Talia hitched up her gown and made a run for it. She slapped the stolen card against the scan pad and slipped through into the utility tunnels.

The walls back there were raw, chipped obsidian. And the doors were painted iron with thirty-year-old tumbler locks. No cameras. With the guard out of the picture, the rest of Talia's work as Finn-slash-Pell's surrogate would be child's play.

She quick-stepped along the doors, searching for the main breaker room. A lightning-bolt danger sticker marked her target. Talia snorted. An OSHA-compliant mob boss. "Safety first, I guess."

The clutch Talia carried was significantly lighter than the one she'd given Darcy in trade. Darcy had emptied most of its contents into the river, leaving only a phone, two tiny black boxes with alligator clips, wire cutters, and a bump key.

Talia pressed the bump key into the lock, applied turning pressure, and rhythmically tapped the head with the wire cutters. On the fourth tap, the lock turned. At the same time, something smashed into the back of her head.

Blinding pain.

Talia's world went dark.

CHAPTER FIFTY-TWO

Club Styx Milos,
Greek Isles
Time Unknown

The boat.

The moonlight on the water.

Finn looking down at her. Talia needed him.

No. Not exactly. She needed him to do something. What was it?

The kids. Hla Meh. Finn had to find the little girl.

"Wake up please."

Light flashed in her brain. Talia groaned. Pain throbbed at the back of her skull. She tried opening her eyes and shut them again, nauseated by the spinning of the world. Was the boat moving? That couldn't be right. Talia had left the boat with the team.

Fighting the urge to throw up, she opened her eyes once more. This time, she held them open, but they did her little good. Her world remained dim and blurry. She sat slumped in a chair, neck limp. Attempting to raise her head brought more pain. On a short pillar of black rock nearby, wavering in her double vision, she saw her phone.

The clock.

The time.

The whole mission hinged on Talia clipping Eddie's boxes to the electrical system to disengage the locks and cameras at the club's seaside loading dock. Had she gotten that far?

A man in a black suit sat near her, their knees almost touching. He spoke with a South African accent. "Wake up. You're almost there. I didn't hit you that hard."

"Yes, you did." The dizziness and pain refused to subside. "What time is it?"

"Why do you care?" He laid her clutch on the pillar, followed by its contents—the cutters, Eddie's black boxes, the stolen ID card, and the bump key. The fifth item he set down had not come from Talia's clutch. He laid a handgun on the pillar behind the rest, out of reach. Her inability to focus prevented Talia from determining the make or model.

After letting her squint at the weapon for a time, the man drew one final item from his belt and leaned forward to rest his elbows on his knees. Light glinted off steel. A knife. Talia felt the cold tip against her cheek, but she didn't have the strength to pull away. "Please."

"Please tell you the time? Please don't kill you?" He laughed. "I saw you slip into our utility hall from the monitor room. I'm sorry, my dear, but none of my people look this good in a dress."

"Just . . ." Talia shut her eyes and opened them again. No matter how hard she tried, she couldn't make the room stand still. "Just looking for the ladies' room."

"That old line? My goodness, I *am* dealing with an amateur." He let out a sigh, as if bored by her bravado. "If there's anything Mr. Jafet hates, it's unanswered questions. Before I let you die, I need to know what you were up to." He pulled the knife away and twisted it back and forth, letting the light bounce off the blade. "By hook or by crook, as it were."

Talia didn't like his phrasing. "*Let* me die?"

"You'll want to before I'm done." He pressed the knife against her cheek again. "Now, before I open the first of what could be many, *many* wounds, I'll give you one last chance to confess your sins." He pushed the tip up, not enough to break the skin, but enough for Talia to feel its sting. "Ten."

The gun. She couldn't get it to hold still in her vision long enough to make a play.

"Nine."

Why would God let this happen to her? Had he brought her all this way to fail?

"Eight."

Talia closed her eyes and opened them again. No change. Where was Tyler? Wasn't this the moment where he always swept in to save her?

"Seven."

Her heart began to pound. Her body tingled,

going numb. The more she fought to regain control, the more control fled from her.

"Six."

Maybe she could scramble, go wild. Maybe she would get lucky.

Lucky.

The idea sounded so utterly ridiculous in the urgency of the moment. Talia almost laughed. She no longer depended on luck, right? Her baptism had made that clear to the world. But what then? If a Christian didn't concern herself with luck, what did she depend on? Herself? That'd been Talia's answer these last few months, despite what she'd said to Val.

"Five."

Her own words came back to jab at her—the story of Christ pulling Peter up out of the water. Talia had battled through storms of late with sweat and bullets instead of faith, never once leaning on God, never once taking his hand and watching him calm the seas.

"Four."

She heard Conrad's voice from a few nights earlier. *You are strong and courageous, my child . . . Joshua, like you, was strong and courageous, not on his own, but because God was with him.*

"Three."

The knife turned. She could feel her captor's muscles tensing through the steel.

Dear God, I trust in you. Hla Meh and the

other children are in your hands, not mine. I trust you have a plan for them. I trust in you, God. I'm leaning on you. Amen.

"Two."

Something changed.

The dizziness evaporated. Talia opened her eyes. Her vision cleared.

"One."

A small whisper inside said, *Go!*

Talia wheeled her left hand up to knock the knife clear—not far, but enough to move. Her right hand went to the gun. She scooped it up by the barrel and lurched clear of a sweeping cut.

The chair fell backward.

The South African lunged, trying to prevent her from turning the gun around. It was a smart move, his only move, and Talia saw it coming. She spun left to dodge the stabbing blade and smashed the butt of the pistol into his temple.

The man collapsed in a heap.

Talia wasted no time in sweeping her tools into the clutch. She stumbled to the door and snuck a look into the tunnel. The utility room where she'd been caught was only two doors down. But before she could make a move, a shadow darkened the corner at the end of the hall.

Talia pulled back and closed the door to barely a slit. The man approaching the utility room looked like a guard. Almost. She pushed out into the hall. "Pell?"

The dizziness returned. Her shoulders fell back against the sharp edges of the obsidian wall.

"Talia." He ran to her side and put an arm around her waist to hold her up. "I was looking for you."

"I got . . . delayed."

"I can see that. You all right?"

She blinked twice. No double vision. At least she could still see. "I will be." God had answered Talia's prayer. He must want her to keep going.

Pell helped her off the wall, and the two ducked into the room with the unconscious security man. "Your work?"

"He started it."

Double rows of folding chairs hung on rolling racks against the wall. Pillar-style obsidian tables were stacked four high in the corner. The room, now that she could see clearly, looked more like a storage room than a holding cell. "I . . ." She touched the bump on the back of her head and winced. Blood darkened her fingers. "I don't think he told anyone about me. Not yet."

Pell kicked the fallen chair aside and lowered her into the one still standing. He worked the man's belt loose. "I take it you never breached the utility closet?"

"Negative. Are we too late?"

"Let's just say we're cutting things a mite close. We'd better get cracking." Pell rolled his unconscious friend over to secure his wrists and found a radio handset had been lying underneath him. He stared at the radio for a moment longer, then looked up at Talia. "This little mishap may work in our favor. Tell me about his accent."

"South African. I'm sure of it."

The chameleon's own accent morphed to match. "That's a good start, miss, but tell me more. Tell about his inflections, the depth of his tone. Tell me every detail you can remember."

CHAPTER FIFTY-THREE

**Club Styx Milos,
Greek Isles
11:23 pm**

A lift carried Talia up to the eighth-level balcony.
On the way, she took a long breath to fight the
nausea from the blow to her head. Thirty-seven
minutes. She had to endure thirty-seven more
minutes and either save Marco or die trying.

With Pell in play and armed with the tools to
handle the utility closet, Talia had returned to
her original mission—intercept Don Marco and
join him on his way to the 11:30 poker game with
Jafet. A date with death.

"Jafet plans to kill him," Tyler had told her.
"He'll do it at midnight, befitting his self-image
as a dark lord, at his private table overlooking the
club."

"Why so public?"

"Many moons ago, Marco was Jafet's biggest
rival. A lot of people remember, and Jafet will
want an audience of lost souls to witness his final
victory and spread the word. But don't worry.
He won't get a shot off. You're going to kill him
before he gets the chance."

That would be a trick without a gun of her own.

Talia had sacrificed the South African's pistol—a Heckler & Koch .45—to solve a cosmetic issue. The blood matting her hair was a dead giveaway that she had not come for a nice evening out. She and Pell had found a faucet in one of the utility rooms, but the water did more harm than good to the updo Val had given her. In the end, she dismantled the .45 and used its recoil spring as a hair screw to rearrange the style and cover the mess.

The gun would have done her little good anyway. The thugs guarding the staircase to Jafet's poker table weren't rocket scientists, but they weren't idiots either. She couldn't exactly waltz past them with an eight-inch .45 sticking half out of her clutch.

"Hurry up." Talia tapped her foot on the lift floor, willing the machine to rise faster. Her hiccup in the tunnels had left her running late.

Marco was not yet in view, but Talia had no trouble getting eyes on Val on the gaming island far below, hanging from Aku's neck like a glittering red stole. The Kongaran raked in a pile of chips at the roulette table. Val laughed and clapped. At least she was having a good time.

Darcy, too, was still in play.

Talia picked the chemist up at the edge of her vision, coming in from the other side of the island and heading straight for Val. The two timed their switch to perfection. Darcy hit Val and the mark in the narrow space between the poker and craps tables, wiggled between them, and came out the other side with a different clutch. If all had gone well, she had also left behind a gift for Aku.

The lift bumped to a stop at level 8. Tyler had predicted Jafet's men would bring Marco out into the open as close as possible to his private table, suspended from the dome by iron bars and attached to the balcony by an orange rhyolite staircase. He was right. At 11:26 p.m., four guards escorted the former Italian crime boss out of a passage less than twenty meters from the steps.

Talia was too far away, but she couldn't run around the balcony. They'd see her coming and read the play. She walked fast, heels clicking. Once Marco was up those stairs, out of reach, the whole game was over.

She was close—maybe ten meters—when a stumbling drunk blocked her path. He grabbed her bare shoulder. "Excuse me, pretty lady. You looking for a—" Whatever his intentions, he bought himself a jab to the liver.

Talia caught his arm to keep him from doubling over and guided him to the rail. "Oops. Are you all right? Maybe you should sit down."

By the time she let go, Marco and his guards had reached the steps. Her heart sank. In a last-ditch effort, she drew a breath to shout out. "Mm—"

Talia swallowed the call.

Marco had tripped on the first step up to the platform. A stall tactic. The guards stooped to steady him. Marco pushed them away, feigning offense at their condescension to his age. By the time the argument settled, Talia had closed the distance.

She scrunched her nose, as if utterly surprised to see him. "Marco?"

"Natalia! *Mia cara.*" He spread his arms.

She blew past the guards to embrace him. They kissed each other on both cheeks. He said something in Italian.

The shortest of Jafet's men—apparently the one in charge—tugged at her arm. "I am sorry, miss. Your friend has an appointment. He must go, and so must you."

"No. No." Talia swatted at him like a cat. Proximity was the key. "I have not seen this man in years. Who are you to part us again so soon?"

The guard clenched his teeth, but Marco intervened in a deep voice, soothing and frightening at the same time. "What are you afraid of, my friends? Hmm?" His dark eyes bored into the lead guard. "She is half the size of your smallest man."

Talia could see where Val got her talent for reading marks. A short man working security for a mob boss had guaranteed inferiority issues. Marco had poked the lead guard right in the soft center of a sensitive psychological bruise.

The guard struggled to find a response, and

the Italian pressed his advantage. "Would your master deny me one friendly face at my final game, hmm? Natalia is harmless. Leave her with me, and let us get on with this."

Before the guard could answer, his radio crackled.

A South African voice said, "Heads up on the ninth circle. The croupier is inbound."

"Copy. Dealer on the way. We will be ready." The guard frowned at Marco, then turned toward the stairs. "Come. We must prepare the platform."

"What about her?" asked the one closest to Talia.

The lead guard glared back at him, now three steps up, a head taller than the rest. "Do you think we cannot handle a woman in an evening gown?"

Talia patted Marco's arm, escorting him up the stairs. "Are we playing poker, Don Marco?"

"*Sì, mia cara.* Perhaps the most important poker game of my life."

"Then I am glad to be here." She faked a naïve smile. "I will bring you luck. I hope."

CHAPTER FIFTY-FOUR

Club Styx Milos,
Greek Isles
11:28 pm

The croupier, an older gentleman with gray hair and spectacles, arrived next to oversee the game and deal the cards, carrying an aluminum case handcuffed to his wrist. He acknowledged Talia with a nod as the men patted him down. "Madame."

She nodded back.

Jafet's men had taken up posts at the four corners of the platform. Standing behind Marco's chair and looking out over an obsidian rail embedded with gems, Talia could see all the action below. Val worked the tables with Aku, who always had a full drink in hand. Darcy had drifted out of sight—as expected. If all went to plan, she'd remain behind the scenes for the remainder of the night.

The croupier placed two trays of chips on the table and pushed them to either end, using a crook-like chip harrow. He set a third, double-layer tray at his right elbow, on Jafet's side.

"Jafet's reserves, I presume?" Marco thrust his square chin at the extra chips. "A show of force. The game is stacked against me already."

The croupier only smiled. He let a machine shuffle his cards and then twiddled his thumbs, waiting.

At 11:38 p.m., fashionably late, Jafet arrived. Marco stood to greet him, and the two met at the midpoint of the table like generals meeting for a parley on the field of battle. Jafet tucked a silver-headed cane under his arm to shake the Italian's hand. "Marco Calafato, how long has it been?"

"Too long, Orien. Too long."

"Indeed." As he returned to his seat, Marco checked a silver pocket watch. "I was concerned for your welfare, old friend. I thought we were to begin at half past."

Jafet made no excuse. His eyes flashed to Talia, standing behind the Italian. "I see you managed to bring a good luck charm, despite my best efforts to keep you all to myself."

"This is Natalia, whom I view as a goddaughter. We met by chance on the balcony."

"Chance, eh?" Jafet did not buy it. The look he cast at the lead guard told Talia the man's job might be forfeit. But then he chuckled. "I'll allow it. What is victory if no one from the losing side lives to tell the tale?"

At the not-so-subtle hint Marco would not survive the night, Talia laid a protective hand on his shoulder.

The old Italian gave her fingers a reassuring pat, never taking his eyes off his opponent.

"Thank you, old friend. Besides, I need her to shield my cards from the roving eyes of your men."

"You wound me, Marco. I would not cheat tonight—not with what lies at stake."

"Honor itself?"

"Just so. And with the stakes affirmed, it is time to begin."

They played five-card draw, the simplest and fastest of poker forms. Marco won the first three hands. Jafet took the fourth, with a larger pot than the first three put together. All the while, the two reminisced. Their rivalry had spanned nations and continents—around the Med and beyond. Sicily. Corsica. Barcelona. Bern.

Jafet's eyes burned with increasing heat, particularly when discussing those cities where his organization had lost ground. But the general flow of the pot to his side of the table seemed to keep his anger in check.

Soon that flow became a flood.

Marco lost one hand after the other. In some, he folded after the first bet, taking minimal hits. But in others, he pushed too far and fell short of Jafet on the call. As his pile of chips dwindled to a breaking point, Talia glanced at the island below to check on Val.

The grifter had pulled Aku to the east bridge, away from the tables. They were arguing—not a heated exchange, but an exaggerated discussion, like teenagers on a third date. Talia watched their lips. In her head, she could hear Val driving the script.

Take one picture of me from the top. Just one.

Why? You'll hardly be visible in the crowd.

A girl wants what a girl wants. Please, Aku. One picture. Get the whole club in the shot.

Aku looked up at the eighth-level balcony. Annoyed but malleable. More than a little tipsy. After a little more encouragement from Val, he set off across the bridge.

A rhythmic splash of chips drew Talia's focus back to the game. Jafet was looking straight at her. "Your good luck charm is distracted, old friend. She is failing at her purpose."

Marco remained cold, his expression unmoving. "Luck is a figment of the imagination. Poker is a skill, a learned balance of risk and reward." Marco's eyes, beneath that heavy brow, looked down at the pot. "It seems you are taking the ultimate risk. You've put me all in."

The dealer scooped all Marco's chips into a neat pile near the pot, and Jafet sat back, laughing without restraint. "You were all in the moment you left Campione. You made a play. I saw it coming. I call." He laid his cards on the table. "Three aces. Two kings. Full house."

Marco held his cards to his chest. "I am afraid I'm not following. What play do you speak of?"

In answer, Jafet reached into his jacket. Talia

tensed, but all he drew out was a miniature tablet. He laid it on the table, started a video application, and nodded for the croupier to slide the device over to Marco with his crook.

On the screen Aku walked along the eighth-level balcony. Talia checked the same spot and saw the Kongaran. The video was live.

Jafet snapped his fingers, and his short lead guard mumbled into his radio. Two guards converged on Aku. They caught him a few paces short of the steps to the platform.

The Kongaran struggled and protested. "A picture. I only wanted a picture."

"I don't believe him," Jafet said, addressing Marco. "After all, he is your man."

"My man?"

"Networks, Marco. The old analog methods you used to best me in Bern and Sicily became obsolete while you languished in retirement. The future is digital. It constrains us, creates choke points, and my network in Club Styx has the best decryption software money can buy." He pointed at Aku with his cane. "Earlier this evening, my sensors tracked a five-million-dollar payment from the account you used to cover your chips to an account belonging to that man—your assassin. Since then, my security force has watched his every move."

Aku's jacket started beeping. One of the guards held his arms while another dug a black orb with a flashing red LED out of his breast pocket. The beeping quickened. The guard's eyes widened, and he threw it out under the dome. The ball exploded with red sparks and a puff of gray smoke, eliciting a shocked *Ooo!* from the crowd.

"Not mine," Aku said, struggling against his captors. "It was not mine!"

The guards dragged him away.

Jafet leveled a silenced pistol at Marco's head. "Midnight is upon us, old friend, and you have played your full hand. Your time is up."

"Have I?" The Italian laid his cards face down on the green felt and checked his pocket watch. "Your clock must be off. There are still five seconds to midnight. Three . . . Two . . . One." He snapped his fingers.

With a synchronous *boom,* blue flashes erupted throughout the club. Smoke filled every alcove where the guards had stood.

The crowd cheered and clapped, thinking the display must be a continuation of Aku's fireworks. They seemed not to notice or care that when the smoke cleared, the guards were gone.

Jafet cared. He glanced around, as if expecting his platform guards to have gone up in smoke as well. They hadn't. His eyes narrowed at Marco. "What have you done?"

"Some of the old ways still work, Orien. The shell game, for instance. It is all about misdirection." Marco nodded at the mini-tablet that had played the live video of Aku. "You wasted your attentions on the wrong cup, and it has cost you."

Jafet's bronze complexion had turned red. "Whatever trick you've played has cost me nothing. A few grunts, perhaps. I still have you under my gun." He tapped his full house with a manicured fingernail. "I'm still holding the best hand."

"Are you?" Marco flipped his cards. All hearts. Ace. King. Queen. Jack. Ten.

Jafet stared at the cards, as if a wish and a hard look could change them, then glared at the croupier. "Those are *not* as they should be."

The Frenchman refused to meet his gaze.

"I will deal with you shortly, as soon as I put a bullet through our guest's head." He thrust the pistol out, finger tightening on the trigger. "Goodbye, Mar—"

"Yeah. Okay. No problem." The croupier interrupted Jafet's big moment. His accent had switched from French to Moldovan.

Jafet gave him a quizzical look, turning the gun sideways. "What?"

The crook-shaped chip harrow flashed out and hooked the mobster's wrist. The gun went off. The lead guard, on Talia's left, let out a gurgling cry and clutched his throat. He dropped to his knees, blood seeping between his fingers.

Pell—the croupier—twisted the harrow, and the gun flopped onto the pile of chips.

At the same time, Talia stepped back to her right, elbow flying. She caught the second guard under the chin and his head snapped back. He collapsed, unconscious.

The last two guards each took a step toward the fight. Pell's hand came down hard, upending the double tray of chips. They flew into the air and exploded with a peppering of blue, green, and yellow pops.

As the guards drew back, covering their faces, Pell freed a gray composite gun taped to the bottom of the double tray and threw it to Talia. She caught it by the grip, slid her finger into the trigger guard, and put two rounds into each man.

Jafet raised his hands. "How?"

"These are my successors, Orien." Marco raised his voice so everyone under the dome could hear. "You've met Natalia." Val came walking up the steps, accepting a second weapon from Pell. "And this is Valerie. Your friends at *the Jungle* know them as the Macciano Sisters. You speak of the future, Orien? These two are the future. And they are taking your seat at the table."

Every eye in the club watched Val and Talia claim their places at Marco's shoulders, standing tall in their black and red evening gowns. And every eye watched them empty their magazines into Jafet's jerking form.

CHAPTER FIFTY-FIVE

Club Styx
Milos, Greek Isles

Jafet fell beside his men, and the crowd of lost souls screamed and shouted in dismay. Talia took full advantage of the confusion. Walking to the railing, she pointed a finger of condemnation at the onlookers below, turned her palm upward, and clenched her fist.

The River Styx exploded into the air. Walls of water crashed down on the gaming tables from all sides, knocking guests off their feet. By the time anyone looked up again, the sisters were gone.

The girls, Pell, and Marco carried Jafet's limp form into the eighth-level surveillance room, now void of security guards. They dropped him ignobly on the floor. On a few screens in the bank of monitors, drenched souls fought over chips. On others, armed soldiers in gray-green tactical gear marched guards and workers through the utility tunnels.

Two men in similar gear were there to greet her. The older one, the Agency's man embedded in the Special Tactics Squadron at Incirlik Air Base, inclined his head toward the monitors. "Once we secured the outer perimeter, we restored the cameras for our own use." He held out two tiny boxes with alligator clips. "I believe these are yours."

Talia accepted the boxes and dropped them into her clutch. "Major Ruiz. Good to see you again."

"Nyx. Always a pleasure." One corner of his mouth curled into a smile, making the black and gray stubble on his chin catch the light. "The men still talk about that business in the Black Sea. And they loved tonight's fireworks display."

"Well, I can't take all the credit. Our team is"— she turned to introduce Val, Pell, and Don Marco, but they had left—"shy, apparently."

At her feet, Jafet groaned and squirmed. The vapor from more than a dozen nonlethal P3Q rounds was finally wearing off, Tyler's own diabolical blend of pepper spray and 3-quinuclidinyl benzilate. The ocular pain and shock of the pepper spray made the paralytic coma effect of the 3Q more predictable and nearly instantaneous. She gave him a poke in the ribs with a toe. "Shut up, you."

The younger soldier knelt to bind and gag the mob boss. "Wait," he said, pausing to blink as he cinched the zip cuffs tight. "This is Nyx? *The* Nyx?" His eyes traveled up from Talia's spiked heels to her sparkling onyx earrings.

She frowned down at him.

Ruiz slapped him upside the head. "Quit

drooling." He lifted the man to his feet by the strap of his tactical vest and shoved him toward the hallway. "Go get Samuels and Bedford and carry this scumbag out to the boat. And make sure his people don't see him. Can you handle that?"

The kid was halfway out the door by the time he answered. "Yes, sir."

A one-shouldered shrug lifted the barrel of the major's M4 carbine. "Sorry, Nyx. Price of fame and all that."

Ever since her first intersection with Ruiz, stopping the launch of hypersonic missiles from a secret base in the Black Sea, Talia's legend in the Special Forces community had grown. Most of the stories had no basis in truth. The men had dubbed her Nyx after the Greek goddess of night—strangely, the mother of the ferryman who'd brought her team into the club. The sudden realization of this connection made Talia blanch.

Jafet tried to roll over.

Talia placed a heel between his shoulder blades to keep him still. "What's to become of our friend here?"

"He's wanted in several nations for a host of crimes, including murder. Once it gets out that we have him, there'll be a massive food fight. Nice of you to spare his life, Nyx. But if the Russians or Egyptians get ahold of him, he's toast."

"Their call. How about we wait awhile, though? Keep him on ice for a bit."

"Oh. We will." Ruiz rested a boot on Jafet's rear end and leaned in, earning a pained grunt. "Dude had his hand in all the wrong cookie jars. We've got weeks of intelligence to pull from his twisted little mind."

On the monitor behind him, a pair of soldiers dragged an unconscious Aku across the outer dock. Talia nodded to direct Ruiz's gaze. "What about the Kongaran?"

"We'll drop him on his boat between the dummy containers, like the drunk bum he is. His men will never see us, and Aku will never remember the last hour. Tell your buddy Tyler I took care of the rest. My man in the Royal Thai Rangers is at his disposal."

"Will do." She shook his hand and turned to go. "Thanks for everything."

"Anytime, Nyx. Godspeed on the next phase of your op."

CHAPTER FIFTY-SIX

Mae Surin Jungle Highlands
Mae Hong Son Province, Thailand

The forest canopy filtered the gray light of dawn, turning everything a shade of green, including Po. The refugee walked a few paces ahead of Finn and Ewan, following the blood trail. Half an hour after sunrise, he stopped, raised a fist, and said something in Thai.

"He found another wire pen." Ewan bent to his knees for a breather and offered Finn a hit from an old-school canteen. "Water?"

Finn wiggled the CamelBak drinking tube hanging at his shoulder. "I'm fine. Came prepared."

"Right. I forgot. Commando."

"Thief."

"Whatever."

The new holding pen looked much like the last two they'd found. Spent bandages and junk food wrappers were strewn about. Po took on a sad expression and raised a small sandal with yellow straps, hanging from his pinky.

Somewhere a little girl—no more than eight, by the size of the sandal—slogged through the jungle with one bare foot, driven by her captors.

Finn's hand went to his weapon. "Look for the blood trail. We need to keep moving."

"There is no trail." Ewan swept a slow path back and forth through the tangled brush beyond the pen's gate. "Whoever was wounded stopped bleeding after this stop." He straightened as Finn came over to him. "Perhaps that's a good sign."

"Or perhaps not." Finn lowered his voice when he said it. He had not forgotten that one of the missing children was Po's son. And the Thai man understood at least some English.

But without the blood trail, how could they continue the search?

They gave it a shot. Using a terrain map, Finn connected the dots from pen to pen. The line curved, but the kidnappers had driven the children generally south. The three took a heading and marched on.

An hour later, the jungle looked exactly the same.

"Water break." Finn nodded at Ewan's canteen. "Drink. You need the hydration."

"You too."

"Yeah, I know. Thanks." As he unhooked the CamelBak tube and set it between his lips, Finn turned in a slow circle, taking in the endless green. But the green wasn't endless. At least, it wasn't unchanging. One sector seemed lighter. He checked the compass clipped to his belt. "Ewan. Look southwest. Tell me what you see."

The Compassion man followed his gaze. After a moment, he nodded. Both men said what they were thinking at the same time.

"A road."

They marched two hundred meters more and stepped out from the trees onto gravel and red dirt.

"Big truck came through here," Finn said, kneeling to draw a finger across a muddy tire track. "A few days ago, maybe. I don't know. Two sets of tires on the rear axle, though—a dually. A sheepherder who dated my mom drove the same type."

Po looked Finn right in the eye and rattled off a few sentences.

"He says big trucks don't use this road. Too dangerous and totally unnecessary. There's a better road to the east that joins all the villages in the region."

Finn gave the refugee a shrug, addressing him directly. "Makes sense for our kidnappers. They'd want to steer clear of prying eyes."

They kept looking, and a few paces up the road, Po found footprints. Lots of them. He'd found the place the kidnappers loaded up the children. "But the tire tracks look the same in both directions," Ewan said. "Finn, can you tell which way they went?"

He wished he could say yes, but he'd never learned proper tracking skills. The frustration of his inadequacy made him a little cranky. "I told you. I'm not a commando. I'm—"

"A thief. We get it." Ewan seemed to let Finn's anger flow right past him. He got down on his knees in the grass beside the road and bowed his head.

"What are you doing?"

"Praying. Hush."

Finn turned to Po. The refugee got down and bowed his head as well.

The thief huffed, shaking his head. "Great. You two gents have at it. In the meantime, I'll try to do something useful." He walked the road.

Fifty meters or more along the northwest track, something silver flashed in the sun. Finn snatched it up and jogged back to the others in triumph. "Oi, fellas! Look at this!"

Ewan made him wait for several seconds while he finished his prayer. As he stood, he eyed Finn's trophy. "It's . . . litter."

"Not just any litter." Finn pulled two more wrappers from his pocket. All three bore the same green and yellow logo on a silver background. "I collected these from the pens. One of our kidnappers is particular about his junk food. And since we know where they loaded up and where this was dropped, we can make a good bet which way they were headed."

Instead of patting Finn on the back, Ewan lifted his eyes skyward and said, "Praise God."

Po raised his hands to match the sentiment.

"God? I'm the one who searched the road. *I* found the wrapper."

"*Because* Po and I prayed and asked for direction."

"I . . . You . . ." Before Finn could muster up an argument, he heard the rumble of an approaching truck. His eyes narrowed. "Po says no one uses this road, right?"

Ewan and the refugee both nodded.

"Into the trees. Now."

They ducked into the foliage and watched as a beat-up Toyota HiLux rolled to a stop a few feet away. The driver leaned his head out. "Come oot, come oot wherever ya are."

"Mac." Finn led the others into the open, waving. " 'Bout time you showed up. Did you have trouble tracking my signal?"

"The mountains make it spotty at best." The Scotsman slapped his door. "Borrowed this beauty from the airfield manager. Whaddaya think?"

The introductions went as well as Finn might have predicted, revisiting the whole Scottish-Thai thing. With that out of the way, Po hopped into the back, and Finn and Ewan crammed themselves into the cab. As they drove off, Ewan looked skyward again and offered up a thankful nod.

"What was that for?" Finn asked.

"I also asked God if he could find us a ride."

CHAPTER FIFTY-SEVEN

Bo Suphan
Suphan Buri Province, Thailand

Gorev despised central Thailand, a sweaty alluvial plain covered in wet fields and little else. No cover. He let the Bentley roll to a stop more than a mile from the cinder-block structures where Panther Five One and his people waited. The two buildings were already visible in the light haze hanging over the rice fields. Five One had not reached his elevated status without some modicum of intelligence. He might be watching. Any closer, and Gorev would give his boss away. "I walk from here."

"Yes, yes. Fine," said Boyd, preoccupied with his phone.

"You drive, da?" They had not discussed that part of the plan before leaving the Twin Tigers. Boyd usually did not sully himself by participating in this end of things. Gorev had never seen him get behind the wheel of a car.

"Yes, I can drive. As long as it's an automatic."

Gorev just looked at him.

Boyd kept working his phone, bristling. "You have something to say about a well-to-do gentleman who can't work a manual gearbox?"

"*Nyet.*"

"Then get out and let me do my thing."

As Gorev opened the door, Boyd touched his bicep. "Wait. The Maltese Tiger is dead."

"The Greek?"

"Guess who took him out." Boyd turned the phone for him to see and played a video. Gaming tables and well-dressed partiers whirled and swung through chaotic footage until the camera settled on three distant figures, standing on a platform beneath an obsidian dome. A pair of women armed with pistols fired round after round into a gray-haired man. The partiers screamed and shouted.

Boyd stopped the playback. "Cobra One Eleven posted it this morning. And there were four others. All claim the shooters are the Macciano Sisters. One claims it was a full-on hostile takeover, involving the daughters of Marco Calafato, the retired crime boss." He snapped his fingers. "Check on our new hawks. Now."

Gorev lifted a tablet from his nylon rifle bag. "Affirmative. Hawk Four One Eight claims she and sister took out Maltese Tiger instead of field mouse. They send thirty-five-million-dollar apology for"—he squinted at the word—"*im-prov-is-a-tion.* Do you accept?"

"I think we can accept," Boyd said after a time. "But the dead Greek leaves us an opening at the Frenzy."

"Who shall I invite?"

"Who do you think? With Jafet gone, we can bring four new panthers to the party. Thirty-five million puts both sisters in the running. Send the new invitation." He flicked his fingers. "Now get out. I have work to do. You have twenty minutes."

As he walked beside the road, rifle slung at his shoulder, Gorev called up the videos of the shooting. None were stable, but one gave him a grainy profile view of the woman in the black dress. He held the screen close to his eyes, shielding it from the sun. *"Intriguyushchiy."* *Intriguing.*

Twenty minutes later, Gorev lay prone among the low stalks of a rice paddy a hundred meters from the rendezvous, feeling what smelled like raw sewage soak into his clothes. The bipod of his FN Ballista rifle would not stay upright in such an environment. He had to support it with one hand, sinking his elbow into the muck.

He sighed. His services were worth more than this.

A thumping sounded in his ear. "Is this thing on? Gorev, you hear me?"

"Transmitter go only one way," he said to the mud. "Idiot."

Boyd's car came into view across the road, pulling into a gravel lot between the pair of cinder-block structures. He climbed out of the

Bentley and slammed the door. Another teeth-rattling noise in the Russian's earpiece.

Gorev put his eye to his scope and set the crosshairs slightly ahead of his boss, adjusting for the quick pace of his gait. How easy it would be to cut the puppet from the strings. But the puppet master would not like this, so he refrained.

A man in fatigues stepped out of the western building to greet Boyd. Satisfied this was Panther Five One, Gorev panned around in a radial search pattern to identify additional targets. There were five—four grown men and a teenager, all armed with Kalashnikovs.

No problem.

"Mr. Boyd," he heard Five One say through his boss's hidden transmitter. "We were expecting your man two days ago."

Boyd gave him a used-car-salesman smile. "I wanted to come out and see the product myself. Hence, the delay. I hope it's all right."

Panther Five One gestured at the door, and Gorev lost sight of them as they entered the building. The transmitter crackled with interference from the cinder-block structure.

"Is this all of them?"

"No sir. Half are here. Half in the other building."

"These look healthy enough, except for that one."

"Yes, but he is not the type of product you

asked for, is he? We'll put him down before we leave."

"I wouldn't waste the bullet. He'll expire soon enough. I think I'm ready to move forward. I'll just need to see the others."

"Yes. Right away."

The door opened, and Gorev saw Boyd for an instant before the Englishman backed into the shadows again. "Please," he heard him say, "after you."

Gorev kept his scope on the door and laid his finger on the trigger. The moment was fast approaching. Five One came out first, followed by the two soldiers who'd gone in with him, and then Boyd.

When all four were in the open, Boyd drew a silenced Beretta. "That's far enough."

Panther Five One shouted in Thai. Two of his soldiers reacted with decent timing, but not fast enough. Gorev pulled the trigger twice. They both fell. The others clued in and raised their rifles high in surrender, except for the teen, who froze. Gorev let out a breath. If the boy so much as twitched, he'd have to put him down.

"What are you doing?" Five One asked. "We had a deal. You said you would connect me with buyers."

Boyd walked two paces closer. "I said I'd connect your *product* with buyers. Tell your men they work for me now."

When his victim hesitated, Boyd pressed the silencer to his forehead. Five One stammered out a few sentences of Thai. His men nodded their understanding. The teen let his rifle hang from its strap. Gorev gave him a quiet grunt. He'd live another day.

"Any of you speak English?" Boyd asked.

One of the soldiers raised a tentative hand.

"Good. Come here." The Englishman stepped out of the way. "Put your rifle to your boss's head and pull the trigger." When the soldier dragged his feet, Boyd thrust his pistol at him. "Don't make me ask again."

"Still," Gorev muttered, drawing his eye from the scope and jerking his elbow out of the muck, "you cannot do own wet work." He had no desire to watch. The echo of the Kalashnikov's three-round burst told him the job was done.

CHAPTER FIFTY-EIGHT

Milos National Airport
Milos, Greek Isles

The crew arrived at the AS2's hangar on Milos in midmorning after a short sleep. Cleanup at Club Styx had taken some time. Talia, along with Tyler, who had shown up at fifteen past midnight, had lingering guests to shoo away.

"Some people just can't take a hint," Tyler had said, using a few well-placed rounds to encourage a pack of drunks to wade off down the ferryman's tunnel.

Eddie had gobs of files to download. Pell and Darcy had weapons and ammo to collect from Jafet's armory, and Val had dozens of ten-sided gem dice to gather from the balcony game tables.

A message was waiting for Talia at the computer station Eddie had set up beside the jet. Finn wanted to talk. She called up the video chat application on the center screen and dialed his number.

"Hey, there." Finn looked down into the camera from the passenger seat of a pickup truck. The image froze, jittered, and froze again, with only fleeting seconds of clarity. "How was the club?"

"The usual. Lots of noise. Self-indulgent patrons. Left me with a splitting headache."

"Headache?" Finn seemed to catch her subtext. "You injured?"

So, he did care. "Bump on the head. That's all."

"Wish I'd been there."

"Yeah. Me too." She shifted the conversation. He hadn't left the message just to check on her. "What about the kids?"

"Still looking. We tracked 'em to a road in the jungle. A goat herder walking the same stretch saw a pair of covered troop carriers two days back. Got pretty riled about it once we got him on the subject. Gave us a pretty fair description. Seems they ran him and his black Bengalis right off the track."

Her heart dropped. Talia didn't know what, exactly, she had dared to hope for, but it was more than a description of some trucks. "Okay." She tried not to sound disappointed. "What's next?"

"We're asking after them at every fuel stop and village. Got a few leads. Looks like they're heading toward Bangkok." He turned his phone so that Talia could see the man beside him, a Thai man in a muddy button-down and jeans. "Helps to have a translator. We'd never have gotten this far without Ewan here."

"I'm sorry. You're breaking up. It sounded like you said that Thai man was Ewan."

The Thai man rolled his eyes and shook his head as Finn turned the camera back to himself.

"Another fuel stop's coming up. Gotta go." The call ended.

Looking past the monitor, Talia saw Val, Tyler, and Don Marco at the edge of the hangar, looking grave.

"But you can't," Val said to Marco as Talia walked over. "They'll arrest you the moment you show up at customs."

The Italian gave her a fatherly smile. "Do you think I did not know this when I left Campione?"

"So avoid customs all together. Your jet—"

"—is not coming back. My orders."

"This is my fault. I should never have called you."

"It was the right thing, *figlia mia*. The only thing. Part of a greater plan." Don Marco took Val's hand in both of his. "And I was glad to be here. Seeing you in this work warms my heart. You will dismantle the evils of Jafet's organization, and do the same to a far greater monster—Livingston Boyd." He raised her fingers and kissed them. "I am so proud."

Still holding her hand, as if unwilling to let go yet, Don Marco turned to Tyler. "You will take care of the house, my people?"

Tyler nodded. "If that is what you wish. But Val's right. You don't have to do this. You don't owe anyone."

"That is where you are wrong, *amico mio*. My eternal account is credited, yes. But wrongs as grievous as mine demand earthly consequences. The time has come for me to face them."

The dismay in Val's expression left Talia puzzled. She had spoken with such disdain of her father before. They'd been estranged for years, yet now she refused to be parted from him. "What about the talk we never had?" asked the grifter, on the verge of tears. "We could go somewhere, sit down for a while."

"I have seen all I need to see—heard all I need to hear." Don Marco took Tyler's hand as well and placed it in Val's. "This, whatever it may be, has my blessing."

A shout from the computer station stole Talia's attention. Eddie slapped his fidget spinner down on the folding table. "We're in!"

When she looked back again, Val had buried her head in Tyler's shoulder. Don Marco was ambling away across the tarmac toward a commercial jet—an old man with nothing but a rolling suitcase to his name.

CHAPTER FIFTY-NINE

Bo Suphan
Suphan Buri Province, Thailand

The days and nights in the cinder-block building had blurred together. Thet Ye couldn't remember how long they'd been there. Aung Thu did not remember either, and he no longer answered when Thet Ye asked.

When the soldiers had herded them inside—a barefoot race from the truck to the building—Thet Ye had seen a matching structure across the road. He could only hope Hla Meh, Teacher Rocha, and Pastor Nakor were in there. They had been taken in the other truck. He hated being separated from his best friend, not knowing if they'd ever see each other again, not knowing if she'd ever forgive him.

Most of the children in Thet Ye's building were boys. They slept on the dirt floor. They ate whatever the soldiers threw at them. They drank from a pail of water left in the corner each morning.

Early in their stay, when the soldiers left them alone, a few whispered of escape. Aung Thu's friend Su Chat even tried to sneak a look through the curtain covering the door. Soe Htun, the leader with the burn scars, caught him. The yelling—the slapping and kicking—was more than Thet Ye could watch. Afterward Thet Ye had gone to Su Chat, but the boy crawled away to hide in the corner. No one spoke of escape from then on.

Thet Ye knew how to pray. Teacher Rocha had shown him, and he liked to pray out loud whenever she asked for a student volunteer. "Prayer is not a list of desires and requests," she would say. "Prayer should be a conversation. We begin with praise and thankfulness because God deserves it, even when we're sad."

In the doldrums of surviving, prayer had become Thet Ye's constant companion. And once he got started, he'd been surprised how easy thankfulness came. He waited in line to scoop a handful of water from the pail, then bowed his head for another. "Thank you, God, that we are alive. Thank you for sending Pastor Nakor and Teacher Rocha with us. Thank you for the food and water we have."

Shouting outside interrupted him, followed by the *rat-a-tat* report of a machine gun. The boys closest to the curtain door scooted backward into the room, pressing against the others—a learned response. Activity meant someone was coming, and no one wanted to be in a soldier's path when he came through.

More shouting.

A long silence.

About the time Thet Ye and the others dared to breathe again, the teenage soldier staggered through the curtain. His weapon hung from its strap, bouncing against his legs. He didn't seem to notice the children. He kept walking, and they stumbled over one another trying to get out of his way. He stopped in the middle of the room.

They watched.

An older soldier came in next. "What are you doing? I told you to get them lined up!"

Shaken from his stupor, the teen tried to obey. He took up his gun and yelled, "You heard him. Get up! Get moving!" But he walked backward as he spoke and tripped over poor Aung Thu.

The teenager toppled into a pack of terrified boys. His hands never left the machine gun. His finger never left the trigger. When his shoulder hit the floor, the gun went off.

This did not go well for anyone.

The bullets etched a line in the cinder blocks above the older soldier's head. The whites of his eyes grew two sizes. He stormed past scrambling children and put the barrel of his gun under the teenager's chin, lifting him to his feet. "I should kill you. I should kill you right now as I killed Soe Htun. Give me a reason not to!"

The same terror that paralyzed the children around him, paralyzed the teen. The older soldier growled, then flipped the rifle around and smashed the butt into his forehead.

The teen crumpled, crying.

In that moment, Thet Ye knew for certain Pastor Nakor had spoken truth. The teen soldier was a captive child like the rest of them, a captive child with a gun.

Blinking in the sunlight, the children from both buildings lined up on either side of the road. Hla Meh was there. Thet Ye tried to call to her but found his voice almost gone. It came out as a hoarse whisper.

She didn't hear him.

"Hurry up. Get them organized." The soldier who'd hit the teenager barked the orders. Had he killed Soe Htun as he claimed? Had he taken over? Something had clearly changed. One of the trucks waited in the road, engine idling. They were being moved again.

The soldiers pulled boys and girls out of each line. Children shuffled across the road with armed escorts in a strange trading game until Thet Ye's line was all boys, and Hla Meh's all girls. He saw no sign of Teacher Rocha or Pastor Nakor.

The new man in charge pounded the side of the truck to get his soldiers' attention. "Good. Now, load up the girls. New boss. New orders."

The men shouted and shoved. Most of the girls complied. The implications did not sink in for Thet Ye until the first of them climbed onto the tailgate.

One truck.

Girls only.

They were taking Hla Meh, and there was nothing he could do to stop them.

A few girls failed to move, too dazed to understand. Hla Meh was among them.

"Round up the stragglers. We have a schedule to keep."

Perhaps to make up for his previous failure, the teen soldier moved in to help. He grabbed Hla Meh by the wrist. "Move it!"

At the force of his jerking, her eyes found focus—and Thet Ye. He saw no blame, only a cry for help. With her free hand, she reached for him. "Thet Ye!"

He needed no other call.

Thet Ye bolted from the line to catch her hand. Their fingers were a hair's breadth apart when the teen soldier punched him in the chest and sent him sprawling back.

He lay there in the gravel, unable to breathe, unable to speak, watching them drag his best friend kicking through the dirt. "Thet Ye! Don't let them take me!"

In seconds, she had disappeared into the darkness beneath the canvas. As the teen soldier slammed the gate into place, the air returned to Thet Ye's lungs. "I'll find you," he called in his hoarse whisper, feeling tears on his cheeks for the first time in days. "I promise, I'll find you."

CHAPTER SIXTY

Milos National Airport
Milos, Greek Isles

The airfield's only tug operator took his sweet time towing the AS2 out of the hangar. He was working on a Greek island clock, which seemed to match the pace of island clocks Talia had experienced in other parts of the world.

Without Mac, Tyler was forced to take the helm of the AS2. "Run the briefing," he called as he taxied the jet toward the runway. "I'm listening."

"Copy." Eddie saluted, even though Tyler wasn't looking. "First item is the new White Lion message."

Seated beside him, Talia blocked his finger to keep him from touching PLAY. "Are you sure it's safe?"

Pell laughed at her from across the aisle. "You do know that we're still on the ground, right? What's the worst that could happen?"

"You weren't here for the last one."

Her tone cowed the chameleon.

"It's fine." Eddie moved his tablet out of her reach and his fingers flashed over the digital keyboard. "I brought this message in before we boarded, and it's clean. Worms,

346

Trojans, polymorphs—I've scanned for every malicious file you can imagine, and a few you can't. Besides"—he finished typing, and the laughing lion materialized in three dimensions over a black ring resting on one of the jet's oak tables—"I'm no longer using the aircraft display system."

"You brought your holographic generator," Talia said.

Eddie grinned.

The laughing faded, and the word *Congratulations* floated around the lion in gold metallic print. Bubbling champagne glasses appeared. "Well done, panther. You've reached the top of the food chain. Now you have a new challenge." The bubbling champagne, the floating text—everything on the screen but the lion—turned blood red. "The Frenzy."

Val pushed a strand of hair back over her ear, and Talia saw a tissue concealed in her hand. Marco's departure seemed to have hit her hard. She hid it well, a cavalier frown on her lips. "Last time, Boyd told us to kill someone. Let's see what he says now."

The whole team fell back against their seats as Tyler pushed the throttles up for takeoff. The AS2 left the runway within seconds, and the video played on.

"How good are you, panther? Time to find out. Take your shot at one of the Jungle's top five positions." The lion's whiskered snout contorted into a smirk. "Even mine."

The video changed to an aerial shot of Bangkok. The camera flew between a pair of ultra-skyscrapers Eddie had shown the group before. "This year's location is the Twin Tigers complex in Bangkok. As always, anonymity holds primacy. Bring no phones or computers. Be warned. The Frenzy competition is as cutthroat as it gets. Opt out, if you wish. Join us at your peril."

Voices whispered in the background. *Law of the Jungle. Kill or be killed.*

"*Eat* or be eaten." The camera turned, and the video settled on the towers and the white marble square below. "Once you set foot in my lair," the lion said, appearing as a ghost before them, "you are committed. That is all." The image faded to black.

"All?" Pell stared at the empty space in the holographic sphere. "He didn't tell us a thing. How does the Frenzy work? What are the rules?"

"Eat or be eaten, yes?" Darcy said. "And somehow, I do not think this is a *métaphore*."

"Hang on." Eddie held up a finger. "The message has a text component. Val and Talia, now Panthers Eight One and Eight Two, are to report to the lobby of the western tower tomorrow night—Val at eight p.m., Talia at eight oh five."

"What else does it say?" Tyler stood in the narrow hallway between the cabin and the flight deck. Concern creased his brow. He waved off a question from Pell before the chameleon could get the words out. "The autopilot's doing fine, Pell. Trust me." As he spoke, the AS2 leveled out on its own. The engines throttled back for cruise.

Eddie shook his head. "Nothing. They each have a seven-digit number. I assume they're entry codes."

Talia read the worry on Tyler's face. Their adversary had given them too little to go on.

Val echoed the same concern. "How do we run the last con if we won't know the rules of Boyd's game?"

"We remain flexible," Tyler said. "We keep the plan fluid and focus on knowns instead of unknowns."

Pell raised a hand. "We know the time and place, right? And you've got contacts. Have the Thai police storm the towers. End of story."

"Too risky. Bangkok cops are notoriously corrupt. They'll tip Boyd off. And the tower chopper pads make for an easy getaway. If we want to go in hard, we use the military, and we wait until the last second." Tyler glanced around at his crew. "Other ideas?"

Eddie brought up the holographic image of the towers. "We can expect comm jamming. The lion said no phones or computers. He can enforce that rule with jammers on the upper floors without blocking signals in the city below."

"Good catch. Solution?"

"I'll put Franklin on it. Right now. "

Talia watched him open a messaging app on his tablet, then looked to Tyler and shrugged. "We also know Boyd himself, right? He's rich. He's a sociopath."

"Narcissist, actually," Val said, tapping her chin. "There's a difference. But you're on to something. Knowing the identity of the White Lion tells us volumes. We have Livingston Boyd, the young energy stock and real estate mogul, and the White Lion, the bloodthirsty crime boss."

"Both sides of his personality," Pell said. "Put them together, and we have a complete picture of the man—a sort of 'What's a diabolical criminal mastermind when he's at home' profile."

Val rocked forward to rest her elbows on the oak table, as if her mind had suddenly gone to work and her hands were looking to follow. "Eddie, show me the layout of the western tower."

"I don't have much." The skyscrapers reappeared in the hologram, and a blueprint overlaid the twisting structure. Most of the floors were blank. "One of Boyd's shell companies handled the development. Whatever he's done with the upper floors is a big secret."

Val walked to the display and used her hands to expand the blueprint, examining a large, open chamber near the tower's top. "What about this? The rest of the building is one-way glass, but these are clear. The video shows greenery inside."

Eddie shrugged. "The blueprint calls it an atrium—actually *the* Atrium."

Tyler pushed himself off the wall, watching her. "What've you got, Val?"

"The difference between a narcissist and a sociopath is the need for validation. Both manipulate others, and both presume they are better and smarter, but a narcissist needs to be *told* he's better." She spun the chamber within the hologram. "A jungle environment, high above the world. Boyd built this to show off, like a throne room. If we pique his interest during the Frenzy, he'll bring us here. This is where we'll get him."

CHAPTER SIXTY-ONE

Aeron AS2
Andaman Sea
Twenty-Eight Thousand Feet
Descending into Bangkok

Three and a half hours after Eddie played the White Lion's message, Talia dropped into the AS2's copilot seat, careful not to disturb the side-mounted flight control stick inches from her armrest. "Finn called. He had news."

Tyler worked a touchscreen panel on the console between them. "Good or bad?" he asked without looking up.

"Good. I think. His canvassing northwest of Bangkok paid off. A street-market water dealer remembered seeing the trucks. She was adamant they were the ones he and Mac are looking for."

"So we know the trucks passed through her village."

"Not exactly." Talia did her best to rein in the hope in her voice. "The shop owner spotted the trucks on her way into town. Parked. She saw them at an isolated facility a good distance from the road."

"And the trucks are still there?"

She shook her head. "But that doesn't mean the

kids aren't. I told Finn to sit tight. He and Mac will keep watch until we arrive."

A radio call interrupted them. Tyler turned a dial on the dash to set a target altitude of fifteen thousand and pressed the dial in to signal the autopilot. The AS2 pitched down a few degrees. He glanced at her sideways. "You committed the team without consulting me?"

"Rescuing those kids is the only thing that matters."

"Rescuing those kids is *important,* and *right,* but it is not the *only* thing, Talia. Our best shot at saving them is to go after the source. Boyd. And we're short on time."

"What if we're wrong. What if the kidnapping has nothing to do with the Frenzy, and this is our last shot before those children are dispersed into the trafficking networks?"

Tyler sighed, closing his eyes. When he opened them again, he pointed to a digital map display on the center console. "The place we call Bangkok is really a dense urban metropolis of interlocking cities. It is broad. It is packed. And traffic is a nightmare like you've never experienced. If we land downtown, we'll never reach Finn."

She couldn't read the subtext in his statement. "What are you saying?"

"I'm saying we need to find another airfield. We'll play it your way. We'll rendezvous with Finn and check out the site."

Tyler landed the AS2 at a Thai military field. When the controller challenged him on his request for an approach, Tyler asked to speak to General Ta Maew. No general came on the radio. The controller immediately cleared him to land. He also offered up a military jeep.

The rendezvous point was an orchard filled with giant spiny fruit. Talia poked at a trio of them. "What do you call these, Ewan?"

"They are *Mong Thong*, meaning golden pillow."

She pressed the tips of the spines. They were hard enough to leave impressions in her fingertips. "Not my kind of pillow."

"Look more like medieval weapons," Mac said. "We could stick 'em on pikes and swing 'em at the kidnappers."

"Or we could use guns." Tyler lifted a pair of machine guns from the back of the jeep. He had brought a case of them from the jet.

"P3Q?" Talia asked as he tossed her one.

"What else?"

Tyler brought out extra magazines for Mac and Finn as well, and the team set to work. Grifter, chemist, wheelman, burglar, and spy—everyone but Eddie the hacker—inspected and readied their weapons like a professional hit team.

Po laughed and said something in Thai. Ewan laughed as well.

"What are you two on about?" Finn asked, stuffing his spare mag into his khakis.

"Po has invented a new word. He says you are not commandos or thieves. You are commando-thieves."

When no one laughed, he frowned and bobbled his head. "Sounds funnier in Thai."

A scan of the compound through a high-powered scope revealed no activity. The trucks were gone. Not one soul moved between the two cinder-block buildings.

Tyler slid in behind the wheel of the jeep. "Let's go see what we see."

On the way, Finn traded his place in the truck with Darcy so he could ride with Talia in the jeep. "How's your head?" he asked, notably failing to add *princess* or *your highness*.

Talia smiled. "Better. Thanks for asking." She touched the spot and winced. "One of Jafet's men left a pretty good bump back there, but the headaches and nausea are gone."

The area surrounding the target compound offered no cover besides a random hill in the otherwise flat plain, terraced for rice. Mac and Tyler parked the pickup and jeep behind the hill, but the team still had to cover a hundred meters of open ground.

Tyler tapped his ear. "Comms on. Spread out. Eddie, grab the scope and hang here. Call out movers and weapons as you see them." He set off from the north end of the hill with Finn and Talia. Val, Mac, and Darcy set off from the south.

Ewan and Po followed Finn, and the thief glanced back, scrunching up his brow. "Where are you two going?"

Po shrugged. Ewan nodded toward the compound. "With you."

"Not on your life. Stay put. Eddie will tell you when it's safe."

A hundred yards was a long distance to cover over a flat, muddy plain, especially when facing armed militiamen. The team fanned out, and Talia kept her eyes moving, senses on full alert.

Finn, however, seemed bored by the whole procedure. "Commando. Thieves . . . Hmm . . . Commando-thieves."

"What about *thief-dohs?*" Darcy said over the comms. "Or how about *comman-ieves,* yes?"

Eddie chimed in with his own idea. "I'm going with *Comanches.*"

Talia's case officer instincts told her not to encourage mindless chatter on a tactical net, but she couldn't help herself. "We can't use Comanches. That's cultural appropriation."

"Don't be such a snowflake."

"You're the snowflake."

Mac unleashed a heavy sigh into the comms. "Not to be a killjoy, but the kidnappers are likely linin' us up in their sights as we speak."

No one said anything else until they crossed the gravel road into the compound.

"The kidnappers should have challenged us by now," Talia said. "Eddie, do you see anything in the scope?"

"Negative."

Finn and Tyler split left to circle the north building. Mac and Darcy split right to circle the other. Talia and Val went up the middle.

Val was the first to spot the dark stain. "Looks like blood." She held her weapon ready and signaled for Talia to kneel and check.

Talia pulled her fingers away with a grimace. "Guys, we have a big puddle of blood seeping into the dirt between the buildings. Still sticky. Skull fragments too. Someone was shot here."

"The term you're looking for is executed," Val said.

"I don't like this. We need to check inside." Talia tried the doorknob on the north building. Locked. Naturally.

The others cleared the perimeter, then Darcy set tiny charges on the main doors of each structure. They split into threes again and breached both at once.

"Clear!" Tyler said, first through the door of Talia's building.

Talia passed to his right, into a large chamber, and made a wide turn into the first of two smaller rooms. The whole place smelled of filth and sickness. "Clear!"

"This room's clear as well." Finn had taken the second room. "Our building's empty."

"Ours is not," Darcy said. "Come over here, and come quickly. Eddie, send Mr. Ferguson."

"Already done. He and Po are on the way."

The second building smelled the same as the first, a scent on the edge of death. Food containers and empty water bottles lay on the floor. Darcy led the team through a cramped hallway to a chamber guarded by a pink and yellow linen curtain. Mac and Val stood on either side, looking stricken. Mac held the curtain back to let the others through.

A man, burned and unconscious, lay on a ragged cot, lit by rays of sunlight streaming in through a high rectangular window. A woman, barely conscious herself, cradled his head. Before Talia could fully process the sight, Ewan and Po rushed past. The woman seemed to recognize Po. She spoke to him in a voice raspy and withered, regretful.

Po dropped to his knees, head hanging.

The woman's eyes broke Talia's heart. "What is she saying, Ewan? Where are the children?"

Ewan choked on his reply. "Gone, Miss Talia. The children are gone."

CHAPTER SIXTY-TWO

Seux Khorng High Rise
Sathon District
Bangkok, Thailand

Tyler pressed a scope against the office glass to minimize the glare of the city lights. He focused the lens on the half city block of new white marble comprising Twin Tigers Plaza, nestled in a sharp bend of the Chao Phraya River.

"Anything?" Eddie asked from the computer station behind him.

"Negative. I don't see our girls."

The mood had remained somber since the discovery of the pastor and teacher from the refugee camp. Ewan had taken them to a hospital to receive care, but Tyler had cautioned him against sharing too many details about their injuries. Fortunately, in Bangkok, doctors weren't generally friendly with local police.

The team had set up shop in an empty office with a view of the plaza, and Tyler had passed the day greasing the wheels he'd set in motion for the con—what wheels he could, with the limited information the White Lion had given his team.

"My cameras are online," Eddie said. "You can watch from over here."

"Copy." Tyler didn't move. When possible, he preferred his own eyes over a digital surrogate. But he did lower the scope a moment later when the elevator let out its telltale ding.

"Pizza's here," Finn said, stepping off with Mac. "Seafood delight and bacon-bit special."

Pell crinkled his nose. "Didn't they have a standard pepperoni?"

"You said you wanted local flavor."

"I was talking about Thai food."

Finn set his boxes on a folding table. "There's a pizza shop every fifty meters in this town. From what I'm seeing, this *is* Thai food."

Mac picked up a slice covered in white cheese and crab meat. "This and Burger King."

Eddie abandoned the computers long enough to grab a slice and a bottle of Mountain Dew. On the return trip, something down in the plaza seemed to catch his eye. He set his food beside the keyboard and played with a trackball. An automated tripod hummed, rotating and tilting its camera to focus on the plaza. The geek sat back, showing Tyler his find. "Did you see this?"

On the screen, showing the base of the eastern tower, workers were busy setting up for a technology convention. The prototype on the center stage looked like a giant drone. "Is that some kind of helicopter?"

"It's a quadcopter Passenger Air Vehicle. The long-awaited PAV. Looks like a medevac version with that open platform underneath." The geek held a hanky to his face, whether for his cold or the drooling, Tyler couldn't tell. "Can we stop by later with your checkbook? I'll take two."

"After the mission." Tyler put his eye to the scope and snapped his fingers. "Look sharp. We've got our first customer. Southern entrance to the square. Black suit. Blue tie. I think it's Atan."

The tripod whirred as Eddie shifted the camera again. "Found him. Locking on." On-screen, the video tracked their target. Facial recognition boxes flashed all over his face, then turned green. "Yep. That's our Albanian friend. Here at the Frenzy, he's the Hyena."

"Why is Atan the Hyena?" Finn asked, mouth half full of seafood pizza. "All the other top positions are named for wildcats."

"A joke?" Tyler said. "Val told me narcissists often have odd senses of humor. Or maybe Boyd's way of motivating his Jungle players to aim higher. Whatever the reason, the name suits Atan."

"Because he is ugly?" Darcy asked. "Or because he is a low-life scavenger?"

"A little of both."

Five minutes later, at 7:40 p.m., another potential competitor appeared, shrouded in a hoodie. Val had predicted five-minute breaks between arrivals. The times given to her and Talia were a clue, plus her profile of Boyd indicated a need for minute levels of control.

The narrow shoulders and hip motion of the new target walking across the plaza spoke of a female, but Tyler couldn't be sure. "Eddie, get me a shot of this one's face. I don't have the angle."

"On it. If Atan was the first of the top-tier competitors, I'll bet this is our Clouded Leopard." Earlier in the day, Finn had set up a remote 10k camera on the roof of a building north of the towers, focused through the gap. Eddie used it to capture the target's face with a nearly straight-on view. "And . . . I'm locked on."

Tyler glanced at the geek's monitors. The mystery guest was definitely female, and Asian, but a good portion of her face remained in shadow beneath the hood, foiling his software. The facial recognition boxes flickered and gave up.

"No way." Eddie slapped the table. "That's Bi Fan, the Hong Kong Hacker."

"How can you tell?" Finn asked. "Facial recognition timed out."

Eddie gave him an incredulous look as the woman passed out of the camera's field of view. "Because she's *famous?* I recognized the scar on her chin." He called up an article on the next monitor over. The headline read MAJOR DATA BREACH. "Bi Fan orchestrated the 2015 hack of the US security clearance records. The Chinese government let her slide in exchange for all the info, but she wound up in Tai Lam Women's Correctional anyway."

Pell, despite his complaints, had stacked several slices of bacon-bit pizza on a napkin. "On hacking charges?"

"Nope. Stabbing. She killed a pickpocket on the bullet train." Eddie pulled up a second article, all in Chinese. The photo showed a body bag being rolled from a train on a gurney. "Boy, did that guy choose the wrong mark. Bi Fan did the same to his convict sister, who came after her in prison with a shiv. That's where she picked up the chin scar."

Finn read the article over his shoulder, pizza sagging from his hand. "Two murders. And the Chinese let her out for . . ."

"I don't know. Good behavior?"

"Violent hacker." Tyler went back to his scope. "Nice. A wonderful addition to the game."

The Snow Leopard came next, aptly named. Like Atan, he made no effort to hide his face as he approached the tower entrance, dressed in an overcoat and jeans. Eddie's facial recognition software pinned him down as one Grygory Rudenko, confirmed by the Siberian prison tattoo on his neck—an eight-pointed star.

Finn finished his pizza and licked his fingers. "This file is pretty thin. Says he's Ukrainian. Deals in antiquities. Can you get any more?"

Eddie tried, working the keyboard, but shook his head. "Nothing here screams diabolical. Other than smuggling stolen artifacts, Rudenko's squeaky clean. I'm surprised he's pulling down enough cash to earn a ranking in the Jungle syndicate."

"Strike two," Tyler said. "Keep watching. Someone in this game is our kidnapper. I can feel it. Either way, get as many IDs as you can. I don't like sending Talia and Val into this deal-making deathmatch without knowing all the players."

No one showed up for the next time slot, 7:50 p.m. And the 7:55 was an unknown panther wearing a hoodie, like Bi Fan. Eddie's software failed to get a match, but the guy was tall, possibly Scandinavian from what Tyler could see via the secondary camera. He checked his watch. "It's almost eight. Our girls are next on the list."

CHAPTER SIXTY-THREE

Twin Tigers Plaza
Bangkok, Thailand

Talia and Val crossed the marble plaza at a leisurely pace. No need to look stressed or hurried—not yet.

Tyler had ordered them to arrive together, despite their separate time slots. He'd pitched the idea as a way to test the boundaries of Boyd's little game from the start. He called it *poking the lion with a feather*. That was an excuse. Tyler was still hovering, using Val as a surrogate. But Talia didn't mind. She had learned her lesson in the bowels of Jafet's underworld. Leaning on her team—and God—was okay.

She and Val both dragged rolling suitcases, and each wore a heavy duffel slung at her hip. Talia's threatened to drag her in a lopsided circle.

They were not alone. The restaurants surrounding the plaza were open. Several pedestrians crossed their path. None of them gave a pair of women in heels and business suits a second look. There was a train station nearby. Luggage was a common sight.

"I wish we had comms right now," Talia whispered to Val. "I hate going in there blind."

The comms were a big problem. First thing upon their arrival in the city center, Eddie had run an analysis of signals in the square and caught Boyd testing a localized frequency jammer on his upper floors. After consultation with Franklin, Eddie and Darcy had gone on a mad dash around the city, picking up parts and pieces for a work-around.

Eddie had briefed Talia and Val when he handed them the finished products. "Boyd will leave the upper end of the RF spectrum free for his own internal security comms and Wi-Fi. Basically, the Bluetooth frequencies—extremely short range. I've modified your earpieces to send Bluetooth comms to a long-range directional relay Darcy and I cobbled together. The relay box will sit in your room and quite literally burn through Boyd's jamming to reach my station."

"If the towers have Wi-Fi," Val asked, "can't we use the signal like we did at Club Styx?"

"Negatory. At Club Styx we wanted to get caught. This time we don't. And Boyd's network security is top-notch. Keep in mind, earpieces are small, so I can make them work on one end of the frequency spectrum or the other, but not both. They won't talk to our SATCOM net without the relay, which has to be plugged into a wall outlet."

Eddie had gone into a dissertation on jamming, VHF directional burn-through, and the resultant power requirements. The short answer was,

Talia and Val couldn't talk to the team until they reached the room and plugged in his device—a rather not-so-subtle oversize hockey puck.

An intense Thai man waited under the tower's curved platinum awning. He said nothing. Val went first. She typed her code into a number pad, and the door unlocked. Talia tried to follow her through, but the guard blocked her path until the door fell closed. He gestured at the pad.

"I get it. No tailgating." Talia used her own code to unlock the door and smiled at the guard on her way in. "You run a tight ship, buster."

She doubted he understood a word.

Lobby wasn't the best word for what greeted her on the other side. *Mall* would have been better. Three stories of luxury shopping space, supported by sweeping gold pillars, surrounded a cylindrical elevator shaft with four cars. Shifting neon lights colored the rippling waters of a pool-sized fountain.

Next to the fountain, Boyd's people had set up a security checkpoint, a backscatter X-ray machine, and a bag scanner. Two carbon copies of the doorman stood ready to funnel the Frenzy players through the checkpoint, wearing the same intense glower. Either Boyd had rigid physical and temperamental requirements for his security men, or he was growing them in a lab. Talia blinked. Maybe that explained the mutism.

Clone One hefted the duffels onto the conveyor

without the slightest grunt. Talia lifted her chin. "You two and your buddy outside must be triplets." She handed her roller bag to Clone Two. "No? Then are the three of you a boy band or something?"

With the roller bags on the move, Talia followed Val through the backscatter machine. No alarms. As expected. They'd hidden all their contraband in the bags.

Clone One watched the X-ray monitor, while Clone Two moved to intercept the luggage on the other side. He unzipped the first duffel, eyeing the rows of Velcro pouches inside. He drew one out, poured a handful of gold coins into his palm, and looked at the girls in relative surprise—a slight change in his glower.

Talia gave him a *hands off the money* frown.

Val backed her up. "That's not a bribe, friend, if that's what you're thinking."

Whether or not he spoke English, they got their point across. Clone Two let the coins slide into the pouch and lobbed it down the conveyer to land in the still-moving duffel.

Talia did her best not to wince. Not everything in that bag was stable.

"You done?" Val asked, yanking her rollerbag down and extending the handle. "So now where do we go?"

Clone One, looking not unlike the Ghost of Christmas Future, extended an arm and a long finger. Talia looked, half expecting to see a gravestone with her name on it. Instead she saw a much more vibrant man waving from the elevators. "I guess we go with that guy."

The clones were mute, but the man at the elevators had a voice, high pitched with some Oxford British mixed into the accent. "Welcome, Panthers Eight One and Eight Two," he said with an exaggerated bow. His silk suit reflected the neon lights of the fountain. "I am the Frenzy's Master of Ceremonies. Let me show you to your rooms."

The MC helped them place their bags on a luggage cart in the elevator, and the three rode up countless levels while Thai music videos played on screens within the walls.

Talia folded her hands in front of her. "You don't seem surprised we arrived together."

"The White Lion suspected you might. You each may have a suite if you desire, or you may room together."

"Can we get adjoining suites?" Val asked.

"Adjacent rooms are not possible."

"Well, yeah, they're possible. You just have to—"

His eyes flashed. "You will understand when we reach the game floors."

Room accommodations were a weakness of Val's. She had a lot of rules, whether on or off the job. Talia nudged her elbow to keep her from arguing. "We'll bunk together. It's fine."

"Very good." The car jolted to a stop, and the MC handed them each a paper-thin tablet, more of a slate—little more than a pane of glass with gold edges. "These will lead you to your room and open the doors. Be inside by a quarter to nine. From then on, your safety is no longer guaranteed."

Safety? Talia squinted at him. "What do—"

"Please." He pushed their luggage cart into a passage with a curving taupe wall and held the door open, indicating in no uncertain terms that they should get out.

A green arrow pulsated at the center of Talia's slate, holding its angle no matter which way she held the screen. *These will lead you to your room.* "Okay. I guess that's it, then."

"Almost." The MC coughed and held out an open palm.

"Right. A tip." Talia laid three one-thousand-Baht notes in his palm, the equivalent of a hundred US. Val added three of her own, and the MC stepped back into the elevator. "Very generous. The mark of competitors with class." As the doors closed, he wheeled his arms, the bills fluttering in his hands. "Good luck, ladies. May you—"

They didn't hear the rest.

Val watched numbers count down as he descended. "May you win? May you sleep well?"

"May you live to tip me again," Talia said. "I'm pretty sure that's what he said."

The two pushed the cart along the tight curve of the passage until they reached an archway that opened into the main hallways. They both stopped in stunned disbelief.

The upper floors were a combination of glass and clear acrylic, held together with steel beams and cables and crisscrossed with brass conduit. Bangkok's lights shined in, captured and refracted in the twisting profile of the tower. Only the rooms—two or three per floor—and a few concrete supports were opaque.

"He's built a transparent labyrinth." Talia felt the blood drain from her cheeks. Boyd had taken the whole video-game boss-level concept a few steps farther than she'd ever dreamed. "He's built a giant death maze in the sky."

CHAPTER SIXTY-FOUR

Western Tower
Twin Tigers Complex
Bangkok, Thailand

Two floors below, Talia could see a figure in a hoodie wandering the acrylic halls, holding a small gray device at arm's length. The figure looked up, an Asian woman with a scar, noted their presence, and moved on. "That's not creepy at all."

"She's trying to work out the maze." Val walked ahead, following the slate's arrow, while Talia pushed the cart. "We should do the same. This whole thing is very dystopian. You think Boyd is obsessed with *Hunger Games*?"

"I think—" Talia grunted as she pushed. The hallway had some slope to it. "I think Boyd is psychotic. To be fair, he's not alone. Boyd and Jordan may share an interior decorator."

"What makes you say that?"

"You should see my office."

The clear walls and floors caused an optical illusion that made navigation impossible. Some hallways were dead ends, others were closed off entirely, existing only to fool the eye. Without the slates, Talia and Val would never have found the room even though they could see it the whole time. And the clear floors did not mesh well with Talia's fear of heights.

At the room, she pushed the cart across the threshold onto the relative normality of a carpeted floor and sank into a black suede couch. "Yes. Praise God for drywall and paint."

Val was less impressed. "Two bedrooms. Kitchenette. Stocked minibar." She waved a room service menu at Talia and shrugged. "I've seen better."

"It's not a spa weekend, Val."

"Truer words . . ." Val fished Eddie's hockey puck out of her duffel. The tungsten core coins—about half of the total in the bags—had served as great shielding, impervious to X-rays. She plugged the puck into a wall outlet, raised an antenna, and flicked a switch.

Talia shoved her earpiece into place and heard Eddie on the comms. "—your signal. Repeat, I am receiving your signal. VHF burn-through is solid. Stand by. Don't say a word. Scanning."

A few seconds passed. Val and Talia exchanged a look.

"You're clean. No listening devices or cameras, and no transmitters other than your own."

Val moved to the other duffel. "Boyd is playing fair—a positive by-product of his narcissism. He wants his players to know they've been squarely beaten."

"Don't be too sure," Tyler said over the frequency. "He might be happy with just the illusion of fair play."

The grifter smiled. "I know I am." She drew two pouches from the bottom of the duffel, both slightly lighter in color than the rest. She passed one to Talia.

Inside, packed in gold coins, was a small plastic pistol with two magazines of P3Q rounds—Tyler's low-velocity, low-noise version. Talia tucked the weapon into her waistband.

Val dragged her suitcase into the larger of the two bedrooms. "Eddie, did you identify any of the other competitors?"

"Aside from Atan, we ID'd a hacker named Bi Fan and an antiquities dealer named Rudenko—the Clouded Leopard and the Snow Leopard, respectively."

"Rudenko?" Val reappeared at the bedroom door. "I know Rudenko. He's a black-market antiquities dealer."

Talia met her gaze. "And I'll bet you've done some acquisition work for him."

"Maybe."

She crossed her arms and frowned. "Anyone else, Eddie?"

"The Maltese Tiger slot is open—you two saw to that on Milos. One of the other two panthers looked Scandinavian. The other never showed."

Val dropped onto the couch. "Chickened out?"

"Maybe. Or he might have been—"

"The trafficker whose blood we found at the compound." Talia closed her eyes. If that were true, they might catch Boyd, but they'd never find out where Hla Meh and the other kids were taken. "Let's hope that's not the case."

At precisely a quarter to nine, while Talia was still unpacking her gear in the smaller bedroom, all the TVs in the suite flickered to life. The White Lion roared over the surround sound system, and the lights dimmed.

"This guy loves a dramatic digital entrance," Eddie said.

"Hush." Talia put on the glasses Franklin had issued her months before, set with a hidden camera and augmented reality data displays. "Make sure you record this."

The White Lion paced into view on a red screen, deep voice shaking the walls. "Let the Frenzy begin. The rules are simple. Close as many deals as you can in twenty-four hours, culminating in the Grand Bazaar. Bring in at least ten million US. That is your ante. At the end, the house will take the ten million, or 25 percent of your earnings, whichever is higher."

A ranking list appeared at the bottom of the screen—four panthers, the two leopards, the Hyena, the Maltese Tiger, and the White Lion. The Maltese Tiger line remained blank. The others each had a dollar sign and a string of zeros. A link symbol joined Panthers Eight One and Eight Two, Val and Talia.

"Mergers are acceptable, as two of our new panthers have demonstrated, but partners must split their profits fifty-fifty, and only one player may hold each position. Greater profits can earn you a top-tier rank for the coming year and a bigger piece of the Jungle pie. Even my position is up for grabs, if you dare to chase me." The lion paused in his pacing to face the viewers. His lion lips curled into a smile. "And on that topic, there is one more rule. Don't get eaten."

The video switched from the lion to the security feed of a penthouse office with a glass floor. A man in a business suit stood behind the desk with his back to the camera, looking out over the city.

"Boyd," Talia said, resisting the urge to reach toward the screen. "So he is here."

"Or was." Val glanced out at the night beyond the suite's windows and back to the screen. "This was filmed earlier. Look at the coloring in the sky. The sun had barely set."

The lion confirmed her assessment. "One of our players attempted an early start to the game, posing as a utility worker. I allowed him to make it as far as my office."

A man entered the scene wearing a maintenance jumpsuit and wielding a gun. The camera angle gave a clear view of his face.

"Eddie . . ." Talia prompted.

"On it. Stand by."

There was no sound, but the fake worker gestured and shouted at Boyd, who refused to turn.

"Got him," Eddie said. "That's arms dealer Riku Ishimoto, one of last year's top panthers. I guess this explains why he didn't show for his time slot."

Talia shot a look at Val. "And now we know he wasn't killed at the compound."

Riku advanced. A third figure—a bear of a man—swept in from off camera and emptied a high-caliber handgun into his body. Boyd never turned from the window. The screen switched back to the lion. "A shame. Panther Six Eight was a good earner. But such is the circle of life." A voice in the background whispered *Kill or be killed, the law of the Jungle*. "Be warned. You are all fair game. If mergers are acceptable, so are hostile takeovers."

In the rankings, the zeros on the White Lion's line rolled down to negative ten million dollars. Those lost millions reappeared beside Panther Six Eight, and the dead panther's line turned red. The word FINAL appeared beside it.

The lion reappeared. "I killed Panther Six Eight—a hostile takeover—so I must cover his ten-million-dollar ante. However, once you've all made more than ten million, takeovers become more lucrative. You keep your kill's earnings, minus the ante. Those are the rules."

He went on to explain the Frenzy's endgame, a lavish party called the Grand Bazaar. There, in a final race to make the biggest deals, the surviving players would hock their illicit wares to high-end buyers.

The digital slates would guide Talia and Val to and from the Grand Bazaar to prepare their merchant bays. All other movement left them at the mercy of the maze and their competitors. But the lion warned against hiding in the room. "Cowering in your den will guarantee a loss. The biggest deals happen at the Grand Bazaar party. There are six of you and only three merchant bays. First come. First served." He paused for the echoing voices.

Kill or be killed, the law of the Jungle.

"Good luck. Let the Frenzy begin."

CHAPTER SIXTY-FIVE

Western Tower
Twin Tigers Complex
Bangkok, Thailand

A green light flashed on the suite's desk—a button labeled PRESS ME. Talia did as it requested, and two touchscreen panels rose from the desktop, canting to an angle. Data windows popped up on the screens.

"Those are resources." Val joined her at the desk, watching over her shoulder as she flipped through the menus. "Tyler, we've hit the jackpot. We have access to every animal in the Jungle syndicate. No names, but locations, activity, and Dark Web messaging. The Frenzy players can wield them like troops on the battlefield."

"Good," Tyler said. "We can use the intel to lean on Boyd once we have him."

"Sure. Or that." Val gently moved Talia aside in a *this is my domain* sort of way. She stretched out her fingers and wiggled them over the panels. "But think of the damage I could do."

Talia shot her a frown. "To Boyd or to pocketbooks worldwide."

"Both."

"Okay, you're cut off. Stay away from the toys."

"Leave her," Tyler said. "This is what Val does best, and the clock is ticking. You two need to show progress soon or Boyd will get suspicious."

A look at the scores, left on the TVs after the lion's video, told her he was right. Atan and the Clouded Leopard already had money on the board. The White Lion had covered seven million of his ten-million-dollar deficit. Talia and Val needed to keep up with the field to maintain their cover, especially with Boyd's big bear running around out there—the one who had killed Riku Ishimoto.

Talia backed off. "Fine. Just make sure she sends all the money to the proper accounts."

She heard laughter in the background of the comms. Tyler chuckled too. "I will. While she works, I need you to head out into the maze."

"To do what?"

"To do what panthers do best. Get out there and hunt some prey."

Talia's glass slate served several functions. After the White Lion's introduction, half the screen had lit up with a Frenzy chat room, including boxes for private messaging and a disturbing game FAQ.

Using the private chat function, cooperating players had the option of sending one another room invites, complete with directions. Otherwise the slate would only lead Talia to her own room or the Grand Bazaar, making her hunt in the maze a challenge, even with her eidetic memory. Talia had to lean on Eddie and his algorithms, sending directions to her augmented reality glasses. But her geeky human navigation aid kept getting sidetracked.

"Kill or be killed." Eddie mimicked the deep voice of the lion. "There is no mercy in this dojo. This guy is like a furry criminal version of the Cobra Kai sensei."

Talia paused at an intersection, waiting for Eddie to send her a direction. "John Kreese was a criminal too. He beat up kids."

"John Kreese. You know the sensei's name. So you're a fan."

"I saw *Karate Kid* once. What part of eidetic memory don't you get?"

"But you did see it."

"Eddie."

"Right. Uh . . ." An arrow appeared in her vision, created by her lenses. "Go straight. I'm directing you to a stairwell. Tyler says the elevators are death traps."

"How comforting. Thanks."

"That's what I'm here for."

The danger early in the game was minimal. As long as Talia's personal score stayed under ten million, any player who killed her in a hostile takeover would be losing money. But once she covered her ante, she'd have a target on her back.

"Heads up, Talia. Someone's approaching above."

Two floors up, she saw the figure. "Jeans. Overcoat. It's Rudenko, the Snow Leopard."

"Let him go. We don't need any stolen terracotta figures or Incan headdresses tonight."

She paused, staring past the Ukrainian antiquities dealer. Above the maze levels, she saw the Atrium. Boyd had filled it with tropical foliage. Something padded across one of its clear walkways. "Eddie. Check the footage. Was that—"

"An actual white lion? Yes. I did some reading about them on the plane. The latest population study I could find was 2018. There were only thirteen left in the wild. But captive white lions show up in smuggling busts and private collections nearly every year."

"Insane." Talia shook her head and kept moving. She needed to find her way to the Grand Bazaar promenade, and soon. With Eddie's profile of earlier Frenzies, Tyler had predicted a physical marketplace, and portions of his plan hinged on the concept. She and Val needed one of those bays.

In the kickoff video, the White Lion had told them the promenade was in the eastern tower. Five aerial walkways joined the two structures. Only one served the Frenzy floors. Talia could see it, glowing blue with high-lumen LEDs, but no matter what she and Eddie tried, she couldn't get there.

After a half hour of wrong turns and dead ends, Talia found a spot with a clear view and checked the scoreboard—a two-story screen on the central cylinder where the elevators were housed. Two of the bays were taken. Rudenko and Atan, veterans of the game, had already staked their claims. Only one remained.

To make matters worse, the lines for Panthers Eight One and Eight Two had each grown to over three million dollars. Val had made their first scores. Talia had to reach the bazaar, claim the last bay, and get back to the room before her partner had made enough money to turn her into a target. "Val, slow down for me."

Eddie answered for the grifter. "She can't. Tyler's orders. You two have to keep up."

"Then make me a map to the bridge."

"Almost there. My computers are analyzing your video, crunching the data. I should have final directions soon." He paused. "I've got movement in your field of view. Check one o'clock low."

Talia looked slightly right and down. Two floors down she saw a woman in a hoodie. "I see her. It's Bi Fan." The Clouded Leopard held the same gray device out in front of her as before. She was heading in the general direction of the sky bridge, one floor up from her and one floor down from Talia. "Eddie, she's heading for the bazaar."

"Concur. Hang on. I don't have a path yet."

"I don't have time to hang on. We lose that bay, we lose half the plan."

CHAPTER SIXTY-SIX

Bi Fan stopped and looked up. Talia watched her, gauging the hacker's intent. "I'm so close to the stairwell, Eddie. How hard can it be?"

The two stared each other down for another long second, then both broke into a run.

"No, no, no!" Eddie shouted into Talia's ear. "Go the other way. The other way!"

He wanted her to run in the opposite direction of her goal, not an easy task for Talia. She slowed, letting Bi Fan pull out ahead. "You sure?"

"The stairwell's a trap. It's a double—one good, one bad, side-by-side so you can't see. Trust me!"

Trust.

"Turning. I'm in your hands."

Eddie directed her back along the corridor twenty meters to another passage. It didn't look good.

"We've been this way before. It's a dead end."

"Not according to the computer. Try running your hand along the wall."

The computer was right. Near a false dead end, Boyd had planted another optical illusion. The wall to Talia's right didn't connect with the back. An opening, wide enough for her to slip through, gave her access to a parallel hallway and an intersecting passage.

"Take the new passage straight to the stairwell," Eddie said. "You're set."

Talia checked on her competition. "Bi Fan got there first. She's on her way up to the bridge."

"I'd bet you your five-point-seven-million-dollar score she isn't."

"Five-point—" Talia shot a glance at the scoreboard. "Been busy, Val?"

"Having the time of my life, darling. Remember, don't get killed."

"Thanks."

Talia hit the stairwell at a sprint and took the clear steps as fast as she dared. A fall and a broken neck would be a dumb way to end the mission. Below, Bi Fan had stopped at the bridge level. The gray device was gone, replaced with a ceramic stiletto.

"Our hacker is waiting to take me out." Talia's hand moved to her waistband.

Eddie read her mind. "Leave your gun hidden. She's waiting because she's stuck."

Trust.

Trust came a lot harder with the threat of deadly action ahead. Talia gritted her teeth and left her gun tucked away. She hit the landing, ready to fend off a blade.

Bi Fan made an overhand stab. The tip hit

polished glass. The barrier chipped but held.

"See," Eddie said. "Two stairwells, placed side by side to make one. Bi Fan chose . . . poorly."

Mesmerized by the strangeness of her circumstance, Talia placed a hand on the glass. Her competition did not reciprocate. Bi Fan took three more jabs at the barrier with her knife. She couldn't break through. She threw back her hood and growled. Talia gave her a *better luck next time* shrug and walked on.

The architects had bent the aerial bridge into a gentle S to meet the twisting profile of the adjoining tower. Talia kept to the center. Walking close to either side made her feel as if nothing separated her from the five-hundred-meter drop to the city below. Looking back at the exterior, she could see lights in the windows of the Frenzy-level rooms. Otherwise, the building's one-way glass kept the maze within a secret.

There were lights aglow in the mid-to-upper levels of the eastern tower as well. "Eddie, the White Lion mentioned inviting whales to the Grand Bazaar."

"Tyler noticed. He's got Darcy and Pell looking into it for us. They think Boyd's using the tech convention in the plaza as a cover to bring in buyers for the players."

"Have you accounted for these whales in the plan?"

She heard Tyler jump in on Eddie's microphone. "It's covered. You stay focused on the game."

Talia stopped talking as she left the bridge, too stunned to speak. Boyd had created an over-the-top Turkish bazaar atmosphere—without the accompanying claustrophobia.

An arched mosaic ceiling hung four stories over the promenade. A bubbling tile fountain marked the center. Along the edges, workers stocked wrought-iron shelving with all manner of tchotchkes. Others set up tables and chairs. Catering carts sat dormant, waiting to be fired up to serve the guests.

"This is surreal." Once she found her voice again, Talia did her best to keep her lips from moving. Armed guards watched from every corner. "He's setting up for a party."

Tyler echoed her thoughts. "A party where drugs, weapons, and children will be sold."

"Do you think these workers know what will happen here in a few hours?"

"Unlikely, but they have some inkling this is a shady job. Guards with submachine guns and whatever premium Boyd is paying them ought to be clue enough. Ignorance is no excuse."

A scoreboard hung over the fountain. As Talia drew near, the screen switched from the tallies to a silent replay of Bi Fan trying to stab her way through the glass. Several workers stopped to watch.

She swallowed and whispered through clenched teeth. "Yep. Surreal."

Two bays opened like caves in the northern wall of the promenade, and one in the southern, adjacent to the fountain. The closest one to Talia on the northern side had a picture of a Hyena on the screen over the opening. The southern bay had a picture of a Snow Leopard. The screen over the second bay in the northern wall remained blank.

"Do you see the pedestals near the mouth of each bay?" Eddie asked, highlighting each one in her augmented reality vision. "They have screens and keypads. It looks like you need to get to the pedestal of the far northern bay and enter your code. I can send it to your glasses."

"No need. I—"

The patter of running feet behind told Talia she shouldn't have spoken so soon. She glanced over her shoulder and heard Eddie slap the table beside his microphone.

"That's Bi Fan! Get going!"

Talia took off, but Bi Fan was already at a full sprint, and it gave her an advantage. She caught up and grabbed Talia's hair, jerking her back.

"Ow!" Talia threw an elbow.

The hacker stumbled back, holding her nose.

The move gave Talia the edge she needed. She reached the pedestal first and typed in her number, which was flashing in her lenses despite her rejection of Eddie's offer. A black panther appeared on both screens—on the pedestal and over the bay—with the number Eight Two in front of it like the number on a sports jersey.

Bi Fan skidded to a stop a few feet away, stiletto up and ready.

The nearest guards raised their machine guns.

Talia gave the hacker a lift of her chin. "I guess this is a no-kill zone."

"Then you had better watch your back in the maze." Bi Fan's English was pretty good. She backed off, signaling her deference to the guards. "You cannot hide here forever."

The knife disappeared. Talia never saw where it went.

As soon as Bi Fan had moved out of range, Talia returned her attention to the pedestal. She selected her language, as if she were standing at an ATM, and a list of instructions appeared. The bay gave her a million-dollar bonus, which immediately split into a half-million each for her and Val on the scoreboard. The money was a staging budget— bay supplies, decorations, and the like. The Frenzy workers would take care of everything.

Tyler coached her over the comms. "Enter a request for twelve eight-foot-by-eight-foot cages. We want to telegraph an intent to sell live products. Maybe the real human traffickers will seek you out."

"Copy." She knew the order was all for show, but

every button-push left a bitter taste in Talia's mouth.

A buzzer sounded through the promenade. On the scoreboard, a message flashed.

ALL BAYS CLAIMED

FRENZY ROUND TWO INITIATED

"What's that supposed to mean?" Eddie asked.

Talia shook her head. "Nothing good."

The *no-kill zone* status made the Grand Bazaar an attractive place to hang out and observe. Talia wandered the promenade. The Snow Leopard, Rudenko, had returned to his bay to direct a crew of locals in gray jumpsuits as they installed a large rotating platform—perhaps for his antiquities. He gave Talia a nod.

She gave one back.

Workers in the same gray jumpsuits bustled about in Atan's bay, but Atan wasn't there.

"Are those refrigerators?" Eddie asked. "What's Atan selling?"

"Not stocks and bonds."

"Pharmaceuticals, remember?" Tyler interrupted them, using Eddie's mic, by the extra distance in his voice.

Talia could see him standing over the geek's shoulder—hovering. She had decided to lean on him and be grateful, but that didn't change the helicopter-mom feel.

391

"Atan has his fingers in a few extra pies. Unless he's selling black-market Kobe beef, those refrigerators mean drugs. The annual market for illicit pharmaceuticals is around seventy billion dollars."

"We have a real pack of winners here," Talia said, watching Atan's workers push another refrigerator into place.

"Tell me about it."

Talia staked out the bazaar for two more hours, but Atan never showed. Either she or Val needed to make contact. He had a part to play in the con. Talia wanted to send him a private message, but Tyler warned her off. "He has to come to us, not the other way around. Otherwise the play won't stick."

By the time she left, the scoreboard hanging over the exit showed her and Val at seventeen million each. The grifter had been too successful for Talia's own good. The others now had a seven-million-dollar motive to kill her, not to mention gain the coveted bay.

She needed to get to the room and stay awhile.

The maze ahead looked darker than before as Talia crossed the bridge. The city lights no longer penetrated the outer walls. And there were colors—pale reds and oranges.

"Something's changed, Eddie. What's happening?"

"The board did say you'd entered Round Two.

I'm guessing Boyd polarized the windows. And with the clear walls and floors, adding colors makes the maze look totally different. No big deal. Use your slate."

She tried. The message board was still running on the glass screen. Bi Fan was in the open chat room as the Clouded Leopard, offering to split a bay with anyone who would help her kill Panther Eight Two and take it. "Thanks, Bi Fan." Talia tapped the arrow icon for directions to her room.

Nothing happened.

She tried again.

ROOM DIRECTIONS ARE CURRENTLY DISABLED
PLEASE TRY AGAIN LATER

Eddie must have read the message through her glasses-cam. "More changes for Round Two," he said. "Boyd is raising the difficulty level. Not to wor . . . We hav . . . y ma . . . After the stairw . . . ake your fir . . ."

"Eddie?"

The geek made no response.

"Val?" Talia touched her ear. "Anyone, come in."

No one answered. The maze no longer registered with Talia's eidetic memory, and now she had lost comms. She was on her own.

CHAPTER SIXTY-SEVEN

Western Tower
Twin Tigers Complex
Bangkok, Thailand

Wandering in the maze was a death sentence. Without directions, Talia couldn't get back to the room. "I can't do it," she said out loud.

A voice answered from deep inside. *Trust.*

"Right. Okay." *Dear God, show me the way.*

Talia closed her eyes. Without the distraction of the red and orange lights, she could remember the path. Once she felt she had a handle on it, she opened her eyes again and pushed herself out of the corner. Patience was the key. One step at a time. She reached the first corridor and took a right. A long passage followed. At the dead end she expected to squeeze her way around the false wall Eddie had shown her.

Prudence told her to use the glow of her slate as a light in the dim and strangely lit hallway. But the glow might also confuse her perception of the maze, not to mention make her an instant target. Instead, Talia put a hand out in front to feel for the back wall.

She stepped into dead air.

With a gasping scream, Talia teetered forward,

flailing for a handhold. Her slate went flying, clattering against artificial outcroppings sure to take her head off if she fell. She caught the glass wall, slipped, and caught it again. Her fingers wrapped the edge. Her body swung sideways toward oblivion. Years of balancing racing shells on the Potomac saved her. Talia used her core muscles to stop her momentum and powered her body back to safety.

She collapsed on the edge. "What is happening?"

Her memory flashed through the labyrinth, looking for something new.

Hinges. Slides. Motors.

Boyd had changed more than the maze's lighting. He had changed the maze itself. The walls were movable.

Not all the walls. Logic precluded it. Talia hadn't seen enough infrastructure to account for much. But Boyd didn't need many moving pieces. One or two per floor, leaving glass cliffs in the shadows, gave the maze a whole new level of deadly.

Talia started again. The missing wall at the back of her current passage meant she had to turn her back to the emptiness to squeeze her way around the false dead end into the next passage over. She moved on, this time keeping her weight on her back foot until she confirmed each step.

"Eddie? Val?"

The comm link didn't return. It had been a jury-rigged system from the start, built from parts scrounged from the Bangkok markets in a half day of searching.

Twenty excruciating minutes later, Talia heard a blood-freezing cry. She knew the voice. "Atan." Who had gotten to him? Bi Fan? The White Lion?

A silhouette hurried through the orange and red light several floors below, but quickly disappeared in the utter black of a darkened hallway. By the speed of the killer's movement, he—or she—knew the maze. Whoever it was would be coming for Talia next.

From then on, every turn felt like a guess. Every dark corner looked like a hooded figure wielding a stiletto. Talia turned the last corner into what she hoped was the final passage, and found a black void.

Thirty meters or so of pure darkness, twisting with the curvature of the building.

Boyd had engineered the new lighting to make certain hallways look and feel like black holes, like the one that absorbed the silhouette of the killer after Atan's scream.

What if the same silhouette, moving with such confidence through the maze, now waited for her in this very hall.

Talia drew her gun and set off. She crept along at a steady pace, one hand on the wall. Twenty meters in, a shadow barred her path. "I see you," she said, and pulled the trigger.

"Don't!" The figure lunged, knocking the gun

aside to spoil her aim. The low-velocity P3Q round smacked against the wall.

Talia didn't fight. She lowered her weapon. "Val?"

The grifter pulled her in close. "I'm so glad to see you. Comms are down."

"I know. What are you doing?"

"I heard you start the journey back before we lost the connection. I came out to help, but—"

"But you couldn't get far in this nightmare." Talia let Val lead her back along the passage. "I understand. Thank you."

"What are fake sisters for?"

In the safety of the room, Talia collapsed onto her bed. She let her gun and her high-tech glasses lie beside her. "I have to get back out there—figure out who took those kids." She barely had enough energy to speak the words, let alone put them to action.

She fought through the exhaustion. "Val," she called from the bed. "We have to figure out what happened to the comm link."

"I think I know. Come see."

The grifter had used the edge of a P3Q magazine to pry the top off Eddie's hockey puck, wisely unplugging the device first. The inside smelled like burned sugar.

Talia wrinkled her nose. "He did say this thing draws tons of power."

"Think we can fix it?"

"We can try."

A few parts were blackened, but only one wire had burned all the way through. Using Val's magazine, Talia scraped away the charred pieces. "They won't reach. We'll have to improvise."

They both looked around the room and settled on the same idea, saying it out loud at the same time. "Desk lamp."

It took nearly half an hour of hard work to saw through the desk lamp's cord with a dull knife from the kitchen and strip away the insulation. Talia wound the ends of her extension piece to the damaged wires. Once she was clear, she gave Val a nod. "Give it a go."

The grifter plugged in the device.

Talia flipped the switch and raised the antenna. Her earpiece crackled.

"Talia? Val? Come in. Do you read?"

"Eddie." Talia pushed out a fist for Val and received a knuckle bump.

The grifter dropped the kitchen knife on the desk. "Your dumb hockey puck died. Nice work."

Continuous static masked Eddie's voice. "It's not a hockey puck. It's an improvised VHF burn-through transmitter-receiver."

"Well, it burned through, all right."

Talia tried not to laugh as she waved her off. "Eddie, the wiring couldn't handle the power draw. We fried one. Do you have a work-around?"

"Figured as much. I came up with a plan. I'll talk you through it."

The kitchen knife and the spare wire from the lamp helped, along with a resistor they dug out of the lamp's base, common in LED lighting, according to Eddie. Soon, they had a solution, and the static vanished.

"The signal's clear," Eddie said, a caution in his tone, "but we've lost range."

Talia didn't like the sound of that. "Meaning?"

"Meaning you won't be able to hear us if you make it to the Atrium, or in the Grand Bazaar."

Val stood above her, arms folded. "That's going to be a problem."

Tyler stepped in on Eddie's end. "Fluid plan, remember? We'll be okay. You two get back to work." There was a long pause, then he added, "Finn and Mac wanted to send in the cavalry, you know."

Talia let out a quiet laugh. "We're not quite there yet."

"That's what I said. I told them to have faith."

"Of course you did."

CHAPTER SIXTY-EIGHT

Western Tower
Twin Tigers Complex
Bangkok, Thailand

With the comms fixed, Val returned to her deal panels.

Talia went to a snack basket in the kitchen and found a granola bar—a sliver of the mundane in what was rapidly becoming the weirdest night of her life. She took a bite and nodded at the grifter. "What are you working on?"

"Something I started before this little interruption. Ever hear of a flash mob?"

"Sure. Pretend crowds suddenly breaking into performance art."

"Now imagine the performance art they're engaging in is purse snatching. I have field mice and jackrabbits hitting cities across Europe. A five-thousand-dollar buy-in gets them a time and place. We've picked up more than two thousand takers."

Talia dropped her forehead into her palm "Val, we're the good guys. You can't—"

"She's okay," Tyler said. "Val is rallying the snatchers. I'm rallying a counter flash mob of my own, of the constabulary persuasion. Cuffs will hit wrists before any purses go missing."

"Great. But all those arrests will make the news."

"By then this will all be over. Your cover is safe. For the moment. How are you holding up?"

Talia didn't want to say, but she was too tired to lie. "I'm worn out, Tyler. Death mazes are exhausting."

"Exhaustion will get you killed. Get some rest."

"But the kids—"

"You can't help them if we don't win this. Get some rest. That's an order."

"Fine. A few minutes. No more." She sank into the couch and watched Val work while she finished her granola bar, and then leaned back into the cushions and closed her eyes.

For only an instant.

When Talia opened her eyes again, light streamed in through the window. The day outside had progressed well beyond the morning hours. How long had she slept? Something buzzed in her lap. "What on earth?"

"Oh good. You're up." Val sat at the kitchen counter, sipping coffee. "I got a couple of hours, but darling, you snore. Anyone ever tell you that?"

Talia rubbed her eyes and glanced down to find a new glass-and-gold slate in her lap.

"A porter dropped that by. Creepy, huh? But you can't argue with the service."

The slate buzzed again. Talia squinted at Val, then checked the screen.

The Hyena. Atan. But Atan was dead.

Talia checked the scoreboard on the TV. By the look of the numbers, Val had been busy. She had run them up to more than twenty-six million each.

"Who did your purse snatchers rob? The Pope?"

Val set her coffee down and stretched, giving her a sleepy laugh. "The purse snatchers haven't struck yet. Most of our money came from Jafet. Eddie and I have been moving it around from account to account to create false deals. What do you think?"

"I think I'm a dead woman the next time I head out into the maze."

But Talia hadn't looked at the scoreboard purely to check Val's work. If the silhouette she saw had killed Atan, his line would be red and empty. It wasn't.

The slate buzzed. "We have a message from Atan."

"When we came back to the room, you said he was dead."

"I think I jumped to a conclusion. Either that, or this is a trap." Talia clicked on the message box.

402

ROUND 3
ROOM DIRECTIONS ARE ACTIVE –
ALL PLAYERS TO ALL ROOMS
WE SHOULD MEET
I HAVE A DEAL FOR YOU

Val sat beside her on the couch. "Do we answer?"

"Do we have a choice? Time is running short. We have to risk this." Talia typed in a response.

OUR PLACE OR YOURS?

The answer came back immediately.

YOU COME HERE
NOT LEAVING MY ROOM
SOMEONE TRIED TO KILL ME
P.S. BRING YOUR BAVARIAN
MERCHANDISE

Talia and Val struck out into the maze together. The outer windows were still polarized, but sunlight filtered in from the Atrium. The colors had changed to blue and green. With the better lighting, Talia saw a moving wall had changed their hallway to a four-foot ledge, open on one side to a forty-foot drop. In the darkness hours before, she could have easily fallen.

Atan the Hyena was in his room. The

leopards, Bi Fan and Rudenko, and the unknown Scandinavian panther were still out there, all potential killers, all with slates now able to lead them to any other player's room. Talia and Val were prime targets, and the heavy duffels they carried made them slow.

Talia let Val handle the directions, while she kept watch, eyes moving. "Where are they all?"

"In their rooms? Setting up at the bazaar?" Val gestured with the slate and the two turned left into a stairwell. "Who cares? As long as they're not here."

Three floors down and a few turns later, they came within sight of Atan's door. His room, like theirs, sat along a ledge, a few steps past an intersection with a blacked-out hallway.

An Asian woman stood at the door in a white dress and black apron. A device strapped to her wrist showed a green flashing arrow. She held a tray with a covered room service platter.

Val let out a nervous laugh. "You think Atan ordered hors d'oeuvres for our meeting?"

The woman kept her body angled slightly away from them. Maybe she hadn't heard them coming, or maybe she was hiding her face.

Talia stopped, catching Val's forearm. "There's no drink."

"What?"

"On the tray. There's no drink. Who orders food with no drinks?"

At Talia's declaration, the woman looked their way, wearing a pleasant smile.

She had a scar on her chin and a cut on the bridge of her nose.

Talia shouldered Val aside and heaved her duffel up as a shield. A ceramic stiletto stuck in the canvas. The hacker had thrown it sidelong from under the tray, all while holding her pleasant smile. Talia charged. The tray clattered to the floor. Bi Fan dodged, but not far enough. Talia clipped her against the wall, swept the back of her knees with a kick, and dropped the duffel full of fake gold on her as she fell.

She pulled the stiletto free and pitched it over the ledge. "You should have learned your lesson after I popped you in the—"

A strained cry from behind cut her short. Eddie shouted into the comms. "Ambush! Val's in trouble!"

"Ambush?" She turned to see Val, caught in a choke hold and fighting to keep her attacker's knife hand at bay. The Scandinavian. He must have been hiding in the dark hallway, waiting for them to pass. Val had a death grip on his wrist, but the duffel was dragging her down.

Talia leveled her gun, walking toward them. "Drop the knife!"

He sneered at the command and fought the blade closer to Val's neck.

What did he see that Talia didn't?

Bi Fan. She glanced back in time to see the hacker coming, but not in time to shoot. Bi Fan knocked the gun out of her hand and the two spun in a standing grapple, each squeezing the other's throat.

The hacker let go and yanked Talia's hair, pulling her head to the side.

Talia punched her in the ribs. She asked a question with each shot. "Really? The hair? Again?"

In her peripheral vision, she saw Val elbow the Scandinavian in the gut. He answered with an "Oof!" and pushed her away.

She reeled back, off balance because of the duffel.

He flipped his knife around for a throw.

"Val, duck!"

Talia gave Bi Fan another swift kick to the knee and turned the hacker's back to the oncoming blade. The knife flew. Val ducked. Bi Fan's eyes widened in pain, and her grip on Talia's hair went slack. She slipped to the floor with the blade embedded in her spine.

Neither Talia nor Val wasted the moment.

Talia dove for her gun and fired.

Val got control of the duffel and came up swinging.

Two P3Q rounds hit their attacker square in the chest. He grunted and winced, but he didn't go down—until Val's duffel full of coins hit him in the shoulder. The Scandinavian teetered, lost his footing, and pitched headlong over the ledge. He bounced off another ledge two floors down and landed with an ugly *thud* at the bottom of the maze.

Talia stared at Val in shock. "What did we just do?"

The door next to her opened. Atan stuck his head out and looked up and down the hall. "Is it over?"

"You," Talia growled. She pushed him back with the barrel of her gun and stormed inside.

CHAPTER SIXTY-NINE

Western Tower
Twin Tigers Complex
Bangkok, Thailand

Atan fell back on his rear end, staring down the barrel of Talia's gun. "Don't shoot!"

"Why not? You lured us into an ambush."

"No!" He scooted backward on his haunches. "I swear. I have no idea how those two knew about our meeting."

"He's not lying." Val dragged both duffels into the room and shut the door. She showed Talia a gray smartphone-size device. "Remember this? Looks like Bi Fan cracked Boyd's system."

"She knew we were coming?"

"She knew *you* were coming. She intercepted the private messages. And she invited the Scandinavian in for some fun." Val scrolled through the data on the hacker's device. "His name was Gunnar Larson. Panther Seven Five. Bi Fan offered him 60 percent of your winnings if she could take the merchant bay at the Grand Bazaar." She laughed. "What a deal."

Talia grabbed Atan's lapel and hauled him to his feet. "You may not have set us up, but you left us out there to die. You could've helped. A third fighter would have made all the difference."

"And get stabbed in the process? No thank you." The Albanian flopped back onto his couch, eyes closed. He laid a hand across his forehead. "So stressful. It is like this every year."

"Then why do you come?" Talia asked, tucking the gun into her waistband.

"Because I make *sooo* much money." He raised his head. "Seriously. The top two contenders will make more than forty million in a single day. Look at the board."

He wasn't exaggerating. Rudenko had generated forty-one million in pre-bazaar deals. If he made no other profits, he'd be taking home more than thirty million after the White Lion claimed his 25 percent.

"And what about you?" Atan made a face. "The *Macciano Sisters*. Bah. You used me to get into the syndicate, then ditched me with your little coup at Jafet's place. They say you're Don Marco's girls. Is it true?"

Neither answered.

"So it *is* true. And you." He pointed at Val. "What happened to your beautiful New York accent? It was so attractive."

"Shut up."

His head fell back again and he thrust his hands toward the ceiling. "Was nothing real?"

Two chimes sounded, drawing Talia's eyes back to the board. The lines marked Panther Seven Five and Clouded Leopard turned red and dropped the ten-million-dollar minimum. Seven million from Bi Fan moved to Panther Eight Two, and nineteen million from the Scandinavian moved to Panther Eight One. Then the two lines balanced out, giving them totals of thirty-nine million each.

Val let out a mirthless laugh. "Two more voted off the island."

The White Lion had fifty-two million. Talia shook her head. "We're closer, but still not within striking distance, and we're running out of time."

The clock on the board read 11:15. Less than ten hours remained. Talia tried to get them back on track. "Mr. Atan, how did you know we brought the gold?" She knew the answer, but Val had taught her to use knowns, rather than unknowns, to steer a mark.

"The airport. I saw your sister fighting with the big black bag at the taxi stand. I thought to myself, these women are not stupid enough to pass fake gold at the White Lion's Frenzy. Ergo, the gold is real. This is how you passed the test at my office. You have the real horde."

Val gave Talia a subtle nod, an affirmation that the mark was showing trust.

Talia kept pushing. "What if we do have the real thalers? That's our affair. Our product. We'll auction them off at the Grand Bazaar."

"For a few million. At most." Atan sat up, rolling his neck and stretching his shoulders as if he'd been part of the fight. He locked eyes with Talia. "With my connections, I can bring in local buyers who will pay five times as much. You know this. My Asian contacts are the reason you targeted me in Prague."

Tyler came up on the comms, coaching. "He's hooked, but don't rush it. Make him fight the line. Keep working him for information."

"Okay. We can be reasonable. Let's work out a percentage."

"A percentage?" Atan snorted. "I want the gold. I will give you ten million. You could quit the game right now. Hole up in your room and most likely go home, each with a leopard position."

"We're doing well enough on our own."

"Too well. Keep going and the lion will think you're attempting a coup, as with Jafet. You won't be safe."

"Safe? We haven't been safe since we entered the maze." Talia would circle back to that question. She needed to close the deal. "Okay. Ten million US for our Bavarian Thalers. Transferred immediately. Deal?" She offered him a hand.

He didn't take it. "One moment." Atan left the couch for the desk and drew an instrument from a small brown case—his XRF scanner. "Fool me once," he said, leaving them to fill in the rest.

The Albanian pulled as many pouches from each duffel as he could carry and dumped piles of gold on the couch. He scanned each pile, spread the coins around, and scanned them again. Atan gasped, as if hardly able to contain his joy. "They *are* real."

Over the comms, Talia heard Finn's Melbourne accent. "Redemption."

What the thief had failed to accomplish in Prague, he had managed at the Bangkok airport. While Tyler was plotting and Eddie was buying tech, the burglar had worked his way into the baggage system of Bangkok's airport and intercepted Atan's bag. He had swapped Atan's XRF reader for Eddie's fake.

Talia hid her smile and touched Atan's shoulder. "I said, 'Do we have a deal?' "

"Yes, yes." He shook her hand, unable to take his eyes off the coins. "We have a deal."

Val coughed into her hand.

"Oh. Yes. Your payment." Atan returned to the desk and worked the touchscreen panels. Talia's slate buzzed. A digital transaction came up, and she hit accept. On the scoreboard, ten million appeared in her account and five filtered into Val's. They were now at over forty-four million each, tied for the number two ranking.

"There," Atan said, returning to his gold. "It is done. Now I suggest you go back to your rooms and hide for the remainder of the competition."

"Why?" Val asked. "We've already been attacked. What else should we fear?"

"Do the accent and I will tell you. Please, for old time's sake."

She drew her gun.

"Okay. Okay. Listen. The Frenzy is *not* a competition for rankings in the Jungle syndicate."

Talia narrowed her eyes. "Isn't it?"

"This is what the White Lion wants you to think. But in truth, he is culling the pride, like a real lion, taking out his strongest rivals. The White Lion uses the Frenzy to identify and eliminate his most ambitious players. Get too close, and you will wind up like Riku Ishimoto."

"We won't. Trust me." Talia didn't explain, but Val and Eddie had nearly exhausted Jafet's reserves. They only had a few more million to shift around for fake deals. The Macciano Sisters didn't have a big enough war chest to threaten Boyd.

Atan walked his guests to the door, and the two stepped out into the maze. The hacker's body was gone, cleared away by the world's creepiest maid staff.

"One more thing." Talia stopped the door before he could close it. "Other than the White Lion, who here are you most afraid of?"

He pulled his chin close to his neck. "Are you serious?" His pupils shifted from Talia to Val and back again. "You. According to the message boards, you beat up the Clouded Leopard at the bazaar. Now you've killed her, along with Panther Seven Five. You two are terrifying."

"Anyone else?"

Atan glanced up and down the hall. Clearly he did not like hanging out with his door open to the maze. "The Snow Leopard. The graceful name does not suit him, nor his dirty business."

How dirty could Rudenko's business be? Talia huffed. "You're mistaken. He sells artifacts."

"No, my dear. The Snow Leopard's smuggling business is a veil, a façade for the Ukrainian authorities. He pays them off. Everyone is happy. No one cares about a few black-market trinkets. No one looks deeper. But at last year's Frenzy, he showed his true spots. His real business is selling children." Atan removed her hand from the door and shut it in her face.

CHAPTER SEVENTY

Western Tower
Twin Tigers Complex
Bangkok, Thailand

"Rudenko's our man." Talia let the arrow steer her and Val through the maze, aware she wasn't paying enough attention to the threat from the remaining players. She no longer cared. "How did we miss this?"

"You mean how did *I* miss this?" The pout in Eddie's voice was palpable.

"Sorry, Eddie. I didn't mean it that way."

"But it's true. I'm the one who did the research. Rudenko's got a solid cover—layers within layers. My computers aren't all knowing. They can only work from the data they're fed."

This sounded like a sore point. Talia had to wonder if Eddie was simultaneously taking grief from Tyler off air. She softened her tone. "Fair point. But now we know, so how do we figure out where he's keeping the children?"

Tyler answered for him, posing another question. "The device Val lifted from the hacker's body. How deep into Boyd's system does it go?"

"Deep." Val matched Talia's steps and held the device in front of Talia's glasses-cam for Eddie to see. "Looks like she had access to every Frenzy communication and transaction. She siphoned a little off each deal. The others were moving so fast they didn't notice."

"What about delivery schedules. Did she hack those?"

"Can't say yet. We'll need some help finding out."

After Talia and Val reached the room, Eddie coached them through a search of the device's functions and data.

"Got it." Talia selected an entry on the device, bringing up times and registry numbers. "Rudenko has a delivery arriving this evening, coming in on two freight trucks."

"Which means train," Tyler said.

"No, I said trucks."

"And Tyler said train." Val took the device out of her hand and set it on the desk. "Bangkok is a packed metropolis with ten times more traffic than its roads can support. Moving freight trucks through this mess by train is more efficient. It's called piggybacking."

"Okay." Talia squinted at Val. "Let's say you're right, and our trucks are coming through the city by rail in a couple of hours. Where does that leave us?"

"With something I've always wanted to try," Tyler said. "An old-fashioned train robbery."

• • •

With the rest of the team preparing to hit the train and nothing left in the Frenzy but the Grand Bazaar, Talia and Val could do nothing but sit tight. Sitting was not in Talia's nature. Pacing was more her style—pacing and praying.

Dear God, place your hands as a shield around Tyler and the team. Help me find the children, and help us bring them safely home to their parents.

"Are you falling asleep on your feet over there?" Val asked from the kitchen.

"Praying."

"Right. I should've guessed. Say one for me, will you?"

The sincerity in the request made Talia open her eyes. "Are you okay?"

"Yes." Val attempted to pour a cup of coffee, but the pitcher rattled against the cup. She set both on the counter and lowered her head. "No."

Her hands were shaking. Talia left her pacing track and went to her. "Val, what's wrong?"

"Weren't you paying attention? Rudenko kidnaps and sells children. By stealing artifacts for him, aiding his cover business and financing, I've been helping him."

In the months Talia had known her, Val kept up a callous veneer. Always shielded. Always arm's length from real emotion. With Don Marco's decision to turn himself in, her veneer

417

had cracked. Now the news about Rudenko had wedged in a crowbar. Talia had two ways to play this—remove the crowbar and add some quick platitude spackling, or tear the fissure wide open.

She chose the harder path. "Yes, Val. You have been helping him."

CHAPTER SEVENTY-ONE

Phra PradaEng District
Samut Prakan City
Bangkok Metropolis, Thailand

Tyler and Finn weaved through traffic on Kawasaki dirt bikes. The four gold spires of Bangkok's Mega Bridge loomed ahead. The helmet muffled Tyler's voice. "Eddie, time check."

"Eleven past. Four minutes to go, assuming the train is on schedule."

"Did the train leave on schedule?"

"Yes."

Tyler changed lanes to dodge a car, gunned his engine, and added some sharpness to his tone. "Too bad we didn't."

Acquiring motorbikes in Bangkok had posed no problem. They were everywhere. The team's delay had come from locating and purchasing a drone that met Eddie's stringent requirements. Tyler and Finn had pushed deep into the Samut Prakan port sector to get the one he wanted, and now they were fighting their way back north to catch the train.

"I told you, boss. If you want me to do this job right, you have to get me quality equipment."

419

"And I told you, this is Bangkok. You can get gear fast or get gear that's high quality. You can't do both."

"We should have held back one of the TACRON spider drones from Milos."

"We didn't know. How many times do I have to say 'fluid plan'?" Tyler took his eyes off the road long enough to check on the drone, keeping pace fifty feet above. "You see the train yet?"

"Coming in from the west at thirty-five miles per hour. She'll turn to follow the new line paralleling the bridge right on time. You might want to step it up."

Tyler couldn't believe the geek had added that last bit. "You might want to hide when Finn and I get back."

The Siam Rail Transport Company had joined its new southern city line to the existing superstructure of the Mega Bridge, putting the tops of any piggybacking freight trucks three feet below the western bridge rail and six feet over. The bridge was the perfect launching point for the heist.

Almost.

The bikes cleared the last building and sped up the ramp of the southern span. As Finn came up on his rear quarter, Tyler made an exaggerated nod toward the forest of support cables. "Those are only ten meters apart. Are you sure you can make this jump?"

"Are *you,* old man?"

Tyler laughed. "So it's like that, is it? I was pulling stunts like this when you were still in diapers"—he popped a wheelie and let the front wheel bounce on the pavement—"driving uphill, in the snow, and firing MP5s with both hands."

Finn didn't answer.

Tyler glanced over his shoulder at the Aussie. "Finn?"

"Sorry. I zoned out at *while you were still in diapers*."

"You're both hilarious," Eddie said. "Here comes the train."

Thai traffic, when following any rules whatsoever, drove on the left. Tyler surged forward between the cars and the left railing. Approaching the second span, the train sped in from the west and turned north beside the bridge. It took the lead, but that was okay. Tyler and Finn wanted to land on the freight trucks, not the diesel engine up front. There'd be no one to hear their bodies slam onto the trailers. During transport, the truck drivers rode up front with the rail company's security guards.

"Ready, Finn?"

"Ready."

They'd have to jump simultaneously to avoid either bike crashing into the other with a rider still on board. Tyler stood on his seat and checked to see Finn do the same. "On my count. Three, two—"

A horn blared. A car swerved to avoid another and smashed into the rail, blocking Tyler's path. He dropped to his seat and steered away. "Finn, go!"

Tyler heard the bike crash behind, followed by angry honking. Through the comm link, he heard the *Oomph!* as Finn landed.

"I'm on."

Parallel to the bridge, the thief hopped to his feet, riding the piggybacking freight truck like an urban surfer. Tyler gave him a salute.

The Aussie saluted back. "You coming?"

"Yeah, yeah. Give me a sec." He gunned the bike past two more cars and swerved back to the railing. The last towering spire passed over him. Ahead, the diesel engine turned under the bridge to follow the northern shoreline. A ten-foot-wide pylon topped with the sculpture of a lotus blossom marked the curve. Tyler made a snap calculation.

"I'm not going to make it."

Talia pounded on Val's bedroom door. "Val, come out. Let's talk this through." She'd chosen the harder path, but she might have been a little too abrupt about it. The grifter had locked herself away. "Val?"

"Complete honesty isn't always the best policy, you know. A little empathy wouldn't hurt."

"Fair point." She had Val talking again. A good

start. Talia rested a shoulder against the door. "I can be harsh. I get it. Eddie reminds me all the time. But I thought you'd want the truth rather than a regurgitation of the same con you've been running on yourself."

Silence.

"This is not new, Val. People have been running this con for years—millennia, even. I call it the . . . the As Wrong Anyway gag."

The door opened, forcing Talia to catch the frame to keep from falling through. Val cocked her head. "You just made that up."

"Maybe. Doesn't make As Wrong Anyway any less of a thing." Val never shared much about her hobbies, but Talia knew she loved grifting lore— the cons, the clever names—made up or not. "Want to hear more?"

"You're playing me."

"Yes I am."

"Fine. I'll bite." Val walked past her and pulled up a stool at the kitchen counter. "Lay out this alleged scam. How's it work?"

"Easy." They both set their earpieces on the counter, and Talia grabbed the coffeepot and two cups. "As Wrong Anyway is a value con like . . ." She racked her memory, searching through all the gags and games Tyler and Val had taught her. ". . . like the Old Violin."

"In which the framer sets the story by decrying his hard times and lamenting the need to sell some dear dilapidated item, and the shill shows up to convince the mark the item is priceless."

"Except As Wrong Anyway works in reverse. It down-values the merchandise, and—"

"And the framer, the shill, and the mark are all the same person." Val accepted her cup and took a sip, eyeing Talia over the rim. "Correct?"

"Nailed it. But keep following." Talia added some milk and sugar to her own cup and stirred it in. "In As Wrong Anyway, the grifter-slash-mark sells herself on doing something wrong by convincing herself this dastardly deed is not *as wrong* as some other crime."

"Variations?"

"Endless." Talia grinned. A moment before, she'd been desperate to get Val talking. Now the two were having fun. "The Wiley Accountant. 'I can cheat on my taxes because it's not *as wrong* as stealing, and the government takes too much money *anyway.*' "

"I like that one," Val said. "I kind of live that one."

"Lots of people do. Then there's The Frenemy. 'Spreading gossip about Mary is not *as wrong* as intentionally hurting her, and *anyway,* the rumor is probably true.' Or"—Talia lowered her chin, raising her gaze to meet Val's—"The Oliver Twist. 'Picking pockets and graft isn't *as wrong* as armed robbery or murder, and *anyway* these rich people have money to burn.' "

Val set her jaw. "Now you're hitting close to home."

"Yes, I am. And you're feeling hurt, betrayed—not because I'm being direct, but because Rudenko's presence pulled back the curtain on your self-con. You can get angry, or you can own the moment and stop treating yourself like a mark."

Val left the counter and walked into the living room, facing the setting sun. She didn't speak for a while. "Is . . . Is this how it was for Marco?"

"And Tyler. And me. Each of us set our own boundaries. I thought my anger at God was not as wrong as outright rebellion in any form. And hey, didn't I deserve to be angry anyway?"

Val remained quiet for a time. "I can see how you'd believe that."

"But by setting my own degrees of right and wrong, I *was* rebelling. I conned myself into believing I was wiser than the one who created the whole universe. I hurt Jenni, Bill, and Eddie, and so many others in the process. Tyler helped me see I was drowning."

"Drowning. Yes." Val turned. Her cheeks were wet. "I've lived a lifetime of taking, Talia. I've hurt thousands of marks—and how many others I didn't know about, like Rudenko's victims. You once said I don't care who I hurt. But I do. I'm sinking under the weight of all my crimes."

"You don't have to." Talia stepped around the

425

counter. Carefully. Slowly. "Remember Peter on the water, how Christ lifted him out of the waves. Trust. Faith. We weren't created to go it alone in this world. I've been learning that since Volgograd. Tyler. Finn. You. You've all been there for me." She stretched out a hand. "Christ is here for you now. All you have to do is accept his help."

Val took her hand, and Talia pulled her into an embrace. The two of them cried together.

CHAPTER SEVENTY-TWO

Ratchawin Riverside Village
Yan Nawa District
Bangkok, Thailand

Tyler jumped the median and cut between oncoming cars. He fishtailed down the bridge's east embankment. A hard right and a spray of gravel left him speeding along the narrow dirt trail beside the tracks.

"You didn't make it?" Eddie asked after Tyler gave him a sitrep. "But you and Finn have to find the trailers and work the locks before Darcy stops the train. Two minutes later, transport security will come running down the tracks from their passenger car. We have a tiny window to get those kids off."

"Fluid plan," Tyler said. "Fluid . . . plan. Finn, report."

"Found the freight trucks. Numbers nine and ten, counting from the back. Working the first lock."

"Keep at it."

The tracks diverged from the riverbank, and a canyon of dilapidated apartment buildings swallowed the train. Tyler inched closer to the railroad ties and sailed through the gap. Every rock and pebble jiggled his front tire, threatening to unseat him, but he sped up. He had to get on board before some larger obstacle sprang up in his path—an obstacle like the utility post materializing two hundred meters ahead.

The bike's engine screamed. The handlebars bounced and jerked at his arms. Tyler closed on the last car, a freight truck on a flatbed like all the rest. With thirty meters to run before the utility box, he reached for the trailer and swiped empty air.

Twenty meters. It was no use.

"Finn, I can't get to you."

"Yes, you can!"

He heard the shout as much from the car beside him as over the comms. The thief appeared from behind the trailer and reached out a hand. "Grab hold!"

Tyler gripped the Aussie's forearm and jumped. The two fell side by side on the flatbed. In their wake, the bike slammed into the utility box, sending up a shower of sparks.

Tyler tossed his helmet over the side and helped Finn to his feet. "I thought I told you to work the locks."

The thief frowned. "You're welcome. First lock's done. Contents were a little disappointing. I'll get to work on the second post-haste."

"Make it post double haste," Eddie said. "You're almost to the market."

The entire plan hinged on being ready to rush the children off the train when it stopped.

According to Eddie's research, Siam Rail Transport had plowed straight through the decades-old Central Bangkok Market to install the new southern line, knocking down tin and cinder-block booths. With the line completed, the vendors moved back in, right up to the tracks. Three times a day, the conductor blew his horn, the awnings rolled back, and the train rolled through at thirty-five miles an hour, inches from the noses of the market customers. The moment it passed, the awnings fell back into place, and business resumed.

A train stopped in the middle of that market would cause all the right kinds of confusion.

Tyler followed Finn from one rolling flatbed to the next, heading for the first truck. "What did you mean when you said the contents were disappointing?"

"I'll show you." They reached the trailer and Finn threw open the doors.

"Clothes?"

"Evening gowns mostly."

Tyler caught the hem of a dress and rubbed sequined polyester between his thumb and forefinger. "Cheap evening gowns. Eddie, how confident are you in those registry numbers?"

"Confident. Please, get to the second trailer. You two are killing me."

The padlock protecting the second trailer proved no match for Finn. He had it loose in moments and unlatched the doors to reveal a wall of cardboard boxes.

"False barrier," Tyler said. "Got to be. Look for a smuggler's door behind." The two hauled down box after box, only to find another row. The horn sounded from the engine. Tyler checked the train's progress. "Darcy, we're approaching the market. Do your thing."

"But of course."

They didn't need to permanently disable the train, only stop it for a time. Darcy had planted a small charge in the tracks to target one of the engine's traction motors—a low-hanging part, easily replaceable with an onboard spare.

With both hands, Finn tore the next wall of boxes away. A few fell open, dumping pottery statuettes on the flatbed. What remained was a roll-up door with a keypad lock. "Found the smuggler's door. We're close, Darcy."

"Copy. I see you on Eddie's drone feed. Stand by for detonation in three . . . two . . . one . . ."

Tyler heard no explosion, not even a pop. He felt a minor jolt as Darcy's charge took out the traction motor, then the conductor laid on the brakes, sending him lurching into the smuggler's door next to Finn. He pushed himself back. "Can you handle that lock?"

The thief gave him a hard look. Finn unzipped

his backpack and dug out a screwdriver and a stun gun.

The train continued to slow. Bewildered shoppers came into view, staring at the two men on the flatbed. A few pointed and yelled.

Finn pried the keypad's cover loose, exposing the guts beneath, and zapped the housing with the stun gun. The hooking latch clicked back. The train came to a stop.

Eddie's drone zipped ahead. "The security guards are out of their car and working their way back along the tracks. We can't involve the authorities, guys. Any word of kids rescued from a train over local police nets will get back to Boyd."

Mac appeared among the growing volume of onlookers beside the car. "How's it goin', lads?"

Tyler pointed up-rail. "Tight. Security is inbound. Go run interference."

"Will do." Mac nodded to Pell, whom Tyler had not noticed until that moment. "Let's have some fun."

As the Scotsman lumbered off with his chameleon sidekick, Finn rolled up the door. "Uh, boss?" He stepped back, allowing Tyler a clear view of the trailer's contents.

Tyler peered in. He bit his lip. "Huh. I didn't see this coming."

CHAPTER SEVENTY-THREE

"What do you mean, they're the wrong kids?" After praying with Val, Talia had reclaimed her earpiece. As she slipped it in, she'd heard the last moments of the train heist.

Tyler was using his *I'm a thief not a magician* voice. "Well, they're not Burmese refugees. That's for sure. We've got fourteen girls in a trailer set up like a bunk room, all in their early teens, all from Siberia, and all mad as bees. I didn't know there were so many ways to say 'You're ruining my life' in Russian."

Talia could hear the girls shouting in the background.

Val gave her a knowing look. "What's the line, Tyler? Did Rudenko convince them they were on their way to see modeling agents?"

"The best in Hong Kong. The girls thought they'd be modeling evening gowns and catching fat contracts. Right now, they're struggling to understand that they're not even *in* Hong Kong. It's a classic bait and switch."

Talia would have laughed, listening to Finn

shepherd a pack of angry teens speaking a language he didn't, except she understood every tearful word. They weren't runaways. The girls' parents had paid Rudenko's ropers huge cash sums to take their daughters off into the glamorous modeling life.

"We got the trailers buttoned up before we left," Tyler said a few minutes later. "Rail security never saw us. Rudenko will know he's been hit when he gets his delivery, but he won't know the who or the why. Pell and Darcy are taking the girls to a hotel to wait out the op. Finn, Mac, and I are headed back on foot. We're a few blocks away."

"What about Compassion's kids?" Talia asked. "What about Hla Meh and the others?"

"We have to face facts. Either their kidnapping had nothing to do with the Frenzy, or the broker involved is Boyd himself. We've eliminated all other options. Keep your focus on the White Lion now. Complete the mission, and let God take it where he will."

Let God. Trust. Faith. Everything Talia had asked of Val, and everything Tyler had asked of her. But leaning and trusting were easier said than done when children's lives were at stake. *Suffer the little children to come unto me.* Whoever took them would pay, one way or another.

Stuck in the room in the middle of Boyd's maze, Talia faded back into the couch cushions.

Her hand came to rest on the bump of an object in her pocket. She drew it out. Val's coin. On Tyler's AS2—on the day Val first flipped that coin to Talia—how sure Talia had been that she'd rush in to save those kids like the white knight in so many stories.

"My coin," Val said. "You still have it."

"I'm sorry. I should have given it back to you in Prague." Talia offered her the piece. "I thought I was teaching you some kind of lesson, but I was being petty."

Val shook her head. "It's all right. Honestly, I wasn't going to ask for it back, not after today. I took that coin from my father's safe when I ran away, along with the first cash I ever stole. In a way, that little piece of gold represents my entire life of crime."

"This coin was in Marco's safe?" Talia swallowed, suddenly afraid to drop it. "It's real, isn't it? I mean, not just real gold. This thaler came from Maximillian's lost treasure."

"I didn't know what I had until years later, when an old collector in Venice told me its history. I used to imagine that single coin would help me track down the rest."

"So the game we ran on Atan—"

"Was me acting out the fanciful dreams of a lost teenager. Yes." Val sat up. "Wait. Atan."

"What about him?"

"He bought our coins, which counted as one of

our deals for the Frenzy. He also told us earning too much would get us unwanted attention from the White Lion."

Talia knew all of this. But they didn't have enough reserves left from the Club Styx job to threaten Boyd, so the point was moot. They couldn't force a meeting. She frowned. "So?"

"So, I'll need my coin back."

Talia narrowed her eyes. "I thought you didn't want it."

"Don't *give* it to me. *Sell* it to me." Val went to the deal panels and worked the screens. On the scoreboard, the link symbol between Panther Eight One and Panther Eight Two broke.

Talia's slate buzzed, as it had during the deal with Atan. Val had made an offer. She raised her eyes to the grifter. "You think this will work?"

"It's worth a shot."

With a light touch of the accept button, Talia took the deal. She passed the Bavarian Thaler to Val. "One gold coin in exchange for a meeting with the White Lion, like handing a drachma to the ferryman for the chance to meet Death."

On the living room TV, the scoreboard gremlins siphoned more than thirty-four million out of Val's account and dumped it into Talia's, leaving Val with ten million—exactly what she needed to cover her ante. Talia's account had grown to the high side of seventy-eight million.

The White Lion's account had grown as well,

but not by nearly as much. Talia now had him beat by a comfortable twenty million, assuming the deal stuck. Boyd was not merely a Frenzy competitor. He was also the referee. Would he allow this little maneuver?

She didn't have long to wait for the answer. The slate buzzed again—a private message from the White Lion.

Talia let out a quiet laugh. "He wants to meet. The Atrium. We've got him."

CHAPTER SEVENTY-FOUR

Jungle Atrium
Twin Tigers Complex
Bangkok, Thailand

The elevator opened onto a glass walkway, etched to emulate a stone path. With the maze lit below, Talia felt like a messenger to Olympus entering a garden high above the world of men. A near perfect memory of her schooling also left her keenly aware that in every mythology, such places were guarded by monsters.

"Tyler, are you seeing this?" she whispered through her teeth. Her comms crackled, but she received no answer. Eddie had warned her the signal from the repaired transmitter-receiver might not reach the Atrium. No audio or video transmissions. Talia took her glasses off. For now, she was on her own.

A stream fed by a four-story waterfall ran beside the path. Something rustled the foliage beyond. Talia fought the urge to touch the weapon holstered at her back, hidden by her blouse—her Agency-issued all-composite Glock. The time for nonlethals was over. She turned in a circle. "Hello?"

"What is your game, Miss Macciano?"

Talia didn't see the speaker. "I don't understand."

Boyd strolled out from behind the waterfall on a steel-grate walkway, two stories up. He crossed his arms, crumpling the vest and tie of a gray three-piece suit. "You heard me."

Talia played her part, feigning surprise. "Livingston Boyd. The energy-stock wunderkind. So, you're the White Lion."

"In the flesh. But I think you knew that." He nodded to her left. "Careful."

A snarling huff punctuated the warning. Talia jumped to the other side of the path. Across the stream, only a few meters away, a full-grown lion shook its white mane, tracking her every move with blue eyes. "Boyd, what is this? You're feeding me to your cat?"

"Relax. He won't cross the stream. There's an ultrasonic fence. The Japanese circus that sold him to me trained him well. I named him Lionel." Boyd shoved his hands into his pockets and shrugged. "I couldn't help myself."

Talia took a step. The lion matched it. She took another. The lion did the same, placing each paw in Boyd's synthetic grass with silent purpose. He licked his lips. She swallowed. "How long has it been since Lionel ate?"

"Two days. Keeps him active. I wouldn't want him passed out in a meat coma when I have guests." Boyd walked along the winding steel grate track, passing between the umbrella boughs of monkeypod trees. "I asked you a question.

What's your game, Miss Macciano? Mine is cutthroat."

"As in billiards?"

"As in everything." He came to a stop above her, where the walkway made an S turn over the path. "I grew up online. Massive multiplayer fantasy games. Resource management simulations. Whatever the arena, cutthroat was the winning strategy. Make alliances. Break alliances. Wipe out the noobs and take their stuff."

Lionel sat on his great haunches, looking up at his master as if hoping for a treat.

Boyd didn't give him so much as a glance. "I found the same applies to the world's markets—black, white, or gray. My game is cutthroat, Miss Macciano. And playing cutthroat has made me billions."

"Your parents must be proud."

"My parents still live in Cardiff and think I'm a stockbroker. I'm biding my time until I can stick them in a home." Boyd rested his forearms on the rail. "So, you ended the partnership with your sister and nearly doubled your money. Betrayal? Collusion? Are you merely vying for my attention, or are you gunning for my title?"

Talia didn't like the way his new position forced her to tilt her head. It robbed her of any awareness of her surroundings. She backed a few paces down the path, grateful Lionel didn't follow. "You tell me."

Boyd snorted. "Sorry. No time for guessing games. In less than fifteen minutes, my proxy will arrive at our off-site warehouse with my biggest buyers. I have thirty or forty million dollars coming in over the next hour. Do you?"

"I still have cards to play."

"Are you referring to the stock you hijacked from Rudenko?"

Talia held her poker face.

"Yes, I know about the hit on Rudenko's shipment. I know everything that happens at the Frenzy, Miss Macciano. Everything. You may be interested to know the stock I'm selling this evening is similar, and much higher in volume. You can't win."

Similar stock. High volume. Boyd had the children, after all. "If you're not worried about losing, why did you call me up here?"

"Curiosity." Boyd descended a spiral stair to the glass path, fingers caressing the rail. Lionel let out another guttural huff, perhaps disappointed the Englishman remained out of reach—a bite-sized beef Wellington on the move. "In years past, Frenzy competitors who came this close wound up lying in pools of their own blood. But you piqued my curiosity."

"How? Is it so surprising to see a pair of women outsmart Atan, Rudenko, and Jafet, or best the White Lion at his own game?"

"I like your confidence, but no. I'm intrigued

by your strange mash-up of do-wrong and do-right. You killed Bi Fan and Larson. You shot—" He laughed. "Forgive me. You *executed* Orien Jafet on behalf of Marco Calafato." He threw his arms out to the sides. "*The* Marco Calafato. Word on the Jungle net is you and your sister are his daughters, and I believed that word. But then I heard a different rumor." Boyd glanced at the foliage near Talia, as if another big cat might appear, stalking her.

But it wasn't a cat.

The huge bodyguard who'd killed Riku Ishimoto emerged from the trees and fake boulders, leveling the same Desert Eagle .50-cal.

Boyd made a simple hand gesture, as if introducing an old acquaintance to a new one. "This is my associate Mr. Gorev. A friend of his told us you're a CIA spy."

CHAPTER SEVENTY-FIVE

Grand Bazaar
Twin Tigers Complex
Bangkok, Thailand

Val arrived at the Grand Bazaar with ten minutes to spare. Atan and Rudenko were already in place, putting the final touches on their bays, and Boyd's master of ceremonies had all his people and decorations set just so, ready for the incoming flood of wealthy customers.

The fountain flowed with a spattering rush. The catering carts sizzled. The air hung thick with the scent of Mediterranean delights. On any other night, Val might have reveled in the glittering gold of this high-end den of thieves. But Aladdin's Cave had lost its luster. A new awareness in her heart peeled back the veneer to show the gold for rusty, painted tin.

The night had lost its luster for Rudenko too. Val stayed out of his sight line, but she kept tabs. Confused workers ducked and dodged around his bay, shielding themselves against a torrent of abuse. Every so often, she heard a sad, airy squeak.

"Eddie, why are Rudenko's bay workers holding armloads of chew toys?"

"Yeah, that." The geek came through with static,

but readable. "I swapped the registry numbers in the cargo database as a backup to the train heist. Don't worry. When this is over, I'll make sure"—he paused as if reading from his computer—"*Beikbān* Happy Pooch Dog Toys . . . gets their delivery."

The Bluetooth signal from Eddie's damaged hockey puck had faded to nil as Val reached the Grand Bazaar. But he had provided a solution. While the cell jammer in the maze was still up, Boyd had shut down the one in the Grand Bazaar to accommodate his guests. Val had found her original SATCOM earpiece taped to one of the many hard-shell cases delivered to Talia's bay. She'd found something else as well—a remote detonator.

Boyd's MC, wearing a sequined tux, stomped into the bay, surveyed the empty eight-by-eight cages, and jiggled the lock on one of the cases. "Open these crates. Fill your big empty cages with whatever it is you are selling. My guests are arriving soon."

"You mean the White Lion's guests?"

"Yes, yes. Whatever." Gone was the goodwill earned by the tips she and Talia had given him. In the elevator the day before, if he really had expressed a hope the two would survive the game, he certainly regretted it now.

"I can't help you. My sister and I dissolved our partnership. This is her bay, and these are her wares, not mine."

This bought her a one-eyed squint. "Really. And where *is* your sister, may I ask?"

"With the White Lion. Go ahead and disturb them. I'm sure he won't mind."

His mouth fell open and snapped shut again. After another heartbeat of glaring, he marched away, thrusting a finger at one of the caterers. "Leave the champagne alone, you idiot! We start with the red. Always the red!"

She watched him stomp past Atan's bay, and the Albanian caught her gaze. He grinned and waved a hand over his central display, a red table with a pile of gold coins.

"Atan has our spare change on display along with his pharmaceuticals. Talia's cargo is in place. We're all set."

"Copy, Val." Tyler kept vigil at the edge of the plaza below, waiting in the shadows with Finn, Mac, and a Thai army colonel dressed in black body armor. "Hang tight." He turned to the colonel. "Wait for my signal as well. If you and your men rush in early, you'll blow the whole thing."

CHAPTER SEVENTY-SIX

Jungle Atrium
Twin Tigers Complex
Bangkok, Thailand

Boyd fingered the waxy leaf of a rubber plant. "The reach of my Jungle syndicate is unending—a product of limitless crowdsourcing and years of acquisitions unchecked by laws." Without taking his gaze from the foliage, he tilted his head, indicating his bodyguard. "I acquired Mr. Gorev, for instance, from a former client. Mr. Gorev had a unique skillset and one excellent contact which I desired. Now he works for me."

"How efficient." Talia shifted her weight, a subtle movement to keep Boyd in sight but refocus her energy toward the bigger threat—the bodyguard and his hand cannon. "And I suppose you had this former client liquidated to make Mr. Gorev a free agent?"

"Oh no. According to Mr. Gorev—the horse's mouth, as it were—the credit for his previous employer's liquidation belongs to you. Isn't that right, Anton?"

"*Da.* Back then she was Natalia Wright, security consultant."

The pieces slammed together in Talia's eidetic

mind, drawn by the cover name she'd used in the mission to stop Pavel Ivanov six months earlier. The Russian's unmistakable voice. His stance. The slight cant of his Desert Eagle—unique to Airborne Spetsnaz. Talia hid her shock behind a flat expression. "Alexi Bazin. You changed your face. It didn't help."

The bear growled.

"Aww, friends reunited," Boyd said. "This is . . . special. Unending reach, Miss Macciano. Or should I say, Miss Inger?"

The use of her real name cracked Talia's hard stare.

Boyd saw the change and grinned. "Yes. Talia Inger. CIA. You changed your appearance, but not enough. Suspicious, Anton put out some feelers. A Jungle cobra in Volgograd linked you to the CIA cover name Vera Novak."

"But you didn't take his word for it."

"No need. As I said, unending reach. My Agency contact, courtesy of Anton, gave me your identity and advised me to kill you. But I'm still wondering, which is the real Talia Inger?" Boyd stretched out his hands, wrists pressed together. Beside him the white lion began to pace again, watching her with hungry eyes. "Are you the dutiful spy, ready to take me in? Or are you the ruthless killer who took out Orien Jafet, looking to become queen of the Jungle."

Talia didn't hesitate. The team had everything

they needed. "The dutiful spy, I'm afraid." She raised three fingers to her temple in a mock salute—a signal to the darkened drone hovering outside. Her other hand moved closer to her Glock. "I'm here to bring you in, Boyd. We all are."

Eddie's call crackled in Val's ear, perhaps affected by the jammer still running over in the maze. "Val, Talia gave me the go sign. You're on."

The patrons of the Grand Bazaar had arrived en masse. A small crowd of Asian businessmen surrounded Rudenko, all quite unhappy. Atan, on the other hand, seemed quite popular. The pile of gold coins and his rainbow of pharmaceuticals had drawn a crowd.

Perfect.

Val palmed the remote trigger and walked out to the central fountain. "Copy that, Red Leader. Three . . . two . . . one . . ." She pressed the button. "Boom."

A blue-white flash and a storm of sparks erupted from Atan's bay. The buyers reeled back. Boyd's security men converged, all talking into their radios at once.

Up in the Atrium, Bazin's radio buzzed with urgent chatter. He took his gaze off Talia to answer, and the barrel of the Desert Eagle drooped—a small opening, but all the opening Talia needed.

She drew the Glock and fired, running sideways into the miniature jungle. The light *crack* of the Glock and the Desert Eagle's hefty *boom* shook the Atrium. His rounds split the air where Talia had been standing a moment before and thwacked into the foliage. She kept shooting. Bazin's body jerked twice and he dropped out of sight.

One down.

Waist deep in rubber plant leaves, Talia shifted her aim to cover Boyd, but he was gone.

CHAPTER SEVENTY-SEVEN

Grand Bazaar
Twin Tigers Complex
Bangkok, Thailand

Darcy's exploding coins caused confusion in the Grand Bazaar but no lasting panic. The crowd in Atan's bay parted. Boyd's guards dragged the protesting Albanian into the promenade.

Val moved behind the fountain, out of his sight line, to avoid the inevitable *She did it!* She turned her attention to the stacks of crates in Talia's bay. "Eddie, Phase Two."

"I'm sorry. Who did you call?"

She sighed. "Red Leader. Phase Two. Hurry up, before we lose the moment."

"With pleasure."

With a ripple of bangs, the stacks of hard-shell crates toppled, lids falling open. Drones poured out like bees from a broken hive. The sight hardly fazed the crowd of hardened black-market buyers. Most only backed up a little as the drones fanned out among them.

The MC helped maintain the calm. "All part of the festivities, ladies and gentlemen. A demonstration of one of our top merchant's wares." He cast a wide-eyed glance at Val, and she gave him a reassuring nod.

"He wants a demonstration?" Eddie said. "I'll give him a demonstration."

The TACRON spider drones with their ball cameras and the sphere drones with their rocket payloads rose to the arched ceiling. The gun drones hovered at eye level and did coordinated flips, earning a smattering of applause.

Val frowned up at one of the cameras. "Stop playing, *Red Leader*."

"Yeah, yeah. A few more seconds. Targeting, sorting, and . . ."

The gun drones opened fire.

What might have been a bloodbath under TACRON's original design became a surreal, but less disturbing scene for Val. The team had loaded the drones' magazines with P3Q rounds. Most of the guards and patrons collapsed in one collective faint. A smattering survived the first salvo, including Rudenko. He ran for the bridge.

"Re-sorting. Re-targeting."

The drones fired again. The remainder dropped. Rudenko fell sprawling beneath the huge Frenzy scoreboard.

Up in the Atrium, the white lion clawed the air, testing his ultrasonic fence. Big cats and gunfire didn't mix.

Talia moved away from him, returning to the

path. "Come out, Boyd. You have nowhere to go."

"Don't I? This is my domain. My kingdom, not yours."

The voice came from the jungle to Talia's right. She pointed her Glock at the mass of green and walked the path, body coiled, ready to spring. She sensed Lionel behind her, mirroring her movements, and prayed the invisible fence along the stream would contain him.

The play of light and shadow in the greenery toyed with her senses. Boyd could be anywhere, working his way toward an exit. She had to keep him talking. "Tell me about the product you're moving tonight. How did you acquire your stock?"

"What do you care? I thought you were here to take me down."

The voice came from behind her. He had doubled back toward the waterfall.

"I am." She reversed her course to follow. Lionel did the same. "I'm just making conversation. Keeping the mood light."

"No, this is something more. You hijacked Rudenko's shipment. Now you're asking about my stock. You came for the children as well as for me. Your priorities are divided. What will you do if you're forced to choose?"

"Won't happen." Talia zeroed in on a grove of short palms. A leaf quivered. She kept her aim low, seeking to wound rather than kill. But as she put weight on the trigger, something felt off. Boyd had to be watching her aim the Glock. Why didn't he run?

The hairs stood up on the back of Talia's neck. She dove for the stream bank an instant before the rhythmic blasts of a 9mm semiautomatic erupted from the grove. Bullets whizzed past, splintering the glass walkway and thudding into the bank.

Lionel pounced.

All the gunfire. All the movement. All the hunger. The ultrasonic fence no longer held instinct at bay. Talia flipped over to see the huge cat airborne, claws extended. She rolled through water and scrambled up the other bank. With incredible agility, the white lion stayed close, swiping at her. Her blouse ripped at the shoulder. Her skin burned. She made for the spiral stair.

Rounds ricocheted off the steps as Talia climbed. The sparks frightened Lionel enough to throw him off the pursuit. He veered away into the green.

She had escaped the lion, but the catwalk left Talia exposed to Boyd's fire. At the top, shoulder smarting, she panned her Glock across the foliage. A third volley hit the steel grate at her feet, and she ran, crouching. Boyd didn't have a good angle, but that wouldn't last long. She made for the concealment of the waterfall.

• • •

"Val," Eddie said, turning serious after the fun he'd been having with the drones. "Talia needs backup. Boyd got the drop on her."

"I'll try the elevators." Val stepped over Rudenko's body on her way to the bridge. She resisted the urge to stomp on his head, but only just.

"Also, I think his pet lion is loose."

"His pet what?" She didn't press for an answer. Another familiar straggler had survived the drone attack. Atan. As Val crossed the sky bridge, he glanced over his shoulder, frantically punching the down button.

He must have escaped his guards when the gun drones struck. When Val reached him, he clasped his hands in beggar's gratitude. "I take it your drones spared me on purpose, correct? Of course they did. You and I are practically partners. The exploding coin gag, very good." He seemed to think all this was another coup, like Milos. "I will make this worth your while. I promise. With the White Lion's resources, we'll be—"

He blathered on, and Val frowned through the windows at the office across the plaza. "Eddie, Talia needs me. We don't have time for this."

"Sorry. Here you go."

A drone rose from behind her and popped Atan with a single round. He collapsed.

Val nudged his limp arms out of the way with

her foot. "Thanks." She tried the up button. Nothing happened. "The elevators are locked down. Can you hack in?"

"Negative. They run on a local server."

"What about the stairs."

A pause. "I can't find you a route to the Atrium from that location. For now, Talia's on her own."

CHAPTER SEVENTY-EIGHT

Golden Tiger Plaza
Twin Tigers Complex
Bangkok, Thailand

Once Val confirmed the guards and patrons at the Grand Bazaar were down, Tyler signaled his colonel friend and sent in the Thai Rangers. He, Mac, and Finn were jogging behind the platoon, heading for the western tower entrance, when he heard the exchange between Eddie and Val. The grifter couldn't get to Talia.

"We can't leave her hanging up there, Eddie. Give me options."

"Already working on them. Option One—I can reroute a police chopper to your position, which will take time."

"Is there an Option Two?"

"Look right."

Option Two sat on a stage at the base of the eastern tower, part of the technology exhibition.

Tyler nodded. "I love the way your mind works, kid." He caught the arm of a young officer in the rear echelon of rangers, slowing him down. "Hang on a sec, Lieutenant. You speak English?"

"Of course."

"Good. You're with me."

Backed by six armed rangers, the thieves ran to the rope line surrounding the quadcopter. The salesman who met them wore a petrified smile.

"Good evening . . . ah . . . gentlemen," he said in broken English, wringing his hands. "You have interest in Thanfa Aerotech Falcon Medical Transport? Lightweight materials. Room for one pilot and two paramedics plus locking gurney for patients. Maximum altitude is—"

Tyler held up a hand to stop the sales pitch. "Lieutenant, ask him if the batteries are charged. Tell him we need to borrow this thing."

The lieutenant relayed the first part, and the salesman gave a nodding reply in his native tongue. But at the second part, his words grew rapid and heated. He waved his arms in the universal sign for *No way, Jose*.

They were burning precious time. Tyler frowned. "Tell him it's a matter of life and death."

"Yes, sir." The lieutenant held up a fist and gave it one pump. With a series of rattling clicks, he and his five companions levelled their machine guns.

The salesman raised his hands and stepped out of the way.

"Right." Finn stepped over the rope. "That's not exactly what he meant, but—you know—whatever works. Cracking on."

"Can you fly this thing?" Tyler asked Mac on the way up the platform steps.

"She's a quadcopter. Any monkey can fly her." The Scotsman squeezed his great form into the open cockpit. "I can make her dance."

More gunfire forced Talia back from the waterfall. She tried retreating, but a fragment from the final round nicked her calf. She fell to her wounded shoulder, twisting to aim a return shot, and saw her target.

"Wait!" Boyd had reached a second staircase, half hidden by the falls. He held his gun ready. With the other hand, he held out a smartphone. On the screen were two simple buttons—cancel and execute. "Keep shooting and I'll set them off."

She used the railing to pull herself up, never lowering the Glock. Down below, Lionel paced the synthetic grass, growling. "Set what off?"

"Your cutthroat game is all an act." Boyd walked up the steps. "Mine, however, is authentic. I'm always prepared to cut my losses and disappear." He waggled the phone. "I had my people place incendiary devices in my warehouse—and in the office above us. They'll burn away all trace of my involvement here, including all witnesses."

"The children."

"And my hosts and buyers—a hard but acceptable loss. The doors will lock. They'll be trapped. Ceramic panels in the walls and ceiling will contain the flames." Boyd made a face. "The effect is like an undertaker's furnace. By the time emergency personnel detect the fire, there'll be nothing left but unrecognizable cinders. Cutthroat, Miss Inger. The only way to play."

He walked forward, slowly, holding his thumb over the button. "If you shoot me, if you so much as scratch me, those children die. Lay down your weapon"—he shrugged, tilting his head and gun—"and I'll most likely kill you, but I promise the children will live."

Eddie and his drone were watching. Where was the team? Talia was leaning, trusting. *Please, God,* she prayed, bending to lay the Glock on the grate. *This is in your hands.*

Talia straightened, palms open at her side, and Lionel roared, giving voice to her frustration. "Now what?"

"Now nothing. You lose." Boyd extended his gun. "Game over."

CHAPTER SEVENTY-NINE

Golden Tiger Plaza
Twin Tigers Complex
Bangkok, Thailand

The shot made Talia cringe. But there was no pain apart from the shallow nicks on her shoulder and calf. And the sound was all wrong, a *boom* instead of a *crack*.

Boyd lowered his gun, eyes wide. He pitched over the rail.

Lionel pounced the moment his body hit the glass.

The *boom* told Talia all she needed to know. Bazin had survived her first attack. She found him on the third level of the catwalk, bleeding from two wounds on the upper right of his torso. All the same, he had her well covered with the Desert Eagle.

"Why?" she asked. "Why did you kill your boss?"

"He is not boss." The Russian let out a weary huff. "Also I want shoot him for some time. He was . . . liability."

"For whom? You?"

"For real boss."

Talia did not have to ask for clarification.

Archangel. Talia and Tyler had assumed Boyd

was Ivanov's connection to the CIA traitor. After all, Boyd had brokered the failed auction of Ivanov's hypersonic weapons six months earlier, and Ivanov had told them the whole plan came from a CIA contact. But Boyd and Ivanov were both young. Neither could have worked with Archangel for long. Bazin, however, was a product of the spy world's post–Cold War bedlam—just like Archangel. Talia should have seen it before.

If Bazin was going to kill her, she wanted answers—the answers she'd been afraid to seek when Tyler first invited her to join the op. "So, Archangel helps you gain the confidence of her marks with the promise of a high-level intelligence contact. In exchange, Archangel gets a few tidbits of criminal intel, enough to make her a shining star at the Agency."

The Russian refused to play along. His stolid frown neither confirmed nor denied the name Archangel.

Talia didn't get the chance to press him further.

Rays of blue, alien light washed over the monkeypod boughs. With a tremendous crash, a section of windows exploded. Glass flew everywhere. Lionel bounded for cover.

Outside, a giant quadcopter hovered, with Tyler and Finn kneeling on its open platform, staring down the sights of their submachine guns. Bazin tried to swing the Desert Eagle to meet the new threat, but Tyler and Finn opened fire on full automatic. The big Russian went down under a hail of P3Q rounds, enough to put a horse to sleep for a week.

Both men leaped from the quadcopter into the Atrium. Finn went straight for Talia, while Tyler swept for additional players.

"Bazin was the last," she shouted, running down the steps. "Except for Lionel."

Finn met her at the bottom. "Who?" He saw the blood on her shoulder and turned her by the arm. "You're shot."

"It's not a gun wound. It's a lion scratch." She nodded at Boyd's body. "He fared far worse."

Finn grimaced. "Real lions don't muck about, do they?" He let his machine gun hang and drew Matilda, aiming the blunderbuss at the trees. "Still out there, is he?"

"Cover me. I need to find Boyd's phone."

A search of the foliage near the body yielded no result, so Talia gutted her way through the gruesome task of rolling Boyd to one side. His phone lay beneath him, screen still active. A timer counted down.

0:03
0:02

"No!" Talia couldn't get a hand on the phone in time.

0:01
DETONATION

Talia, Finn, and Tyler all ducked as fire erupted above. Through the glass ceiling of the Atrium, she saw Boyd's office burning. And if the device in his office had gone off . . . "The children!" she shouted at Tyler. "Boyd set off an incendiary device in his warehouse and locked it down. They'll be killed!"

"Go!" Tyler pointed at Mac and the waiting copter. "Take Finn. I'll get Bazin out of here and help the rangers clear the building."

The copter looked lower than before. Mac beckoned to them from the cockpit. "Get crackin', you two! She's runnin' outta battery!"

The gap between the shattered windows and the copter's platform was bad enough, without it sinking as well. Finn seemed to read the fear in Talia's eyes. "You've got this. We go together, okay?"

"Okay."

He caught her hand, interlocking her fingers with his, and swung her arm in a silent *One, two, three!*

They jumped. Talia landed well inside and caught the medical gurney with her free hand. Finn had not jumped as far. His heels teetered over empty space. His free arm wheeled. She pulled him in, right into a hard embrace. She held him there as Mac descended, until she felt his chest shaking. Finn was laughing.

Talia pushed him away. "You did that on purpose." She should have known. Finn had an insane sense of balance.

He bent over the gurney, holding his gut. "Your face. Priceless."

"I hate you."

"Really? 'Cause you were hugging me pretty tight, there."

After defending himself from a flurry of punches, Finn gave her a new earpiece. She put it in as Eddie was reporting on the warehouse.

". . . location is obvious on my drone's infrared. I've dispatched emergency services. But remember, this is Bangkok. It'll take them a while to reach the building."

"Then it's up to us," Talia said. "Boyd had guards in the building. We'll need armed escort."

"No problem."

A half second later, she saw a yellow flash and an explosion of glass from the sky bridge on the Grand Bazaar level. Eddie's swarm of TACRON drones poured into the night to follow the quadcopter—a mother and her babies.

But the mother was running out of juice, descending the whole way. The narrow lanes and low buildings of the warehouse district came up fast.

Mac held the copter off the asphalt as long as possible.

Finn wrapped an arm around Talia's waist, holding her against the gurney. "Hang on!"

The copter's skids slammed down and scraped along the road until a glancing blow from a corrugated aluminum building sent it into a turn. It hit a curb, teetered, and fell over with an underwhelming *thump*. Finn and Talia crawled out and found Mac climbing from the cockpit.

"I forget," Finn said to the Scotsman. "Did Tyler spring for the damage waiver?"

"Funny." Mac pointed up the road. "Our buildin' is this way."

Eddie gave them updates over the comms. "My spider drones show no windows, but smoke is rising from the edges of the roof. There are guards out front."

Boyd had failed to mention any outside guards. "Can you take them?" Talia asked.

"That's what I'm here for . . . Or . . . virtually there. You know what I mean."

Talia and the others broke out from a cluster of smaller buildings and ran into the warehouse's parking lot. In front of them, Eddie's drones dropped to shoulder level.

The guards turned.

The drones opened fire.

The runners ran past as if the guards had never existed in the first place.

Talia jogged to a stop before a garage-style door and a smaller, normal entrance. "You'll have to blow one, Eddie."

"It's risky."

"Do it anyway." Talia called upon her training for improvised breach devices. Special Forces operators in Iraq and Afghanistan had learned a great deal on that front. She made a quick calculation. "Two rockets. Three meters from the smaller door. The double blast should blow it open without the risk of fragging anyone inside. Darcy, what do you think?"

"I concur, yes? Two rockets at three meters will safely do the job."

Please, God, let us be right. She and the others moved well clear.

Two rockets spiraled down from a sphere drone to blow a crater in the parking lot. When the dust cleared, the door hung from its hinges, blown inward. Smoke and flame billowed out.

CHAPTER EIGHTY

Warehouse Sector
Khlong Toei District
Bangkok, Thailand

Thet Ye's body jerked with fright. But he did not scream like the other boys. He had known the blast was coming.

Fires came with explosions. His father had told him so. On many hot evenings, Thet Ye's father had sat with him on the steps of their hut and retold the story of the fire on the night of his birth. Po would lift his hands high when he told of the moment the fire hit the camp's main petrol tank—an explosion so big many refugees claimed aircraft had dropped firebombs from the sky. "And still, Brave Life," he would say, "you were not afraid to enter this world."

Brave Life. Thet Ye did his best to control his shaking, lest he shame Po and his mother for giving him the name.

The ceiling above had transformed into pure flame. Drops of fire fell like slow rain onto the boys huddled in the cages. There were far more now than at the sheep pens. After the guards took the girls away, the boys had been trucked to this warehouse to join others taken from several camps. Twenty boys per cell. Ten cells in all.

Thet Ye did not know what had become of Hla Meh, but he was grateful God had spared her from this second fire. After what had happened to her father, one was enough.

The guards were equally afraid of the fire, as were the four men and one woman in rich clothes who'd arrived only minutes before it began. They had banged on the door and shouted at the front wall, and the guards had shot it with their machine guns. All to no avail. The teenager had finally sat on the floor, hugging his knees.

When the explosion blew the door from its hinges, one guard was knocked back. Another tried to run out, but Thet Ye heard a shout and a *smack,* and the second guard flew back the same distance as his friend. A huge white man followed him in, and then another man and a woman. They let no one leave until a guard gave them the keys to the cages. Only one guard attempted to raise his weapon. Instead of shooting him, the big man strode up and punched him in the nose.

With the keys in hand, the white men and the woman let the other adults go, although Thet Ye heard shouts of surprise and a buzzing and popping as soon as they ran through the door. In the next moment, a dozen little flying machines entered the warehouse.

The boys in the cages clamored for help, and the big man spoke sweetly to them as he unlocked the cages. His smaller friend ushered the boys out of the building in groups. As they ran, the woman walked along the line, calling a name that made Thet Ye's heart skip.

"Hla Meh?"

Thet Ye bolted the moment the big man unlocked his cage. He dodged the arms of the smaller man and ran to the woman. "Hla Meh!"

The woman scrunched her face in disbelief, as if unsure she'd heard right.

He said it again, nodding. "Hla Meh. She's my best friend!"

The woman didn't understand his Thai, but the message was clear. They were both looking for the same girl. Then the woman performed a miracle. She pulled out a phone—Thet Ye had seen many before—and showed him his father. Not a picture, or a recording, but his real father, speaking to him in earnest.

"Thet Ye." His father struggled to speak.

Another man appeared beside him, the man who had visited Thet Ye's parents before he joined the school. "Thet Ye, this woman is Miss Talia. She is looking for the girls. Do you know where they are?"

"No, I—" Beyond the phone and Miss Talia, he spied the teenage guard. The older boy had not left his place on the floor, knees to his chest. Miss Talia's friends had overlooked him in the confusion. "I know who does."

Thet Ye led Miss Talia to the teenager, and the older boy's eyes grew wide with fear. Covering him with her gun, Miss Talia tore his weapon away and shouted questions in English.

The teenager only lowered his gaze.

Miss Talia grew impatient. She lifted him to his feet, asking again, stern and insistent.

"*Mai chai, mai chai.*" *No, no.* Thet Ye shook his head and waved his hands to stop her. Pastor Nakor had shown him another way. He pushed between them and laid a hand on the boy's arm. "You don't have to be afraid anymore. Look around you." He nodded at the two unconscious guards. "They are finished. You are not their slave anymore. You do not have to be like them."

The teenager met his eyes.

Thet Ye saw him daring to hope. "Yes. You are free. God has done this for you. But he wants the girls to live. Please, tell us where the soldiers took them."

"The girls are here."

His answer made no sense.

At Thet Ye's confused look, the teen pointed at the back wall, entirely engulfed in flame. "There is a second room, with access from the other side."

A second room. The back wall was a divider between the two halves of the warehouse, built of wood and paint like the inside of the camp church. Hla Meh had been near him the whole time.

The fire had opened a gap in the center of the wall, filled with swirling smoke. Thet Ye told the man on the screen what the boy had said, and the man told Miss Talia. And while she spoke in earnest with her friends, Thet Ye stared at the gap.

"I am Thet Ye. I am Brave Life. I am not afraid of the fire."

He spoke the words three times, building his courage, then ran for the wall of flame.

Out of the corner of her eye, Talia saw Thet Ye, Po's son, break away. He rushed the wall of fire before she could stop him. He didn't slow. He didn't falter. He ran at full tilt, leaped through the dripping gap, and vanished.

Talia was at full sprint by the time he jumped. She jumped three steps later. The fire licked at her arms and neck, but the flame could not hold on. She made it through and heard Finn come through after her. The boy turned and gave them an affirming nod.

As Finn caught up to her, he snorted and coughed. "Glad to meet this little daredevil's approval."

The second section of the warehouse matched the first, down to the guards and visitors.

Eddie's drones flowed through the gap and took them down. Talia and Finn recovered the keys from an unconscious guard and began unlocking the doors.

Emergency services had arrived on scene. Sirens surrounded them. Water and soot rained down from above. A team of firefighters broke the door in with a battering ram.

As the firefighter helped the girls out of the building, Talia called for the one who had brought her there. "Hla Meh!" She had to call only once. Thet Ye found the girl first. The two held hands for a few heartbeats, then clung to each other at the center of the chaos.

CHAPTER EIGHTY-ONE

Aerion AS2
Central United States
Forty-Nine Thousand Feet

From his seat in the cabin, Finn glanced at their prisoner, who lay unconscious on a gurney in the center aisle. "He looks so peaceful when he's sleeping."

"Don't be fooled." Talia sat across the table from him. "When he's awake, he's a handful. Tyler said he made a scene in front of the Thai Ranger colonel, tried to convince the man Tyler would kill him."

"How'd that go over?"

"The colonel knows Tyler too well. He agreed to let us smuggle Bazin out of the country in exchange for full credit for taking down Boyd and capturing the whole pod of black-market whales in the Grand Bazaar." She laughed. "Tyler didn't want credit anyway, but he milked the deal. He made the colonel promise to find Lionel a proper home."

The colonel had gladly agreed, and his medics dressed the Russian's wounds for travel and set up a morphine drip. Talia glanced back to check on him. She had little reason to worry. Bazin's wrists and ankles were cuffed to the gurney rails. Darcy poked at the restraints, and Talia gave her a *Stop that* look.

"What?" the chemist asked with a shrug. "I like the clinking sound they make." Her eyes drifted over to Eddie, who swallowed and looked away.

Talia turned back to Finn.

He lifted his chin. "What about the Compassion kids?"

"Ewan's got them well in-hand. He said Compassion's meticulous documentation procedures mean they'll be back with their parents in a couple of days."

He seemed to read the *however* in her tone. "They weren't all Compassion's kids, though, were they?"

"No. Only our thirty-four. The rest face a mountain of red tape. To both Thailand and Myanmar, they are nonentities. It's hard to return children to their parents when those children don't officially exist. But there's a little hope." She allowed herself the hint of a smile. "I know one State Department employee who will take a vested interest in this and work tirelessly on every case."

"Jenni."

She nodded.

"You love your foster sister, don't you?"

"So much."

Finn lowered his gaze to his hands, then raised

it to meet hers. "I'm glad for you. Family's important."

She sensed the pain and longing in the way he said it. Talia didn't know what to say. "I . . . have a new addition to mine. The little girl. Hla Meh. She needed a sponsor—someone to write her letters, show love and care from afar, maybe even visit her once in a while. I'm not the best at letters and such. I barely return texts and emails. Maybe you could help."

He smiled. "I'd like that."

Finn's fingers made a motion toward hers, but Eddie slapped the table across the aisle and shot a hand in the air. "Something's wrong. Something big."

The team gathered around Eddie and Darcy as the geek sent his tablet display to the full-wall screen. Tyler came out of the flight deck, leaving Mac to fly. "What've you got?"

"A message from Franklin—the Dark Web equivalent of a dying rose left on a windowsill." He tapped away at a keyboard attachment. "Franklin left a trail of breadcrumbs—goblin tracks. I'm following them back through the servers and . . . here." He looked up at the wall, where a video window had opened. "It's a live feed. Heavily encrypted. Franklin? Can you hear me?"

The tech guru did not answer. Instead, Frank Brennan's mustache and gristly double chin appeared on the screen, marred by waves of static. He adjusted a webcam to bring the field of view up to his eyes. They were grim, and they settled on Talia. "We have a problem."

"Hello, Frank. What's wrong?"

"You've gone rogue. That's what's wrong."

"Excuse me?"

Tyler stood shoulder to shoulder with Talia. "She took down not one, but two major crime bosses, freed a couple hundred children, and captured the traitor Archangel's agent."

He'd almost made Talia blush. She elbowed him. "*We* did those things. All of us. Together."

He elbowed her back. "Hush. The grown-ups are talking." Tyler frowned at the giant head on his cabin wall. "Is that what you call going rogue, Frank?"

"Not me. Jordan. Always maneuvering. Always the chess queen. She's opened a counter-intelligence investigation into Talia, and she named you as an accomplice. Touch down at Reagan, and you'll find a pack of orangutans from Special Activities waiting for you. I doubt you'll touch tarmac alive."

A groan drew Talia's attention.

Bazin stirred.

She signaled Eddie to cut the feed. "Gotta go, Frank. Thanks for the heads-up. We'll be in touch. Tyler has a plan."

"But I—"

Eddie tapped a key, and the wall returned to live video of the clouds outside.

Bazin rolled his head over. "Miss Wright? Or is it Miss Inger? I forget."

She ignored Finn's signal to leave it be and walked to the gurney. "Then tell me a name I know you remember. Tell me the real name of Archangel."

He gave her a weak smile. "Nice try."

The morphine the medics had given him for the pain would not loosen his lips. Finn had suggested torture, cutting off the drip and digging into the wounds. But CIA case officers didn't operate that way, not the good ones. Neither did Christ followers. No truth serum. No torture. Talia had what she had—her prisoner and her wits. She had a hidden camera on the IV tower, placed there by Eddie for posterity. A glance at the geek told him to hit record.

"Why should I talk to you?" Bazin said. "You shot me."

Talia smiled—an honest smile. "Yes I did." She tried playing the law enforcement card. "We have you complicit in fraud, human trafficking, and murder. When we land, I'll hand you over to the Bureau. Give up your Agency contact, and maybe I can work a deal."

"When we land, I am dead man."

"Then talk to ease your conscience."

"No conscience. Spetsnaz beat this out of me

decades ago." He snorted. "When we land, you are dead too."

Tyler joined her at the gurney. "Explain."

Bazin kept his gaze on Talia, as if Tyler wasn't there. "I heard your friend. The wheels are moving. As they moved before. You are not first. Many years ago, another CIA officer discover her activities. She stop him then. She stop you now." He made the sign of a gun with his cuffed hand. "Bang. No problem."

Many years ago. Could he be talking about Talia's father? She leaned in. "How? How did she stop him back then?"

"She . . . how you say . . . turn tables. She frame him. Rogue spy."

So, Jordan was a slave to her old methods. But Bazin wasn't finished. "She send asset to kill him."

Talia felt Tyler tense beside her. She knew where this was going, a place she never wanted to go again. She had told him so from the beginning.

Bazin gave her a pained grin. "This asset is reason you came to Moldova, no? She call him Lukon."

That name—the myth. A knife to her gut. The old anger welled up inside. Talia felt Tyler's hand on her arm, and she met his eye. She saw the same hurt. For a moment, their anger burned together. The girl whose father had been taken by murder. The man whom Archangel had conned into that bloody act. Together, without words, they gave it to God.

By goading him into naming Lukon, Talia had gained enough intel, perhaps not for the CIA, but for herself. With nothing more to say, she jabbed a needle into Bazin's IV port. His eyes fluttered closed.

She sighed and looked to Tyler. "I told Brennan you have a plan. You do, right?"

He walked off toward the flight deck. "I always have a plan."

CHAPTER EIGHTY-TWO

The Metronome Restaurant
Dupont Circle
Washington, DC

"Contact." Eddie's voice buzzed in Talia's ear. "Subway cam has positive target ID. Point, be advised, Senator Ramirez and one personal security escort are in tow. Target is wearing a green coat and black knit cap."

"Copy. We have eyes on the Metro exit. South side. Standing by for visual."

Tyler bumped her shoulder with his, almost knocking her into the bricks on the east wall of the restaurant bordering the alley where they were hiding. "You look tense. Are you ready for this? It's been a long time coming."

"For both of us." She gave him a thin smile. "Yes, I'm ready."

The green coat stood out among the blur of jackets and overcoats emerging from the Metro station. Talia swallowed to banish the dryness from her throat. In her position—accused of a crime, so close to the op—running point was a rare privilege. "Red Leader, I have a visual. Stand by."

Despite every instinct screaming for her to rush into the circle, Talia waited until Jordan's face was unmistakable to her naked eyes. She raised two fingers pressed together, signaling Tyler, and he matched the gesture, confirming recognition.

Talia let out a breath. *Here it comes.* "Red Leader, Point confirms positive ID. We are a go. Move, move, move!"

Talia and Tyler rushed out of the alley, weapons up. Both carried Glock 26s with real bullets—none of Tyler's nonlethals.

"Mary Jordan!" Talia shouted. "Freeze!"

Tyler covered the senator's personal security guard. "Weapon down! Weapon down! Put it away!"

Any Capitol security man worth his salt would have ignored such commands from a man in an overcoat and flatcap, but Talia and Tyler were not alone.

Red and blue lights flashed. Sirens wailed. Black sedans sped into the circle from P Street and Massachusetts Avenue. Twenty plainclothes FBI agents and two CIA liaisons rushed out from their hiding places, all shouting at the same time.

Jordan retreated toward the Metro, but a pair of plainclothes agents blocked her path.

The senator's security man placed his weapons on the ground, both his primary and his backup, and slowly straightened, hands in the air. Watching him, a few frightened pedestrians also raised their hands, but they were yanked away to safety by local uniforms.

Only Senator Ramirez had the audacity to fight back. "Do you know who I am? Senator Daniela Ramirez, chair of the Senate Select Committee on Intelligence."

"Back off, Senator." Talia kept her Glock trained on Jordan. "This doesn't involve you."

"I'd say it does. Mary Jordan is a good friend. We're on our way to dinner."

"Mary Jordan is a traitor. And she's on her way to jail."

As one FBI agent slapped on the cuffs and another read her Miranda rights, Jordan glared. She didn't let the agent finish reading from the card. "You're going down for this, Talia. I opened an investigation into your activities"—she thrust her chin at Tyler—"and his. This stunt is nothing more than a delay tactic."

"Oh, it's more than a tactic." Talia returned the Glock to its holster. "We have proof you traded criminal favors for intelligence."

Jordan laughed. "Standard Agency protocol."

"Not this time. Your operations were personal, unsanctioned. And one involved an attempted missile attack against this very city."

Several FBI agents glanced her way. Apparently they hadn't read the entire brief.

Talia ignored their questioning looks. "We have Alexi Bazin. It's over."

Jordan played it cool, refusing to react. "I don't know any Bazin. All you have is his word against mine. You'd better come up with something more definitive, honey."

"You think I haven't? Tyler's people were on to Boyd's encrypted network before Volgograd. We couldn't quite crack it, but after gaining access during our infiltration into his black-market competition, we pulled a ton of data. We got everything."

"For instance," Tyler said. "We found an order dating back one week, in which Boyd had a syndicate member bring down half the traffic cams on Route 123. On the same morning, the syndicate dispatched a Bratva hitman to take out Officer Inger. That was enough to raise eyebrows at the Bureau."

"You're talking about communications that have nothing to do with me. You're reaching."

Talia shook her head. "He wasn't finished. We knew we needed to connect you to the syndicate. Yesterday, while I was still inside, the Jungle syndicate received a message warning that CIA operative Vera Novak had infiltrated the White Lion's game, including a picture. The message came from Cobra One Four Seven. You'll remember him as Oleg Zverev."

Tyler gave Jordan an *Ooh that hurts* cringe. "You should have notified your pal Bazin that Oleg was dead. With no body, the Russian cops never got involved. Word never got out. Bazin opened our photo file, and with it, he unleashed a virus engineered by Specialized Skills Officer Eddie Gupta." He glanced back. "Eddie, come over here."

The geek peeked out from the rear doors of an unmarked van. "Really? I thought you might leave me out of this, just in case it goes south. Then I'd, you know, still have a job."

Talia rolled her eyes. "Eddie . . ."

"Okay, okay. I'm coming."

"SSO Gupta's virus permeated the account," Tyler said. "It replicated itself and latched on to all outgoing files, including a new photo of Talia at the Frenzy, which Bazin sent you when he sought confirmation of the tip. The virus is dormant, but SSO Gupta can activate it at will. Would you like a demonstration?"

Jordan had no answer. She looked away.

The FBI commander raised a hand. "*I'd* like a demonstration."

"So would I." Across the street Senator Ramirez raised a hand as well, a skilled politician distancing herself from a bad association. "I'd like one very much."

Eddie unlocked his tablet and tapped the screen twice.

Immediately, Talia heard quiet laughter—the deep, disturbing laughter of the White Lion. Voices chanted, *The law of the Jungle, kill or be killed.* They came from Jordan's direction.

One of the agents reached into her pocket and

drew out a smartphone. He put it to his ear and shook his head.

Jordan's flat expression twisted into a smirk. "That's my phone. No virus."

It was a desperate move. Talia gave her a look of exasperated disappointment and nodded to the agent. "Try the *other* pocket."

He did, and pulled out a second device, screen flashing. Free of the heavy coat, the laughing and chanting filled the square. Eddie tapped his tablet, and the phone went dark. The deep, laughing voice, dying, had one final statement to make.

Game over.

The FBI commander spun Jordan and shoved her toward one of the sedans. "I'd say that's plenty definitive."

CHAPTER EIGHTY-THREE

**Russian Eastern European Division
CIA, New Headquarters Building
Langley, Virginia**

A blue light flashed from one of REED's black marble pillars.

Manila cardstock sheets marked with red and orange classification stamps covered every stack of paper and were taped over every computer screen.

All work had come to a screeching halt.

When the parade of black-uniformed officers—the Agency's Security Protective Services—arrived, Trevor announced their coming with the call, "Uncleared! Uncleared!" like a medieval crier calling *Unclean!* as a leper enters the village.

Such measures had not been taken at the Directorate since the fall of Harold James Nicholson twenty years earlier.

The security officers carried sealed and marked file boxes out of Jordan's office for delivery to the FBI. Talia's fellow case officers had done the boxing and sealing, since Security Protective Services personnel were not cleared for Directorate operations—hence the extraordinary measures during their visit.

Talia had received a great big hug when she stopped for coffee on the way in. Luanne came around her counter to give her the squeeze. "I didn't know, honey. Your own boss? What have we come to?"

"But I did just as you said. I locked her up."

"And for that, your coffee's on the house." Luanne pulled away and winked. "So is the 'I told you so.'"

Brennan lowered his broad girth into a chair near Talia. He set a box of donuts on her desk, laid an old-school briefcase in his lap, and settled in to watch the show.

"Waiting for your new office?" she asked.

He chuckled, digging into the donuts. "Waiting for a new era to begin. A tough era. REED enjoyed success under Jordan, but at what cost? She made deals with more than one devil. She took an easy road."

"And we'll take the hard one?"

Brennan gestured at the parade of boxes with a sour cream glazed. "Starting with cleaning house. This isn't over." He took a bite, continuing as he chewed. "Jordan used to say a recruited agent or asset was the puppet, the case officer was the strings, and—"

"And the section chief was the puppeteer." Talia casually slid the box away from him. "I remember. In this case, Bazin served as the strings for controlling Ivanov and Boyd."

Brennan slid the donuts back to the edge. "But Bazin can't be her only set of strings. Jordan had others, perhaps in this building. We'll take our time unraveling the mess."

He finished his sour cream glazed, picked up a Berliner, and turned to Talia, chair squeaking in protest. "Which brings me to another matter. Someone has to take over Other."

He couldn't be serious. "Don't even think about it. I'm not ready for a desk job, especially *that* desk job."

"Easy, tigress. *That* job belonged to me until a few hours ago." He took another bite, jelly catching on his mustache. "But no, don't worry. I had a different victim in mind." Brennan glanced at the upper level of acrylic offices.

Trevor was up there, taking a seat at his premium-real-estate desk. The REED veteran seemed to feel their eyes tracking him and looked down. His hand went to his bow tie, straightening it. "What?"

"Nothing," both Brennan and Talia said at once.

She lowered her voice. "Trevor?"

"He's a homebody. Hates the field. But he's dedicated. Chief of Other will be a step up for him."

"In title only."

The last security officer in the parade walked out of Jordan's office, carrying the stickman and tightwire desk toy. The little man fell off as he closed the door. He didn't notice, and kept on walking, leaving it lying on the floor.

Brennan heaved himself up from the chair and bent to recover the figure. "That's my cue. One more thing. I'd like to take you and Gupta out to dinner tonight. An Armenian place. Fantastic blackened-pumpkin-noodle-something-or-other. Conrad turned me on to it."

Talia didn't trust the wicked cant of his mustache, jelly-stained or not. She sensed a practical joke. She couldn't go anyway. "Rain check? Eddie and I have plans tonight. There's something I need to do, and I need Eddie there for both moral and technical support."

Bill and Wendy failed to sufficiently hide their looks of absolute terror as they set the table for another meal with Talia's crew. She had asked permission to bring them over again, along with Conrad.

"The police came to the house," Wendy whispered to Talia when the two were alone in the kitchen. Talia caught Tyler glancing over from the living room. Wendy's whispers had always been louder than she knew. "They said you were in trouble."

"I know. And I'm sorry. There was a mix-up at work. It won't happen again, I promise."

Tyler shot her a look that said, *Don't make promises you can't keep.*

She picked up a bread basket and followed Wendy into the dining room. "Well, I certainly *hope* it won't happen again."

Before the meal began, and after the prayer, Talia let her nervous parents off the hook. She rang her glass with a spoon, echoing the phrasing Bill had used a week earlier. "I have a presentation to make." She pushed her chair back, hugging the red box. "I should have accepted this amazing gift the moment you offered."

"So you will?" Wendy asked. "Accept, I mean."

Talia nodded.

Wendy gasped and clasped her hands, beaming. Relief brought color back to Bill's cheeks. "We're so glad. And we understand why you had to think about it. We sort of ambushed you."

"Maybe, but it should have been a no-brainer." Talia walked the box to the head of the table. On the way, without looking, she smacked a roll out of Mac's hand. "I spent so many years spurning the love you showed me. I spurned God's love in self-imposed isolation. But you"—she smiled at her parents and then turned to face the team, looking each of them in the eye—"*all* of you helped me learn to lean." Her gaze fell on Val last. "You helped me realize we're never alone in our struggles, even our failings."

After embracing her parents and Jenni, Talia opened the box. On top of the adoption papers sat a special pen Franklin had engineered for the signing. Nothing technical, a mix of tungsten carbide and titanium. Strong and lasting. The engraving on the side read faith and family.

Talia lifted the pen to sign, but Bill stopped her. "We . . . can't actually sign here. My first presentation to you was symbolic. To make it legal, we have to go to a notary public."

"Taken care of." Talia snapped her fingers. "Eddie?"

The geek left his place at what he called *the kids' table* and joined them, carrying a leather backpack. He drew out a stamp and a seal embosser and rubbed his hands. "Ready to rock." At the question in Bill's eyes, he shrugged. "What? I took an online course." But as he bent to review the papers, he sneezed.

A big sneeze. The sneeze of a monster cold refusing to let go of its victim.

Talia pulled her mother clear of the spray. "Gross, Eddie."

"You can't say 'gross' when someone sneezes." He dabbed his nose with a handkerchief. "It's offensive."

She couldn't help but laugh. Good old Eddie. "It's not offensive. Don't be such a snowflake."

"You're the snowflake." Eddie wiped Franklin's now somewhat less special pen on his jeans and handed it over. "Now hurry up and sign the forms so we can eat."

AUTHOR'S NOTE

Real Heroes

I jumped for joy, right there in the airport, wearing my best business suit. A TSA security guard gave me a sidelong glance, but I didn't care. Compassion International had said yes, and I had the same rush I'd felt years before when ***redacted*** from ***redacted*** tapped me on the shoulder and offered me a special assignment.

With Compassion International's permission to give them a starring role in a spy novel, I had an opportunity to contribute to God's special ops team. Allow me to explain, and when I'm finished, I hope you'll consider being a part of this team too.

Let's talk about unconventional warfare.

Authors are prone to exaggeration, but in this case, the comparison is valid. Unconventional warfare is multipronged and synergistic. Likewise, Compassion combats child poverty along multiple avenues like health care, nutrition, education, spiritual development, and confidence building. They serve the whole child.

Unconventional warfare is quiet warfare. Compassion operates in the background through local churches—more than 7500 in 25 countries at the time of this writing. The local church remains the focal point of love and help in the community. The glory goes to God, not Compassion.

And like any good unconventional warfare team (Talia, Tyler, and company included), Compassion leverages the power of personal relationships to achieve a strategic objective. Through sponsorships, they are defeating global poverty one child—one relationship—at a time.

Unconventional warfare. God's special ops. Real heroes with a major impact.

You can be part of the team.

Becoming a Compassion child sponsor is not just about giving $38 a month. Through the exchange of letters, sponsors build a one-on-one relationship with a child. This love fosters a sense of self-worth and identity that is foundational in the child's battle against poverty and makes them less susceptible to tangible threats like human trafficking.

I write escapist fiction about pretend heroes. The lives Talia and Tyler save are in our shared imagination, yours and mine. But Compassion child sponsors change real lives. They save real lives. A child sponsor is a real hero. If you're ready to become one of these heroes today, visit www.compassion.com.

ACKNOWLEDGMENTS

God is great. God is good. And he demonstrates this to me daily. My ability and opportunity to write are the direct result of God's goodness. Thank you, Lord.

There are, of course, many others to whom and for whom I'm grateful.

I've said it many times. My wife Cindy is my first-line editor, my cheerleader, and my shoulder to cry on. She keeps me on task and quietly shakes her head when I hand her a chapter with a spectacled bear (long story, different series). I love her, and cannot write (or live) without her.

Revell is staffed with amazing professionals. I am blessed to have Andrea Doering, Barb Barnes, Michele Misiak, Brianne Dekker, Karen Steele, and the rest. I'm also blessed to have an agent like Harvey Klinger. As with my other characters, he had a hand in Talia's genesis.

Some unnamed folks helped me with the Agency scenes. They're in undisclosed locations, shaking their collective heads. An old military buddy, Brian Andrews, became my boots-on-the-ground in Bangkok. Dr. Jeremy Evans became my go-to counselor. Thanks to all of you. And thanks to Steven James and DiAnn Mills, who've given so much of their time to mentor me. Come to think of it, DiAnn's critique group members helped with this book as well. It pays to have folks willing to read your work aloud and tell you when it's terrible.

Finally, there are the usual suspects behind my novels: Todd and Susie, John and Nancy, Chris and Melinda, Seth and Gavin, Danika and Dennis, Rachel and Katie, James and Ashton, Nancy and Dan, Steve and Tawnya, Randy and Hulda, and the Barons. So many encouragers. I love you all.

JAMES R. HANNIBAL is no stranger to secrets and adventure. A former stealth pilot from Houston, Texas, he has been shot at, locked up with surface-to-air missiles, and chased down a winding German road by an armed terrorist. He is a two-time Silver Falchion Award winner for his Section 13 mysteries for kids and a Thriller Award nominee for his Nick Baron covert ops series for adults. The author of *The Gryphon Heist*, James is a rare multisense synesthete, meaning all his senses intersect. He sees and feels sounds and smells, and hears flashes of light. If he tells you the chocolate cake you offered smells blue and sticky, take it as a compliment.

Books are produced in the United States using U.S.-based materials

Books are printed using a revolutionary new process called THINKtech™ that lowers energy usage by 70% and increases overall quality

Books are durable and flexible because of Smyth-sewing

Paper is sourced using environmentally responsible foresting methods and the paper is acid-free

Center Point Large Print
600 Brooks Road / PO Box 1
Thorndike, ME 04986-0001 USA

(207) 568-3717

US & Canada:
1 800 929-9108
www.centerpointlargeprint.com